Old Bones Lie Still
Thirteen Stories of the Dark

Terry Kerr

This is for Sarah Smith and Paula Brown.

The following is a work of fiction. No reference to any persons living or dead is intended or should be inferred. Though real locations are used I have taken many geographical liberties.

Contents

4

Author's Note

I was once sat with my good friend David Laing in a canteen at Granada TV unsuccessfully pitching ideas for TV series to an exec. One of these was a notion about reviving the one shot play. Hey, it seemed like a winner to us. 'Nah,' the exec said (maybe she phrased it more elegantly, it was a long time ago), 'anthologies don't sell.'

Well, maybe…

If novels are like a marriage, then short stories are the affairs we have on the side. And while a good marriage is something to be blessed (I'm told) the affairs on the side have their own sordid excitement. And I like my life to be full of sordid excitement.

So maybe that exec was right, and anthologies don't sell. Maybe she was wrong. Who can tell?

T.K. July 2012

Ghost Writer

I

'I am a ghost,' said the big fat lass with Play-Doh skin in front of him.

Brian Palmer nodded, put on his best 'Go on' face, and slid the Edirol closer to her. He didn't have to, it was picking up the levels fine, but if he concentrated on something he wouldn't laugh in her face. That would be bad.

'We all are,' Slimmer of the Year, 1975 continued. 'We all have ghosts within us – our spirits, our souls.'

Arseholes, thought Brian, and coughed to disguise the giggle that popped in his throat.

'Dickens was right,' Tubby McTub-Tub continued, adjusting the Bell tent she was wearing as a dress and opening her piggy eyes as wide as she could – which, considering they were piggy, wasn't very wide at all. 'Our spirits are commanded to walk abroad in life, and if they do not then they are condemned to do that after death. We project our spirits around us and the further they travel, the more they experience, then the happier we are in life. If we keep our spirits within us, then the more miserable and unfulfilled we are. Do you understand?'

Brian, of course, understood perfectly. It was childishly simple. But that wouldn't be playing the game – he'd done enough of these interviews to understand that he must play the idiot so she could establish herself as an expert. 'Are you saying then, that people are…what, like Tupperware boxes? Just containers for the soul?'

'Slightly more complicated than that,' Fatty Arbuckle said, with a patronising smile. *Well done, Brian. Played your part superbly.* 'But in essence, yes. The physical world is unimportant, we have nothing in what the Buddhists call the world of *samsara* that actually *matters.* The world of *samsara* is illusion. All that counts is spirit, and that we allow our spirits to…'

Brian dialled the rest of it to white noise, nodded where he could, put on his *oooh, fascinating* face where appropriate and thought, *what a brilliant way to excuse your morbid obesity. 'It doesn't matter that I eat a fried loaf covered in butter for breakfast and wash it down with a litre of chocolate milkshake and for lunch have half a cow in a sesame seed bun with a large order of fries and for dinner have twenty-six Lion bars. And a Diet Coke. See, my physical self doesn't matter. All that matters is that my spirit "wanders abroad," which is more than I'll ever do since I'm too fucking fat for a plane seat.'*

Who'd have thought it would come to this?

He became aware that she'd stopped talking, and was looking at him like the Delphic Oracle must've looked down on the people of (Delphi, was it?) all proud and holy. He then became aware of the clock behind her, showing almost midnight. 'Well...um,' he groped a bit, then found her name in the mental file marked WHO GIVES A FUCK, 'Nikki, that was really, really interesting. You've really given me some...' *go on, say it,* 'food for thought.' He picked up the Edirol and thumbed the off switch. 'But it's late, I've got a long drive home, and I'm sure you're busy.'

'Not at all,' she said. She had the narrowest mouth he'd seen outside of a mollusc. How the bloody hell she got food down it he'd never know. That mouth now attempted a sexy smile. 'And there's really no need for you to leave tonight. You can stay here if you want.'

Brian dropped the recorder into his pocket, not bothering with the carry case. The recce of her house that he'd done just before the interview ran through his mind. This was a one bedroom flat. 'Well, that's most kind, but I've an early start in the morning and I'd hate to wake you when I left.' He stood, all smiles, and somehow managed not to run for the door, screaming.

'Oh, you wouldn't,' The Blob said, now attempting to sound lascivious. It was like listening to someone who'd once overheard Fenella Fielding from another room through unsyringed ears. 'We'd still be awake.'

Yeah, I would be. Like a little kid scared of the bogeyman. 'Nikki, I'm tempted,' he said, fantastically straight faced. *Tempted to call you 'a fucking fat bitch' and run to the car, tempted to see if you can keep up without having a heart attack and dying therefore affecting McDonald's share prices,* 'but…alas, my lady has my heart. If she didn't…' *Alas? My LADY?*

Tub O'Guts sighed, and all her flab wobbled. Brian wondered if anyone had ever taken her up on her offer. Then he decided that undoubtedly someone had. There'd always be some sick bastard up for a 'fascination fuck.'

'Oh well,' she said, staring at the floor, then raised her Peppa Pig eyes and said, 'if you ever decide to…' then she looked over Brian's left shoulder. 'Dear Jesus *GOD!*'

Brian jumped. A little, but he still jumped. He had, after all, expected this. It was part of the show. There had to be a little steak – or a lot in her case – with the sizzle. 'What is it?'

'Behind you…' she muttered, rolling her eyeballs back so he could see the whites. 'In the shadows. Something…evil…stalking you.'

Brian did as he was expected and looked behind him. All he could see was the greasy worktops of her kitchenette. And a defrosting Sara Lee Poundcake. He looked back. *Give her* some *credit, she's good at this bit.*

Blobby did, indeed, look terrified. Her slack, thin mouth was in a perfect O, her chins wobbling. She raised an arm the size of China and pointed. 'There! Close behind you!'

A frightful fiend, thought Brian. 'I saw nothing,' he said.

'I can,' she wheezed. 'Back, hiding, but getting closer all the time.' She tore her glance (*well done, looking away from that cake must've hurt*) from that imaginary 'thing', then grabbed his arm. 'Please, Mr Palmer – you have to stay! I can get *rid* of that thing – *but you have to stay!*'

Smiling as tenderly as he could, Brian disentangled himself. 'I'm sorry,' he said. 'Things to do, places to go.'

He made his way to the front door, The Thing from the Fridge flapping after him. 'You can't! Please, that thing is *evil!* I can sense it! It's like a cloud! Please!'

You're overplaying the part, sweetheart. He put his hand on the knob and, thankfully, felt it turn under his hand. He wouldn't have put it past her to have locked it. He wouldn't put *anything* past *any* of them. 'If I have any trouble,' he said, without turning, 'I'll be in touch.' He stepped into the Nottingham night, closed the door in her face, and walked nonchalantly to his Honda Civic. *What a crazy, mad bitch. And did I mention she was a* tad *overweight?*

Inside her flat, Nikki Carson watched the car drive off. She was genuinely terrified, more terrified than she ever had been in her life. *How long's he got? A month? Two at the outside? And where did it* come *from?* She'd said she could get rid of it...but could she? She knew what she knew, she'd practised divination plenty of times, she'd spoken to enough emissaries of the dark *and* the light, and she'd always prevailed...but *that* thing? That thing she'd seen following Brian...that thing that was on his trail...oh, that was like nothing she'd ever seen before. It was so much more malevolent. So much darker.

Nikki Carson suddenly burst into tears and ran to her kitchen as fast as she could – which wasn't, in all honesty, very fast at all. She ripped the Poundcake from its box and gobbled it up as fast as she could. It was still partly frozen, but she didn't care.

After seeing something like *that*, a little frozen cake was nothing at all.

II

It was a little after three when Brian arrived back at Stroud Green. He would have made it sooner, but just after he'd joined the motorway he'd been hit with a giggling fit so severe he'd had to pull into the nearest services and pay a month's rent for a coffee. The zombie who served him couldn't seem to understand why Brian was wiping his eyes and having difficulty saying 'large cappuccino,' which only made the whole thing funnier.

There are, at least, some compensations to all this, he thought as he sipped the hot coffee coloured water and stared out of the window at the occasional dots of light that traversed up and down the tarmac. *Precious fucking few, but some.* He pulled the Edirol from his pocket, checked it over, made sure it was OK – those damned things were so fragile – and then checked his BlackBerry. One text, from Natalie. HOPE YOU'RE OK, SEE YOU LATER, LOVE YOU. *There's another,* he thought, and OK, yes, it was nothing short of a miracle someone like Natalie had decided to spend her time with him, and the sight of her name in the MESSAGE INBOX was a nice thing…but where were the emails from the BBC? From Sky? From *any* of them?

Nowhere to be seen, that's where, like my 'frightful fiend.' That brought back the giggling again, the sight of her like a galleon in full sail pursuing him as he'd left, begging him to come back so she could...what, *fuck* the monster out of him? Then the giggling stopped, and he sighed. Then it came back again. He spent a half hour like that, alternately giggling and sighing, then he went to the toilets for a piss.

As he washed his hands, he thought he saw something in the mirror. But when he looked back over his shoulder, there was nothing. It was, after all, half one in the morning and only fools were about at this time.

III

He slid under the duvet, and Natalie muttered something that sounded an awful lot like 'Pixies,' and snuggled over to him. Then she started pushing him towards the edge of the mattress. *Oh Nat, how do I love thee? Let me count the ways. But will you stop hogging the* fucking bed? *Then there'll be one more.*

Brian was tired but far from sleepy. He really shouldn't have had that coffee, but if he'd continued driving while giggling that hard he'd have ended up in the central reservation with blue lights for company. Nothing for it but to stare at the ceiling and ponder this question; *how did it come to this?*

He was going to be a great writer once. He'd had his head filled with brilliant stories and razor sharp insights into the human condition. He was Hemmingway and Faulkner and Hardy (Thomas, not Oliver) in one Economy-sized package. Who couldn't love him? Who *couldn't* love his work?

Well...just about everybody it seemed. Well, everybody who mattered. No, that wasn't fair, Natalie loved his work, and *she* certainly mattered...but was she a publisher? Was she an editor? Was she an agent? No, she was a struggling actress – sorry, actor (or were they actresses again? Brian got lost amidst the terminology maze) – who had earned a grand total of three thousand pounds the previous year. Even he'd made more than that. And all he did was...

Well, write shit for *The Unseen World,* that's all.

Brian turned over, trying to fight for mattress space without waking his girlfriend. She, in turn, spread out like a starfish and mumbled something about 'The Queen's trousers.' *Great title for a story, he thought. Pity I'll never write it. What's the point? I could never sell that to Claude.*

Claude Webb was his editor at *The Unseen World.* Well, *would* have been 'his' editor if Brian had a staff job. Not that anyone there had a staff job. Well, except Claude. And his secretary. Even the cleaners were on short term contracts. *And that's the way of the world in the 21st century. Everybody freelance, that way we can keep 'em on starvation wages. If they don't like it, they can fuck off somewhere else. Except it doesn't look like I* can *fuck off anywhere else, does it? He's the only bastard who'll buy anything I write.*

Ah, such hopes...such dreams...battered into submission – nearly – by constant rejection letters or emails. *Not for us. We regret we cannot take this idea further. Why don't you piss off and stop bothering us, you talentless twat?*

Until, finally, a sale. Of sorts. A spec short story, two thousand words of ghosts and goblins, that he'd sent to *The Unseen World: A monthly look into The Unknown.* He'd no idea if they bought fiction or not, he'd never read the thing. But he'd had an idea for a ghost story, written it, had a look in Smiths to see if there was a magazine that looked a likely taker, and sent it in.

A week later, the phone call came from Claude. No, they didn't buy fiction. They were a factual magazine about the Paranormal (*how can you have a factual magazine about something that's just bollocks,* Brian had thought but didn't say) and they were looking for writers – freelance, of course - to do an article or two. Interviews. *Sittings.* Did he want to try out? Write a spec piece, five thousand words, on his local witches' coven or whatever ('Dig around,' Claude had said, 'there'll be something near you, there always is, you'd be surprised.') and if Claude liked it, he'd buy it, maybe put some more work his way. And he'd pay £750. Per article. On publication, not acceptance.

At the time Brian had been working as a barman in a Slug and Lettuce in Finsbury Park and was barely scraping by on a little over a grand a month. £750 seemed like a Lottery win. A rollover. A *double* rollover. 'Yeah,' he'd said, 'I'll give it a go.'

Natalie said something like, 'I'm out. And on my way,' then rolled away from him. Brian finally closed his eyes and went to sleep, the memories having fought the caffeine to a standstill.

IV

The Edirol was plugged into his computer and files were copying over. The Word Doc in front of him was blank. It had been blank for the best part of an hour.

So Brian typed – for the sake of having something to type – THE BIG FAT BITCH STANK OF WEE. AND SWEATY FANNY. Then he laughed sourly. Then he typed AND YET SOMEHOW SHE COULDN'T GET A FUCK AND WONDERED WHY. Then he laughed again, dragged the mouse over the text and deleted it. *The Unseen World* didn't like its demographic being made fun of.

'Hey babe,' said Natalie, 'how's it going? How was last night?'

Brian pointed at the blank page on the screen. *'That's* how it's going, love. And as for last night, I only narrowly escaped rape at the hands of a human dirigible.'

Natalie's eyes – huge and brown and not at all piggy – widened as she dried her shower damp hair. 'You jest?'

'I jest not. Thankfully I could outrun her. Actually, Stephen Hawking could have outrun her.'

She slapped his arm lightly as she always did when he was being horrible about people. He was used to it, largely because it seemed he was always being horrible about people these days. 'I bet you were tempted.'

'Yeah, I was. Hugely. But I struggled against my baser instincts and somehow managed to do the right thing.'

'You're a saint,' she said. 'An absolute saint, I'm lucky to have you. Any chance I could check my emails? Just a quick scan? Just in case?'

'Knock yourself out.'

He decided not to vacate his chair though. That way she'd have to lean over him and press the keys, and if there was one thing that Brian truly loved in this world, it was Natalie Baxter bending over him. All five foot four of blonde perfection of her, shower fresh and bodywash smelling, leaning over him, tapping away, the odd breast pressing against his shoulder…

'Listen love,' he said, 'since I got nothing last night…'

'Aw, come on. I've only just got out of the shower,' she said, entering her password. 'I don't want to get all messy again…'

'Yeah, but I do.'

'I'll consider it,' she muttered…pressing herself just a little too forcefully against his shoulder. Then rubbing around him. Then breathing in his ear. Then shouting quite loudly *'Yes!'* which made him flinch.

'Watch it, love – I may need that eardrum one day.'

'Sorry,' she said. 'No I'm not, you've got another. Work next week!' She pointed at the screen. There it was, two days facilitative role play in Central College, £150 a day, brief to follow, was she available? 'You *bet* I'm available!' She typed in her acceptance and a thank you, and Brian felt good for the first time in…oh, ages. She was good, Natalie. Talented. Talented and gorgeous. He'd known that when he'd first seen her in that production of *Charley's Fucking Aunt* (he'd checked, and that was, indeed, the working title) at the Bridewell for that theatre company he'd been trying to flog his play to. They, of course, hadn't bought it, but he'd stuck around for the show anyway because he had nothing better to do, and there'd been Natalie, and boom, boom – out went his lights. He'd chatted her up in the bar, telling her he was 'a struggling writer.' She said she was 'a struggling actor' (or had she said *actress?*) and that, pretty much, had been that.

Struggle they continued to do, though. She was better than two days 'facilitative role play.' He was better than the shit he peddled for Claude. But that seemed to be their lot. At least they had each other.

'Cool beans and hot peas,' said Nat as she pressed SEND. 'OK, I'm out of your hair.'

'Not before you at least kiss me you're not.'

'Needy bastard,' she smiled, but kissed him anyway, good and deep, tongues all over the place. Oh, it was too much, it really was. He ran his hands up her body and let them rest on her breasts. *Oh, you can take my liberty and take my life, but don't take my girlfriend's ladybumps away.*

'That's enough,' she said, breaking away. 'You. Write. Meet Deadline. Me Go Shop.' Then she flicked the Vs at him – those tender touches of affection that meant so much - and departed, leaving Brian staring at the screen. Staring at the screen, and desperate for a shag.

V

Horribly, Brian had found His True Vocation – writing about this shite. That conversation with Claude had opened a door – not a door he particularly wanted opening, but a door – and like an idiot he'd walked right through it. Then slammed it behind him. And locked it. And thrown away the key.

Brian had trawled the web as Claude had advised, looking for Weird Occult Nutters in the North London area. And had blinked in mild astonishment at the number of sites he'd found. The Islington Ghost Hunters was one. The Highbury Spirit Seekers was another. The third was gloriously titled The Stoke Newington Phantom Detectors.

Them's the ones for me, he'd decided, and sent them an email. *'Blah blah writer for* The Unseen World (Brian hadn't bothered with the 'probably') *blah blah like to do a story on your group, blah blah good publicity, blah blah and blah de bloody blah.'* At the bottom he'd included his contact details.

He'd been on shift at The Slug that night when his phone had rung. Thankfully it was a Wednesday and the only customers who needed serving were an old man and his dog. The dog had been on the Stella and was getting a bit leery and Brian had been thinking about cutting him off and hoping it wouldn't lead to a fight when the call had come through, saving him from any more insane flights of imagination.

'Is that Brian Palmer?' said an adenoidal voice.

'Certainly is,' said Brian, not even bothering to duck into the storeroom to take the call. 'How can I help?'

'My name's Julian Bleathman,' said the voice. 'I'm the Grand Master of the Stoke Newington Phantom Detectors.'

Brian experienced the first of many odd coughing fits. 'Nice to hear from you…' *Jesus, what do I call him? Mr Master? Or something informal, like 'Grand'?* 'Julian,' he said instead.

'I'm in receipt of your email,' Julian droned on, 'and I must say I find it very interesting.'

'Thank you,' said Brian. 'So, would it be possible to attend one of your meetings and maybe have a chat with you, with the rest of your members, see what you're all about, get your perspective on the world?'

'Yes, that would be agreeable. On certain conditions.'

Conditions? Fuck off, Tannoy Voice, I'm doing you a favour here. If you don't bite I can spit and – apparently - hit hundreds of retards just like you. Then he remembered the money this might bring, and bit his lip. 'Go on.'

'We'd like to see the copy before you file it,' the drone continued. *Here's a man who's watched a couple of old* Lou Grant *episodes on cable, he knows the talk.* 'We've had problems before with reporters who haven't been…respectful.' *Get OUTTA here! Really? Somebody made you out to be a gang of useless bloody lunatics? Who'd-a thunk it!* Then, *anyway, fuck off. I'll write what I want to write.* On top of that, *easy Brian old mate. Think of the money.*

'That must have been awful for you, Mr Mast-*Julian.* I can promise you I'll be nothing but respectful. And here's what I'll do, I'll copy you in on the piece as I send it to my editor, that way you know what I send him is what I send you. Deal?'

'That, Mr Palmer, would be perfectly acceptable. Thank you. Now, we're having a vigil at Abney Park Cemetery this Saturday night, starting at nine. Would you like to attend?'

Actually, I'm working Saturday night. And you can never get shift cover for a Saturday. So no chance, sorry. Then again…I have *got a bit of a cold coming on…* 'Julian, I'd love to.'

That Saturday evening had seen Brian – after phoning up the pub with his best Sick Voice on – freezing his arse off in a cemetery until four in the morning surrounded by the kind of people trainspotters would steal lunch money from. There were thick bottle glasses and greasy hair and dandruff and unbelievable body odour everywhere. One bloke's teeth had been greener than The Incredible Hulk and contained flecks of what looked suspiciously like garlic bread.

The thing they had most in common, however, was their stories. They *all* had a fucking story to tell. The doors that had opened by themselves. The voices that had whispered in their ear. The knockings in the walls. The time they'd seen the headless and bodiless phantom cat. ('If it was headless and bodiless, how did you know it was there?' Brian had asked. 'Vibrations,' one of them had said sagely, while the others nodded.) Brian had listened to them all, nodding, holding the Dictaphone close to catch their weedy utterances (he hadn't moved on to the Edirol then, that was way out of his price bracket) and hadn't laughed in their faces once. Not even when...

Not even when he'd met Julian Bleathman, the Grand Master himself. Who was six feet five, about eighteen stone, had no hair on the top of his head but plenty pouring down his shoulders (like a fatter, uglier Bill Bailey)...and a purple cloak and a wizard's staff.

A purple cloak. A wizard's staff.

'Mr Palmer? So pleased to meet you,' he said, reaching out a hand. There was (of course!) a huge skull ring on his right index finger.

'Likewise,' said Brian, and didn't laugh. It was that moment, more than any other, that set him on his way. When you keep a straight face upon being confronted by someone dressed like that, you can pretty much keep a straight face anywhere.

VI

But on that morning after the Fat Nottingham Escape, Brian was still not writing. He was, instead, spinning on his chair. When Natalie caught him doing this he often said he was 'searching for inspiration.' Sometimes she looked at him like he was a naughty schoolboy and stopped him. Sometimes she joined in and spun the chair for him. Either way, he didn't mind.

On the fourth revolution his eye was taken by something at the bottom of the computer screen. MESSAGE WAITING it said. So he stopped revolving, waited for the dizziness to pass, and clicked on the IncrediMail icon.

In fact, there were two MESSAGES WAITING. The first was from Sky TV. 'We have read your pitch for your TV series *Twist*. Whilst we appreciate its social commentary and applaud your attempt to integrate the current economic climate with a reworking of Charles Dickens' story, we feel that this series is too "high concept" for us. We're currently looking for more down to earth and realistic series ideas that can develop over many series. Regrettably we will not be able to develop it further. We wish you the best of luck with this project.'

'Get cancer you fucking dogs,' muttered Brian, but without any venom at all. It was only the latest in a long line of rejected series pitches to hit his inbox in the last year. His detective idea ('*It's* The Avengers – *but* she's *Steed!*') his sitcom ('*It's an unrequited love story – because* he's a ghost!') and his conspiracy theory thriller ('*There are no conspiracy theories – they're made up by a secret cabal in Washington to control the populace!*') had all been bounced back with similar replies. He'd started to think he wasn't very good at TV ideas. But then he'd watch his set of an evening and there'd be a series about two middle-aged women who were fucking *gardeners* who were also detectives in their spare time and he'd think, *come on, seriously? You commissioned* this? *You thought* this *was worth money? Someone got* paid *for this? There's* got *to be a way in. There's got to be!*

Well…maybe. But not just yet, it seemed. In the meantime there was…

That other email in his inbox. It was from Nikki Fucking Fat Boot. MR PALMER, it read, YOU MUST TAKE ACTION NOW. WHAT I SAW BEHIND YOU LAST NIGHT IS EVIL. IT WILL DESTROY THOSE YOU LOVE AND THEN DESTROY YOU. PLEASE.

Caps lock broken? Come on, podgy-podge, play the game, will you? I'll write the article, give you your fifteen minutes of fame, you'll feel all important in Nottingham, and I'll bank the cheque and take my girlfriend out for a meal. That's the way, uh-huh, uh-huh, I like it.

He deleted her message there and then and stared at the blank screen once more. Then he clicked on the Media Player Progress Bar and saw all the Edirol's files had been copied. Thinking he might get some inspiration if he listened to them, he did so.

VII

The very day after he'd sent the Stoke Newington article off to *The Unseen World* (saying a silent prayer to the God of Money) he'd received two phone calls. One was from Grand Master Flash and His Furious Ring, thanking him for the article and saying it was much better than he expected, but the one he gave a shit about was from Claude, who said he loved the article and it was much better than he expected.

In fact, he'd said, 'This is superb, Brian! Just excellent! It's in, two months' time, no worries on that. Send me your address and an invoice and I'll pop the cheque in the post as soon as the presses run.'

'Thank you,' said Brian, and meant it.

Then Claude had gone on to say, 'I think you've a talent for this sort of work, you know. How about another? In a similar vein?'

Oh fucking hell I can't do that again...still, another £750... 'When d'you want it?' asked Brian.

VIII

Inspiration flowed through him like treacle. Just listening to that voice made him want to weep. Or punch the screen. Or sacrifice a goat on Beachy Head. Anything but write.

'I am a ghost,' he heard her say again. *The ghost of pizzas past, present and yet-to-come. Deep pan, crisp and even.* Then there was all that shit about 'spirits' and 'walking abroad' and bollocks and tit wank and then she said, 'the further a spirit walks in life, the further it goes in death.' He couldn't remember this bit, it must've been when he was listening to the white noise in his head. 'If a person's spirit is kept inside, it becomes sour, chaotic, poisoned. It seeks to wreak havoc in the here and now, to destroy and confuse.'

'offfuckoff.'

Brian jumped in his chair, and slammed the spacebar down, pausing the recording. He dragged the mouse along the timeline and played that section again.

'…in the here and now,' said Doughnut Girl, 'to destroy and confuse.'

'offfuckoff.'

Then Brian was calling his girlfriend's name over and over.

IX

'Yeah,' said Natalie, removing the headphones. 'I can hear it.'

'A voice? A definite *voice,* saying "offfuckoff"?'

'Dunno what it's saying, but I can hear something. A man's voice, I think. Very low. And hissy. So who was it?'

'No idea,' said Brian, smiling. 'But it'll make a kicker for the article. "And I got me an EVP, on a wav. file, living proof of… *The Unseen World!*"'

'Oooh,' said Natalie, all big eyes and teasing mouth. *I just don't care how messy you don't want to get,* Brian thought. *I really, really want to bend you over that desk and mount a charge from the rear.* 'You got a ghost on tape?'

'Have I arse,' said Brian. 'I've got a radio signal from her neighbour or somebody's telly through the wall or even a stray baby monitor somewhere in that block.'

'Do many parents tell their babies to fuck off?'

'Mine did,' he said, still grinning like a Cheshire cat who'd met another Cheshire cat of the opposite sex whose Dad owned a mouse farm and was carrying two FA Cup Final tickets. 'Point is, it's there, and I can theorise to hell and back about what it is, and the readers will love it.'

Natalie had put the 'phones back on again and was dragging the mouse over that bit of the timeline over and over again. 'Weird how it gets all hissy like that, just at that bit, then it clears up again.'

'That's how you know it's interference of some kind,' said Brian. 'If it had genuinely been in the room then the quality wouldn't vary, would it?'

'Suppose not,' said Natalie. She pulled the headphones off a second time and gave him the sort of smile that made his legs go funny. 'I like it when you're happy,' she said. 'Lunch?'

'I'd prefer a fu...'

'I know what you'd prefer,' she said, standing. 'And you'll get it. After the article is finished. But first, lunch?'

Brian sighed. 'OK. Can you bring it in? I've got an idea how to write this bloody thing now.'

'No sweat babe,' she said, and kissed him on the ear. But by the time she came back with the cheese and tomato sandwich, Brian didn't even notice. He was writing.

It was shite, but he wrote it well.

X

That appeared to be both Brian's curse and salvation; he wrote this shite well. He wrote it clearly, concisely and crisply. There was not a shade of the hysterical in his 'cool, point-to-point' prose, as Claude had put it. He somehow managed to tread a line between belief and scepticism, even though every night (and it was *always* night) he spent in the company of these freaks and weirdos he laughed up his sleeve at them. But you'd never tell it from his articles.

He wrote two more on spec; an 'investigation' into the Upper Holloway Grey Lady – a lady, apparently grey, who was alleged to walk the streets of Upper Holloway (Brian had spent two nights patrolling said streets with a gentleman named Leonard Butler and had seen many ladies walking those streets, none of whom were grey and all of whom were demanding cash for services) and a look at The Mystery of Barnsbury Hill, where 'several local residents' had reported over the years hearing the sound of gunfire after dark when the moon was full and it was the second Wednesday of the month with an R in it after a Bank Holiday. Unsurprisingly, all Brian had found was an enormous amount of dogshit and some interesting activity behind the bushes. But he'd contained his mirth and written his articles, and Claude had loved them and published them, and eventually, cheques had started to land on his doorstep.

But then something *truly* remarkable happened.

The month after his first piece – which Claude had somewhat melodramatically entitled *The Abney Park Daemons* – had been published, the letters column of *The Unseen World* was full of praise for Brian's work. In fact, Claude had reported a two hundred per cent increase in the volume of letters and emails received. They'd had a grand total of eleven. 'Excellent, sympathetic reporting,' read one. 'Spine-chillingly accurate,' said another (though since that particular correspondent hadn't been at Abney Park, Brian was more than a little at a loss to comprehend how they'd know that) and – the one that changed his future seemingly irrevocably – 'you've found a star in Brian Palmer. More please, from this author.'

'How about a regular column?' Claude had asked over the phone two days after that issue had hit the stands. 'I'll give you a freelance contract. You deliver one piece per month guaranteed on contract terms and anything over and above that piece is negotiable. Sound good?'

'How much?'

'Five thousand words.'

'No,' said Brian. 'How much per column? Money.'

'Oh,' said Claude, seemingly deflated that Brian hadn't behaved like the winner of a penalty shootout. 'One thousand five hundred.'

A grand and a half per month…not enough to leave the pub. Maybe I could cut down the shifts though, just do a couple of nights a week… 'How long for? Six months? A year?'

'Six months, then renew after another six if the work's still viable.'

*Half a year, grand and a half…*Useless at mental arithmetic, Brian had dug out his ancient Motorola Razr and tapped away at its calculator. Nine grand. No, nowhere near enough to leave the pub. But if he could work reduced shifts, he might get an extra five hundred a month, which would leave him (more tapping) twelve grand. Still peanuts…but much, much bigger peanuts than he was currently earning.

'Still with me?' asked Claude down the line.

'Still with you,' said Brian, then said; 'Nice offer, thank you. How about I make a counter proposal?'

'Go ahead,' said Claude, sniffing a bit.

'Freelance contract, great. Six month option, great. Five thousand words a month, anything on top negotiable, fine. But you get the rights only to my non fiction work in your field; I want a cut of any republishing – annuals, on line streaming, whatever – and its two grand per article.' *Fifteen thousand in six months – if I can still get the bar work. OK, Stephen King ain't going to be losing any sleep, but it's a start.*

There was some harrumphing and heehawing from Claude, but before Brian had issued his ultimate threat – *pay up or I'll take this to* The Fortean Times - Claude had acceded.

From that moment on, Brian Palmer was what he'd always wanted to be, a professional writer. One who still did two evenings a week behind a bar, but hey…he wrote articles and received payment, which made him a professional. He could hold his head up amongst his friends and relatives. He'd made it. He'd achieved what he set out to do.

The fact he was writing crap barely a step above porn for a David Sullivan jazz mag was neither here nor there, really, was it? From now on, all his submissions to TV companies and publishers could include the line 'I am a professional writer,' rather than 'I'm a pathetic hopeless wannabe whose last performed work was *A Day at the Zoo,* read aloud by Miss Begley at Bronswood Park Mixed Infants in 1979 to great acclaim and a Kinder Egg.'

It's a stepping stone, thought Brian as he hung up from Claude that night. *First rung on the ladder, pick your cliché. I'll do this for a while, then something else will come along. You'll see. I'm too good for this shite.*

XI

Except it hadn't, and he wasn't. Two years later he was still peddling five thousand words a month (though the money had gone up to two and a half grand an article) and still working a couple of nights at The Slug. Nothing else had ever sold. Everything else just bounced back into his inbox. He attended séances, he attended vigils, he'd spoken to witches and listened intently to one woman who claimed to have been the victim of a possession when she was a child in Acton. Said possession occurring a week after she'd watched a copy of *The Exorcist*. 'It was divination,' she'd said, 'by watching that film I'd invited the devil into my home.' *Yes,* he'd thought, *just like by watching* Buffy the Vampire Slayer *I invited Sarah Michelle Geller into my home and gave her a right seeing to.* He'd sat overnight in stately homes in Oxford and heard one member of the Paranormal Investigations Group (Oxford) scream 'It's gone cold! Suddenly it's gone cold!' *Yes,* he'd thought, *it's half past pissing three on an October morning. You'd surprise me more if you'd taken your shirt off and said 'C'mon lads, let's get a Solero and jump in the pool! I'm boiling here!'* He'd seen video footage of orbs (or 'dust', as he liked to call them) heard EVP recordings (or someone speaking in another room, as he liked to think) and 'phantom knockings' (someone banging pipes against a wall). He'd even spoken to a few doctors and psychologists (*The 'Facts' Behind Ghosts*, Claude had called that one) all of whom had told him, bluntly, that there were no such things as ghosts. One had even gone so far as to call the readers of *The Unseen World* 'a bunch of tossers who can't get laid so need to invent a secret club full of secret signs and Masonic handshakes in order to boost their own worthless egos.'

'I'm not sure I can print that,' Brian had said. 'Or if I do I may have to clean it up a bit. And grant you anonymity.'

'*Why* can't you?' the psychologist had said, 'it's what you believe. It's written all over your face. You just be grateful you're writing about people who *want* to be believed. They wouldn't know scepticism if it bit them on their arses. Oh, they'll *tell* you they can, they'll probably even tell you their spirit guide can spot it a mile off, but they can't. You keep putting your big eyes and nodding face on and don't take the piss out of them in print and they may well start worshipping you as a God – but frankly, anyone with half a brain can see you don't believe a word of it. And good on you, take the bastards for as much as you can. But I insist, if you use any of this interview, you use that quote about the Masonic handshakes. And give my full name. I'd love to get one of those idiots on the couch.'

Brian had written that article (after all, he was under contract), he had used that quote (though in deference to The Unseen World's writer's guide, he'd substituted the word 'tossers' with 'saddoes') and had given the guy's full name. A little after publication, Brian had rung him to see how things were going.

'Funny you should call,' he'd said, sounding all shaky and little girlish, 'the day after the magazine came out I found a doll in a white coat nailed to the practice door. Ever since then things have been going wrong. Little things, but more all the time.'

'You're joking!'

'Of *course* I'm joking,' the psychologist had laughed. 'Fuck all's happened! Fuck all will *continue* to happen! What are they going to do, send Vincent Price round to beat me up?'

'Tell me,' Brian had asked, a bit miffed he'd even half fallen for that one, 'do you talk to your patients like that?'

'If they can afford to pay my fees,' he'd laughed, 'I call them Sir or Madam.'

So Brian kept on writing, never exposing his contempt for the people he wrote about, a contempt that deepened with every sentence he typed.

Still, it paid the rent.

XII

'Done,' Brian said to Natalie, stepping into their kitchen.

Natalie looked up from stuffing some towels in the washing machine. 'Went it well?'

'As well as it ever goes. Sky have knocked back *Twist.*'

'Bastards,' she said, wrinkling her nose like someone who's encountered a very bad smell indeed. She slammed the machine's door and twisted the dial. 'Got any other ideas?'

'I've got one very good idea,' said Brian, wiggling his eyebrows in a leer.

'Oh, go on then,' said Natalie with her long suffering sigh. 'Tell you what, if you don't go off before the spin cycle I'll take you out for a meal.'

'Safest bet you'll ever make,' he said, wrapping her in his arms.

'I know,' she smiled. 'That's why I made it.'

Just before their tongues locked, Brian thought, *OK, so I ain't the writer I wanted to be. OK, so I churn out shit once a month and have to endure the B.O. and halitosis of people who think* The Vampire Diaries *is a documentary, but I've got a beautiful woman in my arms and she's going to do something very rude to me, so who's actually complaining? It's a* good *life, isn't it?*

XIII

Good life or not, it kept on rolling. Natalie did her work as a facilitative role player and gratefully banked the money. The woman who ran the course complimented Nat on her work and hinted there'd be more in the future. 'Fine,' Natalie had said, 'if I'm available on the dates, I'll happily do the job,' then had run out of the building and rung Brian immediately, so thrilled had she been. Brian, who'd been deeply involved in the intellectual drama that was *The Jeremy Kyle Show* had been thrilled as well. It wasn't what she really wanted to do, he knew that, but it might be a start...a stepping stone...a rung on the ladder...and for her it might actually lead somewhere. God knows he wanted it to.

A week later, Brian travelled to Govan, a delightful and charming suburb of Glasgow. Some walking winnit had contacted *The Unseen World* claiming to have seen the devil himself wandering around his council estate, doubtless looking for a plasma TV to rob and flog down the local for smack money. It was a long haul there, but it was worth it. The guy (whose name was, in fact, Guy) was pure comedy gold.

'I come in aboot half past twa,' he said, not actually talking in such a ludicrous accent but that was the one Brian's subconscious insisted on overlaying on top of Guy's somewhat boring, neutral tone. 'I'd been oot and aboot at the dogs, ye ken? Aye, I'd had a dram or twa o' the harrrrd stuff, I'll nae deny it, but I wasnae drunk, ye ken? An' as I was drrrrawing my currrrtains, I saw him, Auld Nick himself, walkin' abroad – April 30th, ye ken? Beltane, when the Prince is nigh! Thirrrrrrty feet tall, the tail, the hooves – och, the face! Purrrrrre evil, crrrrrruel, savage, like a beastie! Och, I near pappered ma breeks! An' then he looked at me, proper looked and pointed one long arrrrum wi' a bony, turrible funger at th' end o' it, like he wa' marrrrking me, then he walked away towards Parkheed.'

'Parkhead?'

'Aye, those bastid Celtic fans would'a conjured the Auld 'un up, 'cause o' those letters I sent to Neil Lennon, *fuckin' Papist scum!* But noo the de'el himself knows me, knows whure I live, and he'll be oot t' git me, y'ken?'

'Could you show me exactly where you saw him?' Brian asked, making a mental note to Google 'Parkhead' and 'Neil Lennon' when he got home so he could actually understand what this gobshite was on about. Well, to a point.

'Aye,' he replied, and led Brian to 'the windy.' Through 'the windy' (which was apparently the glass thing in the wall, which normal people called 'the window') Brian was directed by Guy's trembling hand to the street, a perfectly boring, slightly dishevelled estate built sometime when Billy Connolly was still funny. 'That's whur the bastid stood, 'tween Poplar Grrrrove and Ash Drrrrrive.'

'And he was – what? Thirty foot high, you said?'

'Aye,' said Guy. *Aye, said Guy, geez a bit o' that meat pie.*

'What was he doing when you saw him? Just standing there?'

'Ye mean, ye believe me?' Guy begged, grabbing onto Brian's arm.

Somehow Brian managed to control the spasm of revulsion that ran through him. 'Of course,' he said, smiling and nodding. He went on to recall, in horrible detail, the occurrences of devil visitations that had been recorded through the ages; culminating in the Aldbourne Hooves of 1971. 'It's not common,' he concluded, hating the fact there were parts of his brain dedicated to remembering this shite, 'but you're far from the first to actually see the devil walking abroad. As you say, April 30th, Beltane and all that entails.' *Mental note, Google 'Beltane' as well as the other kak when you get home.* 'If you have angered some people it's entirely possible they may have...set him on you.' *Like a pet pit-bull.* 'But they're probably in more danger than you – from what we know,' *which is fuck all, as the 'bastid doesnae exist',* 'the devil obeys no one but himself. They may *think* they've called him, but it's likely it was just time for him to have a wander. His voice, they say, is pleasant to hear – he's the father of lies, after all. And anyway, if you had sent some letters to, um... this Papist, I bet he was on his way to thank you for it. Papists aren't his favourites, are they?'

'Aye,' said Guy. *Aye, said Guy, I got sand in me Jap's eye!* Hideously, his eyes were glittering with gratitude. 'Thank ye! Thank ye! Thank ye for believing me! Thank ye for *comforting* me!'

'No sweat,' said Brian, still looking out into the street. He hadn't wanted to see where the Auld 'un had walked at all, he'd just wanted to check the Civic was still there and in possession of all four wheels. Which – oh blessed miracle – it was. *Thirty feet high, with hooves. It is, of course, perfectly logical that no one else saw that. Or heard 'the bastid' clumping about. I don't know why I'm such a cynic.*

As he turned to pick up the Edirol and thank his guest for that cup of piss weak tea (and while he was considering asking for the use of the bathroom before the long trip back) he thought he saw something in his car. In the back seat. Something about the height of a man, sitting down. Then he looked again, harder, and it was just a shadow cast by the streetlight.

Half an hour later, Brian was making his way to the door, when Guy suddenly stopped being obsequious. In fact, he practically jumped back, eyes wide. 'You all right?' asked Brian.

'Aye,' said Guy. *Aye said Guy, I seen the de'el and noo I'll die!* 'Fine. But ye, noo…'

'Me?'

'Aye.' *Oh come on, will you? Start a sentence with 'yes' or something, I'm running out of rhymes.* 'Have ye been tauld…aboot…the thing…'

'Oh that,' said Brian, not having a fucking clue what the stupid bugger was on about, and caring not one whit, 'yes. It's under control. There's someone dealing with it.'

'Gud,' said Guy. ''cause *that* beastie…makes the de'el I saw look like Bugs fucking Bunny.'

'Yeah, he's a rum 'um. Anyway, goodnight.'

Guy stood at the window and watched the Englishman drive off. He'd been a nice enough bloke, listened, set his mind at rest. Pity, really. Guy would have liked to have seen him again, maybe bought him a pint.

Instead he went to bed, and didn't sleep a wink.

XIV

Another day – (it was, after all, twenty past two in the morning) – another motorway service station. Once more, Brian sat with the lorry drivers and murderers and threw something that was distantly related to 'coffee' down his throat. He reached for his BlackBerry (bought with his second cheque from Claude) and Googled 'Parkhead', 'Neil Lennon' and 'Beltane' whilst wondering about the damage to his guts this diarrhoea in a plastic cup was doing. *Ah, so Beltane is 'the greatest occult festival of the year, bar Hallowe'en,' Parkhead is where Celtic FC play – historically a Catholic club – and my old friend Guy has been sending the manager, Neil Lennon, some very sectarian letters by the sound of it. Add some guilt and a 'wee dram o' the harrrrd stuff,' and bingo! Devil hallucination. It's a lemon entry, my dear Watson. Still, wrap it up in some of that other shit I recall and anything else I can rip from Wikipedia and there's your article, Claude – BELTANE BLITZ! THE DEVIL WALKS IN GLASGOW! Attached is my invoice, pay up or I kneecap your kids.*

He shut down Google and rummaged through the inbox – a text from Natalie. BORED, it read. SO BORED I'M GOING TO WATCH CORONATION STREET. LOVE YOU. *Jesus, nobody's ever* that *bored.*

Except me.

Well, that was just the price he paid, wasn't it? He checked his watch again, saw it was still insanely early, and decided the rest of the coffee-coloured water could rot in its cup. He was off home to see his girlfriend.

He zipped his leather jacket right up to his chin as he crossed to his lonely car – early May and still chilly; whatever happened to that Global Warming he'd heard so much about? – and as he opened the door, he jumped in sudden terror.

There was something in the back seat.

No, there was some*one* in the back seat. Maybe five foot nine, medium build – a man, definitely a man...

One of those fucking murderers from the services, he thought in panic, *they've got in the car, hidden in the back, and now they're going to fucking stab me.* For a second, he froze, unable to think of a single thing to do. Then he looked again at the back of the car, ready to run if the bastard struck. *Great thing about a Civic,* his mind babbled, *only a two door, he'll have a struggle getting out – I can be onto the motorway before he's on the tarmac, flagging down a Police car.*

But, of course, when he looked properly, the car was empty. Which it always had been, and was always going to be – except when he gave Nat a lift anyway. And she'd never been in the back seat, except when they'd driven to Margate and had some fun while the sun went down. There was no one in the back seat. Trick of the light, tired eyes, too long spent in the company of nutters and retards who thought the devil could trot around a fucking council estate without being noticed.

Contagious dementia, thought Brian. He'd heard about such things – largely from that cheerfully foul mouthed psychologist. What had he said? Something about mass hysteria? 'You see it at football matches, mainly – but anywhere where there's a gathering of large numbers of people with a like mind and an atmosphere of heightened emotion will do. Look, I've got a season ticket at White Hart Lane, right? And I'm sane and rational – with certificates to prove it. I walk in through the turnstiles with every appearance of a civilised, early twenty-first century man. Ten minutes before kick off, I'm looking around at the rest of the crowd with mild curiosity, I've got some Bovril, maybe a packet of crisps, a pie. I'm chatting to the bloke next to me or sharing a joke with the woman in the row ahead. Being perfectly normal. Ten minutes after kick off, I'm an animal. I'm screaming at the ref because he's missed a foul. I want every opposition player sent off for no very good reason whatsoever, just because they've got the wrong shirt on. And *everyone around me is doing the same!* Listen, we played Arsenal last year – and we *hate* Arsenal. We were two nil up after twenty minutes and there was practically a mass orgy in the stands. I mean it – that woman in the row in front of me is in her mid fifties and maybe a touch on the podgy side, but I was on the verge of asking her for a blowjob. And the thing is, she'd have given me one. But, we went on to lose that game five-three. And by the time the final whistle had ended if the nice middle-aged lady had shouted "let's storm the pitch and hang those Gunner bastards by their bollocks from the crossbar," I'd have done it. We *all* would. We *hated* those bastards! And their fans. I actually wished cancer on them. Truly. Not proud of it, but I did. Lots of people, like minds, heightened emotion – that's how it works. Likewise those religious rallies where people get 'cured'. Likewise your mad mates and their "ghost hunts." They *want* to see ghosts, that's why they're there, they're up late, they're in their pack –

someone pipes up, "Oooh, look, a ghost!" and *everyone* sees it. They're not lying, they really *do* see a ghost. Not because it's there, but because they *want* to, they're in the right emotional state, it's catching. It jumps from person to person. Nobody's immune, not even someone as clever as I am.'

Or someone as cynical as me, apparently, thought Brian as he closed the car door and turned the key. It was disappointing, but not entirely unexpected. Maybe the madness of these desperate saddoes was like cigarette smoke – harmless enough? Ask Roy Castle.

I may need a month off, he thought as he rejoined the motorway. *Take Natalie away somewhere. We could just about afford it. Somewhere sunny. Somewhere fun. Somewhere where no one ever thought they saw the devil.*

All the way back to London, Brian found himself glancing uneasily in the rear view mirror, then calling himself an arsehole. Then glancing at the mirror again.

XV

'Who the fuck's *that?*' Natalie screamed as he opened the door four hours later.

Brian's heart choked him as it leaped into his throat. It had been just after six when he'd pulled up, and Stroud Green was just starting to rock and roll. London didn't sleep, it just dozed lightly between the hours of four and six. So he'd shut the car door quietly (and had maybe taken just another look at the back seat, just in case…and guess what? *There was no one in it!*) and more or less tiptoed to the front door, slid his key in slowly, turned it with infinite care…

At which point his girlfriend had screamed like a banshee from the front room.

He dropped all pretence at stealth and ran to her. She was curled up on the sofa - no, that was too gentle – she was *furled,* like a hedgehog, her eyes wide and a horrible colour of sleep deprived red.

'Nat, it's me,' he said, wholly unnecessarily. 'What's up, love? What the hell are you doing down here?'

She grabbed at him like she was drowning and he was driftwood. 'Jesus, Brian...Jesus fucking *Christ!* God, I'm glad...Jesus!'

He held her close, felt her shaking like a shitting dog. 'Come on, Nat. What is it? Did someone try and break in?' *The joys of living in London.*

'No,' she said, almost crying. 'Not like you mean. There was...a voice, in the bedroom. When I was asleep.'

Brian felt her skin under his arms break out into goosepimples. *My God, she's terrified. Utterly terrified. Who did this to her? I'll hang him by his balls from the crossbar.* 'Easy,' he said. 'Easy.'

'*Easy,*' she screamed again. 'How the fuck am I supposed to be *easy?* I was asleep, in our bed, *on my fucking own,* when I heard this voice – this man's voice - in the room. At first I thought it was you, that you'd got back early, but when I sat up there was *nobody fucking well there! I was all alone!* And *somebody was speaking to me!*'

'It was just a dream, babe,' he crooned. 'Just a bad dream.'

She threw him away from her, and stared back with savage eyes. 'It was *not* a bad dream, you dozy *twat!* I *know* a bad dream when I have one! Someone *fucking spoke to me,* in our room! They *spoke!*'

'What did this voice say?'

She shuddered all over. *She believes this,* Brian thought with some sort of wonder. *She really does.*

'It said, "little girl, I'm going to eat you the fuck up".'

Brian grabbed her, held her, rocked her gently (*rocked her slowly*) crooned some nonsense about it all being over, about there being nothing to worry about, that he was home now and he'd protect her.

He was profoundly grateful she couldn't see his face. He was almost pissing himself laughing.

XVI

It's not that I don't care, he thought three hours later as Natalie slept on the sofa and he was typing up the previous night's notes (generously padded out with some cut and paste shit from Wiki, altered *just enough* for him to avoid a plagiarism suit) *it's just that…I mean, come on,* little girl, I'm going to eat you the fuck up? *Who* wouldn't *laugh at that? Look, she fell asleep, had a nightmare, one so real she thought she'd woken up. That, and all the shit I have to write about just so we don't end up living in a skip behind Morrison's, gets into her head and she has a mild freakout. Well, maybe* not so *mild, granted, but hey – nothing here that can't be explained, nothing to see, move along, ain't you got homes to go to?*

He'd done enough, five thousand words exactly, so he closed the doc and sent it to Claude – long gone were the days of three or four drafts. *Let the sub sort it out. That's what she gets paid for.* He then opened up Internet Explorer and surfed for cheap holidays; with no trouble at all he found a weekend in Amsterdam, three hundred quid. *Fuck it, we're going. Even if I have to write an additional three articles for next month's rag, we're going.* He went ahead and booked it. *Be a nice surprise for Nat when she wakes up, make her happy.*

MESSAGE WAITING, said IncrediMail. Once more, it lied – there were two. One from Claude, thanking him for the article. He'd only scanned it, but thought it was superb, well done, send the invoice and *yadda yadda* yah. The other was – drumroll please! – from Nikki McFatster-Tubby. PLEASE, she'd typed between shovelling pasties, IT IS STALKING YOU. YOU MUST DO SOMETHING. BEFORE ITS TWO LATE.

Too late, you fat illiterate fuck, thought Brian as he deleted the thing. Then he printed off everything he needed for the holiday, went downstairs and waited for Nat to wake up and give her the good news.

XVII

The holiday was a great success – if holiday it could adequately be called. Maybe *dirty weekend* was nearer the mark. Maybe *exceptionally* filthy *weekend* would have been the literal truth.

Nat had still been – well, strained – up until take off. She'd taken a hell of a lot of persuading to actually even *return* to their bedroom on that night after he'd returned from Scottish Beelzebub Hunting. She'd followed him around like a puppy all that day, and by the time night had arrived and Brian – having had exactly *no sleep at all* for thirty-six hours or so – was biting his lip to keep from snapping at her. He really didn't want to, because he loved her, but he was not a man who enjoyed being clung to – which was one of the reasons he'd fallen for Natalie in the first place. She was self-possessed and ever so slightly driven; she didn't need her hand holding when she crossed the road.

But she'd needed virtually dragging to bed that night – and there was *another* first. 'It's going to be OK,' he'd said, over and over. 'I'm here now, you're not on your own.'

'Brian…' she'd virtually whimpered, 'you didn't hear it.'

No, and neither did you. But he'd kept that inside…like he did with the mental patients who claimed to have seen ghosts of invisible cats. 'If I do tonight,' he'd said, 'I'll get up and see who eats whom.'

That had almost garnered a smile, but still, as they'd slid under the duvet, she'd clung to him like a limpet. She'd flinched every time a car drove past. He'd kept calm, despite his raging tiredness, and stroked her hair and her back (and copped the odd feel of her bottom, which made him smile a bit) until she'd fallen asleep. Not long after she'd escaped to oblivion, he'd felt himself sinking too. *Keep quiet,* he'd thought, to the room. *Just shut up. I'm tired and I need my kip.*

There'd been no noise at all, from anywhere – apart from the odd bit of crap that escaped Natalie in the night. *Sleeptalk*, Brian called it, and he loved it. Her brain kept sending things to her mouth, even when the mouth was sleeping. Anyway, he was asleep and didn't hear it.

Not even when she said, 'Offfuckoff.' Not even when she said, 'Eat you the fuck up.'

Anyway, even if he had, he would have just said she was dreaming; unconnected phrases picked up from the recent past, regurgitated from her mouth.

What else could it be, anyhow?

XVIII

But the holiday (dirty weekend, filthy weekend, whatever) went spectacularly well. They giggled together like teenagers from the moment the plane landed at Schipol. *It's like she's taken a really heavy coat off*, Brian thought. By the time they'd arrived at the hotel just off the Damrak, they'd barely been able to stand up for laughing.

What were they laughing about? Nothing, nothing at all. They'd not even had a smoke (though that was certainly on the agenda.) They were just laughing. Until the guy at Reception checked them in. *Then* they had something to laugh about.

'Have you been to Amsterdam before?' he asked in perfect – if ever so slightly accented – English.

'He has,' said Natalie.

'Fifteen years or so ago,' said Brian.

'But me, no. From what I've seen just walking down from the station though, it's very beautiful.' Natalie smiled at the Reception man, her best, biggest, most dazzling smile. *If we ever have a power cut,* Brian had once said, *I'm not going to bother with candles. I'm just going to ask you to smile, because you light up a room.* Natalie's response had been, *fuck off, you soppy bastard.* That, pretty much, was why they worked so well together.

The Receptionist noticed that smile too. He couldn't help it. Any notion of professional politeness vanished out of the window. At that point he would have imitated his fellow countryman and cut off his ear if she'd asked. 'Here, I have a map,' he said, plucking one from the rack behind him, which were clearly marked €2.50. He unfolded it before them, took a pen from his top pocket, and started tracing lines. 'We are here, yes? This is the Vondelpark, down here is the Rijksmuseum...and up here,' he said with a noticeable smirk, 'is the red light district. Very popular with English tourists.'

Several responses went through Brian's head at that. The one he liked most was, *yes, I'm taking her for a stroll around later tonight, see what I can charge by the half hour,* but thankfully he thought twice about it. He wanted his genitals in good working order. 'That's very kind,' he said instead, and pulled the money from his wallet.

The Receptionist waved the money away. 'No, no. It's a gift from me. Now, let me take your cases to your room.' He grabbed the key from the board and flipped open the desk flap.

'There's really no need,' said Natalie, though she didn't do much to stop him.

But the Receptionist waved all that away too, gathered up their bags and led them down a maze of corridors until they arrived at their door, slotted in the key, and showed them around. That took him maybe ten seconds; on Brian's budget this wasn't exactly the Bridal Suite.

Once more, Brian tried to thrust money at him, once more the Receptionist declined. 'Enjoy your stay,' he said, not really taking his eyes off Natalie, and closed the door behind him.

Somehow they managed to wait a good fifteen seconds before bursting out laughing – largely by staring at the faded carpet – but after their eyes met, it was game over. They fell together, howling.

'You total *strumpet*,' Brian managed to say.

'*Me?*' Natalie exclaimed, peering over an imaginary fan. 'All I did was smile at the man. I smile at *lots* of people.'

'Keep smiling, hussy,' he said, enjoying how many outdated terms for *prostitute* he could drag from his memory. 'We might get free drinks in the bar.'

'I'll tell you what you're going to get for free,' she breathed in his ear, then rubbed herself against him. At which point Brian stopped thinking about dated English and started giving thanks to the Lord for what he was about to receive.

XIX

That was the pattern for the rest of it. Silliness, giggling, sex, the occasional smoke, sex, booze, food, sex, and the odd bit of sightseeing. They wandered through the Vondelpark taking in the entertainment, they toured the Rijksmuseum and thoroughly appreciated the Rembrandts ('Damien Hirst can stick his cock up his arse,' said Natalie, 'this bloke could at least *paint*.'), they stood outside Anne Frank's house and Brian found himself a bit disgusted that it was now a tourist attraction. 'I appreciate its historical importance,' he said, 'but Jesus, it's like looking at something from Thorpe Park. Seriously, do you pay extra for the *inside the wardrobe* experience? Do a gang of actors dressed up as Nazis storm the place every twenty minutes and re-enact the capture? Do a...'

But Natalie had cut him off by licking the back of his neck. 'Shut up and buy me lunch,' she said.

So he did.

On their last day, Natalie surprised him somewhat by saying she wanted to see the red light district. 'Oh hon,' he said, 'I went there when I was twenty. It's horrible, really. Tacky – but not in a fun, Bournemouth sort of way. It's dangerous and nasty and really, really shabby.'

'Don't care,' she said, almost skipping across Dam Square. 'Want to go, want to go, want to go.'

'I bet you were a right pain in the arse as a kid.'

'Yep.' At that moment, Brian thought she was glorious. *No wonder that poor bastard at Reception reacted the way he did. Hell, I've been with her for two years now and I'd still sell my soul for her. Imagine if it was all new.*

'All right then,' he said. 'But I want my protest noted.'

'Duly noted it is,' said Natalie. She kissed him on the nose, grabbed his hand, and started skipping along the square again.

So they went to where the tarts and the pimps lived, and in truth, it was even worse than Brian remembered. *Seedy* was the word; no fun or even tawdry glamour showed its face here. This was all business. The sex shops with their goods proudly displayed in the windows ('What's that?' Natalie had asked as they passed one, pointing. 'It's a plastic arse, love,' he responded. 'What's it for?' 'You take it out of the box and stick your cock up it.' 'Of course,' she'd said, after a nose wrinkling pause. 'How silly of me to ask.') the windows with their goods proudly displayed – sad, blank looking women who – upon noticing their gaze – would listlessly perform a bump and grind with all the enthusiasm of a call centre operator.

'The ones with the curtains drawn...?' asked Natalie, rather vaguely.

'They're busy with a client.'

'So behind that window, right now,' she went on, pointing, 'there's a couple shagging?'

'Yep.'

'When you came here before, were you ever...well, tempted?'

Brian thought back to the dim, dead days of his twenties, when he and the gang he'd run with at college had bombed over here to celebrate their exam passes. Brian and Anthony and Mark and Cliff. All of them young, all of them at the centre of their universes, all of them certain that World Domination was just within their grasp. This was their first port of call – live sex shows! Adult fun! Women with their knickers off! How *couldn't* this be their first port of call? But as soon as Brian had set eyes on the place, he'd wanted to leave. It was hideous and ugly, with a nasty vibe thrumming through the cobbled streets.

Cliff, however, was entranced. He had his face pressed against every window like a kid in a toyshop with money in his pocket and a surfeit of things to spend it on. Eventually he picked his whore, despite everything Brian had done to dissuade him. 'Come on,' he'd said, 'how can I go back home *without* having fucked an Amsterdam prozzie? It'd be like going to Blackpool and not visiting the Tower. Think about it, lads.'

So he'd stumped up the money, walked into the building, and they'd all seen him enter the window. He'd given them a manic thumbs up (apposite, really, considering what happened.) But it wasn't the insane enthusiasm of his old friend that Brian recalled with terrible clarity; it was the awful, vacant face of the woman as she drew the curtain. She could have been one of the rubber dolls they'd just seen in a sex shop for all the expression there.

Less than ten minutes later, however, he was genuinely laughing hard – doubled over, in fact – at the sight of Cliff as he tumbled back onto the pavement with a very dazed look on his face.

'Fucking hell,' Mark had said. 'You look like the coyote when Road Runner hits him with an anvil. What happened?'

'Well...' Cliff had said (more than a little unwillingly, it must be admitted), 'first she made me wash my dick in a sink, then she put two condoms on me...'

'*Two?*' Anthony had exploded in disbelief.

'Yeah, *two.* Couldn't feel a fucking thing. Then, right, she lies on the floor, and I get on top – no kissing or nothing – and I'm three pumps in – and it was like fucking the Blackwall Tunnel– and then the dirty bitch sticks her finger up me arse and I go off like a fucking shot!'

That did it, that made it worse. The three of them staggered together, holding each other up.

'Then she pushes me off, says "Goodbye," and I'm out here with me fucking flies still open.'

'How much did you pay for this erotic pleasure?' Brian managed to ask.

'*Fifty fucking guilders!*' Cliff screamed in anger, and from that there was no escape, their legs were useless to them, and they fell to the floor, and Brian had laughed until his stomach muscles screamed in pain.

Old times, good times, good friends...

'Hon,' prompted Natalie from the present, 'you still here?'

'Sorry,' he said. 'Just thinking 'bout the old days. No, never tempted.'

'And now? Are you tempted now?'

Brian reached forward and drew Natalie to him. 'Very,' he said. 'Very tempted. How much do you charge?'

'Oh, you could never afford me,' she said. 'I'm a very top drawer whore.'

But she kissed him, regardless of her price bracket, and they held each other. But a part of Brian was still in the past, wondering what had happened to that old self of his, the one who didn't write shite for a living, the one who saw nothing but greatness in his future.

But it's OK, really he thought, holding his girlfriend. *I've got her, so that's OK, that's fair exchange, which is no mockery.*

XX

He felt Natalie tense beside him as the cab dropped them off at home, but it was only fleeting, and as they fell into bed that night – their own bed – she lit out for the Land of Nod quite easily, Brian not long after. His last thought before the darkness came – in oh so many ways – was, *that was good. We needed that. Now, back to the real world.*

There was a sentence that would have bitter resonances in the weeks to come.

XXI

The morning after they'd returned from Amsterdam, Brian had only just logged on when he heard a cry of pain from the kitchen. 'Fuck *YOU, bastard!*'

He raced downstairs to find Natalie lying on the linoleum rubbing her foot, her beautiful face contorted in agony. Next to her were an unopened ironing board, and an iron. It didn't take Columbo to figure this one out. He knelt by her. 'You OK?'

'Am I *fuck* OK,' she said. Thin tears were squirting down her cheeks. 'Dropped the pissing iron on my fucking foot. Bastard *hurts!*'

'OK babe. Can you stand? Come on, let me help.'

He helped her to stand, but when she put her weight on her damaged foot she screamed again. '*Fuck off!*'

'Right, you're coming to the hospital.'

'I am *not,*' she said. 'I might have work coming in. I can't miss it.'

'Babe,' Brian said, 'you might have broken something. In which case you need X-rays and shit. I am not arguing. Here,' he went on, and swept her into his arms like a bride. She locked her arms around his neck and he gently, ever so gently, led her to the front door. There, of course, he had to set her down to get his keys, and his coat, and unlock the door. All of this accomplished, he reached out to pick her up again.

'Thanks,' she said, still leaking tears of pain, 'I'll pass. You'll just have to put me down again to shut the door, then again when we get to the car, and I gotta tell you, I'm a bit nauseous. Any up and down movement may cause puking.'

'OK, you're the boss. Lean on me then.'

She did so, and eventually he manoeuvred her to the Civic's passenger seat, and off to their nearest A&E department.

Where they sat for an hour and a half, Natalie digging her nails into Brian's arm to avoid screaming, before being seen by a Doctor who looked like he was looking forward to shaving. 'Hmmm, can you wiggle your toes?' Before she could answer, he reached out and tried to wiggle them for her. The language that Natalie produced was poetic, in a John Cooper Clarke sort of way. 'Hmmm,' he said again. 'That'll need an X-ray.' He then wrote out a form, flung it at Brian, then went away again.

'Get that bastard's number,' Natalie said through gritted teeth. 'I'm going to report the fucker.'

Twenty minutes later a nurse arrived with a wheelchair, and Natalie was trundled – with a helpless Brian in tow – to the X-ray department. Where they sat for another hour before she was taken from him and wheeled into a side room with DANGER RADIATION stickers all over it.

Christ, please let it be nothing but a bruise, let her be OK…but frankly, I don't think it's on the cards, is it? Not the way she screamed when that twat played with her piggies.

Half an hour later she was out. 'What's the verdict?' he asked the nurse.

'It'll take two hours for the results to come through,' she said. 'We're very busy today. You can wait in the waiting room.'

Where else? Brian thought, and wheeled his beloved back down the corridors. 'How bad is it, babe?'

'Very bad,' she said, and Brian was once again stung by just how deeply he felt for her. He hated seeing her like that, in pain. *I'd rather it was me.*

It took closer to three hours for their names to be called, by which time Natalie was almost white with agony and frustration. 'Yep,' said another Doctor, one who looked like he'd been in the job for a while. Maybe an entire month. 'Compound fracture of the metatarsal. What was it, an iron?'

Natalie could do no more than nod. *She's going to pass out soon.*

'We see that a lot. Painful, and slow to heal. Sorry.'

'Don't be sorry,' said Brian, almost at breaking point. 'Do something.'

'Nothing much we can do, I'm afraid,' the cheery little cocksucker said. 'Strap it up, wait for the bones to knit, give you some strong painkillers; that's the lot with broken bones. You'll not be walking for a couple of weeks; we'll give you a set of crutches.'

'That's *it?*' Brian asked, wondering how he was going to stop himself from leaping across the desk and pummelling the smarmy get into the middle of next week. 'That's *all?*'

But Natalie, either still compos mentis enough to sense his barely suppressed temper or (more likely) fixed on the word *painkillers,* managed to lay a hand on his arm. 'Thanks,' she whispered.

'I'll write you a prescription,' the quack said. 'Pick it up from the pharmacy on your way out.'

They did so – and that took another half hour. Natalie grabbed the bottle out of Brian's hand, glanced at the dosage, and threw some down her neck, dry swallowing. 'Get me home,' she said.

XXII

It was nearly seven by the time they'd arrived back at Stroud Green and by then the painkillers were kicking in. Natalie refused food, just lay on the sofa staring vacantly at the TV. It wasn't switched on, but she stared at it anyway. *She's more out of it than she was on the dope we had at The Glasshouse.* Brian, in dire need of bladder relief, left her downstairs and legged it to the bathroom. Whilst voiding, he heard a faint hum from the open door of the spare room he liked to call 'the office.'

It was the hum of the computer he'd failed to turn off when he'd heard his girlfriend scream. Realising he wasn't going to be writing anything that day – and maybe not for a while, if Natalie needed a lot of help - he stepped inside to switch the thing off.

But he didn't, not straight away.

Instead he stared at the open Word Doc on the screen, the one he hadn't opened because he hadn't opened anything when he'd been torn from his seat, the one that read in 25 point Arial;

YOU'RE A TALENTLESS FUCK AND YOUR GIRLFRIEND DOESN'T LOVE YOU.

After a long, long while Brian remembered to breathe. *Somebody got in, somebody got in my pissing house and did this! I will find them and kill them.*

There was, in fact, only one suspect; only one person with a set of keys. His landlord, Mr Caveney. And it *had* to be him, because there'd been no sign of forced entry (at the front, anyway, he amended) and no signs of disturbance. Nothing thrown about. Hell, the TV was still downstairs and his computer was still here – so if it had been a thief, what had they taken? The kettle? *Could be, that's one pricey Dolphin model.*

Oh sure, Mr Caveney was *supposed* to give a week's notice before he popped in for an inspection, and no, he'd never *actually* even bothered with one in the three years Brian had been there, but really…who else *could* it be? Maybe he'd been in the area – he had at least three other houses in the same street, decided to pop in, see if his wallpaper was still hanging straight, got no answer, used his keys to let himself in, pottered about a bit, maybe took a dump, then wandered into the office, saw the computer was on and decided to play an *oh so funny* trick.

I will kick your arse out of your nose when I catch you, Brian thought, then closed Word, logged off, and switched the computer off at the wall.

He had a girlfriend to look after.

XXIII

Said girlfriend was asleep and snoring lightly when he returned to the living room. He put a coat over her and kissed her forehead tenderly, then went into the kitchen for some tea.

Hey presto, the kettle was still there, and the kitchen door and window showed no sign of being forced. *Mr Caveney, you are a dead fucking man when I get my hands on you.*

He took the tea into the living room and sat on the armchair, never taking his eyes from Natalie until nearly eleven. Then he woke her, and told her it was time for bed.

'How long have you waited to use that line?' she said, still doped.

He gathered her up and carried her to bed, thinking that it was a good thing she'd worn a skirt that day. Trying to get her jeans off over that foot wouldn't have been funny.

He undressed her slowly. 'Are you getting a boner?' asked Natalie, muzzy and unfocused.

'Yep,' he said. 'Can't help it. You in your underwear; I'm only human.'

'You're a monster,' she said, almost smiling. He slid her under the duvet, noticing how her forehead creased in pain at the slightest pressure. 'A fucking monster.'

'You bet, gorgeous.' He kissed her forehead again. 'But I'm your monster.'

She tried to say something else, but before it formed properly, she was asleep.

XXIV

Not so Brian, who lay awake for quite some time. It had, after all, been quite a day; first seeing Natalie in that much pain and the attendant stress of that insane hospital visit, and second their fucking landlord deciding to play his most amusing little joke. *That's the price you pay for a lovely holiday,* he thought as finally he sank down into the black.

To be awoken some time later by Natalie.

She was moaning in her sleep. *Poor cow must've turned and bumped her foot,* he thought as clearly as he could at – he checked the clock – 3:03 AM. *I'll get her the painkillers.*

But he didn't; he lay there instead and froze as he quite clearly heard her say, 'You're a talentless fuck and your girlfriend doesn't love you.'

How the Christing Jesus does she know about that? I didn't tell her, she never went near the office – hell, she couldn't. I had to carry her up the stairs. So how does she know?

That question went unanswered, however. Instead, finally, he managed to say something. 'Hon,' he whispered through cold lips, 'you awake?'

'Alive and kicking,' said Natalie…but this time her voice wasn't sleep fuzzed. It was wide awake, aware…and not hers. Not hers at all. It was gruff, alien, deep.

A man's voice.

A man's voice, coming from his girlfriend's mouth.

'I'm raring to go,' that voice continued, and Natalie sat up, gracefully – like some reversed film, so quick and fluid were her movements. 'I'm in – in and out and round and about.'

Brian was utterly terrified – for the first time in his life, *ever*, he had simply no idea about what to do. This was lunacy upon insanity, mania, madness, psychosis.

Then Natalie turned and looked at him, and Brian's mental processes took off for a daytrip to the moon. *Sorry pal, we're outta here,* they said, waving.

Natalie's eyes glinted from her beautiful face; eyes so dark naturally that they pulled light itself into them. But not now; now they glittered, like a cat's. *It's pitch in here, that streetlight's not worked in at least six months, so* what fucking light *are her eyes reflecting?*

Natalie smiled at him, a long way from that smile that had destroyed the Receptionist in Amsterdam. This one was the smile of the mad, of the lost, of the small boy burning the ants under the magnifying glass. *'BOO!'* she screamed.

So did Brian. He screamed like a girl.

XXV

'Wha…oh, mother*FUCK*,' said Natalie, as Brian stopped screaming.

She was then rubbing at her foot – or attempting to, but that obviously hurt quite a bit, making her swear even more. 'What the fuck's the *matter* with you?'

'I...I...' Brian stammered, then flicked on the bedside light. There she was, his own gorgeous Natalie, no glittery eyes or supernatural grace. In fact, absolutely no grace at all, as she was bent almost into a question mark with pain. She didn't look magnificently happy, but she *did* look like his girlfriend. 'I'm sorry,' he continued. 'I must've...' *must've what? Been sharing my bed with a demon?* 'Had a nightmare or something.'

'You'll be having *another* if you don't get my *fucking pills*,' she spat at him. 'Christ, this hurts worse than *ever!*'

He muttered something like *yeah, sure, straight away* and left the bedroom, detouring only for a quick kidney tap. *Holy mother of God, that was some nightmare. Never had one like that since I thought Godzilla was in the airing cupboard. And I was five then, what's my excuse now?*

Stress, exhaustion, long weird day, he told himself as he washed his hands. *All that stuff that's gone on, all today's crap, all got vomited out of your subconscious in a bad mind-movie. Put it behind you, get Nat her pills, get yourselves some sleep.*

But the nightmare was hard to shake, even an hour later when Natalie had fallen back into a medicated doze. Very, very real, it was.

So? Films seem real when you watch them, but they aren't.

Yeah, that makes sense. But you see

He was still arguing with himself when he nodded off.

XXVI

All went well – apart from Natalie's agony and alternating patches of doped to the eyeballs tranquillity – for a good twenty-four hours. Brian surfed the net for WANKERS WHO THINK GHOSTS EXISTS, was directed to all sorts of exotic websites – some of which made the shops in Amsterdam seem tame - then tried again, replacing the word WANKERS with PEOPLE. He found a reference to a young woman in Hackney Downs who claimed to have been the victim of a Poltergeist back in the Eighties, events which (apparently) had been well documented by neighbours and the local papers. A little more surfing brought forth (sort of) confirmation of all this; press cuttings, told in that wonderfully dry and uninteresting way that only a local paper could manage. THE RATHBONE POINT SPOOK, one headline read. Blissfully, it refused to name the family involved, but had a photo of their house. *Way to go, boys,* thought Brian as he pasted this gold into a separate doc, *way to guarantee anonymity.*

He typed up a few notes, sent off a few inquiring emails – one to the paper, one to the woman involved – requesting permission to quote and an interview respectively, then spent the rest of the day waiting hand and broken foot on his beloved.

At times, the previous night's dream recurred, and – there was no denying this, so he didn't bother trying – it chilled him. But so what? It was only a nightmare. The reality was Natalie was in pain, she needed help, so he helped her. So wrapped up in that was he that Brian only thought once about driving to Mr Caveney's office and throwing a Molotov cocktail through the window.

XXVII

It was the day after, with Natalie safely doped in front of *Bargain Hunt,* that things started to get out of control.

Once more, Brian was sat at his computer. *They'll bury me here, sitting on this bloody chair facing this bloody monitor, and the headstone will read, Brian Palmer, 1975 – 20??. Did Piss All But Face a Fucking Screen.*

He checked his emails – nothing exciting. No response from the papers or the Hackney Downs Spook Woman yet. *Early days. Still, might as well start rewriting that cut and paste shit, see what I can get away with.*

So he opened the doc labelled BOLLOCKS, but instead of what he'd saved the day before he read,

ENJOY YOUR HOLIDAY? I DID.

And under that, he read,

I SAW YOU LOOKING AT THAT BLONDE WHORE WITH THE BIG TITS

And under that,

NATALIE THINKS YOU'RE A LOUSY FUCK

But the worst was at the bottom. The last line of the document was stark and awful.

THAT'S WHY I'M GOING TO KILL HER. After that, nothing. Apart from a smiley face emoticon.

XXVIII

Brian eventually thought, *so…how do I blame Mr Caveney for this one? What did he do, sneak in during the night, tiptoe up the apples and pears and decide to fuck with my head a bit? Not outside the bounds of possibility, granted – but* probability, *as old Sherlock would ponder? Doubtful. So what does that leave us with?*

Well, me I suppose. Or Natalie – yeah, could have been her, all that dope inside her, she probably doesn't even know what she's doing most of the time. Shit, she's downstairs watching Bargain Hunt *and hasn't once shouted out 'oh, I don't fucking care* how much *it'll make you fucking troll,' like she normally does. So, OK, she gets up in the middle of the night – you know, sleepwalking a bit - comes in here, leaves me a nice message, then pops back into bed none the wiser. Makes sense.*

No it fucking doesn't, he argued back. *She's got a broken foot, in case you developed amnesia in the last ten minutes. She can't bloody* walk *without crutches. And even doped to buggery, one ounce of pressure on said broken foot causes her to yell in pain. I mean, what are you* actually *saying? That somehow, without waking you, she got out of bed, grabbed her crutches, hobbled into here, wrote all this down after deleting the stuff you saved, then hobbled back to bed, got back beside you, fell back asleep – without waking you - and is now happily staring at the telly? Let's get back to old Sherlock – probable?*

No, he reluctantly agreed. *Not really. Which leaves…?*

Who d'you think *it leaves?* You, *numbnuts. Yeah, the holiday was a good idea – you've obviously been…shall we say 'overdoing it'…but it looks like it wasn't quite* enough. *Shall we say it was, at best, a partial solution? You need to quit this ghost shit. Somehow or other it's started dripping into your subconscious. You're the one getting up in the middle of the night and writing kak – and you could do that easily without waking Nat, the amount of dope she's got in her system. You've started packing your bags for a stay at the Laughing Academy. Quit now before they book you in permanently and the next time you see your girlfriend is through a slot in a padded door.*

Brian kept staring at the screen throughout all of this, his eyes never leaving those awful words. ENJOY YOUR HOLIDAY? I DID. I SAW YOU LOOKING AT THAT BLONDE WHORE WITH THE BIG TITS. NATALIE THINKS YOU'RE A LOUSY FUCK. And at the bottom, THAT'S WHY I'M GOING TO KILL HER. And that bastard, smiley fucking faced, twatting emoticon.

Yeah, quit, he thought eventually. *Makes sense, I'm obviously running on fumes here. Something's not right in my head. So yeah, quit, give it all up, phone Claude – no, I'll email him, less hassle – tell him I'm hanging up my crucifix and leaving the graveyards behind. And then I'll…well, I'll…I'll…*

What? What *would* he do? Go back to the pub full time and pull pints? If he worked double shifts for seven days a week he might almost make the money he was making now. OK, he'd never see Natalie, but at least he'd be sane.

Yeah, because that job was so stimulating. I'd never go mad there, would I? It's like the Garrick Club after all – endless inspiration.

I think you might be overlooking a very important point here, Bri – you're sleeptyping. I think you're in a slightly unhealthy place right now. Remember when you quit smoking after you got that cough that wouldn't go away and you got really scared? This is like that; you're facing an issue. Head it off now before it becomes worse.

All of which made a sort of sense. Brian could see that, even as he dragged the mouse over the text before him, highlighted and then deleted it. But he was a *writer,* for Christ's sake, a *professional* writer, that was all he had ever wanted to be and now he *was* one. This...whatever it was...was just a blip, a little mental hiccup, like that cough that had never developed into lung cancer, that was, in the end, just a cough.

I'll be all right, he thought as MESSAGE WAITING scrolled across the screen. *I'll be fine.* He opened the email – and as if to confirm how right his course of action was, it was from Janet McEverleigh, the Hackney Downs Spook Girl. An interview, she said, would be perfectly acceptable. She wanted her side of the story made quite clear. And look at this! She'd read his work in *The Unseen World* and thought it was excellent. 'Clear and level headed,' she'd typed. 'In fact,' she'd gone on, 'you're the only reporter I'd consider speaking to.'

So there, he thought as he typed his reply – thank you, when, where, whatever's acceptable to you – piss off *with your notions of quitting. Like it or not, this is what I do. What I have to do. I may hate it, but it's all I'm good for. Leave this and I'm good for nothing.*

XXIX

That night, in bed, Natalie beside him, muttering sleep trash such as 'that baby's got a hat' and 'leave the sausages in the pan, doughnut,' Brian may or may not have heard faint knockings in the wall. Little light raps, *one-two-three, one-two-three.* They may or may not have come in clumps of three, then a gap, then a threesome again.

He turned over, screwed his eyes shut, and decided he didn't hear them at all. And if he did, they were outside, from the street. *Some kids mucking about, for a laugh – honestly, eh? Did they still give out ASBOs? They should, for that lot. Bastards.*

Then he was either asleep or those faint knockings in the walls stopped. One or the other.

XXX

The day after he did or didn't hear the faint knockings, Brian may have thought he saw something in the mirror while he was shaving. He didn't, obviously, because he was alone in the bathroom, and anyway, even if he did see the outline of someone about five foot nine at his shoulder, and even if that did cause him to jump a bit, it was only a trick of the light.

There were two things that he could absolutely, verifiably guarantee happened. One was that Janet McPoltergeist replied, and suggested meeting up the following Thursday, eight o'clock at her house. Brian had said that was fine by him, thank you very much, he was looking forward to it.

The second was that Natalie was offered a job.

'I can't,' he overheard her saying into the phone as he walked into the living room, choking for some caffeine. 'I really *can't*. I've broken my foot. Yeah, dozy of me. Dropped a bloody iron on it.' Pause, while she listened. Then, '*How* much?' Another pause. 'Where is it?' More silence. Brian hung around in the doorway, not wanting to interrupt. 'Oh, but Miriam, I can't...it's too much...oh, did she? *Specifically* me?' Silence, then; 'No...not in a chair, but I'm on crutches. And out of it on painkillers most of the time.' More listening. 'When is it? Next Thursday? Gives me a week...but, hey I can't drive or...' Pause. 'That's an inconvenience for *you* though, isn't it? Oh, right, yeah. Expenses. Got it. Um...look, can I think it over?' Pause. 'I *know* they can't discriminate, but we've got to consider how practical it is.' Pause. 'Yeah, it'll obviously be accessible. And the money *is* good...How long do you need?' Pause. 'Give me an hour, I'll call you back.' She clicked the close button, then – without turning – said, 'Brian, never attempt to become a secret agent. You've all the stealth of a bull elephant.'

'Not to mention the sexual equipment,' he said, stepping into the room. 'Job?'

'Yeah, next Thursday. Ashworth, in Kent. Working for the NHS, training newly qualified doctors in how to break bad news. Run by the same mob that got me the last day's work – Miriam says they specifically asked for me.'

'You doing it?'

'Oh, how can I?' she moaned, pointing at the crutches resting by the sofa. 'I can hardly walk, I'm more stoned here than I was in Dam Square...'

'Though you seem lucid now,' said Brian, knowing she wanted this job, knowing she wanted him to talk her into it...not that it was a problem, he wanted her to take it. Broken foot or not, she loved her work and Brian loved her; that was the way the world worked.

'Yeah,' she said, a little surprised. 'But, that's just the tablets wearing off. In a minute I'll be screaming in pain again.'

'But this job's not for a week, you'll be better then. Better enough, anyway.'

'Yeah,' she said, agreeing despite herself. Or so she probably thought.

I'm pushing an open door. 'How much are they paying?'

'Five hundred. For the day.'

Brian whistled. 'Not bad at all, babe.'

'No. It's not, is it?' She smiled, that smile that had reduced the Dutch bloke to jelly. *Can I have sex with her now? I'd avoid the foot, honest.* 'And Miriam said she'd take me there, bring me back…they'll pay her expenses…'

'And she's got that Range Rover,' said Brian, in a *there's the deal sealed* sort of way. 'Plenty of room. Phone her back, tell her you'll take it.'

'I don't know…' she demurred, biting her bottom lip, the way she occasionally did when she rode him to orgasm, 'what if I'm not well enough?'

'You'll be fine,' he said, desperate to nail her there and then. 'You, phone back. Me, boil kettle. Tea?'

'Love one,' said Natalie, already pressing the green button on her phone.

See, thought Brian *as he made his way into the kitchen. Everything's fine.*

He even pretended he didn't hear the voice that said 'you fucking think so?' in his ear.

XXXI

But as he lay in bed that night, listening to Natalie talk to an elf about shoes, a stray, random thought decided to take a walk through his brain.

Listen, it said, *I don't know if you've* really *paid attention to what's going on here. Odd messages keep appearing on your computer screen. Faint knockings in the walls, a faint figure in your car, a little voice – maybe a man's, maybe not – whispering in your ear. And the thing that spoke to Nat while you were up in Bonnie Glasgee. Suppose…just* suppose, *mind…that all this* is actually happening? *What then, oh wise one? What* then?

But it isn't *happening,* he answered himself, and rolled onto his back. *Tricks of the light, nightmares, tiredness, tinnitus, a computer virus. Th-Th-That's all, folks!*

He continued telling himself that even as those low knocks started again, *one-two-three, one-two-three,* preventing him from sleeping until way after four, when the first pale signs of daylight began to filter through the curtains.

XXXII

The rest of the week passed with absolutely nothing of value whatsoever; Natalie received her brief and learned it, sat on the sofa with her leg in the air as the foot gradually healed, and Brian did some background reading on the Hackney Downs case, which turned out to be more interesting by the second. It really *was* incredibly well documented; witness statements from everyone concerned, neighbours, some passers-by, a lollipop lady who happened to be stationed opposite the house, police officers who'd been called, a Council Housing officer who thought this might be some kind of re-homing scam; there was even supposed to be some audio recordings of Janet 'speaking as an old man' for hours on end.

This isn't an article, or an interview…this is a fucking series, Brian thought as one web link led to another. *Maybe even a* book. *Hey, think of it…a real by God* book *at last, one you can take from a shelf and walk to the checkout with. An advance…royalties…signings in my local Waterstones…*

His head filled up with these dreams as the appointment with Janet McGhostygirl approached, so much so that he totally ignored the occasional YOU CAN'T WRITE FOR TOFFEENUTS FUCKFACE that appeared on his computer screen, or the knockings in the night that never woke his girlfriend, or even the gruff 'I'm on my way, tosser' that he'd heard one morning as he was parking his breakfast.

Sod all *of that,* he thought. *I'm going to make it. At last, I'm going to* make *it.*

XXXIII

On the Thursday that she died, Natalie hobbled to Miriam's Range Rover supported by Brian and a crutch. 'I'm not sure I should be doing this,' she said as she stood by its door, ignoring the fact that they were almost twenty minutes late already and Miriam – who had once worked as a phone whore for Playboy TV Chat and was not noted for her patience – revved the engine.

'Shut up,' said Brian, in his best *getting down to business* voice, 'and go and be brilliant. Work the injury into it. When they tell you the cancer's terminal, just look down and say, "but I only come in with me foot."'

Natalie gave him a half-hearted punch on the arm, then kissed him on the cheek. 'Love you,' she said.

'And you babe.' He helped Natalie into the passenger seat, watched her clip the belt across her wonderful chest (Miriam's was much bigger – it was, after all, what got her the Playboy job – but since it was actually just two bags of glue Brian paid it no nevermind). 'Drive safe, you two,' he said to Miriam.

'Always do,' she said, having already thrown the car into reverse and started backing out.

'See you later,' Brian called to Natalie. She waved back, then the car was away into the traffic.

That was the last thing he ever said to her.

XXXIV

'It was hell,' said Janet McEverleigh at eight o'clock that evening.

She was utterly unlike anyone Brian had met in his time writing shite for a magazine that peddled lies to gullible losers. Small, trim, 'plainly pretty' – almost as if a Pretty Woman mould had been corrupted somehow in the People Making Factory. Her light blue eyes looked shyly at him over her round John Lennon glasses, she fidgeted a bit in her just-past-its-best sofa that resided in the front room of the modest semidetached house she shared with her husband and two daughters.

She's not self-aggrandising, that's what it is, Brian thought as he listened – actually *listened. Everyone else has been full of their self-importance; kings or queens of a universe that just doesn't matter. Social inadequates who can't get along in the real world, so have to create one full of ghosts and goblins just so they can be the centre of something. She's not like that. Bollocks or not – and it* is *bollocks – it genuinely meant something to her. And not something good.*

'Everything that happened,' she went on, gnawing at her thumb, 'everything people saw. It was just hell. Couldn't go anywhere in the street for people pointing at me. Got taken out of school 'cause the other kids were bullying me. Mum had a breakdown, had to go into hospital. My sister Lianne still won't speak to me...' Janet trailed off, staring into the past.

'Look,' Brian found himself saying, 'if this is too upsetting, we can call it a day.' *What about your book?* a stern voice spoke up inside his head, but Brian ignored it.

'No,' Janet said, as firmly as she could. 'It's time I had my say. My kids...I've never told them about what went on when I was their age – my husband knows, of course – but...there's all that stuff out there now, isn't there? Websites and stuff, full of what went on. Maybe they should hear it from me, through you. Before someone else points it out to them. Before they start to get bullied.'

'OK,' said Brian. 'So just relax, tell me what you can remember, and if at any time you want to take a break, or it gets too much for you, let me know and I'll turn the recorder off.'

'Thanks.' Janet took a deep, steadying breath, then said, 'it started when I was thirteen. Not long after I, y'know, got my period.' She blushed and looked away. 'First thing was the knockings, little raps in the walls.' She tapped at her armchair, a rapid *one-two-three, one-two-three* tattoo.

Brian twitched a bit at that, but kept silent. After all, 'phantom noises' were a common enough phenomenon at 'hauntings.'

'I shared a room with Lianne back then – she's two years' younger than me – but they never woke *her* up. It was only me who could hear them. Then stuff got moved around, like. Things were never where I could find them. I thought she was taking the piss, right? You would. Kid sister hiding your homework or your brushes or whatever.'

'And the knockings? What did you think they were?'

'Didn't think much about them, really. Kids outside, maybe mice – our old house backed onto a railway line, there were hundreds of the bastards about.'

'When did you stop thinking it was your sister or mice?' *You're actually interviewing this one,* he marvelled. *Asking questions and listening for the answers. Normally you don't get a fucking word in edgewise.*

'When the bed started shaking.'

Not a flicker from those somehow sad eyes. That sentence had come out with all the calm boredom of 'it's raining out.' None of the desperate pleading or strange arrogance that the others – *all* the others - had demonstrated.

'That was about a week after the knockings started. Went up to bed at ten so Mum could watch the news in peace, and when I lay down the thing started thumping up and down. Not by much, couple of inches. It was like there were people either side lifting it up and slamming it down. Even Lianne saw it. That's when I started getting scared, like. There was only me and her in the room, see? Just me and Lianne. No one could have been messing about. And Mum came legging it up the stairs, ready to bollock us for making a noise, and she saw it too. Me lying on me bed, crying, the thing bouncing up and down...'

She trailed off then, no longer living in her own body, now deep in the memories of her past. Something very strange happened to Brian then. He felt a lump in his throat, and a stone in the pit of his stomach. He was *moved* by this. For everyone else he'd spoken to since accepting this gig – well, embracing the easy money, to tell the truth – he'd felt nothing but a mix of contempt and amusement. But he felt deeply sorry for this woman, and had no idea why.

'After that,' she continued at length, 'it all went mental. The telly kept changing channels – and there was no remotes in them days, was there? You had buttons you had to punch. But there we'd be, watching *Blue Peter* or something and then we'd be watching the news in Welsh on BBC2. No one near the bloody thing and it'd turn over. One night we got woken up by this woman screaming, screaming really loud like she was being murdered. Neighbours heard it too, called in the police. But it wasn't us screaming. The knocks got louder and louder, and they were at all times of day, didn't matter if there was people around or not. Just bloody knocking all the time. The lollipop lady across the street said she was looking right at our house one day – the crossing's right outside where I used to live – and she saw me in the living room, looking at her. Then…she said I…lifted my skirt and started, you know…masturbating.' Another flush to the cheeks, another look away. Then she looked at him again, almost angry. 'But then she turns and sees me next to her, wanting to cross the road, 'cause I'd just come home from school, like. And she nearly drops dead, looks back at the house, and there's no one there. She packed it in the next day. Poor cow.

'And then I got possessed, like.'

Brian held her gaze, wouldn't let her look away. Janet stared back – she didn't cut her eyes to the right or open them too wide or tug at her earlobe. She didn't give any indication that she knew she was lying.

'Go on,' said Brian.

'It's hard,' said Janet, in a small voice. 'I don't remember what actually happened when…I wasn't me, like. But by then it was all over the local papers. Oh, they never gave our names, but they did publish a photo of the bloody house! Brilliant!'

I know, I've seen it.

'Anyway, someone had got in touch with someone else from the SPR – Society for Psychic Research – and they'd sent some people round to investigate. Practically lived with us, they did. Nice men, didn't laugh, seemed to be trying to help – but still, strangers living in the house all that time...wore Mum down even more, that did. So, one of them kept a tape recorder going all the time – nothing like that,' she said, pointing at Brian's state-of-the-art Edirol, 'like one of the ones we had that you played your tapes on. And one day this thing's running, and he says "Janet? Janet," 'cause he said later it looked like I was dead, all glassy eyes, like, and...' a hard swallow, 'this man's voice comes out of me and tells him to fuck off, 'cause I'm going to eat him the fuck up.'

Brian twitched involuntarily, and shivered a little. Had it grown colder in there? *Eat you the fuck up.* Exactly what Natalie had said she'd heard from the man in the bedroom...

Except that was a nightmare, except that didn't really happen, because there are no such things as ghosts!

'Next thing I know,' Janet continued, 'all the people are staring at me, horrified like. "What?" I asked. Never knew a thing about it. Never, ever. Kept on happening though. It was like I'd...black out. One minute I'm feeding the budgie or eating my tea and the next everyone's staring at me 'cause I've told someone I'm gonna shit down their neck.'

Despite himself – and, yes, it was colder in that room – Brian laughed a bit. To his relief, Janet joined in.

'I didn't even swear back then,' she said. 'Neither did Mum. Nothing stronger than "bloody" anyway. But there I was, calling people "cocksuckers" and stuff. Yeah, I'd heard that stuff in the playground, but...still...it wasn't like me. And the voice they reckon I used...'

'Did you ever hear the tapes?'

Janet stared at him in horror. 'Why would I want to do *that?* I don't want to hear…to hear…' She paused again, wiping a hand across her nose. Her slightly red nose. She shivered. 'Parky, isn't it?'

'Yes.'

She reached out and touched a radiator, then pulled her hand back quickly. 'Heating's on.' Then she shrugged. 'Be a draught. Those windows are nearly falling out, we can't afford to get them replaced.'

She's looking for a rational explanation…no, not looking for, has accepted *the rational explanation. All of the others would have been screaming 'it's a g-g-g-ghost!' by now. She just says the house is tatty. Odd. No, normal. But odd for one of the Spook Brigade.*

'How did it end?' asked Brian.

'End?' asked a man. Brian *really* jumped then. In terror. He saw his breath hang in the air. Goosebumps ran the length of his body. His testicles decided to set up camp in his throat.

For no one else had entered the room. There was still only him and Janet, this trim, nearly pretty, middle-aged woman who was utterly convinced she'd once been the victim of a haunting, a woman he'd decided he quite liked as a person.

But now she sat opposite him and those timid light blue eyes blazed with a flat hatred and violence.

And she spoke in the voice of a man; a terrible, old voice.

XXXV

'It *hasn't* ended, fuckwit,' the voice went on. 'It *never* ends. I'm in this bitch until she *dies*. Why? 'Cause I can. For shits and giggles. Because Y is a crooked letter and it'll never be straightened. Because I can do what the fuck I want *when* I want. You'll see, you talentless fucking *hack!*' Then, even more terrifying, Janet leaned over to him and leered. 'You wanna fuck, son? You may as well, 'cause you're getting nothing from that slag of yours ever again. May as well. Get it in before it's too late.'

Brian simply couldn't move. He'd never experienced anything like that before. It was Janet, but it *wasn't* Janet. That voice – somehow familiar – was awful, gruff, and most definitely *male*. It wasn't an impersonation, he was sure of that – but if it wasn't…then what was it?

Then she blinked, cleared herself somehow, and looked at him. She took in the look on his face and said, 'What?' When he didn't answer, she burst into tears, and through her sobs he heard her say, 'Christ no, please. Not again. *Please.*'

But Brian could do nothing to comfort her.

XXXVI

He was in his car half an hour later, just sitting outside Janet's house. He couldn't drive, his hands were shaking too badly. *If I try to drive I'll plough this thing into a lorry.*

After she'd regained some control, Janet had virtually thrown him out of her house. 'I can't,' she'd said, 'I can't have this happen again. Go, get out, never speak to me again! *Never! Never!*' Brian had been too stunned to react, he'd just allowed himself to be bundled to the door. Now he sat behind the wheel of the Civic, emasculated. *I have no idea what to do, none. None at all. Was that…was that really…something supernatural?*

No, his rational side spoke up. *It can't be. Such things just don't exist, do they? In two years of digging around this pool of dog diarrhoea, what have you actually* found? Ever? *Nothing, because there's nothing to find.*

That *wasn't an act. It* did *get colder in that house. She* did *change her voice, her whole personality.*

Draughts. She even did that old confidence trick thing of pointing it out so you didn't deduce it for yourself. 'Oh, she must be on the level, she said it was a draught. And she changed her voice, her personality? Jesus Christ man, you live with an actress! *Or actor, whatever. What does she do for a living? Changes her voice and personality, numbnuts! Yeah, this Janet was good, better than any of them, and I'm sure you could wire her to a polygraph while she unravelled her awful tale and it'd stay flatlined, but that* don't make it real! *Real is overdue bills and empty cupboards, so go home, start writing, and earn some fucking money. Got that, Jeeves?*

Got that, strength five. But before starting the car, he pulled the BlackBerry from his pocket, looking for a text from Natalie to say she was home. But there was nothing.

Odd. *Still, maybe they've stopped off at some services on their way home. I believe it's the thing to do.*

Controlling his hands as best he could, Brian turned on the engine, let off the handbrake and started off home. With every rotation of the wheels, he felt better, calmer, more in control. By the time he turned into Stroud Green Road he was even whistling a tune.

Until he saw the police car outside his house, that is.

XXXVII

This is not going to be a practical joke, Brian thought as he walked to the two officers standing on his doorstep. *No twat from TV is going to jump out and say, 'Gotcha!' This is horribly, horribly serious.*

'Can I help you, gentlemen?' Brian asked. He saw them glance at each other, then the older copper asked if he was Brian Palmer. Brian said he was. The older copper asked if they could go inside. Brian said they could.

Five minutes later, Brian was sitting on his sofa, the older copper opposite him on the armchair. The younger one was standing at the doorway. Brian couldn't tell if it was the perfectly normal paranoia that innocent people felt when confronted by the Rozzers or not, but he was sure that the kid was preventing Brian's escape.

'Mr Palmer,' said the older man. 'Could you please tell me where you were this evening, at about seven o'clock?'

'Yeah, sure.' Why? 'I was here. I had an appointment in Hackney Downs at a quarter to eight. Didn't leave till seven twenty.'

'An appointment?'

'Yes, with a lady called Janet McEverleigh. I'm a writer. For *The Unseen World* magazine.' Brian went on to give McEverleigh's address and phone number for good measure. 'May I ask why you want to know?'

'Of course,' said the elder copper. But he didn't answer straight away. 'This Miss McEverleigh, she'll verify this appointment?'

'Yes.' *Unless the demon's got her.* 'Even if for some reason she doesn't, I've got the whole thing on here.' He produced the Edirol from his pocket.

'Hard disc?'

'Smart card. Dates and timestamps everything. So, there's your proof. So once more, if you don't mind, why are you asking?'

A puzzled glance passed between the two officers of the law. Then the older one fixed Brian with a professionally sympathetic gaze and said, 'Mr Palmer, did you know a young lady called Natalie Baxter?'

'Yes, I do know...' But for the second time in less than two hours, Brian felt pure terror. 'Nat...?'

'There was an incident on the M20. The Range Rover Miss Baxter was travelling in swerved across the road. It was hit by several other vehicles. I'm afraid both Miss Baxter and Miss Carlin were killed outright. We found this address among Miss Baxter's personal effects. We're sorry for your loss.'

Numbness rolled over him like a blanket. He welcomed it, ran for it, jumped into it. 'Incident?'

Another look between the officers. 'Yes. We can talk more later. Mr Palmer, is there someone you can call…?'

'Incident?' Brian repeated. His cold, numb brain fixated on it. *Incident, they said. Not accident,* incident. 'What does that mean?'

'Mr Palmer, you've had a shock. This would be better left to…'

'*Incident?*' Brian almost screamed.

The two coppers once again shared that imperceptible look. The younger one – a little more relaxed now – shrugged, as if to say, *your call, boss.* The older one gave a sour *thanks a bunch, mate* look back, then turned to Brian. 'It's very early days, Mr Palmer, but the best guess we have at the moment is that they picked up a hitchhiker. Witnesses report a man of medium height with dark brown hair leaning over the back seat and wrestling with the steering wheel.'

The numbness wasn't numb enough. This punched the air from him. 'They were…what? Murdered? Is that what you're saying?'

'At this moment, we're not saying anything definite. That's just what some witnesses reported. The car went off the road at seven this evening, ambulance crews and police were on the scene in fifteen minutes. Miss Baxter and Miss Carlin were pronounced dead at the scene. There was no sign of anyone else, but we, of course, have to check on everything.'

'Yes. Yes, of course you do.' Brian very shakily got to his feet. For a second he thought he would fall, but somehow he kept upright. 'Would you gentlemen excuse me,' he said with the politeness of a man at a formal dinner party. 'I think I'm going to throw up.'

He made it to the sink, and everything came out in a gush. With every heave, he felt himself thinking, *Natalie. Jesus God, Natalie.*

XXXVIII

He switched off the bathroom light and tried not to think about the empty bed he was about to climb into. The police had left about an hour ago, after formalising an appointment to identify his girlfriend's body. Since then he'd sat and stared at the blank television set, trying to figure out what exactly was going on.

Natalie's dead, he thought. *I'll never see her again, hold her, kiss her, fuck her, get on her nerves, watch her eat, listen to her talk shit in the dark. Natalie's dead. She has joined the choir celestial, she's pushing up the daisies, she's –*

Oh, stop quoting Monty fucking Python, will you? YOUR GIRLFRIEND IS DEAD! Possibly MURDERED. Murdered by some twat they picked up at the side of the road, Natalie and her bleeding heart, Natalie with her…

No, Natalie hadn't even been driving. This was that bitch Miriam's fault. Hey look at him, *she'd have said,* he's cute, I reckon I could get a casual fuck out of him. After all, I used to get paid listening to men tug themselves off, so I'm a whore, so I fuck anyone.

Yeah, a whore. Like those in the windows in Amsterdam, the ones he and Natalie had pointed at less than a month ago. A good weekend – no a *great* weekend. And now…

Now Natalie's dead because that bitch got a wet patch that needed sponging. Now Natalie's dead because her friend needed some meat up her and picked up a fucking psychotic that drove them off the road and just walked away.

If I find him, I will kill him. I will kill him twice.

The first of what promised to be a great many tears fell then. It brought some friends, and they invited their families. They partied on Brian's face as he sobbed.

But the tears passed, and Brian went upstairs to wash his face, and think about the future.

XXXIX

Before he went into his bedroom, Brian heard the hum of the computer from the 'office.' Of course he looked in, and on the screen of the Dell which he had left switched off and unplugged before he had left for his appointment a million years ago was an open Word Doc, with the words HA FUCKING HA written on it in clear 36 point Arial.

I am so spectacularly not arsed tonight, he thought, and pulled the plugs without closing the thing down properly. *I hope I've just lost everything.* On top of that, *yes, I have. Haven't I?*

XL

He lay awake all that night, listening to the knocks in the walls, and the gruff voice that spoke from the shadows, the voice that told him what a laugh this all was, what a great fucking laugh, didn't he just love it?

But Brian didn't care about any of that. He lay in his huge, empty cold bed and stared at the ceiling. *Let me get my hands on that bastard, just for five minutes. Let me alone in a room with him. Let me even up the score.*

XLI

At ten thirty the following morning, a haggard, unshaven, barely washed and red eyed Brian Palmer stood in a viewing room at North London Coroner's Office and braced himself as a man knocked on a wall. A shade behind the window he was facing opened. 'Yes,' he said, almost inaudibly, 'that's Natalie Baxter.'

The shade was closed, and Brian was glad. That car must have been going at a hell of a rate when it...happened. His beloved was bashed and bruised, the greyness of her face making those atrocities stand out all the more. Her nose canted to the left. Her mouth – the mouth that had made him sing to the angels – was ripped in two.

I will find the cunt who did this and rip his fucking face off and piss in the wound. Then I will rub salt in it, stitch the face back on, then rip it off again. I will do this world without end, amen.

But first, he broke down in tears and was escorted to a side room until he was fit to go home.

XLII

An hour and a half later, Brian entered his house thinking *I am going to get pissed. I am going to get so pissed I pass out. I'm going to hang a DO NOT DISTURB UNTIL JUDGEMENT TRUMP notice on my house and drink until nothing matters any more.*

Heavy, heartsore, weary Brian trudged through his living room. Then he stopped cold.

He could hear someone in his kitchen. Someone ferreting around in his fridge. He could hear the chime of bottles being moved around.

Brian's first thought was *who the hell...?* His second thought was *how the hell...?* His third thought, though, broke through the terrible wall of Novocain that had engulfed him in the last day. *It's him. The bastard who killed my Natalie. It's him, he's here, maybe to kill me as well – no, I don't know why, but one thing I do know is it* has *to be him. And here's where I take my revenge. I don't care if I go to prison for life and am raped in the showers by Mr Big who's in with the warders; I'm going to stamp this bastard's lights out. And sing while I do it.*

He heard the fridge door shut, and with a low, animalistic growl, Brian Palmer ran for the kitchen, not caring that was where knives lived, not caring he was armed only with his fists.

Payback's a bitch, was virtually his final coherent thought.

He somehow skidded to a halt on the lino as he came face to face with the man in the kitchen. The man was standing there, smiling, a can of Carlsberg in each hand, untroubled, unfazed, at ease, at home.

And why wouldn't *he feel at home,* Brian's rapidly disconnecting brain wondered. *It is his house after all.*

'Hey, Brian,' said the intruder. 'Fancy a beer?'

The intruder was Brian.

XLIII

'Shall we go into the living room,' said his double, 'make ourselves more comfortable?'

Brian said nothing. He just gaped at the sight. It was him. He was looking at himself. Same height, same weight, same hair, same clothes, same voice…somewhere in the deep recesses of his skull he felt several axons firing off sparks of electricity as they overloaded and burnt out.

'Suit yourself,' said the twin, shrugging. He walked past Brian into the living room. Brian stayed where he was, spittle leaking down his chin.

'Don't make me force you,' said his voice from the other room. 'I can, you know. It's just…well, I understand it can be unpleasant, and there's been enough of that already, hasn't there? C'mon, mate, take a pew. Let's sit, and tell sad stories.'

Brian twitched into life and somehow managed to walk into the living room. Uncomprehending, he stared at himself, sat across from him, sprawling on the sofa. 'That's the way,' his other body said, patronisingly. 'C'mon, to the chair, you can make it.' His double pulled open a can and foam spilled out in a gush, covering his hand. 'Shit,' he muttered, setting the beer down on the coffee table and waving his sodden right arm in the air. 'Don't you just hate it when that happens?'

Brian just about made it to the armchair before his strength gave way.

His double sipped the Carlsberg, then grimaced a bit. 'They reckon this stuff is probably the best lager in the world, but between you and me – literally – I still think it tastes like piss.'

'It was Natalie's,' Brian heard himself say.

'Yeah, I know. Of *course* I know, dickhead. I'm *you*, understand?'

Brian just sat there, staring.

His double sighed an *I've been expecting* this sort of sigh. 'No, you *don't* know, do you? You *still* haven't figured it out, numbnuts. All those clues I've been leaving you, all those messages from the sad bastards you so graciously patronise...and you *still* can't piece it together, can you? You want to know the irony, the bit that's just so funny it makes me want to scream? Any of them, even the one we called Fatty McFat-Fat, could have twigged it in a second. In fact, me old China, if you'd only listened to the pizza-guzzling bitch instead of making up insults in your head, maybe all of this could have been avoided, maybe Natalie would still be swallowing your dick instead of worms. Who knows?'

'What...what do you mean?'

'*Jesus Christ,* man,' said his avatar in exasperation, then took a deep breath and steadied himself. 'OK, sorry. Yes, things are moving a little quickly for you, I got that, and your brain's packing up.' He stopped, contemplating. 'I can actually *feel* it going. Odd…like an itch inside your head. But before it packs up completely, just have a go, will you? Start with Mrs Blobby and work forwards. Here, I'll give you a hand.'

Brian felt a pressure inside his head grow; synapses which had been unravelling came together. Pictures formed before his eyes.

He saw the fat boot from Nottingham staring off behind him, terrified.

He saw himself in the M1 services, glancing into the mirror because he thought he'd seen something behind him.

He heard the fat lass talk about spirits, some that walked abroad and some that stayed at home.

He thought about the two times he'd thought he'd seen someone on the back seat of his car; the second time quite clearly in the service station car park on the way back from Scotland…someone about five foot nine.

He heard Natalie saying she'd heard a voice from the dark, telling her he'd eat her right the fuck up. Saying she thought it'd been him.

He saw the computer screen with its awful messages. His computer. His *password protected* computer.

He heard the police, questioning him about his whereabouts when Natalie had died, about the man that witnesses had seen in the car. A man of medium build, about five foot nine.

He heard the voices from the dark that had spoken to him, he heard the voice that had come from Janet McEverleigh's mouth. The same voice, he realised now. The same, awful gruff voice.

The fat cow again, *If a person's spirit is kept inside, it becomes sour, chaotic, poisoned. It seeks to wreak havoc in the here and now, to destroy and confuse.*

'No,' he muttered. '*Please…no.*'

His double nodded, like a teacher who's seen the thick kid add two and two. 'Yep,' it said.

It had been *his* voice from the dark, *his* voice whispering in his ear, on the Edirol recording. It had been *his* voice that had spoken to Natalie that night as he drove back from Glasgow. '*I thought it was you,*' she'd said.

It *had* been him; his *spirit,* kept inside. Sour, chaotic, spoiled…misanthropic. His spirit, wreaking havoc, destroying and confusing.

He, Brian Palmer, all five foot nine and medium build of him, had been haunting himself. His spirit had been in the car with Natalie, somehow corporeal as it was now, it had – *he* had - turned the wheel that had caused the car to lose control.

He had killed his own girlfriend, his beloved Natalie, the only bright point in this wretched, terrible, trapped life he led. His sour, poisoned spirit.

He had done it all, himself.

'Sorry,' said his spirit as it sipped some more beer. 'Nah, who am I kidding? No I'm not. I mean, how *could* I be? I am what you made me. It's like when people say cats are cruel because they tease mice before killing them. They're not cruel, they're just what they are. Cruelty implies intelligence, and I – like cats – am a slave to my instincts. Your instincts. Well, *our* instincts. Gets confusing, doesn't it? Anyway, gist is, you made me the man I am today. A man who pretty much hates everything, including himself. All of that *poison,* all of that bitterness and rage, building up inside you…created *me.* The way everyone on this stupid, pointless planet creates their own ghost. Like Tubster said back in Nottingham, *the further a man's spirit wanders in life, the healthier it is.* Yours – which is me – didn't get further than your own – *my* own – fingernails. You ever wonder why some people see ghosts and some don't?'

Brian said nothing. Silent tears leaked down his cheeks.

'I'll tell you,' said his ghost, relaxing and giving an expansive stretch of the arms, 'I haven't a fucking clue. But, I can tell you what ghosts *are.* Ghosts are the projections of our own selves, our personalities. Sometimes you fleshbags can't quite process it properly so you filter it as a headless horseman or a chain-clanking skeleton, but all you're actually seeing is a *reflection.* Take that Janet, for instance – truthfully, she's a bit of a bitch. Worked hard to keep it covered, granted, but when she went on the rag – bang, out it all came. She hated her sister, blamed her Mum for the divorce – which she kept quiet about, I noticed – and so, when given the opportunity, her spirit popped out of the body and went a bit mental. She even did that wank show to try and give the old lollipop lady a fright.' More beer went down the ghost's throat. 'I'm not saying she did it deliberately, because she didn't. Her spirit just got out, had a bit of a play, then she shut it inside again.

'Effectively, it comes to this; nice people see nice ghosts, the nice ghosts they've created, that are part of *them*. Nasty people see nasty ghosts. And you're a *very* nasty fucker, so you've got a very nasty ghost. I mean, *look* at me. I'm *you*. You're so narcissistic you can't even be bothered to turn me into a hooded monk or a grim reaper. You've just *got* to look at yourself all the time.'

'Why?' moaned Brian eventually.

'Why what, numbnuts?' asked his ghost.

'Why kill Nat?' Brian's voice was hardly above a whisper. 'I loved her.'

'Yeah, I know,' said the ghost, dismissively. 'You love a Bargain Bucket on a Friday night, too. But you know what? You hated her a little.'

'No.' Brian wanted to scream this, but couldn't.

'Yeah you did. You always thought she was too good for you. You always thought she'd leave you some day. You were terrified of that – and don't bother denying anything, I'm you, remember? So I killed her. That way she'll never leave you. Us. And you know what? When I popped up behind the wheel and gave it a shake was the furthest I've *ever* been without you! And having taken a look around, frankly I can see why you kept me inside. Bluntly, the world of the living is a fucking shithole. Then I jumped into Janet's head and made her think she was possessed again, just for a fucking laugh.'

The ghost tipped the last of the can down its throat, then picked the other one from the table. He offered it to Brian. 'Sure I can't tempt you?'

Brian didn't even look at it. *Did I really hate her like he – I – said I did? Was I so scared I didn't deserve her that I…pushed her away?*

Does it matter? the fading, small voice of his sanity said. *For the record, yes you did. You'd have never harmed her, never – not intentionally, though* intent *doesn't seem to matter right now, does it? This seems to be all about instinct – but you so hated yourself you thought you were impossible to love. Following that line of thought to its conclusion, what* else *could you think but that she'd leave you sooner or later?*

Brian moaned again and shivered. He wanted to cover his face with his hands, but that seemed like far too much hard work.

'So,' said the ghost, brisk and businesslike, 'that's all the exposition out of the way. Now there's just the problem of – as they used to say on *A Question of Sport* – "what happens next?"'

'What...do you mean?' said Brian. He was tired. Very tired.

'Well, I'm out now,' said his ghost. 'Out, about and all around. Unlike things of no importance, which are neither here nor there, I'm both here *and* there. Which isn't on, is it – we can't *both* be Brian Palmer, it'd confuse the Electoral Register. So, here's my proposition. Why don't I take a try on the outside for a bit, see if I can manage what you failed at? You pop down into the depths of me and shut the fuck up for a while. Deal? Or no deal?'

'I don't...what do you...what are you saying?' asked Brian, awfully tired now, terribly confused, completely unable to think.

'Oh, piss off you fucking whiner,' was the last thing he heard his ghost say.

XLIV

Natalie was buried a week later. An inquest into her death reported it was the result of 'person or persons unknown.' Brian stood at the graveside and cried. Everyone who saw him remarked on how devastated he looked.

Her killer was never found.

When he returned home from the funeral, Brian wrote up his article on Janet McEverleigh for *The Unseen World,* and when that was done, he opened up a new Word Doc and started typing.

XLV

A year after Natalie's death, Brian received a letter. It was from a publisher. They'd accepted his book for their line and would pay him a generous advance against royalties. They'd be interested, they said, in reading more. Brian, who had been writing a *lot* since the funeral, printed off two chapters and a synopsis. Then he rang Claude and told him to stick his fucking job up his fucking arse, twat.

XLVI

Brian's first book, about a ghost in the Cotswolds, sold like a bastard. Four months after its release, Dimension Films picked up the movie rights for a sum so large it would barely fit on the contract. With that money he bought a house in Islington.

His second book, about a ghost that haunted an actress, was even bigger than the first. Paramount picked up the rights to that one.

His third, about a demon from another dimension, was sent off to a publisher's auction. His agent – whom he'd handpicked from the host who'd come swarming round him after his first book had done so well – sold it for one million pounds to Hodder. Hodder recouped their investment in six months. Brian sold the house in Islington and bought one in Barnes. A big one. The film made from that had a Royal Premiere at the Odeon, Leicester Square. Brian shook Kate Middleton's hand, and from the way she looked at him, she'd have quite liked him to do a little more with that hand.

Five years after Natalie died, Brian had become a rich and successful author. Not a writer, an *author*. TV companies begged him to come up with series ideas, and he told them all to get fucked, dickhead. He was banging an actress who commanded a six figure salary, and had a string of affairs on the side. He appeared on chat shows and breakfast television.

He had everything he'd ever wanted, and he loved it. He revelled in it, wallowed in it like a pig in shit. He laughed and laughed and laughed.

Well, most of him did. For deep down, buried and scared, was a small part of Brian that looked out through his eyes and cried, cried for his life, cried for Natalie, cried for what he could have been.

Still, Brian would think when he would feel that small, sad presence lurking. *Fuck it, eh, numbnuts? What did you ever do with my life?*

I Hear Talk

Wait.

You hear that? Talk. Upstairs. But there's no one upstairs. No one lives there anymore. But there's talk.

In the dark, in the night. Talk. They talk to distract me, keep me awake. Wear me down. They say

We know you know. We're coming.

Sometimes they laugh.

But not like we can laugh. They copy it.

Wait.

That's not my mirror. I know my mirror. That's not it. It's not my face in it. I have marked everything in this flat.

Everything.

With an infra red pen. This pen? See it? See it? That's what I mark things with. I outline cups and ashtrays and furniture and mirrors. My mirror. That mirror. It's not mine. That's not my face in it.

When I come home I shine my black light on the things I've marked. I know that they've moved things. The things they move I don't touch.

They come in through holes.

I destroy what they touch so they don't get me.

There are three levels of them and they are everywhere.

They teach in schools. They say

Kennedy was shot by Lee Harvey Oswald.

They say

There is nothing in Area 51.

They say

Men landed on the moon in 1969.

Ha! HA!

Stanley Kubrick made the moon landings in a studio in LA in 1969 with actors. The flag flutters in the breeze. I'd show you but I can't. There are no stars. Neil Armstrong wouldn't go along with it so they shot him and you never see him now. That's not him if you ever see him. That's a double. It's two inches taller.

Wait.

They come in through holes, did I tell you?

There are three levels. One looks like us. That's the top level. The level beneath that looks like us but wrong. They have pale skin and never see the sun and stand in bus stops and go *eh laaaaaaaaaa*.

Cigarettes do not cause cancer. Cigarettes PREVENT cancer. But they don't want you to know that. There's too much money in the lobby.

Through holes.

They say

Muslims flew planes into the twin towers on September 11 2001.

Kennedy was shot because he knew. But not in Texas. That wasn't him. He was shot in 1961 in his bed. Then a double said *we will go to the moon* and that was to scare the Russians. Then they shot the double. He was 4lbs thinner than Kennedy and the hair was wrong.

I would show you but I can't, it would give you cancer.

Do not use TV or radio or computers or phones they give you cancer. They have put RAYS in the TV and radio and internet. Turn them off. All of them. You see? You see? That's how they get you.

They meet in places and say things.

Their third level is like weasels. That's their true form. They live in sewers. They come up through pipes and get in through holes. People have seen them but they die. From cancer through TV.

They have been here a long time.

I wear tinfoil to stop them GETTING MY THOUGHTS. In my hat so they don't know.

They won't get me.

They won't.

Wait.

There is a spaceship in Area 51 but it is a fake. It was put there by them when they took over the government in 1961, so that when people eventually break in we will think AH A FAKE but it is all true. They play the double bluff.

You know that game?

They play it well.

They talk. I hear them. They know I'm onto them. I would show you but I can't.

At night they come through the holes and whisper. *They say not long now* and *they think you're mad.*

You cannot block up all the holes. You have to poo but they eat your poo, it is their food.

The twin towers were blown up by them. And the Pentagon. The twin towers were the distraction. A man in the Pentagon called WALTER M DISCHEL knew and was about to blow the whistle but they killed him with a plane so we didn't care.

Listen.

So we didn't care they DISRACTED us with the twin towers and a controlled explosion but no one died. They were all robots controlled by them. The phone calls were made in Texas by them and bounced by satellite all over the world.

The satellites are theirs.

That's not my face. I will tell you.

On YouTube you can see a woman falling from a window on September 11 but it is not a woman it is one of their robots. I would show you but I can't. If you slow the footage down and single frame you can see the light glint off the metal.

Wait.

The Prime Minister is one and the President. They start riots to scare us, but I am not scared.

And the Leader of the Opposition.

All the police and army too.

Listen.

You hear? Talk.

I could not block the holes. They came in last night

Listen.

Listen.

And gave me an implant. They put me in a drugged sleep so I could see but not move. They slithered like weasels from the toilet and put an implant in my head.

That's why it's not my face.

See.

Or my mirror. They have a camera there so they can watch. There's one in the TV too and the computer so they can watch you when you watch things.

It looks like my face but it's not. It looks like my mirror but it's not.

The implant is in my eye. The right one.

That's why you're here.

Wait.

Hold my head. Hold it. Hold it fast. Don't let me move.

Hold it.

This spoon is mine and it is clean. They have never touched it.

I will get this implant out.

I will tell the world what I told you.

I will dig it out with this clean spoon.

If thine eye offend thee, pluck it out.

Wait.

10:59

One

For the hundredth time in the last hour, Becka Goodman thought, *It just isn't going to happen. It's impossible. It's madness. Everything will be OK, you'll see. That clock will turn to eleven and you'll still be here to see it. So don't worry, it's fine.*

Which, of course, made sense. How could it not make sense? Everything would always go on the way it had. The clock on the mantelpiece – which currently read 10:38 – would tick on and on, just as it had for years. She would sit on her sofa, just as she had for years. And when 10:59 clicked over to 11:00, she would laugh (which she didn't normally do), call herself a Silly Becka (which was slightly more common behaviour), make her usual hot milk and tramp up the wooden hill to Bedfordshire, sleep for eight blissful hours, then start another day at The Card Factory, stacking cards and arranging teddy bears.

That's exactly what will happen, she thought. *I will not die at 10:59 tonight, no matter what the paper said.*

Trouble was, she didn't believe what she thought.

Two

When pressed to describe her, Becka's friends (well...*friends* was probably too strong a word. *Close acquaintances* was probably nearer the mark) would have described her thusly: *good hearted, sweet natured, a lil' angel.* Those who were perhaps of a slightly harder nature would maybe add, *not too sharp, a little slow on the uptake, just a wee bit too trusting,* but on one thing they all agreed, Becka Goodman was basically a nice person to have around.

'There's no side to her, is there?' Helen Reece, her manager at The Card Factory, had said on many an occasion. 'You never hear her bitch about anyone – not even the customers – you never hear her complain that she's tired, she never moans about getting stock; she's just...well, nice to have around.'

Fundamental niceness had been bred in the bone in Becka. Her parents had instilled this virtually from birth. 'Manners cost nothing,' her father had said – and, indeed continued to say. 'Remember "Please" when you want something, remember "Thank you" when you get it, don't forget to smile when you meet people; and if you've nothing nice to say, say nothing at all.'

These homilies – and many others, such as 'always leave a little on your plate for Mr Manners' – had been driven in with such gentle ferocity that by the time she'd left school, she'd gained something of a reputation. Perhaps not the best reputation, however. People basically thought she was a bit thick. The world, after all, did not embrace niceness easily.

She'd been on the receiving end of a fair bit of teasing and some medium to heavy bullying at school, and this often perplexed her and made her sad. Why did the other girls (and a fair percentage of the boys) want to stand in a circle around her and chant rude words at her? Why did they want to use such words at all? Becka didn't, neither did her parents. She – and they – were quite capable of holding a conversation without a lot of (as her father put it) *effing and jeffing*. And why were they always talking about that *thing* that thing boys did with girls? Why were they...well, *obsessed* by it? Why was there all that *giggling* in Human Biology when Mrs Rouse took them through the facts of life? It didn't seem a giggly or dirty thing to Becka. It was just something God had made for the human race to continue, that's all. On top of that, it was bad manners to giggle in class.

By the time she was fifteen, she could stand these questions no longer, and so took them to her mother. Becka stood in the garden, watching her mother hang out the washing, and asked her this question; 'Mum, why are some people mean?'

'Mean with money or mean as people?' her mother asked back through a mouthful of wooden pegs.

'Mean as people,' said Becka.

'That's a good question. One your father and I often ask. Answer is, we don't know. Maybe God didn't make enough nice ones. Or maybe it's the fault of the Free Will Covenant. "Go where ye list," it says it in the Bible, and that means "make your choice." Like Eve.' Becka's mother put the fourth peg in the sheet, then walked over to her. 'Have people been mean to you?'

'Yes, sometimes.' Becka never even considered lying. Not to anyone, but especially not to her mother.

Her mother didn't ask *who*, or *what have they been doing* or *should I go up to the school and have a word?* She just settled onto her haunches and looked Becka in the eye. Some might have thought her glance harsh, but not Becka. It was just her mother's love. 'It seems to me,' she said, 'that when God gave us free will, He gave us two choices; be nice or be mean. Mean, I think, is easier. It takes no imagination to be cruel – to pull legs off spiders or shoot dogs with air rifles or to tease someone and make them sad. But to be nice, to be courteous and to think of others...well, that seems like hard work, somehow. And most people are scared of hard work. But you're not, are you Becka?'

'No Mum!'

'No, you're not. Because you're a good girl. And when those people are mean, I want you to remember that they're weak, and you are strong, because you've resisted the temptation to be mean. Don't succumb to those baser desires, no matter how appealing it may be. For that way is the route to Hell. "A soft answer turneth away wrath," that's what the Bible says.' Then her mother stood, pulled another sheet from the basket and more pegs from her pinafore pocket. 'You got homework?'

'Yes Mum.'

'Then go on, tea will be at six.'

Nothing much changed for Becka after that – the mean kids were still mean – but instead of feeling perplexed by their behaviour, she now felt...well, pity. It was such a shame they weren't stronger. It was such a shame they couldn't resist the temptation to be cruel.

Still, maybe she could set an example.

Three

10:40.

Becka sat on her sofa and stared at the clock. No TV, no radio...just the clock, ticking...ticking...ticking, like that old song they'd sung in Infant School. The one that had stopped. Short. Never to go again, when the old man died.

Except that's not *a grandfather clock, I'm* not *an old man, and newspaper horoscopes* never *came true.*

Well...these days it seems they did.

Four

One of her father's less stringent aphorisms had been *nobody's perfect*. About this, and about all other things, he'd been right. Everybody human had their little vices. Her father, for instance, would sometimes take a glass of whisky or smoke a cigar. Not often, but sometimes. Her mother was hooked on a daytime soap opera from Australia. These weren't major vices of course – certainly not compared with certain other people in their street that they could mention but didn't because that would be improper – but they were enough to *reassure* Becka in some strange way. *We're only people,* she'd think, *and people are weak sometimes.*

With Becka, it was horoscopes.

She'd been born on May 25th 1980, which made her a Gemini. She was supposed to have a twin nature – pragmatic, hard headed and hopelessly romantic at the same time. She wasn't. In fact she shared none of the traits that the newspapers said she should...so obviously it was all nonsense...but, well...it was *harmless* nonsense, like the magicians they had on TV, or the Chuckle Brothers. 'Nobody human,' her father had once said, 'can completely live *in* this world all the time. We *all* need the edges blurring slightly. A little relaxation. As long as it's under control, then it's fine. As long as it doesn't become an addiction or an obsession. After all, even the Good Lord took a day off.'

So there, she had approval. She could read her horoscope and not worry. *Today is a good day to work on your people skills,* it would say one day. *Persevere with a project that you feel is worth it,* it would say on another. Some days it would say *a certain someone special has their eye on you,* and that was quite *clearly* nonsense...but still, when she'd read something like that, she'd feel a tingle in her belly and a blush on her cheek...and when it came down to it, what was *wrong* with feeling like that?

So Becka left school with a whole string of GSCEs – she wasn't naturally particularly clever, but she applied herself – and within the week she'd found herself working at The Card Factory in Stockport. It may not have been a brilliant job, it might not have been that well paid, but it was good enough and she liked the people she worked with and it was close to home...and, really, who needed ambition? Where did *that* get you? Lucifer had been ambitious, and it hadn't worked out so well for him, had it?

There she worked, there she stayed. For sixteen years. After a while she'd saved enough to put down a deposit on a little house. What could be better than that?

Five

10:45.

Becka had a sudden urge to get blindingly, horribly drunk. Hot on the heels of that, she had a sudden urge to smoke a packet of cigarettes. Then, overwhelming both of those desires, she had an urge to go into the street, find a man, and get him to put his penis in her.

In less than a quarter of an hour I'm going to die, and I have never done any *of those things. I've never been abroad, I've never placed a bet on a horse, and I've never been with a man.*

Stop it, stop it, she scolded herself. *You are* not *going to die tonight. This is just madness, a…test, maybe, to see if you'll give in to temptation, the way God tested Abraham. Just sit quietly, ride this out, and how you'll laugh later.*

But still, she was scared.

Six

No, she would never get drunk or smoke or be with a man. As the years rolled by, none of those things happened. Despite the times her horoscope read *you may meet someone special* or *take note of who's watching you, it could be someone extraordinary* and despite how often her tummy would tingle and her face blush, this never happened. It didn't really matter though. Becka just kept going. It wasn't in the plan for her.

She had her job, she had her home, she was kind and considerate and did no one any harm, she was inoffensive and mostly liked…and every day, at lunch, she sat in the Sayers across the road with a ham and tomato sandwich and read her horoscope in the paper. *You may feel like you've been burning the candle at both ends,* it may say, *so think about taking things easy. Or you may have too many things cluttering your life, why not remove some obstacles to success?* Under all of these, an 0800 number promising a fuller reading. Becka never rang them, not because of the expense, but because she thought that might be taking relaxation into obsession. Besides, those things in the paper never came true.

Until the day they did.

Seven

Exactly a week before Becka was sitting on her sofa, staring in terror at her clock, she was sitting in Sayers with her ham and tomato sandwich staring at her paper and read, *you will find a ten pound note in the gutter on your way home tonight.*

Startled, she blinked. She even rubbed her eyes, half expecting those words to magically vanish and be replaced with something wonderfully generic like *all work and no play makes no one happy – find time for yourself.* But no. They stayed. *You will find a ten pound note in the gutter on your way home tonight.*

How very strange, she thought, turning the page. Gypsy Tamara must be having an off day. Of course, there wasn't *really* a Gypsy Tamara – there was just a sub editor somewhere at a desk knocking these out, she wasn't *stupid* – but, still…what an *odd* thing to write.

She really thought no more about it – other than to vaguely wonder if that poor sub editor was going to lose his job – until she left work that night. The heavens decided to open when she was halfway home, and she had to fumble in her handbag for the umbrella she always kept there, just in case. While she was looking downwards, she saw something in the gutter.

It was a rather soggy ten pound note.

Becka stared at it. A splash of rainwater ran down her face, into her eyes, blurring her vision. But when it cleared, there it was still.

A ten pound note. In the gutter. Which she had found. After work. Like it had said in her horoscope.

She did what came naturally to her, and took the dripping note to the nearest police station. The duty officer took her name and address, commended her for her honesty, and said if no one claimed it within seven days then, legally, it was hers.

How very odd, she'd thought on the way home that night. *How very, very odd.*

Eight

10:49. In her living room, where no man had ever sat, Becka gave that barking laugh again. *Just think, tomorrow I can go down to the station and claim my ten pounds. If its rightful owner hasn't collected it. And if I'm still alive.*

Of course *I'll still be alive! What rubbish! I am* in no way *entering the last ten minutes of my existence! And to prove it, I will stop looking at that clock and go to the kitchen where I will make a cup of tea. With sugar.*

But she didn't. Becka didn't even move. She seemed welded to her sofa, watching the seconds tick by.

Nine

'Good morning, Becks,' Sally had said the following day. 'How're you?'

Sally worked on the counter with her. She was nineteen years old and as pretty as a picture. She had long blonde hair and big blue eyes and a string of boyfriends – but she was kind, and Becka liked her. She *effed and jeffed* every other word like all the young people did, and that made Becka a bit sad, but hey – that just appeared to be the way of the world.

Becka removed her coat and told Sally the story of her horoscope and the ten pound note. 'That is odd,' Sally agreed. 'Nice odd, but odd.'

'Yes,' agreed Becka. 'It was nice, wasn't it?'

That lunchtime, she was back in Sayers with her sandwich, flicking through the paper…and with a slightly apprehensive hand she turned to Gypsy Tamara's column. *Gemini (May 21 – June 22)* it read. *Today you will be barked at by a Staffordshire Terrier called Butch – but it won't bite, it's a softie.*

I think the poor man who's writing these is heading for a breakdown of some sort, she thought. *Poor dear.* On the heels of that, *doesn't his editor* read *these columns?*

By six thirty she was making her way home, walking through the Stockport streets the way she had countless times. Then, towards her, a brown streak rushed, all blurred legs and bullet shaped head, an angry, brutish noise erupting from its throat. *Oh my,* thought Becka as she stopped cold. *That's a* very *angry dog indeed! What if it bites? And where's its owner?*

As if in answer, a voice even louder and angrier than the dog's came to her ears. 'Butch,' a man screamed. 'Butch! Get 'ere, y'little bastard!'

Butch (*oh look, Butch, his name's Butch*) took no notice whatsoever. He came running on at full pelt, barking like crazy, as if Becka's very presence on the pavement had affronted him. At her feet, he dropped down low on his haunches, his mouth open in what looked like a terrible grin. *Oh dear, he's going to jump and bite and I'll not be able to protect…*

But he didn't. Butch just lay there, front legs down, back legs up. Incredibly, Becka realised that, if he had a tail, he'd be wagging it. 'Um...hello,' she said, making a smile appear on her frozen face. 'Hello, doggy.'

His owner – the man with the angry voice – ran into view. He was in his early twenties by the look of him, shaven headed and red-faced. He grabbed Butch by the collar – not violently though, just to make sure he didn't get away. He looked down on the animal with a sort of exasperated love, then up at Becka, all apologies. 'Sorry, sorry,' he panted. 'Me little girl left the front door open and he got out,' down at the dog, 'didn't you, you naughty Butch?' The dog's backside waggled even harder. Back to Becka. 'Sorry if he scared you, he's all bark though. He wouldn't 'ave 'urt you. He's just...'

'Yes, I know. A big softie,' said Becka.

Ten

That night Becka had found it hard to sleep. Maybe one odd thing in the paper was a coincidence. But *two? Maybe...maybe they're a sign of something,* she thought. *Something maybe miraculous. I mean, think about it carefully, Becka. There are millions of copies of the paper printed each day. Somehow, you've managed to pick – not once, but twice - the exact copy that speaks to you – that has something in it that* literally *came true! How likely is that? Maybe...maybe someone...or* Someone*...has decided to make some form of contact with you. Maybe this is your reward for being nice all these years.*

And with that comforting thought, Becka fell asleep.

The next day, she decided to try an experiment.

'You've got two copies 'ere, love,' said the man in the newsagent.

'Yes, I know,' said Becka.

'Just sayin'. Don't want you comin' in 'ere askin' for a refund. Gettin' one for a mate are you?'

'Something like that.'

She virtually raced to her seat in Sayers, and ripped through the pages until she found the one with the cartoon strips and the star signs. Hers read, *you're feeling underappreciated, both at work and at home. Make them see you're someone special.*

Sudden disappointment ran through her. *Oh dear,* she thought. *I thought I was someone special, but it seems like I'm not.* Though her hunger had vanished, she took a bite out of her sandwich anyway and opened the second copy of the paper, flicking idly forward. Then she nearly choked as she read, *at 12:59 the man to your left will sneeze so violently he will bang his knee on the table.* She checked her watch. It was 12:58. A glance to her side took in a man of nondescript appearance with salt and pepper hair wearing a leather jacket. He was drinking a coffee. Back to her watch. As 12:58 became 12:59 he convulsed with a sneeze so apocalyptic his entire body went into spasm and – *clang!* – his kneecap struck the underside of the wrought iron table. '*Mother-FUCK!*' He cried out in pain. Then, seeing Becka look over at him, he apologised.

'Don't mention it,' she smiled. 'Are you all right?'

'Fine,' he said.

Becka finished her sandwich in peace. There appeared to be one newspaper in *all* of the batches that had something unique in it. And it was for her, it seemed.

Eleven

10:52. *Thanks for that,* Becka found herself thinking. Her first ungrateful thought at the age of thirty-two.

Twelve

She carried on experimenting – well, she had to be sure, didn't she? If this was some kind of miracle, she had to be absolutely *certain* before she took it to the Vicar. She went to different shops to buy her paper, but at each one she found a special horoscope. At church on that Sunday, sandwiched as always between her parents (to whom she had not said a word about this) she prayed very, very hard. *Lord, if You are speaking to me in this way, I am very grateful. I am grateful You have chosen me to be Your vessel. I will do your bidding. Just let me be clear what it is You want me to do, and I will do it.*

But the one maddening thing was that there didn't seem to be anything the Lord actually *wanted* her to do. He just (if it really *was* He) kept sending down cryptically specific messages. On the Monday, *a six year old boy will accidentally kick a football towards you at 18:27.* And he did. On Tuesday, *you will see an argument in the street between a man and a woman at 22:30.* And she had, that night as she closed her curtains before climbing into bed. Wednesday, *you will drop a box of Famous Friends Teddy Bears down the steps at 15:48, but none will spill out or be damaged.* She had, and they hadn't.

But none of these messages actually told her to do anything. None of them read, *Right Becka, now I've got your attention, I want you to go to Africa and become a missionary* or *OK, now you know it's Me talking, get thee to a nunnery.* They just imparted these…well…bland messages. Special, but bland.

Until that lunchtime, when she'd opened her paper and read *you will die at 10:59 tonight.*

Thirteen

'Jesus Christ,' said Sally, as Becka staggered back into work. 'What's up? You look like shite.'

'Sally,' said Helen the manager. 'Customers!' Then, to Becka, 'she's right though. You look a bit pale.'

'This...' Becka managed to say, waving the paper at them. 'This...'

Then she fainted.

She'd come round in what they called the 'staff room' (in reality a cupboard with two chairs and a coffee machine in it). Both Sally and Helen were with her. 'Who's minding the shop?' she asked.

'*Fuck* the shop,' said Sally. 'We've pulled the shutters down. We're worried about you.'

'No, I'm...' But then she saw Helen holding the paper, and Becka remembered everything. She moaned.

'What is it,' asked Helen. 'What happened?'

'Th-that,' Becka stuttered. 'My...stars.'

The two women exchanged a glance. 'What d'you mean?' asked Helen.

'Please,' moaned Becka. 'Read them.'

Helen flicked through the paper and did. Her face grew pale until Becka thought she was going to faint as well. 'Oh Jesus,' the older woman muttered. 'Oh holy God...'

'What's up?' asked Sally, and pretty much snatched the paper out of Helen's nerveless hands. Then, as she read...'You're fucking *shitting* me!'

On one score, Becka felt slightly relieved. At least other people could see them. At least she hadn't actually been going mad.

Fourteen

Helen had wanted to call the Police. This was, after all, some terrible hoax, an awfully cruel trick. Becka talked her out of it. Who, after all, would they charge? Sally wanted to 'find the miserable fucker who did this and kick the living shit out of him,' but frankly Becka didn't think that was possible. In the end, they simply called a taxi – for which Helen insisted on paying no matter how hard Becka protested – and sent her home. Sally had offered to come and sit with her all night, and for a moment Becka had been tempted, but in the end she'd turned the girl down. She was however profoundly touched.

I'll miss them, she thought as the cab pulled away. Then, *No I won't. I won't because I'll be in again tomorrow and I'll make Helen dock the cab fare out of my wages. I'll be in tomorrow because...well, because I'm* always *in.*

But all the same, 10:59 rushed towards her like a tidal wave.

She hadn't eaten. She'd drunk several cups of water, but hadn't eaten. At seven she'd rung her parents, the way she rang them every night. She gave no thought to telling them what had happened. Why worry them? After all, she'd be there – still – the next day. As she rang off, she told them she loved them, just the way she always had.

Then she sat back on her sofa to wait.

Fifteen

10:58.

There was no *way* she would die in sixty seconds' time. It was impossible. She'd led a good and blameless life. She'd indulged in no vices. Why would God let her die? What reward for a good and blameless life would that be?

Unless there are *no rewards,* she suddenly found herself thinking. *Unless this is it, a pointless life and a pointless death. Unless maybe it doesn't really matter what you do or what you say or how you act on Earth, you're just going to die anyway.* 'God is cruel,' people would say sometimes. Maybe He is. Maybe this is His ultimate act of cruelty. Maybe it matters not one tinker's cuss how you live, sooner or later something divinely awful happens to us all.

No! No, that can't be!

And anyway, what was that you were saying about having indulged in no vices? But you did, *didn't you? Your horoscope was your vice. Maybe this is God telling you how wicked you were for that vicarious thrill?*

'No!' she screamed aloud. 'No! They were harmless! Just harmless! *Just a bit of fun!*'

Still think they're fun, Becka?

The clock turned from 10:58 to 10:59.

Becka stood bolt upright. '*Oh you fucking cocksucking son of a FUCKING WHORE!*' she screamed.

Then she said nothing else. Ever.

Sixteen

By ten o'clock the following day, Helen Reece had become so concerned about Becka's non arrival at work that she called Becka's home. There was no answer. She then called Becka's parents – Becka having left their number 'in case of emergencies' many years ago. Becka's parents said they'd spoken to their daughter the night before and she'd sounded fine...no, she'd said nothing about any newspaper.

Becka's parents, worried...well, scared...had called the Police. The Police sent two officers, PC Morgan and PC McFadden, to Becka's house. They knocked. There was no reply. They knocked louder. Still nothing. The curtains were drawn and they couldn't see in. PC McFadden checked the lock on the front door.

'Easy,' she said.

'We can't break in,' said PC Morgan. 'We've no warrant or anything.'

'She could be lying on the floor, gasping for breath,' said PC McFadden. 'If you break in and save her, you'd be a hero. Something to talk about in that Church of yours.'

PC Morgan sighed, then put his shoulder to the wood. She'd been right. It *was* easy.

They made their way into the living room, calling Becka Goodman's name. There was no answer, which was unsurprising really as they found her on the carpet, cold and as stiff as a board.

'Flip you for who tells her parents,' said PC McFadden, reaching into her pocket.

Of course, PC Morgan lost. He broke the news in person an hour later as, across town, the coroner removed Becka's blameless body from her house. He told the weeping parents he was sorry for their loss. The father said something about their daughter being with God now, and PC Morgan had agreed. She was. Maybe there was some comfort in that. Then he went back to the station and wrote up his report. That finished, he went into the canteen, poured some tea, and opened the paper. He skimmed through the news and the cartoons and the TV Guide until he came to his favourite bit. Reading, PC Morgan sat forward and frowned.

Leo (July 22-Aug 22): Today you will find a ten pound note in the gutter on your way home from work.

Heaven is Paradise. Isn't It?

I used to be a troubled soul, but I'm not anymore. At least, I won't be soon. At least, I *hope* I won't be soon. I had – well, still have, really – a question. It was a question that kept me awake at night, a question that got in the way of doing stuff in the day. The question is this; If Heaven is so great, why do people struggle on down here on Earth?

I mean, think about it. Down here you've got the benefits office and cancer and stubbed toes and Tourette's, and up there you've got fluffy clouds and peace and eternal life. If you look at it that way, what's the point of being down here at all? Eh? Why don't we all just pack up and move Upstairs tomorrow?

Unless, of course, Heaven's not *really* like that at all. I mean, that could be so, couldn't it? I mean, no one who's been there has ever told us what it's like, have they? Not directly. Or I've never seen it. There's been no one on *The Wright Stuff* or *The One Show* saying 'I went to Heaven and it was great.' Yeah, I know, some people have said there's a tunnel and a white light and all that, but what does that actually *mean?* Is *that* Heaven? A *tunnel?* I don't like tunnels. We went down one on a school trip to Llandudno once and it was crap. Damp and everything, it was. Set my asthma off. The other kids laughed.

I don't want Heaven to be a tunnel.

So I had my question – still have – and it really started to bug me. So I went to St Luke's and I asked Jesus in my head. *Dear Lord,* I asked, *what's Heaven really like?* And I listened truly hard. My Dad used to say that if you listened hard enough Jesus would speak to you in a small, still voice. I listened and listened and listened. I didn't breathe in case I didn't hear Him. In the end I nearly fainted, but I didn't hear a dicky bird. Maybe He's at lunch.

See, there's another thing. Do you get hungry in Heaven? And if you do, what do you get to eat? I hope you don't get wafers like you do at St Luke's. They're yuk. All flat and dry they are and they stick to the roof of your mouth. Who wants *that* for eternity? In Heaven you should be able to get whatever you want at a click of your fingers – a Happy Meal with Large Fries and a Thickshake, for instance. See, *drink!* There's *another* thing! What do you get to drink up there? At St Luke's we only get wine that tastes like poison. (I imagine. I haven't actually tasted poison.) Can you get Stella in Heaven? Stella that doesn't make your head hurt?

Hang on...wasn't Jesus a shepherd or something? He had a Lamb of God, right? Right? Am I right? So maybe you get lamb in Heaven. That's good. I like lamb. New Zealand is best. I reckon in Heaven you can get any lamb you want.

I should find out soon enough anyway.

So, Dad's words were no help at all and Jesus is at lunch (do you think His lunch breaks are longer than ours? Who'd tell Him to get back to work? Well, yes, God, OK, God would. But what if time is different up there? What if an hour to Jesus is a million years to us? What if?) So I went to Father Mackie. He's the Vicar at St Luke's. Nice man. We had tea and scones with blackcurrant jam and everything. And we sat in his front room with pictures of Jesus and the Apostles and the Last Supper and all that, and I asked him my question.

But he wasn't much help. Which was a shame. He said he didn't really know what Heaven was like either. He said we spent eternity with our loved ones, but I *knew* that, that's *accepted*. I wanted to know what the *place* was like and what you did there. So I asked him that. I asked him if Heaven was like the paintings, were there fluffy clouds and harps and angels with wings and were there 50" Plasma tellies with all the channels and all for free and was there a magic telescope or something like that so you see down to Earth. But he just blinked a bit and said that we needed to have faith in the Lord our God. Faith in the Lord our God, he said, was a wonderful thing. So I asked him about that, what faith really *was* because *I want to know,* and he said faith was belief, faith had made him want to be a Vicar and spread God's Word and Truth. He said that one day a small, still voice had spoken up inside him and it was God, saying become a Vicar, which proves two things. (1) My Dad didn't lie and (2) Jesus gets back from lunch sometimes and picks up His messages.

But the one thing I *did* learn from Father Mackie is that Heaven is Paradise. Yeah, OK, granted, I'd read that in The Holy Bible, but I'd read other stuff in there too and...well, you know. I mean, Lot's wife and Noah's Ark! I mean, *come on!* A boat big enough to carry two of every animal on Earth? (Except unicorns.) And how did tigers and lions and penguins and polar bears all get to the same place? They live *miles* away from each other! Was there a shuttle bus? And why didn't the lions eat everything? And Lot? His wife got turned to salt! I mean, *salt!* Stone, I could believe that, but *salt?* Why do that unless God wanted Lot to have something to sprinkle on his chips?

But Father Mackie, he said it right out. 'Heaven,' he said, 'is Paradise.' And Jesus had spoken to him, hadn't he, he said so. He *must* know then, he must know what he's *talking about.* Right?
Right?
But I'll know too, soon enough.

Not thanks to Father Mackie though. Thanks to Old Mrs Wallace.

Old Mrs Wallace lives in the ground floor flat and she's a million but she's OK. Smells a bit of wee sometimes. Doesn't always put her teeth in. Her hair is cotton wool and her cardies have holes in, but she's OK. Calls me by the wrong name sometimes, but that I don't mind. Who *wants* to be called Thomas? He Doubted. Old Mrs Wallace used to have a cat called Millie, but Millie died and Old Mrs Wallace was sad. Millie was a nice cat. Stripey and not too fluffy so she didn't set my asthma off too much. (I didn't ask Father Mackie if cats went to Heaven. Heck, everyone knows animals have their own Heavens, where cats can sit on radiators and dogs can sniff each other's bottoms and hamsters can run round in wheels – *everyone* knows that! I'm not *stupid!*)

I'm *not!*

Old Mrs Wallace and I would have tea in her flat sometimes. Tea and Battenburg cake. Or Jamaican Ginger cake. I'd buy the cake. I'd make the tea too, because Old Mrs Wallace's hands hurt with arthritis. Well, not just her hands. Everything hurt with arthritis, she said.

And that was a shame, because Old Mrs Wallace was a nice lady. We'd sit for hours and we'd talk. She'd talk about her husband (in Heaven with Jesus) and what a nice man he'd been, but *oh!* he didn't hold with them Tories, oh he *hated* them Tories! We'd talk about her daughter (in Lincoln with a man) and how Old Mrs Wallace didn't see her much anymore, just at Christmas every other year. She'd talk about Millie (you know where *she* is) and how empty the flat was without her. We'd talk about the house she and Mr Wallace used to have and how there'd been parties sometimes and arguments other times and her brothers and sisters and friends and parents and how they were all gone, all gone to Heaven, and she sometimes forgot things and that upset her and sometimes she would start crying and I'd say there there, Mrs Wallace and she'd say there was pain all the time. Pain. And she'd say I was a good boy for coming to see her so often. A good boy.

A good boy to bring an old lady cake.

A good boy to make her tea.

A good boy to sometimes do the shopping (Old Mrs Wallace called shopping 'messages' for some reason) because oh my, my bones do hurt and I forget what I want or I make a list and forget that.

A good boy.

We had nice chats, me and Old Mrs Wallace.

See, she was old.

She missed her husband. And her cat. She forgot things. She was in pain – a *lot* of pain. She was very lonely.

The last time we had a chat, I asked her my question. 'Mrs Wallace,' I said (I didn't call her '*Old* Mrs Wallace,' that would upset her) 'Mrs Wallace, if Heaven is so great, why do we struggle here on Earth?' Mrs Wallace said she didn't know. 'Mrs Wallace,' I said, 'when you…go…would you do me a big favour?'

'Yis,' she said. She always said 'yis' when she meant 'yes.'

'I just want to know what it's like up there. Would you...you know...find a way to come and tell me? Please? As a sort of...thank you for the cake?'

'Yis,' she said. 'Yis.'

She meant it too. I know she did.

I *know* she did.

So four hours ago I went downstairs and I knocked on her door. Old Mrs Wallace answered and seemed pleased to see me. She was happy. At the end, she was happy because her only friend, her one good boy had come to see her. She was still smiling as I closed the door and put one hand over her mouth and the other on the back of her head. I pressed down hard. I covered her nose and mouth. She was only little. She struggled a bit, but not much. She was old. There was a bit of drool against my palm that wasn't nice. Then she wet herself and that wasn't nice either. After a while she stopped struggling but I held her there for half an hour before I took my hands away.

I sat her in her favourite chair and held a mirror to her mouth. I'd seen that on the telly. It didn't fog. I mopped up the wee and wiped her drool on my shirt and went back to my flat to wait.

Do you think Jesus will let Old Mrs Wallace go on a day trip to Cat Heaven so she can see Millie every so often? She loved that cat. Maybe she can take Mr Wallace. I mean, that's possible, isn't it? *Isn't* it?

Isn't it?

Hey, I'll know soon enough. I'll know it *all*. Old Mrs Wallace said she'd come back and tell me everything, what it was like. She *said*. So, sure, it's been four hours since she died...but, hey, who knows how long it takes to get to Heaven? Maybe Heaven's a really, really long way away. Especially if you've got arthritis.

But...then again...there's a worry, isn't there?

I mean, Old Mrs Wallace forgot things. I told you that. I *told* you that! I mean, she couldn't remember my name or what to get in the shops...so what if she forgot her promise? What then? What *then?* Or what if she remembered but forgot who *I* was? What if she told someone else?

Well, never mind. I've got a plan. If Old Mrs Wallace doesn't come through, I'll ask another old lady. There are lots of them out there, aren't there?

Lots and lots and lots.

You *bet* there are.

The Start of Another Week

Neil swiped his card and listened to the hum as the doors swung open. Mondays, he thought, could be tricky. It was the time away. Settling back into the routine wasn't always easy.

He shifted his briefcase to his left hand as he walked to the lift. A glance at his watch brought his first smile since Friday evening. 7:45. He'd be first in again. He could sit behind his desk and stare through the glass walls of his office as the drones filed in. He would see the smiles dying on their lips, their inane chat about soap operas and football evaporating into silence as they beheld him. Then they would scurry to their workstations and click their computers into life and type in passwords without a sound. And silence would descend. Neil loved silence. After a weekend at home with his Father, silence was – excuse the blasphemy - sacred.

The lift arrived with a gentle ping and a recorded woman's voice floated out of the speaker. 'Doors opening. Lift going up.' He stepped inside and pressed the button for the eighth floor, his smile becoming an actual grin. The Lift Refurbishment Programme had been his project – some ten years ago now – his first big success, the one that had really got him started at System Four. Strip out the old cars and replace them with state of the art computer driven new ones complete with Braille buttons and SpeakTech circuits. It had cost a fortune and raised some high level eyebrows, but Neil had stood his ground, arguing right up to MD level that just because they didn't have any visually impaired employees now, it didn't mean they wouldn't in the future, did it? And the 21st century was the era of Political Correctness, wasn't it? How better to advertise what a caring, considerate company this was? Wouldn't it make them appear – pardon the pun – far sighted?

The MD had smiled at that, produced a big rubber stamp with the word APPROVED on it, and said the three magic words. 'Good plan, Neil.'

'Eighth Floor,' said the recording. 'Doors opening.' Neil swept through the open plan area, eyes to the left, eyes to the right. A used and unwashed Smarties mug on a windowsill. A report on a desk in contravention of the Clear Desk Policy. He noted these things. He noted *everything*.

He arrived at his office door and, because there was no one else around, he took a handkerchief from his trouser pocket and polished the brass nameplate until it shone. NEIL MORRISON SUPERVISOR CORPORATE ACCOUNTS. He stepped inside. His domain. His world. He wished he could show it to Father, he wished he could throw it in the old man's face during those rows that seemed to spring up hourly these days. He wanted to be able to shout 'See? This is what I'm doing! This is what it's all about! *This is what I'm worth!*'

But that, of course was...well, if not impossible, then inadvisable.

The thought of it still made him smile as he logged on and started checking his emails. Three smiles already. Not even eight o'clock. Maybe it *would* be a good day after all.

He was immersed in this and that until almost nine. He had tremendous focus, did Neil – something else his Father never gave him credit for. He would almost zone out while he worked on a project. His Father, of course, ran amok – half starting this thing, then running off to half start another – and that just drove Neil insane. His Father often looked like one of those circus plate spinners. Yes, the old man had been successful, no argument there, but it just wasn't the right way to go about things. You had to start one thing and then see it through to the end before you started another. That was the logical way to behave. That was how business succeeded these days.

Nine o'clock. Well, nearly. Coffee time. Neil hated coffee – just as he hated tea or cocoa or hot water – but it was important to be seen with some in his hand from time to time. It was the little human touches that kept him ahead of the game. Besides, on his way to and from the coffee machine he could check the desks, see who was doing what, like a spy in some old movie.

As he opened the office door, he froze, eyes down to pinheads. He could hear someone talking. He could hear someone sharing a joke. He could hear someone *not working*.

He slid into the open plan, silent as death. He could feel the rage – his Father's *true* inheritance – building up inside him. He clamped it down as best he could. He saw who was slacking off. Peter. Of course. Who else? Peter, that stupid, arrogant son of a whore! How many arguments had they had down the years? Too many. Peter was old school System Four. He'd been here nearly twenty years now. He thought Neil was an upstart. Peter was a dinosaur, a survivor from some earlier epoch where it was OK to drink three pints at lunchtime, where it was OK to dick around, where it was OK to screw some secretary behind the filing cabinets. Peter was a problem. Peter flicked V signs behind Neil's back and mimicked his voice. Peter didn't show enough respect.

Peter had to be dealt with.

There he was, at it again, chatting to that vacant lump of flesh called Lin. He was finishing off some oh so humorous story, his voice *buh-bubbling* with laughter. 'At which point,' he said, 'she opened the tent and told me to stop fiddling with her flaps!' Then they both dissolved into mild hysteria.

Neil ghosted up to Peter's shoulder, honestly puzzled. What was funny about that? Lin caught his eye, coloured up and started tapping keys at random. Peter noticed her change in attitude and spun round. Neil assumed a huge grin (but not a genuine one like earlier), clapped Peter on the shoulder and said, 'Hi Pete! Good weekend, mate?'

Peter flinched a bit in surprise (which was good) and there was apprehension in his eyes (which was better)...but he showed no fear. *Sorry Peter*, Neil thought – although he wasn't – *that's your last mistake. Should've been afraid. Then I might have spared you.* 'Yeah,' he said. 'Not bad. You?' *Like I care*, Peter's eyes said.

'Great thanks. Went home to see Dad. He's knocking on a bit, you know?' Peter nodded with sympathy every bit as genuine as a six pound note. 'Listen, what time you clocking off tonight?'

'Bout five.'

'Smart. Could you bring me the Justman figures before you go? I'd like to see how they're going.'

'Sure. No problem.'

Neil's fake smile nearly ripped his face apart, but he clapped Peter on the shoulder again, called him a 'good man,' and wandered over to the vending machine where for fifty pence he was rewarded with a plastic cup full of warm mud. He was well aware that behind him Peter was puffing his cheeks out and wiping an imaginary sheen of sweat from his forehead, thinking he'd got away with it. *Dream on sunshine*, he thought as he walked back to his office, carefully miming drinking and hearing nothing but the soft clack of keyboards. *Dream on.*

He worked away the rest of the morning – hitting 'save' on some things and 'send' on others – and at twelve he met the MD for lunch in the staff canteen. Not the executive dining area, the staff canteen. Neil wanted to be seen as a Man of the People...sort of.

The MD was in a fine mood. 'Productivity's up,' he said, 'client feedback is up, errors are down, and absenteeism and disciplinaries are at an all time low. The board is very happy, Neil. As are our shareholders. As am I.'

Neil waved this away as he was supposed to, but once more he thought of his Father. *You see, I am someone! I am someone! I AM NOT WASTING MY TIME UP HERE!*

'So what's your secret, young man?' asked the MD.

For an awful second, Neil thought he was found out. Something in his chest – not his heart, exactly – loosened. He almost felt a stab of fear. But then he looked at the flabby bald man before him and relaxed. The MD, like them all, was so stupid he virtually needed a note on his desk that said 'BREATHE IN' and another underneath that said 'BREATHE OUT.' He had not been found out. He faked a bemused expression and said, 'Secret?'

'Well, when you arrived here from…' The MD's face became slack, the flab hanging limply like dough. His eyes were flat, unfocused.

'Oxford,' said Neil. 'Thirteen years ago.'

'Oxford, thirteen years ago,' the MD said with confidence, now entirely back in the world, 'the board took one look at you and said, "Well, he's intelligent. He's keen. But he's inexperienced. How can he cope in the real world?" Now, there were two ways of finding out. One was to ease you in, give you some low level work at first, increase your responsibility gradually. Then there was the other way – and I'm pleased to say, this was my idea.'

Neil smiled and pretended to eat a sandwich. *It wasn't your idea. It was mine. I just made you* think *it was your idea.*

'I decided to give you a division that was failing,' the MD droned on. 'Low morale, unhappy clients, bad debts. A division that was maybe a year from being closed altogether. In no way did we expect you to turn it around. We wanted to see how you handled failure, because that's the true measure of a man, isn't it? But you *didn't* fail! You *did* turn it around, and now Corporate is showing the highest profits this company's ever seen! And all in...' Again, that blankness came over him.

'Thirteen years,' said Neil.

'Thirteen years! Which, frankly, is far too long for you to be sat in one desk, young man!' The MD leaned forward, whispering like a convict. 'It's probably time you...moved up, shall we say? Say nothing, but there could well be a seat on the board coming free in a week or two. And it might – just might - have your name on it.'

Father...did you hear that? Did you? Wasting my time, am I? Turned my back on the family business, have I? Oh no, I'm more of a success than you'll ever be.

'Go on then,' said the MD, 'divulge your secret.'

'No secret, sir,' said Neil, holding the MD's gaze. 'Just hard work. Graft. Nothing more than that. See, this company is a football team, sir. The department heads are the team captains, the board is the manager. Corporate just needed a strong captain, that's all. No secret. Nothing special. Once I got your message across then we started to win games. And I like to win. Don't you, sir?'

The MD said he did, and went back to his food. He had no idea that Neil had captured some of his soul. *Still, what did he keep calling me? 'Young man?' I'll have to watch that, I missed that. I've been here thirteen years. Maybe I need some grey...a receding hairline...OK, Father, I'll grant you that one. You'd never have missed that trick, would you?*

It was OK though. Stopped him becoming complacent.

At four fifty that afternoon, Neil was disturbed from his work by a knock at his office door. He looked through the glass walls and saw Peter, folder in hand. Neil beckoned him in, and a genuine smile snaked across his jaw. He was looking forward to this. Perfect way to end a Monday.

'The Justman figures,' said Peter, closing the door behind him.

'Cheers, bud,' said Neil. He gestured to the chair opposite. 'You got a minute to go through them? Been ages since we had a chat.'

Peter looked at his watch. 'Well…'

'Won't take long, promise. I quite fancy getting home myself.' Wide smile, body eased back in his chair…Neil would have bet the family fortune that he'd never looked more approachable.

'OK then.' Peter sat. 'What do you want to know?'

Neil nodded towards the folder. 'How much time do they take up these days?'

'Hardly any. Things come and go pretty much on time.'

Neil made himself whistle in mild astonishment. 'Well done, bud. They were in a pretty bad state at one point, weren't they? Thinking of pulling the plug.'

'Yeah,' said Peter, puffing his loathsome chest out. 'But I put the hours in. Turned it around. Glad I did, too. These guys are big spenders.'

'You should be pleased with yourself.'

'Yeah, I am.' Smiling like a lunatic.

'Is that why you think you can dick away your time mucking about?'

Peter's smile vanished – a joyous sight. He'd forgotten all about this morning, and why not? Didn't he have a million laughs a day? 'Sorry?'

'You and that empty headed slut Lin,' said Neil, giving his widest, most genuine smile. 'I see you, Peter. I see her. I see *everything*.'

'Hey, you can't say things like that!'

'Wrong, arsewipe. I can say what the fuck I like. I'm the boss.'

'OK, that's it.' Peter stood and marched stiffly to the door. 'I'm getting the Union in on this. See what you have to say to *them*.' He grasped the handle and turned. His hand slipped off. He tried again. The handle didn't budge. He pulled. He pushed. Nothing. He turned to Neil. 'This is jammed.'

'Is it?' Neil was biting the inside of his cheek to keep from laughing.

'Weren't you watching? We're stuck in here. Get on the phone to maintenance.'

The smile vanished from Neil's face this time. Inside, he could feel his Father's nature bubbling. 'Are you telling me what to do? You? *In my office?*'

'Oh for God's sake, drop the rank shit will you,' said Peter, moving for Neil's phone. 'We're locked in.'

The part of him that was and always would be his Father popped. In less than a second Neil was out from behind his desk, moving so fast he was practically invisible. He slapped Peter backhand across the face. Peter recoiled, eyes watering. The sound was delicious. On another occasion Neil would have savoured it, but now he was truly his Father's son and the rage was loose. He wore it proudly, a black shroud. 'Don't say that name,' said Neil. He advanced on Peter who backed away towards the door. 'Don't you *dare* say that *name.*' He kicked out and caught Peter a good one on the shin. Peter howled and fell to one knee. 'Don't you know who I *am?*' he roared on, kicking out again, catching Peter under the chin. Peter flew backwards through the air with all the grace of a crippled elephant and cracked his head on the carpet. Blood started to trickle from a wound back there. Neil strode to him, rolled him over, kicked him again in the kidneys. Peter made a noise like a deflating balloon. 'I'm the fucking *boss,*' he said. He rolled Peter back, uncoiled him from that foetal position and kicked him again, square in the balls. Neil swore he could hear one pop like a grape. 'You *respect* the boss!' A kick to the ribs. 'You respect my *position!*' A stamp on the chest. Peter was coughing blood up now. *'That's* all I ask, me and Aretha,' he ranted, stooping to pick Peter up by the hair. 'Just,' he said, smacking Peter's face on the desk, 'a little,' he did it again, 'fucking,' once more, bone and blood flying everywhere, *'RESPECT!'*

Neil picked up the bloody tangle of limbs that had once been a man and hurled it across the room. It hit the glass walls but didn't shatter them. It rebounded, leaving a viscous smear, the sort a spider might leave when splattered across a wall by a newspaper (only much, much bigger) then flopped to the carpet and lay motionless.

Like magic, the rage was gone. Neil smiled at the wreckage. *How* many smiles that day? Oh, enough. The smile turned to a grin as he looked out through the goo-stained glass to the workers beyond. None of them had turned a hair. They sat still, typing away, silent and good. If any of them had happened to look up during the last few minutes, they'd have only seen the image that Neil had projected into their minds – two old buds sitting in chairs, shooting the breeze about business. It was a small trick, one of the first his Father had taught him – cheap parlour magic – but it worked. Maybe not everything about the old ways was outdated.

A coughing moan from the floor. Incredibly, Peter was still alive. *Lucifer, you humans are hard to kill sometimes.* Still, his Father wouldn't mind too much. He liked the live ones even more than the dead, apparently. They screamed louder. Neil crossed to the mess that had once laughed and joked and shown disrespect and dropped to his haunches. 'See, that was your mistake bud,' he said, almost regretfully. 'I get enough shit at home from Father, I don't want it here from the likes of you. He says all of *this* is a waste of time.' He chuckled. 'Time! We've got *eternity,* mate! He says – Father – that I've abandoned the old ways. But I haven't. I've just *updated* them. See, all he does is sit and watch people *burn!* All day! *Every* day! And laughs. Which is fair enough, bud, it *is* quite funny – I mean, your Mum, she makes me howl with laughter – but all day, *every* day? *Nah!* See, bud, that's Father's problem; a lack of vision. He's happy with what he's got, that bloody fiery pit thing with the demons and the prongs and that, and it *works,* don't get me wrong...but it's all a bit, *Medieval,* don't you think? And you've got to *wait* for all of that! The new way – *my* way – is to bring all the despair and misery up to *your* level – y'know, to make your job *hell on Earth,* get me? You see the *brilliance* of it all? Despair and misery *every day of your working life! That's* what I'll take with me *everywhere I go* – and trust me, bud. I'm going *far.* All people have to remember is this – *NO FUCKING LAUGHING AT WORK!!'*

Some hours later, Neil dragged the remains of Peter's body to the lift doors and pressed the call button. There were bits of Peter missing, but Neil didn't think Father would mind. He'd only pretended to eat lunch after all, and he was hungry.

The lift doors opened with a gentle ping and Neil threw the body inside. He pushed the lowest button, the button only he could see. Neil was a happy camper. It hadn't been a bad old Monday after all.

'Doors closing,' said the recorded woman. 'Lift going down.'

Once more Neil thought what a good idea the Lift Refurbishment Programme had been – one even his Father had approved of. New meets old. An express delivery service. 'That's right, sweetheart,' said Neil. '*All* the way down.'

Whistling, Neil went back to collect his briefcase, hoping that Tuesday would be even better.

New Message.
Read Now?

Dusk of a March evening, 2002. The sun – having put in a full day shining – decided it was quitting time and made its way to the horizon. Its fading golden light fell on a quite unremarkable semidetached house on the outskirts of Liverpool.

Inside that house, all was calm and all was quiet. A man in his early middle age was hunched over a coffee table, a glass of wine to his left, a stack of books in front of him, a red pen in his right hand. No TV or music disturbed the air. The man frowned as he read something, leaned forward and made a correction.

A noise like a Police siren split the air.

'Shit,' screamed Christopher Tulloch as his arm spasmed in surprise. 'Shit,' he said again as his pen turned a red X into a jagged, stabbing line. 'Shit,' he said a third time as he reached for the mobile phone that had made the noise but missed and knocked the glass of Chardonnay over, pouring its contents over the Year Seven exercise books he'd been marking.

But despite all the profanity, he didn't really care about the mess. He might possibly be bothered that in the morning he'd be handing alcohol smelling homework back to his students and they'd laugh behind his back calling him *pisshead* or *boozeface,* but just at that moment he was fixed on the noise, on his text message alert, and his heart was singing.

He righted the glass with his right hand and wafted the drenched book with his left. The ink was smudging a bit, but frankly Cathy Brodie's handwriting was only improved by it. He looked down at the Ericsson's display, and there they were; the words he'd been longing to read. NEW MESSAGE, the screen said, black over green. READ NOW?

Nicole, he thought. He smiled as he flipped open the phone's cover. He pressed the YES key and there in front of him were the words BCK. THNK GOD. HME SOON. MSS ME?X

Bless the phone, Christopher nearly said aloud as he entered his reply. *Bless the phone for* contact. *No matter where, no matter how far, bless the phone for stapling two people together. Bless cellular technology and satellites. Bless the only decent thing invented since the Compact Disc. Bless the mobile network. And most of all, bless SMS texting.*

Yeah, a sappy, soppy thought – he knew that. He just didn't care. He'd been alone for five days and now his new wife was back in England and he'd missed her like crazy, so bless the phone and *fuck* soppy!

COME HOME, COME HOME, he keyed. Slowly. He was used to a QWERTY keyboard and this bizarre arrangement of numbers and letters would always fox him. I'VE MISSED YOU! WHERE ARE YOU? Then Christopher pressed SEND and the words vanished, in their place a crude graphic of two brick shaped receivers sending wavy lines to each other. Then that too was gone and the words MESSAGE HAS BEEN SENT popped up.

He'd met Nicole barely a year ago at a party given by his friend Rob. Christopher and Nicole had been the only single people there and when the word 'matchmaking' had been mentioned to him a few weeks later, Rob had widened his eyes and protested his innocence just a little too much. Not that Christopher cared by then. By then he was stone in love.

It was Rob's girlfriend who had provided this explosive catalyst. She'd been rather drunkenly attempting to force a copy of *ABBA's Greatest Hits* into the CD player and Christopher had been begging her not to. 'Please, Claire,' he'd said. 'I'll *pay* you not to put that on. I'll do a wine run. *Anything.* Just not *Dancing Queen.* Please. Haven't you any Elvis Costello or Ian Dury? Something with a bit of…well, *honesty?'*

'Or even The Boomtown Rats at a pinch,' a woman's voice said behind him, and Christopher turned, meaning to say that it'd have to be one *hell* of a pinch, but there she was, Nicole Bishop, five foot six, credit card slim, light brown hair cut into a bob, slight turn to her right beautiful navy blue eye and the *cutest* button nose. Christopher Tulloch didn't actually say a word right then. He just gaped a bit.

A noise like a Police siren. JST PSD DOVER, Nicole's new message read. WITH U 3HRS. MSD U 2.X

Ah Nicole, he thought as he deciphered this. *I love you with all my heart, soul and worldly goods – such as they are – but that elision, now. What are we to do about* that? Nothing, that was what. Nicole elided her texts. It was as much a part of her as the thousand shampoo bottles in the bathroom or the *Sex and the City* boxed set she watched and rewatched. Unlike him, Nicole hadn't decided that the world had ended fifteen years back. Unlike him, Nicole had moved forward and embraced the twenty-first century. Elided text messages, emails instead of proper letters and foul mouthed whores on late night TV.

Sometimes she'd call Christopher an old fart, especially when he would proceed to lecture about the fact that the kids in his class couldn't spell any more, about how an entire generation would grow up and not know how to communicate personally. 'Can you imagine these kids going for a job interview?' he'd once said. 'They'd have to have the questions sent to their phones and text back the bloody replies!'

'But *you've* got a mobile,' she'd countered, wrinkling that cutest button nose, 'you text.'

'Yes, but that's different! I text you and *only* you. That mobile's for us, exclusively. And I use the actual *words!*'

'Yes babe, I know you do,' she'd said in that mock-patronising tone that just made him want to pick her up, smear her with ice cream and lick it all off. 'And it takes you hours. My way is a lot quicker. And you always understand what I'm saying. We communicate, don't we? And we always will, no matter what.'

There'd been no ice cream in the freezer, but they'd licked each other all over anyway.

He looked to the clock on the VCR. 18:20, it said, green over black. At a little after nine he'd hear her key in the lock and hold her in his arms and kiss her and...well, maybe just lick her all over again. DRIVE CAREFULLY LOVE he sent back. HOW DID IT GO?

He'd spent the whole of Rob's party at Nicole's side, all the time expecting a bloke the size of a house to appear and sling an arm around her waist and say *sorry I was so long on the toilet, babe. Who's your friend?* At that point Christopher would sigh, shake the man's hand (assuming he'd washed it first), accept defeat gracefully, hang around and make some polite conversation so it wasn't *too* obvious he had the hots for this woman, and then slink off into the night, sad but not surprised. It was the story of his life after all. Why it was, he didn't know. It just was.

But it didn't happen. No one turned up to claim this vision of beauty as his own. No one came to spoil his night. The party went on and on and they kept talking, and at some point near midnight he'd drunk enough wine to believe that the impossible might have *actually happened* – that he'd met a single woman who liked him. Or was at least lonely enough at a party to *pretend* to like him.

But eventually the party wound down, because they do, they always do, and Christopher had found himself escorting her to a taxi and he'd *known,* he'd just *known* that if he hadn't screwed up all his courage and asked this gorgeous woman for her phone number *right at that very second* then she would simply vanish into the night and be nothing more than a memory.

Nicole never knew the agony he'd felt as he opened the cab door for her and somehow managed to squeak, 'Listen...I...um, really enjoyed talking to you tonight and I...um...well, maybe I could give you a ring and we could...maybe...do this again? If you're not too busy?'

Nicole said, 'Thanks, I'm very flattered, but my boyfriend just wouldn't like it, sorry. He's twenty feet tall, built like King Kong and very, very jealous.'

Nicole said, 'Sure, great – give me your number and I'll call you.' Then the taxi drove off and at the top of the road Christopher saw her throw the scrap of paper he'd written his number on out of the window and heard a faint laugh.

Nicole actually said *neither* of those things. Instead, she reached into her handbag and pulled out a business card. It had a photo of a Jaguar car on it. NICOLE BISHOP it said. There was a phone and a fax number underneath the photo. She flipped the card over and wrote a number on the back in eyeliner. 'I'd like that,' she *actually* said. 'Any time after seven. If I'm not there I'll be on the office number.' Then she'd kissed him on the cheek, jumped into the cab and Christopher stood on the kerb, staring at the card, then at the tail lights, then back at the card, grinning like a chimp.

A noise like a Police siren. TUFF BUT GT DUN. LNG DYS THO. HOW U?X

How badly had he slept after that party? Very. How stupid had the grin been on his face as he replayed every sentence of their conversation? Very. How happy had he been? Who needs to ask?

I'M OK, he sent. DON'T TEXT AND DRIVE!! SEE YOU LATER. LOVE YOU.

Christopher decided to screw the rest of the marking. Instead he would take a long bath, light some candles and give his wife a proper welcome home.

A noise like a Police siren. LUV U 2.X

Love you! No matter *how* they were spelled, were there any finer words in the English language than that? No, there were not and never would be. Words that a life without wasn't worth living and a life *with* was pure heaven.

Half an hour later he was soaking in the bath and remembering their first date, the time he'd become truly aware of *just* how remarkable Nicole really was. A quick post work drink around the corner from his school was all he'd proposed on the phone (and how nervous had he been when he punched in her number? See earlier questions) but they'd ended up staying till closing time. Sometimes he talked and she listened, but mostly she'd talked and *he'd* listened, and the more he listened, the more in love he had fallen.

She talked about herself, her family, her job. She talked about her parents' divorce, her bitterness towards her father who'd run off with another woman, never to be seen again. She told him she'd run wild as a teenager and though her mother had done her best, there'd been three other kids for her to juggle, all of them younger than Nicole, and not enough time or money to cope. So Nicole had been left to her own devices, and had specialised in Truancy and Drinking. But by some sheer fluke, she'd managed to leave school with two CSEs; Maths and English. Just.

But those C grades had been enough to secure her a Youth Opportunities position at the Jaguar factory at the other end of town. Up at five every morning, two buses and a twenty minute walk to file letters, open envelopes and make tea for the princely sum of thirty-five pounds a week. But one Thursday, bored out of her skull, Nicole had Made A Discovery. One that was to turn her life right around.

She'd been looking for an invoice from a parts manufacturer in Oldham. It had to be stapled to something else for reasons she never truly understood. So she'd gone to the filing cabinet and looked under *I*. There was no tab marked *Invoice*. Baffled and a bit irritated, she'd looked under *P*, for *Parts Manufacturers*. Nothing there either. She looked under the company's name. Empty. Almost screaming in frustration she'd looked under *O* for *Oldham*, and lo and behold, there it was.

An hour later, Nicole's Office Manager had returned from lunch to discover the files neatly arranged in a sensible fashion. *Invoices* were under *I*, then tabbed in date received order. *Purchase Orders* were under *P*...and so on. The Office Manager asked Nicole what she'd done. Nicole had told her. The Office Manager said that wasn't part of Nicole's job description. Nicole said she knew, but it would help make everyone's life easier if they could actually find things. The Office Manager said everyone knew where things were anyway and Nicole had ruined it. The Office Manager told her to put it all back the way it was.

'*That's* when I discovered what I had, who I was,' she'd told him that night, smiling. 'I'd done *nothing* with my life up till then, except skip school and drink Thunderbird until I was sick. But I saw the look on that snotty cow's face and I was *determined* to prove her wrong. I was *determined* to make the bloody thing work the way I *knew* it would work!'

Determination became Nicole's keyword. She persuaded the Office Manager to trial the system for a week, *see how it goes* – and it had worked like a charm, just as Nicole had been determined it would. The Branch Manager commended it himself, then offered Nicole a permanent contract on the spot. She accepted and signed on as a Clerical Assistant. Within a year she was promoted to Clerical Officer. Two years later, she replaced the Office Manager. And three years after *that,* Nicole was offered the job she currently held – PA to the Managing Director of the marketing division of Jaguar UK.

'It's scary, Chris' she'd confided that night. 'In only six years I've gone from a virtual slave to someone who jets off to Paris or Rome and sips champagne while making appointments and sorting out meetings for a bloke who holds so much *power!* And I left school a virtual illiterate! All I've got are two low grade exam passes and a desire not to make an idiot of myself.'

'No,' Christopher had said. 'You've got more than that. You've got determination.' *And the world's most beautiful face.*

'Yeah,' she'd agreed. 'I do worry about that sometimes. I don't want to be the kind of woman who eats people up and spits them out just to get my own way. It's just…I don't want to be *beaten* at anything. Does that make me horrible? I don't want to be horrible.'

'You're not,' he'd said, and she wasn't. She was just a success. A success at whatever she put her mind to.

They were married four months after that date. The pride he'd felt as he kissed Nicole in front of the congregation, the pride he'd felt as he took the most beautiful, most wonderful, most determined woman who had ever breathed as his wife, was beyond his capacity to describe. The closest he could come to it was *bliss*.

A noise like a Police siren distracted Christopher from the candle lighting some time later. He'd dowsed himself in the FCUK aftershave Nicole had bought him for Christmas and ordered in some Chinese food; this was going to be a welcome she'd *never* forget. NEW MESSAGE, the Ericsson read, black over green. READ NOW? He hit YES and prepared to hear his heart sing again.

But the message read LOST. DARK. HELP ME.

What the hell? he thought, a faint tingle of unmanning fear running down his spine. *What's up? Where is she?* He was about to call her – stuff texting – when there was a knock at the front door. *Can't be the food already, it's only*, he checked the VCR clock, green over black, *half past eight. Who the bloody hell is it then?*

Troubled, he opened the door. There were two Police officers, a man and a woman. They asked if his name was Christopher Tulloch and he said it was. The woman asked if they could come in and he let them. The man told Christopher to brace himself for some bad news. The woman made a speech about Nicole – about his *wife* – which contained the words 'lorry' and 'jacknifed' and 'central reservation' and 'your wife's Jaguar' and 'probably instantaneous' and 'so very sorry for your loss.'

Through it all, the phone remained in his hand.

*

Dusk of an April night, 2002. A lonely man sat on the bed of his semidetached house crying soundless tears. Tough times had come to Christopher Tulloch. No doubt about it, tough times had come. Now he sat, some three days since his wife – his beautiful, beautiful wife – had been lowered into the ground, wondering if the tough times would *ever* go away. What if they didn't? Oh, if only grief was like a function on a mobile phone, something you could DELETE with the press of a thumb.

Mobile phones, text messages, gone forever. Christopher sat on his bed and sipped some whisky and thought about that. No more sounds like a Police siren signifying some elided words that would make him smile. Oh yes. Tough times indeed.

Texts, a faint thought said. *Texts and times.* That made no sense to him, so he drank a bit and cried some more.

Tough times, and tough times to be faced on his own. Oh, there would be support; his family, Nicole's family, Rob – Rob whose party had brought him that brief, shining happiness – but Christopher wasn't a stupid man. An old fashioned man, maybe, but not a stupid one. He knew that after a while, all those who offered support would have to take up the reins of their own lives again, they'd have to get on with more pressing matters, and after a while he'd just slip out of their Hot One Hundred, and he'd have to deal with things alone.

Alone. Such a horrible, awful word. One that rhymes with phone.

Ah, the phone. The Ericsson on the bedside table, silent since the night two weeks back when his world had ended. That had been for Nicole and Nicole alone. That had been how they communicated. Text messages. Sometimes it was important stuff like GOTTA WRK L8 SOZ HUN.X or sometimes just I LUV U. X

He looked at the phone and cried some more. Silent phone never to send its tone into the night ever again. No more I LUV U's.

Except that last message, he thought. Then, *texts and times.*

Yes, that last message had been…well, wrong, hadn't it? Scary. And…

He picked the phone up, flipped the cover open and there it was, that last message. LOST, it said. DARK. HELP ME. More tears. *Dear God, where was she when she sent that? What was she seeing when –*

When…
When.

The message was sent at 20:30, almost two weeks previously. Christopher thought as hard as he could through the grief and the drink. The text alert, the message, about to call her back, knock on the door. Is that the food? Can't be, it's only – checks the VCR clock – half past eight. It wasn't the food. It was the Police. Who told him –

Who told him that Nicole had been killed in an accident at around seven o'clock on the motorway just outside Birmingham. She'd been taken to hospital by air ambulance and pronounced dead at the scene.

But the message in the Ericsson's memory was timed at 20:30. Half eight. Ninety minutes after the accident.

The accident in which his wife died – how did the Policewoman put it? – 'probably instantaneously.'

A terrible shiver ran through Christopher's body. *What's going on? How does this work out? What's –*

A sound like a Police siren. But it *wasn't* a Police siren. It was his text message alert. NEW MESSAGE, the words read, black over green. READ NOW?

Moving like a badly wound toy, Christopher crossed the bedroom and opened the wardrobe door. At the bottom was a box with Nicole's possessions in it – the ones the Police had recovered from the crash. Her Nokia was on top. It was battered. Still. Silent.

He looked down at the Ericsson in his hand and numbly hit the YES key with his thumb.

SOZ L8, the message read. GOT LOST. HM SOON.X

Spittle dripped from his open mouth. *Dear God. Dear God…*

A sound like a Police siren. NRLY THERE. MISS ME.X

Was that a car engine? Faint but growing louder? A *Jaguar* car engine?

A sound like a Police siren. I C THE LIGHT. U IN BED? WAITING 4 ME? NORTY BOY!X

The car pulled up in the drive. He heard the door open and close. Slow, dragging footsteps made their way to the front door.

I just don't like to be beaten at anything, she'd said, back in the pub, all those months ago. *Does that make me horrible?*

A sound like a Police siren. TK SUM TIME BT HERE I AM READY OR NOT. LUV U.X

How horrible was she now? How horrible was she now? HOW HORRIBLE WAS SHE NOW??

That *determination…*

At the sound of her key in the lock, Christopher Tulloch screamed.

Putting Meat on the Table

Lindsay Fisher sat on her bed and looked at the face that stared back from the mirror. Mousy hair. Bags under her pale blue eyes, no matter how much foundation she slapped on. Fading jawline. First signs of wattling on the neck. It'd do. Just. She unscrewed her lipstick – Scarlet Blush – and listened as she wound the greasy tube round her thin lips. From across the hall she could hear Ronnie at his PlayStation. Murray Walker was screaming his excitement as Fernando Alonso's Renault landed in a gravel trap. *Jesus,* she thought. *Ronnie's right. That game is old. I know fuck all about Formula One and even I know Alonso doesn't drive for Renault anymore!*

Well, it wasn't just the game that was old, was it? It was the console as well. A PlayStation! When did you last see one of those? Ten years ago? Fifteen? The years tumbled so fast when you were…well, past your first flush. And the TV the console was plugged into? A CRT Phillips model, so heavy that if she ever replaced it they'd need a block and tackle to lift it off the stand.

So yeah, the game was old, the console was old, the TV was old, and Lindsay knew all of those things, but that didn't excuse Ronnie, did it? It didn't excuse the way he'd nagged and nagged at her the other night, about his mate Richard at school, about how Richard had got a 50" LCD telly and a Blu-Ray player with 5.1 Surround sound and Mum, you should see it, you should see it! It hadn't excused him as he'd gone on and on about Richard's new XBox or whatever the fuck it was called, it hadn't excused him as he'd whined endlessly about how great *Harry Bastard Potter and My Goblin's on Fire* had looked and sounded on Richard's telly, it hadn't excused him as he'd…

No, it hadn't. But Ronnie was only ten, and sometimes ten year olds didn't see things properly.

Lindsay should've understood that. No, she *did* understand that, but it was early and she'd just come back from work and it had been a difficult night, a night in which she'd almost been caught, and she was still shaking with fear at the thought of that Police car and how close it had been, and Ronnie had started nagging, and she'd snapped.

She *shouldn't* have snapped. She should have sat down, hoisted her child on her lap and calmly, lovingly, explained the facts of their lives. But snap she did. In doing so, Ronnie had seen her as she *really* was, and he'd cried. He often did that when he saw her properly, and she felt sad. But that sadness was tempered by the terrible fear that was her constant companion since Steve had died – that and the close call with the coppers had forced her to snap.

Well, not snap. *Rage* would be more appropriate.

'Where do you think the money comes from, eh?' She'd shouted. 'Do you think there's a Magic Money Tree in the park across the road? Do you think I just go and shake a branch and tenners drop off? Since your Dad died I've had to work like a slave – like a *slave* – to put meat on the table for us! There's rent and food and clothes and bills to be paid, and *I'm on my own!* I've got to do it *all!* So don't talk to me about some stuck up kid whose *Mummeh* and *Daddeh* can afford to buy him everything he wants! I do my *best* for you, I do *all I can! I…*'

The red mist vanished like her true self as she finally saw Ronnie's hitching tears. She ran to him, hugged him, picked him up and spun him round. 'I'm sorry baby, I'm sorry, your old Mum's sorry,' she said, over and over like a mantra. 'I know you want things, I do too, and maybe one day, eh? Maybe one day. I'm sorry, your old Mum's so very, very sorry.'

After a while she'd got him to smile again and she'd made him his favourite tea – kidneys and mash washed down with Tizer – and by the time he'd gone to bed they'd been best friends again. That was good. She loved her son. He looked so much like Steve it burst her heart.

The following morning, as she'd laid her head on her lonely pillow in her lonely bedroom, she'd breathed a huge sigh of relief. Thank God she'd seen that look on Ronnie's face when she did.

If she hadn't, she might have just gone on and on, told Ronnie of the risks she took every time she left the house. About the way that every time she stepped out into the Kennington night there was a really large chance she might never come back. About the things she'd had to do to pay for that ancient TV or the out of date games console or that second hand bike. Oh yeah, she was being careful...but her luck was bound to run out sooner or later, law of averages, and what would Ronnie do then, poor thing? With no Mum or Dad to look after him? Where would he go? Who would – who could - take him in?

Oh, Lindsay's life was hard. No easy choices. Through one door, a tiger. Through the other, a bigger tiger. Oh it hurt to see her little boy decked out in threadbare jeans and a too large Bart Simpson T-shirt, but it would hurt more to have him alone in the world. It would crucify her to think of him making his way through the minefield that was Social Services. Ronnie in a foster home? What would they do when he reached puberty? What would they do when they saw *who he really was?*

She really had no other choice, did she? She *had* to keep doing what she did. She had to do it to bring in the money and put meat on the table. She had no other option. Or if she did, she couldn't think of it.

Trapped, she thought as she stared into the mirror. She ran the brush across her cheeks, taking the edges off her makeup. *But then, we've always been trapped, haven't we? All of us. Steve, me…Steph…*

The doorbell rang. Lindsay checked her watch. 9.30. 'That'll be Steph,' she called across the hall. 'Let her in, hon, will you?' No answer, but she heard the game pause in mid rev and the thump *thump thump* of her beautiful but graceless son as he made his way downstairs to the front door. *Steph,* she thought as she rifled through the pitifully small collection of going out clothes in her wardrobe, *there's always Steph. Ronnie would be safe with her…*

But Steph's one of us, she answered herself as she picked out the black mini skirt, the black stiletto heeled boots and the red halter top. *Steph takes the same risks I do. Oh, why can't things just be simple for the likes of us?*

From below, she heard Steph bellow her greetings and Ronnie's mumbled hello. Then she heard her son giggling, and one set of footsteps up the stairs. Steph was piggybacking him again. 'The wine's in the kitchen,' Lindsay called. 'Be out in a minute.'

Steph sent back a distant 'Ta,' and Lindsay finished dressing. *I'll tell you why things can't be simple for the likes of us,* Steve said from her memory. They'd had this conversation a lot before he'd died – and things had been much, *much* easier then. *Because we shouldn't be here. Because there's three classes in this world, angel. There's them, the ones with the jobs and the money and the BMWs and the holidays in Thailand. Then there's the underclass, the ones with the pot addictions and the fortnightly appointments at the Job Centres. And then there's us. The* **under-underclass.** *We're not wanted. Not needed. They'll hunt us down should they ever find us. Kill us, one by one. So we have to keep under the radar until we can…well, you know.*

Yeah, she knew. She tried not to tear up – that would glue those fucking false eyelashes together – and checked herself out in the full length mirror. *You'll do. For your age. And frankly they're not too fussy around here anyway.*

She stepped into the living room and saw that not only had Steph poured a generous glass of fizz, she'd joined her son in a game of *F1 Max!* 'Right, I'm off,' she said. 'You two going to be OK?'

'Of course,' said Steph. 'Well, Ronnie will cry like a baby when I batter him at this game, but…'

'You wish,' muttered Ronnie, not taking his eyes off the screen.

'You got my number?' Lindsay asked Steph. 'Just in case?'

'What, the one I use to call you on, you mean? Just bug out, Lindsay. Leave me to humiliate your son.' But their eyes locked and there was no smile there. *Be careful,* sent Steph. *I will,* Lindsay replied.

She bent and kissed Ronnie on the cheek – well, just brushed it. She didn't want to smudge her lipstick. Scarlet Blush didn't come cheap. 'Be a good boy.'

'Oh *Mum*,' Ronnie howled as a scarlet car hit a wall and bounced into the air.

'See?' said Steph. 'Humiliated.' Then, 'Bags?'

'Jesus,' said Lindsay, and almost ran into the kitchen. She pulled some Tesco carrier bags from the cupboard under the sink. 'Forget my head if it wasn't screwed on,' she said as she re-entered the living room.

'Yeah,' Steph said, and gave a knowing grin. 'Good job it *is* screwed on, isn't it?'

The woman's laughter followed Lindsay down the stairs and into the hot August night. She scurried to the bus stop, waited, then boarded the 231 into town. She ignored the smirk on the driver's face and concentrated on remembering Steve. She remembered him as he was, on the trip over, those long days and nights as they'd stared through the porthole. She remembered his smile, his easy temper, the way he took care of her. She remembered how easily he'd assimilated himself into this strange place, how quickly he'd found that factory job, working all the shifts he could get, the shifts the English didn't want to do. She remembered him at night, tired, worn out, but somehow still finding the energy to take her to bed and put their baby inside her. And then, when Ronnie was born, he'd found the energy to play with him, to make him laugh – with enough energy left to make *her* laugh in the bedroom. She remembered how he'd looked out for them, how he'd kept them out of trouble. How he'd kept dark the things that needed to be kept dark. She remembered the way he'd kissed all her anxieties away with a simple *It'll be all right, I'll take care of us.*

She tried not to remember the day the Police had knocked on her door. That was too scary. The way she first thought they'd been found out. Then somehow keeping her face fixed as they'd told her that her husband had been run over by some fucking drunk driver and could she please identify the body?

She tried not to think these things, but she did anyway.

She tried not to think of her husband's body on that slab, or the way she'd nodded, or the way she'd thought *please, let it stay just long enough for the funeral. Don't let it break.* She tried not to think of the way she'd thought *so who takes care of us now, Lindsay?* And the answer that had come back, *why, you do.* You *do.*

The bus pulled up at her stop, and she hurried off, once more ignoring the glance that bastard of a driver was giving her. She looked at the pavement and crossed the road to the pub, halted outside the door, took a deep breath, then swaggered in. The timid rabbit that had left the flat was gone. Through that door, she was confident, sexy, aloof, almost arrogant. *Changing comes easily to me.*

She oozed her way to the bar, knowing that the men in that place – that awful, stinking place – were fixed on her. They were hungry, desirous, lustful. Oh, she needed that. Oh, she *counted* on that.

The ape behind the bar poured her Tia Maria and Coke and never made contact with her eyes. Lindsay sipped from it, slowly, seductively, licking the tip of her glass. Sooner or later one of them would screw up the courage to screw her. *The underclass. And we're the* under-*underclass. Them, with their pot and their fortnightly Job Centre appointments. They're the forgotten. We're the* not-known. *Not yet, anyway. But these…these dregs of the human race…they can be useful to us. Until it's our time.*

'How much?' said a man's voice on her left. Lindsay turned, and there stood a small man in his fifties with acne, black teeth and scum-smeared glasses. *Brad Pitt must be at home watching the telly,* she thought. *And why not? There's a good documentary on Channel Four.*

'Twenty for a handjob, thirty for oral, sixty for the works. In advance.'

The twitching homunculus dug deep into his wallet and pulled out three twenties. Lindsay took them and made them vanish. 'Where?'

'Alley,' she said, standing. 'Round the back.'

She walked from the pub, her client right behind, breathing like Darth Vader after a half marathon. *He'd better be careful or he'll come in his jeans,* she thought. *Dirty fucking fucker. Jesus, these people!*

She led him halfway down the alley then leaned against the wall, beckoning him on like she'd seen whores beckon clients in films. He leapt to her, slobbering, his hands up her top and rubbing hard at her braless chest. Then his lips replaced his hands and he sucked greedily at her nipples, sounding like a pig at a fucking trough.

The he raised his head, doubtless to ask her to do something to him, and his face locked in utter terror.

Cruel though it was, Lindsay couldn't help but laugh. She *always* laughed at this bit, the bit where they saw her as she *really* was, all her masks and tricks aside, the face that she wore for her and her alone these days, the face that she'd let Ronnie see accidentally, the face he hadn't grown yet.

But he would.

The underclass, Steve said in her memory. *The forgotten...but useful to the likes of us. Our food and drink, you might say.*

Lindsay Fisher – who never was and never would be Lindsay Fisher, there *wasn't* a Lindsay Fisher, not really – reached out with a hand like a gnarled branch and punched a hole through the four eyed freak's chest. He died instantly. Blood flew like a shower. Her dark, primordial eyes watered with laughter and she ripped him from top to bottom and gutted the bastard.

That night all those years ago, on the ship over, as they'd watched their destination grow bigger and bigger through the endless night, Steve had reiterated their plan. *We settle in. We settle down. Make a niche for ourselves. All of us. We're only few, but if we're careful, if we're clever, we can bed down and breed. We have to be watchful. Kill only the ones they won't notice, the ones they don't care about. And while we wait, we smile. We change to look like* them, *we're nice neighbours who never make too much fuss.*

But after ten years or so...we'll kick the shit out of them.

And he'd laughed. And so had she. *But until then…careful.*

She ladled the dead pervert's organs into a carrier bag and set off into the night.

Before going home she visited four other pubs and by midnight she had a hundred and fifty pounds in her purse and three full carrier bags. The bags contained two hearts, four livers, a pancreas and three kidneys. *Kidneys,* she thought as she clambered aboard the night bus. *Ronnie's favourite.* Her bags were dripping with blood and gore but Lindsay didn't mind. The mask, the illusion, their one great secret – hell, their one great *power* – was up again, full force.

She was home by one and Steph told her that Ronnie had been as good as gold. 'Rough night?' Steph asked as Lindsay munched on a piece of human heart.

'Piece of piss,' she said. She held out the dripping organ, licking the blood from her fingers. 'Want some?'

'I'll pass,' said Steph. 'Chucking out time in Tottenham. I'll cruise around, see what I can find.'

'Be careful,' said Lindsay.

She sat at her kitchen table, fully intending just to have a nibble, just to take the edge off, but the next time she looked she was down to the aorta. *Steady, don't want to get fat, do we?* She put the rest of the food in the fridge and smiled. *Do us for a while…maybe five days if we don't go mad.* Then she smiled harder. *The things we have to do to put meat on the table, eh?*

She looked in on her son, fast asleep, curled like a ball. *Soon it'll all kick in. Soon your hormones will rage and your glands will burst and your true heritage will out.* That made her feel a little sad…oh, the years did tumble…but also a little excited. *She* may not live to see the day they inherited this world, but Ronnie might.

She went to her room, undressed, and spread the money on her dressing table. Twenty was for the electricity meter. Twenty was for the gas. Thirty was for vegetables and potatoes. The rest she stuck in her Bible.

Rainy day money, she thought as she eased under the duvet. *Maybe for emergencies…maybe a holiday, somewhere warm.*

Maybe, one day, enough for a 50" LCD telly. And an XBox, or whatever they were called.

As she clicked off the light, she wished Steve was there to cuddle.

When You're Five, You Call Them Quack-Quacks

September 1

I had the dream again last night. Again and again, like a cycle. Imogen was looking up at me from under the lake, eyes wide. Terrified. Bubbles bursting from her open mouth. Blood like red poster paint from the wound in her head. And she screamed to me. She was under the water and drowning, but it was a dream and I could hear her perfectly. Of course I could. 'Help me Mummy,' she screamed. 'Please help me! I'm cold and wet and I can't breathe! Help me! Come and save me! You're my Mummy, you keep me safe, please help me!'

I tried to speak, I tried to tell her my ankle was broken, I tried to tell her that actually I was unconscious when it happened, but no sound came out. Of course it didn't.

Imogen's eyes went all glassy then, and the bubbles stopped and she sank below the water. That's when I woke up, half past three this morning. My face was soaked, but John was still asleep beside me so I don't think I cried too loudly. Maybe that's a blessing.

A blessing!

My ankle throbs and my head still hurts and my heart is broken. Oh Imogen. Oh my love.

September 3

I don't know what to do with her clothes. They're still in her room, in her wardrobe, in her drawers. Her bed hasn't been made since...since. All her teddies are on the windowsill. They line up and stare at me accusingly. Where were you, they say. Why didn't you protect her?

Do we burn her clothes? Do we take them to a charity shop? Do we just throw them out?

What do we do?

I have to talk to John about it. I will talk to John about it. I will.

In the dream last night Imogen said nothing as I watched her drown, but the look on her face was enough. It was frightened and lonely.

What do we do?

September 4

John went back to work today. He squared himself up before going out of the door like a soldier going over the top back in 1915. I hate myself for this (for this!? For everything!) but a part of me is glad. I think he thinks it was all my fault. Fair enough. It was all my fault. Yes, he put on a show of support for the Inquest and he said all the right things to people, but since...

Crying again. Won't be able to read this back for the smudges. No, won't ever read this back anyway. Just need to get it down, get it out.

Since it happened, since June, he's been cold. Not hostile, not angry. Just cold. Distant. If only he could put his arms around me like he used to. If only he would tell me it was all right. If only he –

Oh listen to me! Me, me, me! John's lost his only child too, hasn't he? Isn't he entitled to grieve for his daughter? Isn't he entitled to be cold towards the woman who killed her? Isn't he?

I spent most of the afternoon in Imogen's room. I took her dresses from the wardrobe and laid them on the bed, one after the other. Cried a lot. Why shouldn't I cry a lot? It was warm and I took down all her teddies and held them all and cried some more.

I opened the window and held Mr Bunny, because Mr Bunny was her favourite, and I sat on the windowsill. You can just about see the lake from there. I held Mr Bunny and we heard the ducks and then we heard a little girl laughing. She sounded so happy that I cried again.

September 5

Mum came by with flowers this afternoon. She said her and Dad were worried about me. She said I was too pale and too thin. She said I shouldn't shut myself away. She said life went on even after…accidents.

Mum was worried about me but I worry about her. She looked eighty not sixty-five. I bet she doesn't sleep much now. She loved Imogen. Everybody loved her.

Mum held me and we cried together, then kissed me and went away again. I think we're OK.

John and me…no, we're not OK. He sits far away and won't talk. I ask him how his day in work has been and was it OK and I just want him to…

To say something!

He doesn't. He sits and grunts monosyllables.

September 6

Last night I decided to hug John. He was sitting in his chair not reading the paper and I went over to him and hugged him. He froze. Didn't pull away, just froze. I stopped hugging him and went to Imogen's room.

My house is silent now. Once it held noise and bustle and John would watch football and Imogen would have her Girls Aloud on and sometimes I would say 'Keep it down, you two, I can't hear myself think' but now it's silent and I want the noise back. Any noise.

I sat in her room and held Mr Bunny. Though the sun was nearly down I opened the window. I heard that little girl again – maybe it was another little girl but she sounded the same as the one I heard the other day. She was laughing. Maybe she was feeding the ducks. That's how Imogen sounded when she fed the ducks. She loved the ducks, especially the ones with the green heads, they were her favourites. She called them 'quack-quacks.'

She was only five.

How many tears can a woman have inside her?

September 9

Woke up after the dream and walked to the bathroom without too much of a limp. I think my ankle's healing. Drank too much wine last night – at least, that's what John said to me. 'You're drinking too much wine.' It may be the most loving thing he's said to me since the Inquest. But that's why I needed the bathroom. On the way back the door to Imogen's room swung open and I thought I saw her shadow on the wall but when I looked in I decided it must have been the birch tree outside.

September 12

Went to the lake today. First time since she died. Didn't tell anyone, just went. The ankle bore up OK. I'm limping a bit more heavily than I was yesterday and it's throbbing a bit, but I can live with that.

I was steeling myself for the lake, I thought it would be bad. But it wasn't. Not really. It was hard at first looking at the water, looking at where my baby drowned, and my heart was beating like crazy and it was hard to breathe…but then I remembered how it was before. Before she died. I remembered Imogen throwing the bread on the water and the ducks scrabbling for it. I remembered her dancing with joy at how funny she found them.

Some ducks swam up to me as I stood there. Maybe they remembered me. Maybe they were wondering where the little girl was who gave them bread.

As I looked down at them my eyes tricked me into thinking I could see Imogen's reflection standing beside me.

I felt suddenly at peace. The lake was her happy place – maybe even her best place – where she laughed and danced and fed her funny friends. Why should I allow what happened to spoil that for her?

I love my daughter.

Is it wrong to put that in the present tense?

September 13

Bad move, I think, going back to the lake. Bad dream last night. Not the usual one. I was in bed and I woke up and Imogen was standing in the doorway. She looked so sad! So lonely! I reached out to hug her but she turned away and went to her room. I followed her and she was looking out of her window. Guess what? I was crying again. 'I'm cold, Mummy,' she said and I ran to her, wanting to warm her, but when she turned I saw she was all puffed and black, rotting, rotting because she was dead, rotting because I killed her, and she would never be warm again.

I knew nothing else until morning when John woke me. I was on her bed. He asked me what I was doing there. I told him about the dream. I said it seemed very real (and it did, not like the other dream at all.) He grunted and said something about sleepwalking and went to get a shower.

Oh I'm lost and confused and tired and unhappy.

September 16

John doesn't come home straight from work anymore. He used to when Imogen was alive. On the dot, five thirty, with a cry of 'Where are my girls?' But now it can be half eight, maybe even nine before I hear his key in the door. I've tried, but I can't smell drink on his breath, so I don't think he's sloping off to the pub. Maybe he's having an affair. I've no reason to think that – no whiff of alien perfume or strange lipstick on his collar but wouldn't that be the perfect way to punish me? I mean, we don't make love anymore and why should we? I killed his daughter, our daughter, so why should he make love to me? Why shouldn't he find warmth in some other non-child-killing woman's arms?

Except I didn't kill Imogen. It was an accident. I know so, the Coroner said so, that's all it was, just an accident and I'm sorry, I'm so sorry; yes, she was in my arms just before it happened, but that doesn't make it murder, does it?

Does it?

Came downstairs from my bath last night and John was just standing in the living room. Just standing there. No TV, no radio, no sound at all. Just standing there. Like a statue. He must be in such pain! Why won't he let me help him?

No, I don't think he's having an affair. I just don't think he can bear to come home.

Before I fell asleep I thought I heard Imogen, as though from far away. I think she was laughing though she may have been crying. It was difficult to tell.

September 19

I will write this but never say it. But it is true. In my heart I know it is true. That's where it counts, in the heart. Never mind the rest. My heart says it is true and no one will ever read this so I will write it.

I heard the little girl laughing by the lake again today. Mr Bunny and I were sitting at the windowsill and the window was open and I heard her laughing. The ducks were quacking and I heard the little girl speak.

She said, 'Quack-quacks! Silly old quack-quacks!'

It was Imogen. It was my daughter. It is my daughter. I heard her laugh and speak and I know my daughter. I don't care if she's been dead since June.

My daughter, Imogen, is down by the lake sometimes. Laughing at the silly old quack-quacks.

(Later)

Why does she laugh at the lake but is sad in my dreams? I've been asking myself that all day. Is it because of the quack-quacks? Are they her friends during the day but asleep at night and so, cold and lonely, she comes to me? To her mother? For comfort? Is that it? Is that it? Oh Imogen, why can't you tell me?

September 25

I saw her today.

I spent days agonising over what my heart had told me. I know she's dead. I know that! Of course I do, I'm not mad! It was me, wasn't it, who crawled to the lake and fished her out? It was me, wasn't it, who held her broken, sodden body and tried to warm it? It was me, wasn't it, who wiped the blood from her shattered temple? It was me, wasn't it, who leaned on her crutches and watched that box, that so tiny box, get lowered into the ground?

No, I am not mad. Yes, I know she's dead.

But I know her laugh. I know how she spoke. I'm – was – her mother. And no one knows a child like their mother.

I went to the lake to see.

There she was, at the lake, her back to me, staring out towards the water. The quack-quacks were fluttering about her. Once again, that sense of…peace, of rest, came over me. She was wearing the pink jacket with the bunny on the back and her pink Wellingtons just as she had on that day and as I spoke her name, she turned, and there she was, she broke my heart, because she was beautiful and there, there! And she was my child and my love and she was there! She was happy and her cheeks were rosy and she said, 'Mummy! Mummy! I love you! Come and play! Come and feed the quack-quacks like we used to!'

She held her arms out to me but as I ran to her a dog barked quite close and I looked to it, but when I looked back Imogen had gone.

I waited an hour, but she didn't come back.

September 26

In my dream last night Imogen sat on my bed and told me it was lovely to see me again. She said she loved me. She said, wouldn't it be fun to see me once more and play down by the lake, like we always used to, like before she went to heaven?

Tried to get to see her again, but Mum came round and stayed for hours and then Dad came round to pick her up and he stayed for hours and then John came home so I couldn't. It would have been too dark then. The quack-quacks would have been in beddy bye.

Tomorrow, my love. Tomorrow. I'll bring some bread and we can feed your funny friends again. I love the quack-quacks too. I love you. Tomorrow, you and me.

Just like it was.

Just like before.

21 Grassmere Lane
Moreton, Cheshire,
CH4 3XL.
19th October

Jean & Phil,

I found Prue's diary last week as I was going through her things. I thought it might help if you saw it. It explains a lot, I think. But I must warn you now — a lot of what she set down here is deeply disturbing, and it may upset you. God knows it upset me. Please, THINK TWICE about reading it. I hope I'm doing the right thing by sending it to you. I've agonised about it endlessly. I've still no real clue. I'm just flying on instruments these days.

Oh, how much I regret how I was to her! I'm sorry. Truly, heartily sorry. I know that sounds pathetic, but I just can't think of another way to put it. I'm sorry.

Please believe me though — I never blamed her. Not once. I loved Prue. I just…in my grief…forgot how to show it, I suppose. I know she just tripped over that branch while carrying our poor baby Imogen to the lake, I know she broke her ankle and was knocked out when she hit that rock. I know our darling hit her head and drowned. I know. I ALWAYS knew, I promise you! My poor darling Prue! How much she suffered, thinking I blamed her! Bad enough to lose our daughter in the first place…but then to think her own husband blamed her! Oh Prue! Oh my poor love!

They were in my dreams last night, both of them, standing in the bedroom doorway. I tried to tell them I was sorry but they turned away.

So that's how it ends then. My life as a husband and a father; my wife and only child claimed by the same lake. One accident, one suicide. Maybe I should move, get away from the place? What do you think?

But...I don't know. There just seems so much of them still here, somehow. How can I leave that?

Prue was right about one thing, though. If you sit on the windowsill in Imogen's room with the window open, and you're very quiet, you can hear sounds from the lake. I was in there yesterday and I heard a little girl and her mother as they fed the ducks. Laughing they were. Very happy. It made me a little sad, to be honest.

Anyway, I'll see you soon. And please, THINK CAREFULLY about the diary.

Your loving son-in law,

John.

The Time of Your Life!

(Only £9.99!)

Justin trudged down Islington High Street and tried to erase Jacqui's crying face from his mind. He tried instead to think of all the lyrics to *Bat out of Hell,* but gave up after the first chorus. He then tried to think of Ten Great Films Starring Clint Eastwood, then realised with considerable dismay that there were, in fact, only five films that were even passable, and he was actually being over generous by including *Magnum Force,* which Jacqui had hated...

Arse biscuits, he thought as the pitiless July sun battered his hatless head. *Stop it. Stop thinking about her, stop thinking about how much she cried, stop thinking about her blue eyes puffed with tears, stop thinking about her gorgeous red hair clumped in bunches from having sweaty hands running through it over and over again, stop thinking about those runners of snot dangling from her nostrils. Think about something else. Think about how funny that dog is over there or the Knights that Say 'Ni' or anything, just* anything *but her and why she was crying.*

He walked to the kerb and leaned against the railing, the metal burning his skin. He took a deep breath and decided that, since filling his mind with stuff obviously wasn't working, he'd take the opposite approach and try that relaxation technique his mate Dave the Hypnotherapist had shown him. Take a deep breath, fix it to a thought, exhale slowly and completely and the thought is gone. Could work. He fixed his eyes on the Tube station entrance opposite. Deep breath, fixed to a thought, exhale. Once more. Twice more...

Oh, look at that *geek!*

Blinking in the light across the dual carriageway was the dictionary definition of 'Dork.' He was wearing a faded Red Dwarf T-shirt, khaki shorts and white socks under Jesus sandals. The whole relaxation thing collapsed in a struggling heap and Justin felt a grin break out under his nose. *Wanker. OK, so I may have fucked up big time, but at least I'm not* him.

So, of course, the *moment* this thought crossed his mind a stunning blonde woman in a cotton summer dress that was decent by half an inch ran up to this arsehole, jumped in his arms and rammed her tongue down his throat. Justin's sigh began in his ankles. *What a world.*

Then Jacqui was right in front of him, sobbing helplessly, asking *why. Why?*

Suddenly angry, Justin slammed his fist on the railing (which hurt) and stormed off down the High Street into Market Lane. Here the air was thicker, the crowd a homogenous mass as they writhed around the stalls. *Maybe this'll do. Maybe here, pushing people aside and being assaulted by the shrieks of the barkers and the stench of the fruit, vegetables and fish might- just might – blot out her face.*

For a second or two, he actually thought it would work. Uncaring, he brushed people aside. He looked neither left nor right. He let the noises, the sensations batter him, eat him up, make him unreal, make him a ghost; and that suited him just fine. Ghosts had no feelings. Ghosts weren't crippled with guilt. Not feeling guilt was as right as rain with Justin.

Then he heard the voice. It cut through the low roar of the crowd like a klaxon. Strong, well-modulated, almost accentless, it came from his right. 'The time of your life,' it called. 'The hour you always loved! Sixty of your finest minutes all over again! Bargain! Under ten pounds!'

What an odd thing to say, thought Justin. He stopped in his tracks (and was nearly rammed by a harassed looking woman with a pushchair, who muttered 'Cockend' as she steered around him) and turned to the voice.

There was a wooden barrow, much like the others that filled the lane. Except for the fact it was completely bare. Not a single item upon it. No batteries, no mobile phone covers, no dodgy-looking DVDs with photocopied covers, no apples or oranges, nothing. Nada. Zip.

Then, behind the barrow, Justin saw the vendor. As their eyes locked, Justin felt something like a low voltage electric shock spasm his muscles. The vendor was a tall man, maybe six foot four, stick thin and dressed in an immaculate grey suit, white shirt and a red tie. *How the hell is he not sweating a river?* Justin wondered, but there he was, apparently as cool as a cliché. His dark black hair was swept straight back from the forehead, and his gaunt, high cheekboned face bore more than a little resemblance to the actor Michael Rennie. The vendor's face broke into a smile, and it was so warm, so *infectious,* that Justin couldn't help but return it.

That smile faded, however, when Justin suddenly realised he couldn't hear the crowd any more. No, that wasn't quite right – he *could* still make it out, but only if he strained. It was like someone had got hold of a global remote control and pressed the NIGHT button. A mild panic gripped him and he gazed around. The crowd was still there, still going about their insane business, but now they sounded like someone had stuffed their mouths with cotton wool. Oh, and another thing; he'd been standing still for maybe four or five seconds now, and no one had bumped into him, no one since the Cockend Woman had swerved around him…no one, in fact, seemed to notice he was there at all.

Unnerved, he looked back at the well-dressed vendor, who met Justin's gaze with his slightly cheeky smile. Then he beckoned.

Slightly stunned, Justin crossed in what felt like slow motion, avoiding no one, for no one crossed his path. 'Now then, my fine sir,' said the vendor, 'if I'm not mistaken – and I'm *never* mistaken – you present to me the air of a man with a problem. Am I not right?'

'Um, sorry,' said Justin, totally at a loss. 'I just…'

'Just what, sir?'

Justin held his nose and blew hard, hoping that his hearing would clear. It didn't. 'Sorry, things are a bit...well, I dunno. Maybe I've got a sinus problem. Or a cold. Or something.'

'Summer colds are the worst,' the vendor sympathised. 'Still, you seem to be hearing *me* clearly enough. Am I not right?'

With a start, Justin realised that this man was, indeed, right. Whereas every other sound seemed to be reaching him from another room, the vendor's voice was as clear as day. 'Well, yes. But I'm not sure how.'

The vendor waved his hand as if this was the least important thing since the Earth had cooled. 'All the rest is static anyway, utterly insignificant to what will happen here. So, before we go any further, let me introduce myself. I'm Paul.' He thrust his hand out.

'Justin,' and as he took the hand and shook it, Justin felt that odd, low tremble again.

'Good to make your acquaintance, young sir! And now that we know each other, let me tell you that I am in possession of the one thing guaranteed – *absolutely guaranteed* – to make this problem you're dragging around with you fly away like an autumn leaf.'

'OK,' said Justin. 'But I think I should warn you, if you're selling blow, the coppers are up and down this lane every five minutes. Also, you could be more subtle.'

'Drugs, Mr Rooney? No, no drugs. I offer a *solution,* my friend, not a disguise! Look at my stall and tell me what do you see?'

'Well, nothing.' *And when exactly did I tell you my surname?*

'Yes, nothing. It's as clean as a nun's conscience, as they say where I come from. No fish, no fowl, no fruit, no vegetables. That's because what I have to sell can't be displayed. Or, more ontologically, it *is* being displayed, right at this very second. That's because I spoke nothing but the literal truth when I shouted out. What I sell, Justin my friend, is Time itself.' Paul leaned forward and spoke in a tiny conspiratorial whisper that still sailed into Justin's ear unopposed. '*Time.* Not in a clock from Switzerland. Not in a knock-off Rolex or a sundial or even an hourglass. Time. *That* is my commodity.'

Justin blinked.

'Not the whole thing of course,' Paul went on, straightening up and speaking normally. '*Goodness,* no! I couldn't sell eternity, even if I wanted to!' Then back to being a con in a Warner Bros. movie. 'I mean, don't pass this around – but eternal life? Mostly it's pretty dull.'

'I'll keep it to myself,' said Justin in a small voice. Even though this guy was fairly comical and even strangely likeable, he was quite clearly a nutter. Justin started planning his exit strategy – though glancing at his left wrist and saying, 'Oh, is that the time?' was probably a non-starter. God alone knew where *that* might lead.

'Good man,' boomed Paul. '*Knew* I could trust you! Knew it as soon as I *saw* you! I told you, I'm *never* mistaken. So here's the deal, Mr Rooney. In return for the rather pathetic sum of nine pounds ninety-nine pence, I will provide you with an hour of your life *all over again.* Sixty entire minutes of your past for you to re-experience. *Any hour you wish!* And with change from a ten pound note! Now, how does that sound?'

'It sounds like you're fucking Looney Tunes,' said Justin, the words out of his mouth before he could stop them. *Bad move,* he thought. *You're supposed to humour madmen. Confront them with their delusions and they're apt to run amok with an axe.*

Paul, however, just laughed. 'Mad? Heavens, no! I am very, very far from mad, friend Justin. And don't you worry about offending me. I know your race, I know it well. You've always been cynical. Once, many long years ago, I would offer this service for free, for gratis, and you know what? *I never had a single taker!* Your lot will not accept something for nothing – well, some of you will, but we don't really bother about them. But even if offered a genuine miracle on a plate, the human race will look upon it and say, "Where's the con? Where's the angle?" So I began to ask for some payment – a nominal one, but a payment nonetheless – and things started to turn around. It at least guaranteed some interest. Oh yes, sure, the response is always "You're crazy" or even a more colourful variation such as the one you've just offered, but what you actually mean is "Prove it." Which I will.' Paul held his right hand up, as if taking an oath. 'Watch closely,' he said. He then spread his fingers like that salute Mr Spock used to give in *Star Trek,* forming a V.

In that V, suspended in mid-air, a picture formed.

Justin leaned forward, squinting, struck dumb with astonishment and wonder. *Jesus Christ almighty! Am I seeing this? Really? How can I be? This is…this is…*magic.

The picture was of a small boy, maybe eight years old, with a pudding bowl haircut and short trousers standing on what looked like a school stage. Then – faint, but still clearer than the muted hubbub of the crowd – he heard the small boy say, 'Abou Ben-Adhem (May his tribe increase!) awoke one night from a deep dream of peace…'

My God. My God…that's… that's me. *That's me! Eight years old, was I? Runner up in that bloody poetry recital thing at school. I was so scared I nearly pissed my pants waiting for my turn. But Sister Francis said I was a very good boy, and everyone clapped, and Mum and Dad were so pleased, and I didn't care that I came second, I was just so happy to have got through it…*

Then a terrible fear ran through him. *What is this? What's he done? Hypnotised me? Done a Derren Brown thing? Wait till I tell Dave about* this! *He'll shit a brick and give up the hypnotherapy and open a newsagent's. This guy's a* real *talent. But if he can do this…what* else *can this crazy motherfucker do?*

At that, Paul snapped his fingers shut. The picture disappeared like a bursting soap bubble. 'That's your proof,' he smiled. 'And Mr Rooney, it was no trick. I promise you. I have just shown you a fragment of your life. But if you decide to accept my offer, you will be able to crawl *inside* that fragment – *or any other fragment you choose!* You can live it *all over again!* But there *are* conditions of sale – aren't there always? *You* and *only* you will be aware that what is occurring is a replay of a previous event. Anyone else in your fragment will be experiencing it for the *first and only* time. You will be unable to *alter* any event or word that happened in that fragment – Time will not be corrupted in that way. Time *cannot* be corrupted in that way. You will have sixty minutes *exactly.* Not a second more, not a second less. And finally, *this is a once in a lifetime offer!* You may decide to take me up on it. You may decide to walk away. The human race has, after all, free will. But if you decide to re-live an hour of your past, you must be *absolutely sure* that it is an hour you *really* want to re-live! There are no second chances here, no margin for error. Not with miracles. Now, do you understand what I have said?'

Numbed, shocked…more than a little scared…Justin could only nod.

'Good,' said Paul, rubbing his palms together briskly. 'Now, of course, I don't expect you to decide upon your hour now. Take some time, think it over. Take a day. If you decide it's a good idea, meet me back here tomorrow at the same time. If you decide it isn't, stay away. Sound fair to you?'

Once more, Justin only nodded.

'Hope to see you tomorrow then,' said Paul, and with a terrible suddenness, the sound of the world flooded right back to full volume, and Justin clapped his hands over his ears.

'What...what *is* all this?' Justin heard himself shouting.

'A business deal, what else? You go home now, my friend. Think it over. Carefully.'

On pipe cleaner legs, Justin wove his way through the throng, making his way towards the High Street. Just before stepping back into the punitive light he turned, hoping to catch a glimpse of that strange, strange man. But he couldn't. There were far too many people in the way. *Fuck me, I need a drink.* So he went off to find one.

*

That night he sat in his kitchen, looking out through the open window, nursing a Jack Daniels and Coke so large it could've dwarfed Paul Bunyan. He felt extremely strange, like he'd been hit on the back of his head with a shovel wrapped in a blanket. He thought of that man Paul, of the way all the noises had been muffled except for his voice. He thought of the way he'd known Justin's surname. He thought of his offer. He thought of that strange picture, hanging in the air – but mostly, he thought about Jacqui. *How odd, even after all that...that madness, the first thing I wanted to do was pick up the phone and say, 'Hey Jacks, guess what? I met some weirdo today right out of* The Twilight Zone!'

But he couldn't do that, could he? He'd dumped Jacqui a month ago. He couldn't call her about this. He couldn't call her about anything anymore.

He finished his drink and had another which, if anything, made the first look like Kenny Baker. He wondered if he should call Dave, see if Dave could give his girl Anne the slip and the two of them could go on the piss, maybe see if Mrs Rooney's eldest was still the Pull King of North London. Then he decided that was too much effort. Besides, what was *Jacqui* doing at that very moment? Supposing – and this was a big suppose – that she hadn't found someone else to share the duvet with, wasn't it likely that she was just sat in on her own, listening to her soundtracks of West End musicals or watching something mindless on the telly? And if she was, what gave *him* the right to go out and enjoy himself?

The second drink was followed by a third, and this time Justin merely waved the Coke at the bourbon. *C'mon, will you,* he tried to scold himself, *it's been a month since you two split up. Time to forget it and move on, right?*

Split up? You didn't split up. *She was dumped, wasn't she?*

Well, yeah, she was dumped…but so what? That's what people mean when they say 'split up.' One person dumped the other. I just happened to dump her. *Could've easily been the other way round.*

Yeah, right.

Justin sipped – well, gulped – his drink, and looked over at the kitchen chair opposite. That's where Jacqui had sat on their last night, sobbing her heart out. She'd asked him to move in to her place. They'd been going out for over a year, she'd said, and they loved each other, so why not? Made sense. And his place was too small for them both, so…

Justin had said no.
Jacqui had asked why.
Justin had said because.
Jacqui had asked because why.
Justin had said just because, that's why.

Jacqui had started to cry. She'd asked him if he still loved her.

Justin had said nothing.

Jacqui had moved from crying to sobbing, asking why not, what had she done, what had happened, why didn't he…?

Sitting in his kitchen, halfway to being drunk, Justin had an appalling revelation. He had *no idea* why not. No idea *at all*.

*

'Mr Rooney,' said Paul, the following day, and Justin was very, very glad of the diminished crowd noise. He had a bit of a headache. 'So glad to see you again! Now, do you wish to take me up on my offer?'

Justin said he did,

'Do you have a time in mind?'

Justin did, and told him so.

'Can you remember the conditions of sale and repeat then back to me?'

Justin could, and did.

'Excellent! And most importantly, do you have the money?'

Justin handed over a ten pound note. Paul held it up to the light, stuffed it in his pocket and flipped Justin a penny. 'Hey ho,' he said. 'Let's go.'

*

'Over five hundred years,' said Jacqui to his right, her voice low, musical and sexy.

Justin rocked back on his heels a little, stunned. He was no longer in Islington in June, 2012. He was…he was…*in York, my God, I'm in York and it's September 20th, 2011, and it's…oh fuck, it's real…it's real…it's fucking real!!*

'Are you listening to me?' Jacqui asked, but Justin didn't turn. He *wanted* to turn, pick her up, carry her off to bed somewhere, but he couldn't. He tried to move, he tried with every ounce of his strength to move, to turn, to tell her exactly what was happening...but he couldn't. Of course he couldn't – hadn't Paul said that everything must be just as it was? That he may *know* it was happening again, but he couldn't change anything? 'Oi,' she went on, rapping him lightly on the head with her knuckles, 'cloth ears, I'm pontificating here, and I need an appreciative audience, yeah?'

Now he *did* turn to her, because he'd turned *then*, but back then...had he had his breath taken away by her the way he did now? Oh, *man*...azure blue eyes, hair of flame tied back with a butterfly clip, that naughty, irreverent mouth turned up at the corners. Yeah, Jacqui, back again, beige jumper straining at the front, tan leather jacket, blue jeans and ankle boots that were totally impractical for walking...yeah, Jacqui. *Oh boy. All that and a bag of chips.*

'Earth to Justin,' she laughed. 'Come home, Captain Kirk. The crew of the *Enterprise* need you.'

'Sorry love,' he said, just as he had back then. 'But you were talking so I got bored and thought about a squirrel having a fight with a badger.'

'Oh, I'm *such* a lucky woman,' she said, but smiled and linked his arm as they walked around the ruined monastery. 'Of all the men I could have picked to cleave unto – and there were hundreds, Justin, literally *hundreds* – I had to end up with you, a man who showers me with compliments every waking moment.'

'You are truly fortuitous,' he said to the woman he had so callously dumped.

'Come on,' she said. 'Let me educate you.'

My dear God, Justin thought as they negotiated the ruins. Everything the same as it was. But then it was...stuff, just the stuff we did, the stuff we said, that's just how we were. And I...I took it for granted, didn't I? I took this *for granted...*how? *How could I have* done *that?* Look *at her!* Listen *to her! How could I have let her go? How? She's...she's...ah God, this is* wonderful!

So he let her guide him through the place he'd let her guide him through once before, and she told him once again of eras, of kings and queens, and she used words like *Jacobean* and *Reformation* and he interrupted her over and over again, just as he had done back then, making jokes, making puns, and she'd punched him on the arm just as she had done once before, and she said that if you'd just actually *listen* for a change, you might be less of a thicko, and he'd pretended to be outraged at that and had chased after her, and they played hide and seek through the columns and colonnades or whatever the bloody hell they were called, and once more he caught her, held her to him, and kissed her and kissed her and kissed her some more, and every time his face pressed down on hers, he wanted to cry for things lost. But he couldn't, because they weren't yet lost.

Once more, she suggested an ice cream, and once more he bought her a mint King Cone and had a Strawberry Split for himself. Once more, they sat on a bench and ate them, once more she rested her head on his shoulder.

'Do you know something?' he said.

'I know *lots* of things,' she said, snapping a bit off the bottom of her cone and dipping it in the ice cream. 'One for teddy,' she said.

'Teddy hasn't got a mouth,' he replied.

'I eat teddy's for him, he doesn't mind. Anyway, things I know; the names of Henry VIII's wives – in order. The *exact* wording of the American Declaration of Independence. And you are desperate to get me back to the hotel so you can slake your filthy desires upon my defenceless body. Now, do *you* know something?'

'I know that if I buy you a frighteningly expensive meal, you'll let me.'

'*It's a bullseye!*' Jacqui laughed and squirmed closer to him, and they munched on their ice creams and said nothing more. Justin *wanted* to say more, but he couldn't. He wanted to tell her he was sorry. He wanted to tell her he loved her. He wanted to tell her that he had finally realised – way, way too late – that there was *no reason at all for them to have broken up!* This hour, this *re-lived* hour, had shown him that *something could have been worked out!*

Why? She had asked him when he'd said they weren't going to move in together. And he'd given no answer, because there hadn't been an answer to give. All he'd thought was, *uh-uh, no way, that's not what I do, is it?*

How pathetic. No talk, no discussion, just the shutters in his brain slamming down and saying, no.

But it was all too late now. Far, far too late now. So he cherished the feel of her next to him and begged with all his heart that he could stay, stay here, stay in the past, change it all, change it all for the better.

*

'Welcome back, Mr Rooney,' said Paul from the depths of the crowded, noisy Islington market. 'Did you enjoy your hour?'

Justin couldn't speak. There were tears on his face and a lump in his throat. All he could do was nod.

'Excellent, a satisfied customer! They're *always* satisfied customers! Now, remember what I said to you yesterday? That what I sold could make your problem blow away like an autumn leaf?' Another nod from Justin. 'Well, it can. If you take what you've learned here, and use it. Pride, you know, isn't *always* a bad thing, it's not always a sin. But *misplaced* pride – or arrogance, as it's sometimes called – is *always* a bad thing! *That* can sometimes stop you seeing what's really in front of you. But I think you understand that now, don't you? So, why don't you toddle off and put what you've learned to use?'

Justin wiped his face, nodded, and started to move off. But then he turned, swallowed the blockage in his throat, and somehow managed to ask, 'Paul…who are you?'

But Paul just smiled and tapped the edge of his nose with his forefinger. Justin nodded a final time, expecting no more. He turned and walked towards the High Street. He didn't look back, and never saw the tall man with the Michael Rennie face again.

Half an hour later, Justin stood in front of Jacqui's front door, wondering. He wondered about Paul, about who he was and where he came from. He wondered about Jacqui, and had she found a new boyfriend. He wondered what she'd do when she saw him again. He wondered what would happen next.

He raised his hand and rang the bell.

If What Were Horses?

What was it Martin had said to her that night? *Oh yeah. I don't know why you waste your time in that café. You got a brain. You got looks. You've probably got hidden talents. You're better than that job.*

Arsehole.

'Bacon and eggs and a black coffee please,' said the Anthony Perkins look-alike at table five, and Sandra Jones gave him the smile and wrote on her pad and wished him cancer. *Push,* she felt. And there it was, done. She dropped the order down the dumb waiter and slopped coffee from the Silex, knowing – *just fucking knowing* – that Perkins' eyes were on her arse the whole time. *Christ, some bastards will stare at any arse, no matter how much it's growing. Maybe they can't help it. Maybe it's in their genes or something. On the other hand, who gives a fuck?*

She took him his coffee and smiled at him, and he leered back, eyes no higher than her nipples. *Jesus, I hate bank holidays. Every perv, gimp and general arsehole flees to the North Wales coast. Fuck off, Perkins. Fuck off to the beach and have a tug over the sixteen year olds in their thong bikinis, eh? Who knows, their tits may still be somewhere above their knees.*

'Enjoy your coffee,' she said. *And your pointless chemotherapy.*

Wasn't that men all over? They may spout about equality or women's rights or *blah* this or *blah* that but they *all* turned into Benny Hill at the sight of a pair of tits. Even Martin. Oh, fuck that, *especially* Martin. Except, of course, that wasn't fair and Sandra knew it. Martin had been no worse than any other man. Trouble was, he'd been no better, either.

'Can I have two cheese omelettes, a fish burger, a side order of chips, a tea and a strawberry milkshake please?' said the titanically ugly troll at table three. *Now here's something you don't see every day,* she marvelled. *A REALLY FAT woman in lycra leggings and a council facelift haircut! With her EQUALLY FAT and HIDEOUS CHILD!! Who's got a phone? I need a shot of this! This could make me a fortune!!* But Sandra smiled, wrote the order, and with a *push* wished a traffic accident on the boy and a brain embolism on the mother. On the same day. *It's a two-for-one deal,* she thought, almost laughing. *It's on the specials board.*

The only thing she could honestly say in Martin's favour was that he had, at least, been honest about his marital status from the start. Though really, when you thought about it, was that a plus point at all? Could you have an 'honest adulterer?' Was such a thing possible? Who knew? And who gave a fuck, anyway? All she knew was that three hours after meeting him in that club in Colwyn Bay where she'd been celebrating her mate Gillian's hen night, she'd been in the back of a taxi with Martin's tongue down her throat as they sped back to her flat here in Llandudno.

One thought and one thought alone rang through her head that night. *Married,* it went. *Married, he's married, he wears a ring and he told you, he came right out and told you, so what are you doing Sandra? Well, yeah, I know* what *you're doing. But why? Why?*

Oh, but the answer was simple and awful enough. The words. The words he'd said to her. 'Look, I'll tell you right out,' he'd said, 'and if you want to walk away, fine. If you want *me* to walk away, fine. I'm married. I have two beautiful daughters. And I have never, *ever* wanted to cheat on my wife. But tonight I do. Because you are the sexiest woman I've ever seen in my life.'

'A ham and cheese toastie and a coffee please,' said the four eyed piece of shit with the *Twilight* T-shirt and the hideous acne at table four. Sandra smiled, wrote on a pad, and with that little push wished the fucker AIDS from a dirty needle.

Yeah, right Sandra had thought in that club. *The sexiest woman you've ever seen. Left the house much recently? Had your eyes tested since 1999? And a married man, at that! Oooh, what a future we have! Seeya, wouldn't wanna be ya, I'm off.*

But she'd stayed.

She'd stayed and talked to him and they'd danced and they'd talked some more and he'd bought her drinks and once he even made her laugh. Almost. And when, at the end of the night, he'd asked if they could go back to her place, she'd said yes.

Why? Because of the words, that's why. The words he'd said, the words no one else had ever spoken to her. She was almost thirty-five and no one had ever said that she was the sexiest woman they'd ever seen – and if it was a lie, who cared? Who really, honestly, *cared* if that was a lie? (Who actually cared if it was true?) The words were out, they'd been said, and deep down – despite what she could do with her wishes - Sandra was no different to anyone else.

She just wanted to feel special to someone.

So they'd snogged all the way back to her flat, they'd snogged at the door, they'd snogged up the stairs and they'd stumbled to the bedroom and they'd ripped each other's clothes off and he'd…well, then he'd…well, he'd done his best, and it was OK…she supposed…but…

Well, it was a bit quick.

'Was it all right for you?' he'd asked in the dark, and Sandra had told him it was, of course it was, because he was just a man and needed to feel he was the Shag King of All Britain. And it hadn't been *appalling,* after all. Just quick. But she'd told him it was wonderful, that he was the best, that he was a champ, and he'd nodded as if he expected no less, then climbed back into his clothes and called a taxi. As she heard the door close behind him, she'd thought *Well, that's that.*

But that hadn't been that. The very next day he'd walked into her café and asked to see her again. And she hadn't even thought about it, she'd said yes. Despite the disappointing sex, she'd said yes. Because of what he'd said, because she was old, because there was no one else, because it was him or her 10" Rabbit.

Sometimes Sandra wondered why that was. OK, sure, she was past her best, but she wasn't *repellent.* Much worse than *her* found someone. She had a brain – well, maybe it had atrophied through lack of use – but there was one in there *somewhere.* So why? Why was there no one for her but a married man? Why was there no one of her *own?* No one *special?*

Ah, who knew? And who gave a fuck?

'Just two coffees please,' said the female half of the impossibly good looking couple at table ten. She had the most gorgeous raven hair and eyes the colour of jade. He was square jawed and looked a little like Robert Downey, Jnr. They were young – mid-twenties maybe – and so much in love they were on the point of bursting. It was in the way they looked at each other, the way his hand absently stroked hers, the way their chairs were angled inwards. Sandra smiled, wrote on her pad and wished them…nothing. Nothing but a love that would last forever. But as hard as she tried, she knew this wish would never come true.

Maybe that's why you're alone, she thought as she made her way to the Silex. *This...power or whatever it is. This thing you can do, this thing that's been inside you ever since you were a little girl and you made Jenny Flood fall off the pier and drown just because she was laughing at your dress...it's all bad, isn't it? Only the bad things come true. This weird bitterness and rage and anger that you can...well, inflict on others, I suppose...do you think that's twisted you? You think that's possible? You think people can sense that somehow? Do you think that's why you're alone?*

Ah, who knew? And who gave a fuck?

So the pattern of her life was work, and foul wishes, and Martin sneaking to her flat whenever he was free. The two of them on her sofa, his hand up her blouse, hers down his trousers. Or him pontificating on one thing or another as if he knew the answers to everything. Or the two of them grinding in bed for all of five minutes before he shot his wad up her. And all the time she would pretend she didn't see how often he'd glance at his watch, she'd pretend not to care about the fact they could never be seen in public, she'd pretend she'd never think about his wife and two beautiful daughters, she'd pretend she never asked herself *what does he look like in the morning* and *will he ever be mine and mine alone?*

For a month, that was the pattern of her life. Sandra sort of actually liked it, despite all the problems, despite the mediocre sex and the fact he was (let's face it) a bit of a bore, Sandra was almost happy. It was, after all, that or nothing.

But, of course, the pattern changed. It changed, of course, with a phone call. (*A phone call! Such class, Martin!*)

'I'm sorry,' he'd said, and who knows, maybe he even meant it? 'But I think Denise is getting suspicious. She's asking questions all the time. I think...I think it's better if we don't see each other again.'

It was a Sunday morning, and she was naked. The bastard had got her out of the bath to tell her it was all over. The bastard had interrupted her nice, warm soak to tell her she was on her own again. The bastard had...

The *bastard*...

The bastard with the wife and two beautiful daughters.

The bastard who had someone to talk to, *someone to fuck!*

The *bastard*.

She'd hung up, not saying a word after her initial hello.

Bastard.

So she *wished*, she *wished* with all her might, harder than she'd *ever* wished before. It went out with a push, into the world, out to *him*, out to that *bastard*.

Then she felt better and went back to the bathroom to dry off.

It was in the paper the next evening, and as she cut the piece out and pinned it to the cork board in her kitchen Sandra laughed like a drain. She'd underlined the words MERCEDES and BLOW OUT and WRECKAGE and DECAPITATED in red. She'd double underlined the words WIFE AND TWO DAUGHTERS BURNED and HOSPITAL and CRITICAL CONDITION in red.

What had Martin said to her that night? *I don't know why you waste your time in that café. You got a brain. You got looks. You've probably got hidden talents. You're better than that job.*

Oh yeah. She had hidden talents, all right. Ask Jenny Flood, who bobbed up and down in the sea for hours before anyone could get to her. Yeah, Sandra Jones had hidden talents, all right.

But she was still working in this fucking café, she was still alone, and the only thing that made her day worthwhile was wishing people to death. Why *was* that, exactly? Why *couldn't* she find a way out? Why couldn't she *change*?

Ah, who knows, thought Sandra as she took the bacon and eggs to Anthony Perkins. *And who gives a fuck anyhow?*

Anthony Perkins thanked her very much and stared at her chest. He started to eat as the cells in his lymph nodes turned black and started killing him.

Maybe It's The Will of God
of God
(The End of the World I)

In a farmhouse in Yorkshire, a man too large for the small bedroom chair he sat in shifted his bulk. He removed the shotgun from his lap and rested it – gently, the safety was off – on the floor. The figures on the bedside alarm clock read 03:33, but the large man wasn't tired. He was a man of the land, was Bernard Cook, and when you worked the land you just accepted long hours.

A cry – not too loud, but a cry nonetheless – from the room down the landing made him glance towards the door. Wendy, his wife. Bad dreams. Hardly surprising, this was a bad dream night for sure. The two Valium he'd ground into her ten o'clock cocoa hadn't done much good. Not that he'd expected them to.

The moon peeked out from a cloud as if to see whether it was all over yet. It lit up the room with a death light, picking out the posters on the walls – TNA Wrestlers, *The Saturdays* and Andy Carroll in his England shirt. It shone across the portable TV with the Wii plugged in the back. It picked out the tiny hunched figure that lurked under the duvet. The very quiet, very still figure. The one Bernard was staring at. The one he was waiting for.

The moonlight also illuminated one side of Bernard's face. His left eye glittered mercilessly. There was no compassion there.

He was a farmer, a man of the soil, Bernard Cook – and compassion had no place in his world. He knew of it, he'd heard of it, he thought it was fine for those who could afford it, but Bernard's world was harsh and unfair and gruelling. It was a world of long hours and short money, of price hikes and no subsidies and fuel duty and compulsory purchase orders and back pain and cuts and cows who sometimes died and buggered your profit margin; a world of protesters and trendy, lefty veggies and animal rights activists and *Oh I want ORGANIC milk!*

But it was *his* life; he was a farmer – a third generation farmer at that. Despite all of the above, it's what he did, it was what he loved. Why? Because his life kept him in touch with the reality of the world – never mind your Global Warming and your Toyota Prius; here's your *real* environmentalism for you; the soil. The land. *That's* what mattered – that's *all* that mattered. Everything came from the soil, everything went back to the soil. Bernard had a reasonable education and he made bloody well sure his son had one as well, but really, the only thing anyone needed to know was this; death, life, death. And death wasn't something to be feared, not on a farm, not where it happened daily; death, after all, gave life. When an animal died it became food. When a person died they went into the ground and gave nutrients to the plants which fed the animals which fed man...and so on and so on, world without end, Hallelujah. That's what he'd learned from his father, it's what he'd passed down to his son, Andy.

Though not without a bit of a struggle.

He thought about that as he stared straight ahead, looking for signs - thought about that day when he'd taken his son to his first lambing. How old had the boy been? Four? Five? Something like that; a long time ago, anyway. As the first child had popped out of its mother and lay trembling on the ground, Andy's eyes had lit up and said, 'Oh Daddy! What shall we call it?'

'Son,' Bernard had replied, 'you don't give a name to something you eat.'

That night Andy had refused to eat the steak Wendy had made them. He said he didn't want to eat lambs or cows or chickens any more. He said it was cruel. Wendy had first begged him, then cajoled him and then finally shouted at him, which was wrong of her. Understandable - after all, she'd worked hard to provide her men with a fine meal and there was her son all but calling her a murderer - but wrong. So Wendy had shouted, and when the shouting was over the boy was in tears but still refused to eat, so Wendy had sent him to bed. Bernard had watched, but didn't intervene. He chewed his food and kept his thoughts to himself.

Later on he had gone to his boy. Andy had been sitting up in bed, eyes puffy. 'Son,' he said, 'you're old enough now to understand how the world works. You may think it's harsh, but it's not, not really. It goes like this; big things eat little things. That's it, that's all you ever need to know, that's how things *are*. The only things that don't get eaten are us - and that's because God put Man at the top of the chain. He put the things on this Earth to feed us - the cattle, the sheep, the lambs. What we do on this farm is to put God's plan into *action,* you see? Now maybe when you're older you can think about changing what you eat - lot of folk do, even though it seems foolish to me, to go against God like that - but you ain't a man yet, you're a boy - *our* boy - and boys live by the rules of their parents and by the rules of God. Understand?'

After a day or two, Andy had gone back to eating meat.

Bernard Cook, a man of the soil, a third generation farmer, lived with his family in the house his grandfather had virtually built with his own two hands. Oh sure, there was electricity and central heating and inside toilets and even television sent down from space, but mostly it was a life the long corrupt David Cook would have recognised – big things eating little things and God in Heaven making sure that Man was the biggest thing of all and that nothing fed on him.

Until, that was, the plague struck.

The very first reports had come out of the television set less than four months ago – muddy, confused stuff from Africa where people had apparently started dropping like flies. 'No surprise there,' Bernard had said. 'Them niggers will allus have trouble. Look at that land – look at that *soil*. Thin, way too thin, that is. Can't grow nothin'. Course, you can't *tell* 'em that – oh no, they just keep poppin' out kids who starve to death 'cause there's no food for them 'cause there's no food for the animals 'cause of that soil! Well, into every generation a plague will fall.' Andy and Wendy had agreed with that wisdom.

But it wasn't the soil; it wasn't famine. Nor was it anything like dysentery or any other disease spread by unsanitary conditions or lack of clean water. All the doctors agreed on that. Trouble was, of course, that was the only thing they could agree *on*. No, that wasn't strictly true. They could agree that thousands were dying by the day. They could agree that the disease first showed up as raised glands on the neck and a strange purplish discolouration on the palms of the hands...but both of those symptoms faded very quickly, maybe in evidence for only a couple of hours, which made diagnosis a bitch. Between an hour and an hour and a half of these symptoms vanishing, the victim contracted a sudden high fever which literally boiled the poor bastards alive. Death was agonising, but mercifully swift. It took less than twenty minutes.

If all of that wasn't unsettling enough, there were the autopsies. For a while – a week, in fact – these details were marked NOT IN THE PUBLIC INTEREST and kept very, very quiet indeed. Even by the neurosurgeon who'd run screaming from that Mombassa operating room, his hair literally standing on end. The fact that he ran straight into the road without looking and was splattered across the tarmac by a Kia Cee'd had something to do with it. But by the time events started to get out of control, just about everybody left alive knew that the plague liquefied its victim's internal organs into some kind of mush that resembled blancmange. Pink blancmange, coated in jelly. But the brain...*that* was what had sent the neurosurgeon screaming to his appointment with his Maker.

The brain appeared to…well, *grow*, even after death. Strange alien ganglions sprouted from the cortex and buried themselves into the top of the spinal columns. They looked like tree roots. Or plant stalks. Or *anything* bar a natural part of the human brain. At a second autopsy, someone attempted a biopsy. The scalpel wouldn't cut through, just bounced off. A saw was tried. Same result. After a while they ran out of things with blades and tried to cut something off it with a laser. The laser passed right through. An MRI scan showed massive electrical activity passing down these ganglions, even though the brain they were attached to was inert.

One surgeon turned to another as they held these results and giggled like a schoolgirl. 'It's like something's trying to jump start the poor dead bastard.' The other surgeon giggled back. Then they stopped giggling and looked terrified.

Two days later, they had good reason.

Bernard Cook and his family watched the end of the world from their Yorkshire farm. Beamed via satellite, in glorious LCD colour and surround sound, the Cooks found out that those people killed by the plague *just wouldn't stay dead.* They lay in cold rooms or in the ground for less than a week, then they decided to get up again and walk around a bit. They didn't look that much different than they had when they were alive. You could've probably passed one in the street and not really noticed the difference…well, apart from the smell.

The smell, and the fact they were very, very hungry. For meat, mainly. Any meat. Even human meat.

Actually, *especially* human meat.

No one – not the best medics in the world – could find a way to stop the plague spreading. No one could decide whether it was airborne or spread by human contact. Containment was impossible. No combination of antivirals so much as slowed it down. It thrived in every environment it appeared in. Two months after the first reported case, the plague was out of Africa and making a world tour.

By the time it arrived in England, the entire planet was insane. Authority was a bad joke, panic became the new order – rioting and anarchy were rife. What else could people do when they saw the Prime Minister eaten by a pack of the bastard things outside Downing Street live on BBC *Breakfast?* What else could they do when a two year old girl sank its teeth into its mother's neck and pulled chunks of flesh from the bone, wolfing then down with a greedy, smacking sound? How could debate and reason prevail against *that?*

Individually, of course, the monsters could be stopped. Blowing their heads off worked well enough, as did dousing them in petrol and setting them alight. But there were thousands of them, and more every day as terrified people felt the lumps on their necks, saw the blotches on their hands and knew their days were numbered.

Through it all, the Cooks kept on. Bernard made the farm into a fortress. As soon as the first case was confirmed in England, he took Andy out of school. He told the few staff he employed to get the hell away from the place – a point he made eloquently with his shotgun. They left. He shut all the gates and barricaded them as best he could.

They continued to work the land. They would have enough for a while – the animals didn't seem to get this damned disease. They could isolate themselves, wait it out, keep this madness confined to the TV. *God willing,* Bernard thought, *we can get through this.*

God didn't appear to be willing. Wendy had come to him three days ago and said, 'Andy's got it.'

Bernard had stared back at her, long and hard, had taken in her shivering body and quaking mouth, then dismounted his tractor and walked to the boy, who was feeding the chickens. 'Let's see them hands, boy.'

Andy put down the pail and held his palms out to his father. Ugly purple blotches spread across them both.

Without speaking, Bernard reached out and felt the boy's neck. Nothing out of the ordinary there. But those marks...

'Filthy, they are,' said Bernard, voice level, eyes clear. 'Get 'em washed, Ma's makin' us tea.'

His son had trotted to the house, whistling. Wendy came up to Bernard, still shivering. 'Our little boy,' she'd said.

'Nothing wrong with his neck,' Bernard had replied.

'But his hands, the marks...'

'Aye, he's got them.'

'So this means...'

'I know what they *say* it means,' Bernard had said. He also knew of the vague advice the Government had given out. Anyone showing the marks on the hands or the neck was to be executed – or 'euthanased' as they put it – and their body burned, to 'prevent further spread of this disease.' Like that'd help. 'But how can we be sure?' he went on. 'We don't know what those marks are – could be bruises for all we know. And *there's nothing on his neck!* How can we...how can we do what they *say* we should do if we're not sure?'

'So what do we do?' Wendy asked.

Bernard took a deep breath and ran his hands through his hair. He looked at the farm, at the land, at the soil. 'We place our trust in the Lord,' he said at last. 'He'll see us right.'

For two entire days they'd watched Andy like a hawk, and he seemed fine. Just his own normal self, in fact. He did his chores and ate his food and slept in his bed. The marks…bruises, whatever…didn't fade in the way they had on those others. *Please God*, Bernard kept thinking, *please, show mercy on my son. He's a good boy and never set his face against us or You. Please God, mercy. Please.*

He was almost starting to think they were going to get away with it, when yesterday Andy had entered the kitchen and said, 'Dad, I feel hot.' Then he'd collapsed on the floor, jittering like a fly on a grill.

Bernard held him while Wendy did everything she could to take her son's temperature down, even to the point of throwing a bucket of water over him. But it didn't work. The water just turned to steam. In less than an hour, their boy was dead.

Wendy had howled, howled in grief and fear and outrage. Bernard had said nothing.

Nothing at all.

After a while he had picked his son up and carried him to his bedroom. He tucked the boy under the duvet and went back down into the kitchen. He helped Wendy to her feet, held her for a time, then went to the cupboard and removed his shotgun. He put two cartridges inside and another two in his pocket. Then he led Wendy to the kitchen table and let her continue crying.

They sat like that for some time, next to each other, Wendy in tears and Bernard silent. He ran his hand over the wood of the table, a table his grandfather had built, a table that was a time traveller. Once, when they had been newly married, he'd been so overcome with desire that he'd taken Wendy on that table. She'd cried when she came. Back in the day when Man ate the animals which ate the grass, and no one ate Man.

'You know what…' said Wendy eventually. 'You know what we have to do now?'

'I know what they *say* we have to do,' said Bernard. 'But maybe what happened to *them* won't happen to our boy. Maybe God will reward us for our lives by taking him straight to Heaven. Could you face doing…*that* to him if 'twere were the case, lass?'

Wendy looked at him, wet eyed, with wonder and love and grief and exhaustion. When was the last time he'd called her 'lass?' Ten years back? More? 'And if he is…like them?'

'If he is,' said Bernard, 'I'll send him to God myself.'

A rustle from under the duvet – was it? It was so quiet, so…stealthy. Had he heard it at all, or just imagined it? *Never mind, just be ready. Just in case.* He reached down and picked up the shotgun, remembering that horse that had gone lame, just before Andy had been born. The way it had looked at him just before the trigger had been pulled.

A definite noise from under the duvet…a low sigh. Bernard pulled the hammers back.

'Who's there?' said a young voice. It sounded a bit like his boy, but it wasn't. Not anymore. *All true then,* Bernard thought, and looked along the barrel. There was no compassion on his face. When you worked the land you could laugh and you could love, but compassion was not an option.

The thing in the bed sat up and looked straight at him. Bernard's heart skipped a couple of beats. He almost dropped the gun. It was dead but alive; it was his son but not his son. It gave an awful, ghastly smile. 'Daddy,' it giggled. 'Daddy, is it you? Daddy…I'm really hungry.'

Bernard Cook blew the thing's head clean off its shoulders.

The sound was enormous in the still night. Blood splattered the headboard in a torrent; grey flecks of inhuman brain flew like shrapnel. The smell of blood was everywhere. The thing that had once cried at the thought of eating a lamb convulsed horribly and tumbled out of bed, hitting the floor hard. Bernard stood and marched to the body on clockwork legs, looking for signs of life. There were none. It was still. He lowered the gun and stared at the abattoir that had once been his little boy's bedroom, a bedroom where Bernard had once explained the nature of God's plan.

Except it seemed that God now had a new plan.

He heard the thump of their bedroom door as it was flung open. Wendy didn't need to see this, not yet. There was a job for her to do first.

She ran into his arms at the doorway to Andy's room. 'Is he,' she slurred, voice heavy with drugged sleep, 'was he…?'

'Aye,' Bernard said. 'Everything like they said, everything true. Now we know, don't we? Now we know for sure.' He untangled himself from her embrace, and she sagged against the wall. If not for the Valium she'd be wailing already. Bernard broke open the shotgun, ejected the smoking cartridge cases and loaded the two from his pocket. He snapped it shut and handed it to Wendy, who stared at him, befuddled, uncomprehending.

'All things serve the Lord,' said Bernard. 'I told Andy that, years ago. Big things eat little things but nothing eats us, 'cause God put us at the top of the chain. But now we're not at the top of the chain no more, now something *does* eat us. Maybe that's God's plan too, I don't know. We can't see the mind of God and it's a sin to try. One *other* thing I told him that night; a boy must obey the will of his parents and the will of God. But I am not a boy. I'm a man. And if this is God's will, then I choose to set myself against it.'

He held his hands up to his wife, palms out. There was just enough moonlight for her to make out the purple blotches on them.

Gettin' Smarter
(The End of the World II)

The car threw itself round the country lanes like a lion with its tail on fire. Inside, April hung on to the door strap while Tony didn't bother to slow down for a bend. He took a swig of Bud, driving one handed. Theirs were the only lights on show.

She was going to ask him to slow down, going to tell him it wasn't safe, then didn't bother. What did it matter anyway? He was coked up and pissed, the car was doing over eighty, sooner or later they'd miss a turn and hit a tree and the car would explode and they'd burn inside it and, really, that'd be a blessing.

Of course, he *also* wouldn't listen to her. Even now, he wouldn't listen to her.

'Tunes,' said Tony, but not to her. 'Gorra get some fuckin tunes.'

The radio would be no good, of course. That was blank now across all bands, like the telly. But he had his iPod hooked into the stereo, so that was OK. He took both hands off the wheel and fiddled with it. There was a bend coming up. A sharp one.

'Tony,' said April, in her loudest, strongest voice. It didn't even register over the engine.

He didn't look. Just kept scrolling. The bend was very, very close – beyond that, a ditch. Probably. Yorkshire country lanes were Ditch Central. She was going to die in a ditch, just like Mum had said. 'You could have been dead in a ditch somewhere for all I knew,' that's all April ever heard when she'd been younger as she came in at four o'clock from whatever club she'd been at.

But suppose they *didn't* die straight off? Suppose they just got hurt? Suppose they just broke bones or got cut? There were no hospitals now, so who'd help them? Yeah, dying, that'd be a good thing, that'd be a blessing – but *pain?* Who needed *that?* How *long* would they be in pain for? How *much* pain?

April didn't like pain, which was surprising considering how much she'd put up with in her twenty-two years.

So she reached across to the steering wheel – Tony not looking from his iPod – and tweaked it a little so the car made the bend. 'The fuck're you doin?' Tony muttered.

'Bend,' she said.

Tony shrugged, found something he wanted to hear, dropped the iPod on the floor and resumed driving. Something loud and horrible burst through the speakers; some nig nog shouting about bitches and guns and stuff. 'Don't touch my fuckin' car again. Fuckin' bitch.' Tony said, not looking at her. *Bitches on the stereo, bitches in the car.*

And all around them in the night, unseen, dead people walking.

They were on the way back from a 'party' (or 'wake', as Tony's friend Joe had called it) in Bretton. Joe had a big house. It wasn't his, though. Joe had lived in a squat. Well, he was still living in a squat, just a big squat in Bretton instead of that bedsit in Leeds. There were loads of empty houses now. Joe had found one. And even though the mobile networks were patchy, he'd got through to Tony and invited them up. 'A big fuckin' wake for the Earth,' he'd said. There was booze and dope and coke and H and everything.

April just drank, She didn't like the rest of the stuff. Tony had hit just about all of it, except the H. 'H is for cunts,' he said.

'We gonna party like it's 1999,' Joe had said, which April didn't understand because it *wasn't* 1999, but everybody laughed – there were maybe a dozen people there and she didn't want people to think she was thick, even though she was, so she laughed anyway. Tony had looked at her. He knew she didn't get the joke.

There were some girls there. They might have been fourteen. They might have been twelve. Who knew? They had makeup on that made them look like dolls. They had big, scared eyes, even though they were doped to fuck. They looked like the people in Tony's Nip comics. The girls walked around the people with drinks and drugs. Every so often a man or boy or even one of the other women would take them into another room. Sometimes there'd be the sounds of punching. Sometimes there wouldn't.

It seemed like she'd been at the party for a long time.

She'd gone to get a drink from the kitchen – feeling her way because there was, of course, no power, there or anywhere, just the torches people had to carry – and had passed Tony in the hallway, somehow smoking a spliff and snorting Charlie at the same time.

'Still with that thick cunt?' Joe had asked Tony.

'Yuh,' was the noise Tony had made, which April decided meant yes.

'The fuck you see in her, dude?' Joe came from Bradford and sounded funny when he said *dude* but April never said anything.

'Big tits, great arse. Swallers.' Tony had said.

There was a mean laugh then, but April had heard those laughs before, so it was OK.

She'd heard them most of her life. Even her own brother had said stuff like *you're one thick cow but Jesus April you'll never go hungry*. April didn't understand what he meant, but that was OK because she was thick. Ever since she'd grown tits that's what people had said to her. *C'mon dumbo. Hey jugs! Jesus, the fuckin' rack on you. If them's puppies* (and this one she *really* didn't get) *I'll have the ones with the pink noses.*

Ever since she was fourteen, that's what men had said. Ever since she was fourteen they'd crowded round her like dogs. Big tits, great arse. Swallers.

She took her drink back into the living room. Joe and Tony came in. Joe had champagne. He said he'd found it in the cellar when he'd 'moved in.'

'A toast,' he'd said, then necked a load of it. 'To the end of the world!'

That much April understood. Well, sort of. Bad stuff was happening all around. Dead people didn't stay dead no more. No one knew why, which meant even doctors were as thick as she was.

'These are the last times,' Joe had said. 'The great plague has fallen upon us, and as it says in the Bible, brothers and sisters, *we are fucked!*' Some people had laughed at that. April did too.

Just in case it was funny.

'An' it's speedin' up,' Joe said. 'Least it was, last I heard.' He pointed to the big telly that hung on the wall. It was smashed. 'Fuckin' *'mergency* band's even off air now. Now if you get bit, you don't even have to lay on the slab for couple a days. Now if you get bit, you're one of them pretty much straight away.'

'Kiddin'?' said one of the other people there. 'But the marks an' stuff…?'

'No marks, no more,' said Joe. 'Them bastards just keep comin' and bitin' and when you're bit, you're one of *them.*' He gave a scary laugh. No one else laughed though so April didn't either. 'If they don't eatcha there an' then. Last I heard, they reckon whatever it is had…dunno the word…*changed,* like. No marks on the hand, no lyin' in no morgue, just a bite and then you're one of the motherfuckin' livin' dead. So drink up, drug up, shut up and fuck up, cause *this may be your last chance to dance!*'

There was a cheer then, so April joined in.

A couple of hours later, Tony had come to get her. She was standing outside, looking at the moon. A boy – maybe eleven, maybe eight, who knew – had asked her to fuck him. He was crying. She said no and he cried even more. She didn't like to see little boys cry so she'd gone outside to look at the moon.

'We're goin',' Tony had said.

April nearly asked him who he'd fucked, but didn't. That way Tony got mean. 'OK,' she said.

He led her back through the house. Joe was by the front door. His jeans were round his ankles and one of the Nip comic eyed girls was sucking him off. 'Goin'?' he asked.

'Yeah,' said Tony.

'Aw man, why? Stay. We got all stuff here.'

'Cause you're out of coke and you're a cunt,' said Tony, opening the door.

'Thank you for a lovely party,' said April. Thick, but well mannered.

Now they were heading back to Tony's place in Wakefield. It was dark but it was dark everywhere now. There were bends but he didn't care. And he said nothing to her.

The end of the world, April thought. *Shit, that.* She'd wanted to grow a bit older. Maybe marry. Get a job somewhere nice – like Argos or something. Now she wouldn't because there were dead people out there who wouldn't lie down and it had just…well, *happened,* hadn't it?

But then, everything had *just happened* to April. She'd *just happened* to grow tits. She'd *just happened* to get men. And she'd *just happened* to meet Tony in the pub, and he was the sort of man she liked. Tall and dark. She was thick and he knew it, he told her often enough. But it was OK, really, because he made all the decisions, he told her what to eat and drink and wear and think and she did them. That was, after all, what she was there for.

On the iPod, one nig nog gave way to another. One bend gave way to another. Tony actually steered round this one.

Only now there was a man in the road.

'Fuck,' Tony said mildly, and they hit him at eighty miles an hour.

The impact was tremendous. April was slammed forward, the seatbelt cutting between what Tony called her *funbags,* stopping her breath. Her head jerked back and forwards, her neck a savage wall of pain.

Tony was struggling with the wheel. It didn't seem to be turning the way he wanted it to turn. They were spinning on the road. The headlights picked out the ditch they were heading for.

You were right, Mum, thought April, *here comes the ditch,* and the car left the road.

But April didn't die. Nor did Tony.

The crunch was the world, the loudest sound in the history of sounds. Once more, she was thrown forward, once more her enormous tits feeling like they were cut in two, once more her head bounced around like it was on a spring.

Then silence, pain, and the fact they were at an angle, canted forward.

'Tony,' she said eventually. 'You all right?'

'Don't be so fuckin' thick, dozy cunt,' he said. He didn't ask after her. He wrestled his seatbelt free and kicked open his door. 'Fuckin' Volvos,' he muttered. 'Fuckin' *tanks.'*

He got out and slid down the ditch on his arse. 'Bastard,' she heard him mutter. She would have laughed, but that would have got him mad, and anyway her chest hurt. She somehow managed to unclip her seatbelt, but the door appeared stuck. 'Tony,' she called, but she couldn't get much breath.

He didn't answer, just stood looking at the car. 'Fucked,' he said. April rattled the door again. Still nothing. She called his name as loud as she could. He didn't answer.

Then she *screamed* his name.

There was a man behind him. Well, no. Not a *man*. Not anymore.

There was no way of knowing if it was the same man they'd run over, but April was sure it was anyway. He was picked out in the still working headlights. His suit was grimy, torn. His face was pale. A huge cut ran across his forehead. One arm looked broken.

And he was right behind her boyfriend.

Tony looked at her as she screamed, then followed where she was frantically pointing. He turned and saw the 'man.' He put his fists up, the way she'd seen him put his fists up many times. He threw one fantastic punch, right from the shoulder. It hit the 'man' right below the jaw. Once, on a night out in Leeds, she'd seen Tony do that to someone who'd 'gave him shit.' The fact he was a player on the same rugby team made no difference. No one gave Tony shit. The other man had gone out like a light, eyes rolling backwards, and had hit the pavement like a bag of shite.

But not this 'man.' This 'man' just rocked on his heels, then put out his own arm. He grabbed Tony by the throat and lifted him in the air. He started shaking Tony back and forth.

Over Tony's shoulder, the 'man' looked at April.

He smiled.

Somehow, April managed to find the strength to open the car door.

She stood there for a second, wondering what to do. Tony was making some awful 'glug glug' noises. Should she help him? She *had* to help him, he was her boyfriend.

Just one bite and you're one of the motherfuckin' livin' dead, Joe spoke up in her mind. Tony was going to be bitten, right enough, and then he'd be one of 'them.' And when he was one of 'them', who'd he come after…?

Who was the only fresh meat about the place?

So April ran.

Well…perhaps 'ran' didn't quite describe what she did. Her chest hurt, her neck hurt and one of her legs seemed to be a bit numb. So she kind've limp-staggered up the ditch, and kind've limp-staggered down the road, as quickly as she could, with no idea of where she was, where she was going, how many of 'those' were around, or what she was actually going to *do.*

The only light was the moon, and that didn't show much. As she kept going, panicked, grief stricken, she tried to make out shapes in the darkness. Nothing. Nothing but more country road and ditches and trees and a field or two and more country roads. *Fucking country, fucking stinks and full of fuck all. What did Tony call it?*

But the thought of Tony made her cry, the thought that she had abandoned her boyfriend who she loved made her cry, so she stopped thinking about him.

How long later was it that the stitch ripped across her ribcage and caused her to scream? She'd no idea. Maybe half an hour. Maybe a year. All the breath was forced from her and she collapsed to the tarmac, fetching her knee a *fuck off* wallop. She hissed.

Pain. She hated pain. Suddenly she hated *everything;* the world, her tits, the pain, the dead people who just wouldn't stay fucking dead, even (for a split second, anyway) Tony, who had brought her this way, miles from anywhere, miles from home.

She sank back on her haunches and cried in pain and fear and grief.

When she'd finished and wiped her eyes, she saw the farmhouse.

It was maybe a mile down the road. Two floors high, barn behind it, fields, and a big wooden gate. Her first thought was to find a phone and call the Police. Then she realised how thick she was (the worst thing about being thick was constantly forgetting you were thick). There *were* no Police now. Still, it had (probably) doors and windows and stuff and…well, maybe even food. If she could get in, she'd be safe. If there were other people – people like *her* – they'd take her in and look after her. If there were people like the 'man' who'd killed Tony – she stifled a sob – then she'd go away.

It's somewhere to go, thought April.

Slowly, each step agony, she made her way to the farmhouse. Once there – and keeping an eye out for those 'others' – she knocked at the door. 'Hello?' she called as loud as she could. 'Is anyone in? My name's April.' She paused, thinking hard. 'I'm normal.'

Nothing. The place was in darkness, but hell – *everywhere* was in darkness now, even in the daytime. She knocked again. 'Hello?' Nothing.

She tried the door, just knowing it would be locked. But it wasn't.

It led into a kitchen. *Funny people, farmers. Got their front door on the wrong way. And they fuck their animals, Tony said. Dirty bastards.* There was just enough light through the leaded windows to make out a huge table, the chairs that surrounded it, and the woman hanging from the light fitting. There wasn't enough light to make out how long she'd been there.

Suicide's a sin. Still, enough people had done it recently. Hardly surprising, even if Tony had called it 'the coward's way out.' She wondered if he still felt the same way. Then she started crying again.

Through her tears, April said, 'Sorry missus. Am I OK to, like, crash out here a bit? Stuff's gone to shit, you see. Expect you know that.'

The corpse said nothing, just kept swinging. Still crying, April rooted through the cupboards and found some crisps. Cheese and onion, but beggars weren't choosers. She munched on them as she cried and left the kitchen.

Through the doorway was a staircase. *Bed.* It seemed horrible to think of sleep with Tony either dead or...worse...and that poor bitch swinging away, but she was tired and sore. She climbed the stairs, not scared overmuch at what she would find. That had been one thing Tony had liked about her. They'd watch his *Saw* and *Hostel* movies over and over and April was never scared. 'That's cause you're too thick to scare,' he'd said.

On the landing at the top of the stairs was a man. Well, *had* been a man. His body ended at his neck. There was stuff all over the walls. In the bad light it looked black. There was a bedroom to her right. April looked in. It was a little boy's room. Posters of footballers and a girl band and those wrestlers on telly. There was a little boy in the bed. Well...like the man on the landing, there was most of him.

'I'm sorry, little boy,' she said, thinking of the little boy at the party, the one who'd wanted her to fuck him.

She stepped over the man's body and found another bedroom. This had nothing in it but a bed, and she lay on it, curled up tight like a baby, missing her boyfriend. She cried herself to sleep.

But not for long. It was still dark when she heard the crash, the noise that jerked her awake. *The fuck AM I?* This wasn't her room.

No, it's the farm. Remember? The party, the car, the 'man'...Tony...

The crash again, from downstairs, like something bumbling about. Something lost.

Fuck fuck fuck it's one of 'them,' she thought, and sprang out of bed. Well, tried to. She had, of course, forgotten how injured she was. The pain in her chest and her leg (also her knee) caused her to bite her lip lest she scream and let whoever it was know she was there. *Maybe if I'm quiet, it'll go away.*

She stood as still as she could, listening to the 'thing' blunder about below her. Horribly, she discovered she wanted a piss. Never could go more than two hours, Tony said.

The 'thing' kept moving around. *Please don't find the stairs.* Bang…thud thud thud…bang. Crash. *The fuck's it* doing? Thud thud thud…then silence.

Has it gone?

Nothing, no noise at all. A terrible silence, pregnant, ready to pop.

Has it? Jesus, please, I'm bursting.

She tiptoed to the window and peeked out, not that she could see much. There didn't appear to be anyone moving about. *Has it gone? Can I go to the bog now?*

Then, terrifyingly, the sound of shuffling feet on stairs. Suddenly April didn't need to go to the toilet any more. The stench of her urine filled the room. *Sorry missus,* she found herself thinking. *I'll clean that up later, I promise.* Then, *oh God it'll smell that, like dogs do, Jesus, it'll smell* me, *what am I going to do, what am I going to do?*

There was only one door into the room. She had to barricade it with something. But the only thing she could see was a heavy wooden chest of drawers. She tried to push it in front of the door but couldn't – even if she'd been at her full strength she couldn't have shifted that.

Footsteps, shuffling…then stopped. She heard a wet, ripping, smacking noise. *It's found the dead man. Is it…snacking on him, like I did on the crisps?*

The thought made her sick, but if it was, that just might give her a second or two. She had to get out...but that thing was right outside...

Almost whining, April looked around her. The window. That was her only hope. It opened outwards by the look of it. She threw the thing as wide as it would go and looked down. Of course, there was a flagstone driveway some – what? Fifteen feet below? Twenty? *Break your fuckin' ankles,* she heard Tony say.

Either that or be eaten, she heard herself answer him back. And even as she climbed awkwardly and painfully onto the bedroom chair, she thought, *how odd. I've finally answered him back.*

April wiggled onto the windowsill, then lowered herself down, hanging on, the night air cooling her hot face. Then she let go.

The pain was excruciating, and she screamed plenty, but she didn't think she actually broke anything as she landed. All the same, she had more agony to add to the list. She rolled over and landed on her back, staring up at the window she'd dropped from. A head stuck out from it. The 'thing' that had been in the house. A girl, maybe just a little older than April. There was a sort of 'd'uh?' look of confusion on her face that April almost wanted to laugh at. *You're thicker than me!*

But then the girl's head vanished from sight, and April knew she was on her way down. *Got to shift your arse.*

Easier said than done, but she managed to scramble her way to her feet and hobble off, in the direction of the barn.

April had some idea she could maybe hide in there. If these 'things' were like dogs, if they did hunt by smell, then maybe all the animal smells in the barn would confuse them? *I mean, that makes sense, doesn't it?*

So on she went. And even though the barn was only ten feet from the house, she didn't seem to be getting any closer. Any minute that back-to-front door would open and that 'thing' would be after her – and right now, April didn't have a speed advantage.

She risked one look behind her. Nothing yet. But surely it wouldn't be long...

The door was flung open, and there she was, the girl in dirty pigtails and a filthy dress, shuffling towards her, aimless, hopeless...but it knew where April was, all right.

April put the best spurt on she could, no longer looking back. She had to keep her eyes on the door to the barn. Maybe when she got there she could shut it, bar them out, hole up. The only thing she could hold onto was, *they're thicker than me! They're thicker than even me! They're thicker than*

Her left ankle gave way.

She actually *felt* the bone shatter. The pain was unlike anything else she'd ever suffered, ever. She fell to the floor, unable to get her hands out and broke her nose.

See, you thick bitch, spoke Tony in her head. *Told you you'd break your fuckin' ankles.*

April lay on the gravel, too tired and in too much pain even to cry, and felt the girl's pigtails as they brushed her neck.

Then she felt her teeth.

Wrong, ma, she thought as a million daggers pierced her throat. *Wasn't a ditch I died in after all.*

*

Dawn was breaking over the barn. There was no sign of life at all. No cock crew, no birds sang, no aeroplanes or microlights disturbed the silence.

Then a voice, a man's voice, harsh, tired, strained. 'April! The fuck *are* you?'

Tony staggered up to the house, crushed, bloody...but alive. He'd managed to beat that fucker down, all right. Took some doing, but Tony never took shit from no one, least of all some cunt who didn't know when to stay dead.

Dead they may be, but the fucker had still folded up when Tony had kicked him in the balls. *No one* tried to strangle Tony. *No one!*

So the bastard had gone down and Tony had kicked and stamped his head for hours. Little crash like that wasn't going to slow *him* down. Not Tony. Not a prop forward. By the time he'd finished, that dead fucker's head had looked like jam.

Now he needed to find April. Well, not *needed* to exactly...but she had great tits. And she swallered.

'April,' he called again, as loud as his ragged throat would allow.

'Yes, Tony?'

He swivelled around. That was her all right – but where was she? 'Get out here now, bitch! Let's see you. Gonna rip this bastard's car off if he's got one! Get the fuck home.'

'OK.'

Did she sound weird? Nah, no weirder than ever. Little thin, whiny voice on it, little thin, whiny, thick *what do we do now* or *why* wasn't *it a goal?* Thick, dumb, big titted bitch. But still she was nowhere to be seen. 'Now!' he called.

There she was, coming out the barn. Covered in shit and staggering a bit. Christ. Without him to look after her she couldn't remember how to take a dump.

'Tony,' she said...and, no...there *was* something different about her voice. For no very good reason, Tony found himself suddenly very, very scared indeed. He just wished he could see her face more clearly, but she was in shadow.

Then it occurred to him. She sounded *sly*. Like she had a secret. She was holding her left hand out.

'Y'know you always said I was thick?' she went on, walking towards him, closer and closer to the light. 'Well…I think I'm cleverer now.' He saw what she was holding out to him, but couldn't really take it in. *It's a joke, a fuckin' joke, she's a thick bitch, she can't…*

'I got me more brains,' said April, fully into the light, her slack, dead face…well, *smiling* at him as she reached down and bit a mouthful of the pink, jellylike thing she held in her hand. 'Mmmm…num nums!'

Tony goggled at her.

'Can I pick *your* brains now, please?' April asked. Tony screamed.

Thick, but well mannered.

The Ones We Love Come Back in Dreams

He's nineteen years old in 1984. It's summer, early June, and England's baking in a heatwave, and he's nineteen. They sit in their pub, the seven of them; him, Howard, Sophie, Joe (who they call George), Brian, Emma and Carol. They're young, all of them young, all of them at the start of things, and there's smoke in the air because people smoked cigarettes in pubs back then. There's smoke and there's talk and there's jokes and there's music – not just music though, because this is 1984, he's nineteen, this is the avatar of music, and there's a video juke in this pub (technology so advanced you can't distinguish it from magic) and it's playing 99 Red Balloons by Nena, it's playing All Night Long (All Night) by Lionel Richie, it's playing The Longest Time by Billy Joel, it's playing them all, all the songs he knows, and he's nineteen, nuh-nuh-nuh-nuh nineteen, and he's sat by Carol, and as Brian tells another of his jokes (he's always got jokes, Brian, always) her hand steals into his under the table, and it's 1984, he's nineteen, and he'll never stop smiling.

But then he wakes it's to the damp dawn on a September morning in 2009, and he's forty-four, and he's crying. Just a little, but a little's enough. And as he makes his way downstairs and says good morning to his wife and his daughter, he thinks, 'Why did I wake up crying? What did I dream?'

Chapter One

'Wake up, lover,' she whispered into his ear, low and soft. He muttered something and tried to stay asleep. Oh no, she wasn't having that. She prodded him. 'Lover, hey,' she said, louder. 'Wake up. I want some fun.'

Reluctantly he opened his eyes, tried to focus, looked around him, registered what was happening, then tried to bolt upright and escape. Louise giggled.

She giggled because he *couldn't* escape, she giggled because he was handcuffed to the kitchen radiator, she giggled because the polythene made a delightful crinkling noise underneath him. She just giggled, giggled because she was a happy bunny.

'What'll it take to make you *see* it's your fault?' Louise asked as she held the knife to his throat. She liked the way his eyes bugged and the whimpering he made from beneath the gaffer tape that sealed his lips. When all this was done she'd maybe play with Polly for an hour. 'Do I have to draw you a diagram? Do a shadow play? Sock puppets? Or is it worth my effort? Would you *ever* actually see it was all your fault?' She prodded the knife forward, stuck him with it a little, just under his Adam's apple. A thin bubble of blood bloomed like a flower. Oh, he was wide awake now all right. His jerked his head back and forth, *no, no, no* those *huh-UGE* eyes of his saying, *PUH-LEEZE don't hurt me Massa-boss!* Then, delightedly, she thought of that old film. *Ooo-dat-man!*

'No poppet,' she crooned. 'Keep your head still. I'm really close to your jugular with this and – I gather – if I open it the mess will be awful. So important safety tip, George…don't waggle your head, otherwise,' she held up the knife, held it close to his eyes, so close she could see those *huh-UGE* orbs reflected above the words SHEFFIELD STEEL, 'otherwise I carve you a second mouth. Got it?'

He nodded, head on a string nod, bouncy and trouncy like Tigger (should she play with Tigger as *well* as Polly? Would Polly mind? Ah, she could ask) and Louise giggled again. She giggled because that nod was just so comical, all *huh-UGE* eyes and sweat and corkscrew hair – I mean, a *table* would laugh at that sight!

She giggled because dear old George looked like he thought he could get away with it.

Why he would think that when she'd let him get a very good look at her was another thing altogether. How could she let him go into the night, screaming and shrieking to the Police, pointing out her house, giving her description? *I mean, honestly, some people!* Maybe later she would ask Polly and Tigger and Pooh and Basil (she was beginning to think she'd play with them all – to celebrate) and see if they had any ideas. Because as soon as Louise started speaking low and comforting and using words like *safety tip,* she'd seen it in his eyes, the look that said, *just agree with anything and she'll let you go,* and – Lord! – that made her giggle.

'So,' said Louise, *'was* it your fault?'

His head bounced again and again. *Yes! Yes! Yes!*

'Do you mean it?'

Yes! Yes! Yes!

'Do you accept *full and total blame* for everything you did; do you *refute* provocation and justification? Do you admit that *you* and your *friends* were responsible for it *all?'*

Oh now, *look* at him – his top really *was* made out of rubber! Up and down and up and down! And bug eyed? If he was to bug any more his eyes would be on his *cheeks!* And how red was his face? As red as a poppy, as red as a Manchester United home shirt, as red as…well, you know, blood.

'Sorry,' said Louise, leaning forward, 'I didn't quite hear that.'

Then it struck home. Then he *finally* realised that there were no more clubs for him, that he'd never more sit in a chair, fumbling in his trousers as a Dirty Lady did a wriggly dance in front of him.

She saw it blaze into those *huh-UGE* eyes, the final realisation he would ever have. *I'm going to die,* it read. *I'm going to die, I'm going to die, I'm going to –*

He shrieked as much as he could through the tape, he brought his feet down on the kitchen floor in some kind of drumming signal to whoever would hear (but they were miles from anywhere, the only things who could help were Polly and Pooh and Tigger and Basil, and they obeyed her and only her), he whipped his head from side to side, he tried to pull the radiator from the wall, and Louise let him. It was the last thing he'd ever do after all, and she saw no point in depriving him of his fun. Once she'd seen a dog run over in the street by her house. Nine years old she'd been. It hadn't been a clean kill, the wretched mongrel had howled and roared in pain. The man who'd run it over had climbed out of his car and placed his foot on the dog's head and stamped hard. Grey stuff had squished from its ears and then poor Bowzer had shut up. When she'd asked her Mum why the man had done that, her Mum had said that the dog was in pain and that the man had ended its suffering. Her Mum had made it sound like the man had done a Good Thing, but Louise thought he'd been a spoilsport. After all, how did he know the dog didn't *enjoy* making all that noise, being the centre of attention? So Louise let George crawl and crab and make his noises – for all she knew, he was having the time of his life.

In the end though, she grew bored and took the knife and stabbed him six times through the heart. He was almost certainly dead by the third, but she was a woman who believed in redundancy. Blood exploded everywhere – it flew up the walls, it cascaded across the floor, it smelled like pennies in the pocket. It smudged her eyes, but the yellow sou'wester and Wellington boots she was wearing ensured nothing reached her clothes.

But it stopped. *He* stopped. George, at the end of his pointless, evil life. He grew weaker and weaker, the torrent from the gash in his chest stilled, his head (bouncy and trouncy no more) flopped onto his chest, his eyes a mirror, the eyes of Basil. And when he was no more, Louise leaned in and used the knife to hack his heart out. She unclipped the handcuffs and rolled him up in the cellophane, singing a song as she did so. A song about balloons, a song about *red* balloons, ninety-nine of them. She dragged the messy parcel to her car and dumped it some miles away, in the country, in the dark, and when she came home she showered and took Polly and Tigger and Pooh and Basil and even – for it was a Very Important Day Indeed - Bounce the Bear from the shelf and made them tea.

Well, water. But they all pretended it was tea, so that was good enough.

Chapter Two

Colin Bryant attempted a smile as he hung his coat on the office hanger and sat down before his computer. It must've looked OK as Nicola, his twenty year old and impossibly beautiful PA, simply said, 'Good morning,' and not, *God almighty, what's the matter with you?*

'Heads or tails?' asked Colin as he entered his password with his right hand and fished a 10p from his trouser pocket with his left. His voice certainly sounded normal – but then, really, why shouldn't it? *Dreamed something heavy, that's all. Weighs on my shoulders.* But just what it was he couldn't remember.

'Tails,' Nicola said, finishing emailing over his schedule. She looked up and smiled at him. Long blonde hair, big blue eyes, figure that would stop a clock…Colin liked to make her smile. Ordinarily that smile of hers would solve a lot of problems. Just not today for some reason.

He spun the coin, caught it, lifted his hand and said, 'Hard luck.' He stuffed it back in his pocket without letting her see it. *There,* he thought, *jokes and fun, fun and jokes…that'll lift the weight. That and her beauty.*

But the weight wouldn't go. It wouldn't even lift a bit. It pressed him down remorselessly. Even when she shouted 'Hey!' and 'You cheat!' Even when she giggled and walked to the kettle and he got to check out her arse through her skirt. *Old man, married man, father of a girl about her age,* a voice whispered inside, *what would they think of you at home if they knew what you were doing? There's a register for people like you.*

'Mr Pearson's late,' she reported from the window as she waited for the kettle to boil, breaking his chain of thought. Nicola couldn't help reporting on what she saw through the glass. Colin couldn't tell whether it was endearing or not. Even after three months he couldn't.

'Oh yeah?' Fifteen emails in his Inbox. None of them spam, and none of them fun.

'Yeah,' Nicola went on, 'and he's smoking a fag as he's legging it. Dunno what'll get him first, cancer or a broken leg.'

'Open a book, I'll put a fiver on cancer.' Click. *Dear Mr Bryant, with regard to your email of 21st August, please excuse the delay in replying. I've reviewed your comments and would like to make the following observations…*

'OK,' she said, and she poured them coffee, and they drank as they sat opposite each other, both typing onto keyboards, and the weight just didn't roll off Colin's shoulders at all, and he had no idea why.

Chapter Three

Colin pulled into his driveway, switched off the Focus's engine, and sat for a moment, unable to bring himself to open the door. Monday night, Helen at her amateur dramatics, Tasha at dancing, just him rattling around in the house, a tired old man with thinning hair, an expanding waistline and a shrinking mortgage. That weight on his shoulders hadn't lessened at all as he'd plodded through the day, email after email, meeting after meeting, coffee after coffee, stolen glance at his PA after stolen glance at his PA – rather it had deepened into some terrible, bone deep weariness that left him feeling every day of his forty-four years.

What's up with me, he thought as he stared at the front door of his Formby semidetached house. *Why do I feel so...useless?*

He wasn't ordinarily a man given to such feelings. Helen sometimes described him as a 'man with no corners.' He thought that meant she considered him straightforward, uncomplicated, reliable – maybe a little dull, but not the sort of man given to sudden bizarre behaviour. He drank a little, but not to excess, he supported Liverpool FC (but didn't go to many games and it didn't obsess him, unlike that clot Pearson in Accounts, who would recount every second of every game with military precision, and tell you where the manager was going wrong and who he should be signing at the next transfer window)...Colin was just, well...ordinary.

And ordinary people don't sit in their driveways unable to open their car doors, so climb out and go inside otherwise Clifford in Number 26 will see you. And it'll be all round the Drive in 16.4 seconds flat that Colin Bryant's going a bit funny.

He gave a sigh and stepped out. *Get changed, have a bath, eat your tea...maybe have a small drink...and you'll feel better. You'll feel like yourself again.*

Oh yeah, and who am *I anyway?*

It was after ten when he heard the door open.

He'd taken his advice, and it had sort of worked. The bath, the very small brandy and the chicken and chips had *almost* restored his equilibrium. The one compensation for his wife and daughter being absent was he could feed the CD player whatever he wanted without complaints – and when it came to Bruce Springsteen and Billy Joel the complaints tended to be vociferous. But these songs were his soundtrack, these tunes were his life, they washed over him like emollient, and by the time Billy was telling him about how he'd once made it with a red haired girl in a Chevrolet, he was very nearly back on track.

Except...except when he'd heard the first few notes of Billy's *The Longest Time* a strange ghost voice had spoken in his head, a ghost voice accompanied by the murmur of conversation, the clinking of glasses, raucous laughter; 'Oh *FOR FUCK'S SAKE,*' the ghost had said, 'not again! *Please,* not again!'

Who was that? A man – no, not quite a man...exasperated, but laughing. Who?

But there was no answer, not even a hint, so he ignored it and listened to the album (skipping *Uptown Girl,* of course. He might have been a Philistine, but he was no fool) until the door opened and Helen and Tasha tumbled in, all laughs and jokes.

'Dad,' Tasha glowered, 'please, the neighbours will hear.'

'Now dear,' said Helen, dropping her script (the Formby Players were doing *Dangerous Corner* by J.B. Priestley, though not for another nine weeks) and planting a kiss on Colin's forehead, 'your father's entitled to his rotten music while we're out.'

'I am delighted to know I'm a figure of fun to you both,' said Colin, flicking the STOP button on the remote.

'It's not just us,' said Tasha, settling down on the sofa and turning on the TV. There was a *Big Brother* double eviction on that night, and there was no way she was going to miss it, 'you're a figure of fun to everyone on the street.'

'You know,' Colin said to Helen as he nuzzled her neck, 'I would never have talked to my father like that.'

'She doesn't mean it,' said Helen.

'Police identified the man as forty-three year old Joseph McGovern of Crosby, and are appealing for witnesses,' the ITN newscaster said in the background, but that was all he said before Tasha hit the button and the room was filled with the ear splitting roar of Davina McCall.

'Down,' said Colin. Tasha wrinkled her nose at him…but thumbed the volume control. A little. Then, to his wife, 'You want a drink, hon?'

She did, and he poured it for her – a very weak gin and tonic – and she followed him into the kitchen and told him about her rehearsal and the new girl who had joined the company who seemed very good, and they found themselves kissing up against the sink, and it was good, it was fine, he loved his wife and daughter…

But the ghost voice…*please, not again. Whose* was *that?*

He woke in the night, thinking *Joseph McGovern.* Helen was a sleeping lump beside him. He looked at the ceiling thinking, *Joseph McGovern.*

He knew no one by that name. He'd *never* known anyone by that name.

After a while, he fell asleep again.

*

They're in The Windmill now, opposite the Catholic Church on Bleaker Street. Except they're not in *it at all, they're* outside, *it's 1984 and oh dear God is it hot, so they're at The Windmill, The Windmill is exotic, The Windmill has benches outside, you can sit outside and drink your beer, and it's 1984 and there are few places in Southport like that, and Sophie laughs and tells people it's like being in Italy, and Howard throws a beer mat at her (but laughing, they always laugh, they never stopped laughing) and tells her to* shut the fuck up *about her holidays abroad, tells her to stop reminding them of how fucking rich her Mummy and Daddy are, tells her that her shit still stinks like that of a pauper, and they all roar, they roar with laughter, even Sophie because there is no malice here, they are young, they're free, and they're friends.*

From the pub he can hear Limahl sing Never Ending Story, *he can hear Imagination sing* Body Talk, *Colin can hear them* all, *the hits of his summer, it's hot, it's blinding, and he's laughing and repeating the favourite bits from* The Young Ones *and when Carol puts her hand in his it's a little sweaty, a little clammy, but that's OK, because it's summer and it's 1984 and he's nineteen, and clammy and sweaty it may be, but it's Carol's hand, and Carol is his girlfriend now, and she is mighty fine indeed.*

Mighty fucking fine.

And George comes back from the bar with the tray laden high; he's got four bottles of Colt 45 for the men and a gin for Emma and Sophie and a cider and blackcurrant for Carol and there's crisps and nuts, it's 1984, he's nineteen, and everyone claps and cheers because George has not spilled one fucking drop and…

But not everyone's *clapping,* not everyone's *cheering. Because Carol leans into him, whispers in his ear (and in his sleep, twenty-five years later, Colin moans a little at how good that feels), 'George is heartless, you know.'*

'What do you -' he starts to ask, but then he doesn't need to. For blood is pouring down George's Choose Life! T-shirt in a cascade. A red, sticky puddle forms at his feet. And on the left hand side of George's chest there's a gaping, ragged hole, a hole right through him, a hole big enough to put your face into, and George doesn't notice, George doesn't care. No one else notices either, just Colin and Carol, 'the two Cs' as Howard calls them. The rest just clap and cheer and remove their drinks from the tray. Horrified, nineteen, he turns to Carol who just widens her blue eyes and shrugs her shoulders. 'Heartless,' she says again.

He remembered that dream no more than he did the other, but the name *Joseph McGovern* ran around his head for days, like a hamster in a cage.

Chapter Four

'Oh *please,*' said Louise to Tigger. Tigger was having a naughty day. Tigger was 'copping a deaf 'un,' as Louise's old Mum had been prone to say. 'Please get back on the bed. Please, Tigger, *please!*'

Tigger didn't listen, Tigger just bounced across the carpet. Pooh and Basil and Polly looked disapprovingly but made no attempt to stop him. They were GOOD TOYS today.

'*Ti-GGER,*' Louise pleaded, 'I've got to go, I'll be *late.* He *hates* me being late!'

I don't care, laughed Tigger, bouncing high and low, bouncing hither and yon, looking for Roo's medicine which was, as everyone knew, Tigger's favourite thing. *I'm having a good day, I'm having fun!*

'You're being *naughty,*' she scolded. 'You're being very, *very* naughty! And if you don't come back *right now* I won't play with you *EVER AGAIN!*'

That stopped him. Tigger liked to be played with. Tigger liked the games. Of course, they *all* did, but Tigger liked them best of all. Tigger, after all, was the naughtiest. Tigger bounced and trounced. The thought of sitting unplayed with forever struck him dumb. He turned to face her, head on one side. *You wouldn't?*

'I would too,' said Louise, scowling. She found it hard to scowl at any of them, because she loved them, loved them with all her heart and soul, but sometimes love had to be tough.

That was something her old Mum had taught her.

Oooh, OK, said Tigger and he stomped back to the bed, his tail drooping, his mouth turned down. He climbed awkwardly in and made a space next to Pooh. Pooh cuddled him a bit. Pooh had Very Little Brain, but a yard of heart.

'*There's* a good Tigger,' she said, kissing him on the head. 'Now Mummy's going out, but I'll be back in six hours. That sounds like a long time, but it isn't. Not really. You have a big sleep, all of you, and when you wake up, I'll be home. OK?'

OK Mummy, they all said, even Tigger (because Tigger didn't stay upset for long) and then they settled down to sleep, Polly saying her prayers and Pooh trying to repeat them but getting them all muddled, and then all was quiet and Louise could concentrate on her makeup.

He *really* hated it when she was late.

Chapter Five

Emma Fillion dragged herself into her kitchen, dropped the two Sainsbury's bags onto the counter, and tried to tell herself to wait until after her tea for the ice cream. Then she reasoned that if the pie took forty-five minutes to cook, which it did, then it would be an hour or so before she had her ice cream. She looked at the Krazy Kat clock on the wall and its elongated body and rolling eyes told her it was half past five. Which meant no ice cream till half six or so. Which *further* meant that Kevin and his new girlfriend would arrive, assuming they were on time (and he was *always* on time, her baby didn't do late) while she was stuffing pistachio into her mouth. And though her baby loved her, oh yes he loved her, she would see that look in his eyes, the one that went *Oh Mother, must you embarrass me so?*

And Emma did not want to embarrass Kevin. Not ever, but most *especially* not today.

Not when he was bringing his new girlfriend home for the first time.

So in order not to embarrass her son and his new – well, his *first* – girlfriend, Emma opened the Ben & Jerry's tub and dug right in.

His first love, she thought. *Baby's all grown up now.* It was simultaneously a sad and exciting thought. There truly was nothing warmer than a first love, first love grew hotter than the sun...but it burnt out fast. Hers had, Kevin's would too. It hurt when a first love died.

Of course, it hurt worse when it wasn't even reciprocated. Oh, how she'd loved Howard. Oh, how he hadn't noticed. Or maybe he had and just hadn't fancied her – in the days when Emma Fillion had been Emma Richards she'd been *big* (not as big as she was now, but big) and maybe he just didn't like big lasses. But...still, how she'd loved him. How she yearned.

Reciprocated or not, love was still love, and he'd been her first. In a way, they'd *all* been her first, the whole gang, none of them laughing at her, none of them cruel, her gang, her friends, her loves.

Now her son had reached that age, his *first love* age, and what would become of her? So often alone in the house with only the contents of the fridge to talk to, her husband on the rigs for months and months at a time…what would become of *her?*

No matter, thought Emma as the oven timer binged, announcing her steak and kidney was nearly done, time to put the veggies on. She stuck the by now half empty tub in the freezer and boiled a pan of water. *No matter as long as Kevin has as much fun as I did, back then, back in the heatwave.*

Emma Fillion, lost in the past and a little scared by the future, ate her pie and vegetables on that Tuesday in mid September 2009, and never mind the imponderables, the food was, as ever, mighty fine.

Considering that was her last ever meal, it's just as well she enjoyed it.

She heard the lock turn at six forty, just as she knew it would, for Kevin was never late. Kevin had a clock in his head that counted the seconds and marked them, and she stood to welcome her son and her guest, her son's first girlfriend, that marker that said that time was on the move, that 1984 was done and long dead and would never return.

'Hi Mum,' her son said as he entered the living room. A big man, like his father, like his mother, but unlike both of them a man of intent, of purpose – a man who really applied himself to his studies, a man who was going to go places. Just now though, as he stepped aside to admit the smaller figure she could see through the frosted glass door that led into the hallway, there was an expression she hadn't seen on his face since he'd been ten years old; an expression of shy pride. It was the way he'd looked as he'd shown her the schoolbooks he'd brought home, the schoolbooks marked with A pluses and comments such as *Excellent work, Kevin!*

He really likes this girl, Emma thought. *He's really in love!* And her heart burst for her son. To see that look on his face…oh, it made her sing inside.

'This is Louise,' he said, the last sentence she would hear him utter. He stepped aside and the girl entered, small, vulnerable looking, her hair tidied up in a woollen cap…

And *familiar?*

Just in that last second, Emma really, really thought she'd seen this girl before.

But then this Louise was pulling something from the pocket of her combat trousers – the *very deep* pockets of her combat trousers – and running at her. Running and yelling, a scream of anger and rage that contorted those pretty features into something evil, some kind of demon, and she saw Kevin's face gape in surprise – no, shock - and Emma had a second to see that this girl had some kind of hammer in her hand, but before she could run the hammer was descending in an arc towards her temple, and there was a bright, flaring spark and a bitter wall of pain, and the world went into the black.

Chapter Six

'Emma,' said a voice from nowhere. It rolled in the dark, echoing and trebling, the voice of a giant, the voice of God.

No, not God…this voice was…

Was…

Familiar.

But there was pain where the voice was, so she tried to ignore it, to sink back into the dark where nothing hurt.

'Emma,' the Giant Voice said again, impatient. 'Emma-bemma.' There was a sharp pain in her ribs. She moaned. 'Emma-bemma-mi-mo-memma,' the Giant chanted, 'you got to *wake up*, Emma-fomemma, you got to wake up *RIGHT NOW!* Little Kevvy faw down and hurt hisself, Emma-momemma, wickle Kevvy needs his Mummy-bunny, wickle Kevvy wants you to kiss him *ALL BETTER.*'

The mention of her son's name was enough. It didn't matter what had happened to her. It didn't matter what pain she was in, if her son was hurt, *her son –*

Emma forced her eyes open, then shut them again straight away. Searing white light bit deep into her retinas, tears streamed onto her cheeks.

'Oh Emma-Nutella,' the Giant said – though it was less Giant now, the voice seemed to be settling down in her head – 'don't you think you've started your crying a *little* too early? I mean, it's like not taking your coat off in the pictures. You'll not feel the benefit when you leave. That's what *my* Mummy used to say.'

Struggling, Emma opened her eyes. This time she kept them open, despite the glare of the fluorescents in this…this…*kitchen?*

Yes, kitchen. She could make out the worktops – though they seemed covered with some kind of wrapping - behind…behind…

That girl!

'Hey,' the girl smiled. 'That's the way, sleepyhead.' Once more that maddening *familiarity* crawled across Emma's mind. She felt sure she knew this kid from somewhere. Maybe if her head didn't hurt so bad from where…from where…

From where this kid hit me with the hammer, Emma remembered, and jerked forward in panic. She made it maybe four inches before she felt something dig into her wrists and pulled her back.

'Sorry,' the kid – Louise – said. 'Got you handcuffed to a radiator. Now, you're a pretty big Heffalump, Emma-Fruitella, and I've got me a feeling that if you really, really tried you could probably do some damage to the Hundred Acre Wood, so just in case you get yourself some funny ideas – and I'll know, Emma-salmonella, I'll know - here's a good look at what people who get funny ideas end up like.'

The girl moved her head to Emma's left. That gave her a clear field of vision. It gave her a clear field of vision of her son, her Kevin, her only begotten child propped up before the polythene encased fridge with his eyes gouged out, her child who she had created with her husband John, *her* child; quite dead, her son with ripped gaping holes where his beautiful baby browns had once been.

Her dead, dead son.

Horror so intense Emma had no idea such a thing existed consumed her, and she opened her mouth to scream in anguish and sorrow and alarm. Just as she did, the girl stuffed a packet of frozen peas in her mouth.

Did you hear about the dyslexic rock star? Louise's Mum asked from her head. And when Louise had shaken her head, she'd continued, *he choked on his own Vimto.* Had they laughed then? Oh, yes! Hard, but quiet, covering their mouths with their hands to keep from annoying Dad who was downstairs doing something boring.

Oh, her Mum knew jokes! Her Mum *always* had jokes! Her Mum's jokes came from her past and she carried them in her heart and passed them to Louise when she felt the time was right.

That's what Mums were for.

It was a shame she didn't have any Vimto to choke this fat bitch with, but hey- you made the most of what you had.

That's *another* thing her Mum had told her.

'You see,' Louise said, stuffing the packet of peas as far down Emma's throat as they would go, '*nobody's* eyes are bigger than their belly! People *say* that, they say that *all the time,* but they're not! Kevvy's eyes were really, really quite small. *Tiny!* And yours; oh yeah, them's a-bugging and a-bopping, but them's *no way* bigger than your belly, right?' She leaned in then, speaking low into Emma-Fenella's ear. Not that Emma-kinella was listening. She was too busy spitting foam over the bag of Bird's Eye specials, too busy trying to cough, too busy drumming her feet in a horrid tattoo, too busy trying to draw breath. Stupid fat Heffalump couldn't even see she had two perfectly functioning nostrils that would do that job for her. 'You always had a big jelly belly, didn't you Emma, even then, back in the day?'

Emma-umbrella wasn't listening, Louise had really rammed that bag of peas down her throat. *Now* she was choking, *now* she was gagging. Soon she would trip the vomit reflex, and oh dear oh me, everyone would be out of the pool. 'See, Emma-Cruella,' said Louise, crooning softly, 'if only you'd all just *admitted* it, straight off, straight away, then do you know how much of this would be necessary? *None of it. None.* And you'd have kept your son and your life and I wouldn't have to *bother* with all this fuss. But you *didn't,* did you? None of you. So, really, it's *all your own* fault.' Then lower, sweeter; 'Will you? *Will* you admit it? Will you say it's all your fault, little Heffalump?'

But Emma-Princella was long past caring what Louise was saying. So Louise just sighed a little – not much, it's not as if she expected any different – and reached out her little finger and popped the last inch of the Bird's Eye bag into Emma-Manilla's mouth.

Then she sat and watched as Emma-Spinella tried to vomit past the obstruction in her throat, as her eyes burst from their sockets (like Mother, like son) as thin dribbles of mucus escaped her nostrils, as her face turned black, as she died.

Hey, thought Louise, laughing. *Ooo dat man?* Still chuckling, she went to the bedroom to fetch Pooh. Pooh had never seen a Heffalump in the Hundred Acre Wood, but he'd see one here all right.

Here in his own kitchen. What a lucky *bear!*

Chapter Seven

Colin sat bolt upright in bed. 'Whuzzup?' muttered Helen beside him.

'Bad dream,' he said after a second, but that wasn't right, was it? It hadn't been a dream, nor had it been bad. All it had been was a phrase that rattled in the dark. Not from his subconscious, not from his memory, but from…from…?

Ah, he didn't know. But somewhere deep. Somewhere outside.

That phrase? *'Why that's the most ridiculous thing I ever hoid!'* Groucho Marx's voice…except it wasn't Groucho's voice at all. It didn't even really sound like it, but they'd pretended it had…

Who had?

No answer to that, no answer in the night.

'Come here,' said Helen, still half asleep, and he let himself fall into her, into her dozy warmth and she enfolded him and drifted straight into the land of Nod again. But Colin lay awake a little longer, thinking, *Who pretended what and when to whom?*

Chapter Eight

'What's up with you?' Nicola asked as he slumped down at his desk and typed in his password.

'Bad night,' Colin muttered. 'Hardly slept.' *Still, if ever there was a sight to cheer you up…*

Stop it. Stop being a cliché. You're a middle aged man, she's hardly out of her teens. You're a happily married *middle aged man. With a daughter. A daughter nearly the same age as your PA. So stop it, OK?*

Ah, come on, he argued back as he dug the 10p from his pocket. *It's not like I'm going to* do *anything. It's not like I'd get the* opportunity *to do anything. Like she's going to look at* me *twice. She's young and she's beautiful, in her prime, and you're an old wreck. Everyone's free to check out the display. Maybe even Helen does. She does that Am Dram after all. Who knows what she thinks about the men she acts opposite? It's only window shopping. It's when you step inside to buy that the problems start. Probably.*

He spun the coin. 'Call.'

'Tails,' said Nicola as she tucked a long stray blonde hair behind her ear.

'Heads,' he said, tucking the coin away before she could see it. 'Hard luck.'

'I hate you,' she said, narrowing those cobalt eyes and pursing her delectable mouth. A rush of lust caused Colin's stomach to spasm. Then she stood, allowing him a fine view of her pert, full chest as it strained against her blouse. 'Ow,' she said suddenly, her right hand clutching the small of her back.

'You OK?'

A blush ran across her cheeks, making her look younger and more girlish than ever. She giggled. 'I think I've put my back out.'

'Oh? How, or shouldn't I ask?' *The things you don't know, the things you never ask,* Colin thought. *Who do you turn to in the small hours, Nicola? Who takes you to Heaven when he puts his head between your thighs? Who's the lucky bastard?*

Nicola straightened, pushing her chest forward, massaging her coccyx with both palms. *My dear Lord.* 'No,' she said, 'you shouldn't ask. But I tell you, he'll pay.' She tipped him a wink. 'He'll pay big time.' She made her way awkwardly to the kettle. He tried to avoid checking her arse out again, but just didn't manage it. Where her body was concerned, his eyes were the boss. *Jesus Christ, get a grip. No – not on her! Check that agenda she's emailed over. Now. Before you get caught.* He tried to focus on it and almost succeeded until he heard; 'Ha!'

'What's up?'

'Jeffers from Sales has got his coat caught in his Micra,' she said, laughing. 'And he can't get to his keys!' A fit of giggles exploded from her. 'He's spinning around like a dog looking for somewhere to sleep!'

'Why,' said Colin automatically, 'that's the most ridiculous thing I ever hoid!'

Nicola turned from the amusement in the car park and stared at him. 'What's that?'

This time it was Colin's turn to blush. Not because his impression was poor – it was, but so what? – but because of the blank look on his PA's face, the expression that told him she had no idea of what he was saying, the expression that told him he was a fossil, the expression he used to wear when his Dad had talked about *The Crazy Gang.* 'Groucho Marx,' he muttered. 'He was in old films when I was young. He made me laugh. Sorry.'

'Oh,' she said. 'Gotcha.' But she hadn't got him. She was a blank. A big, blue eyed, blonde haired, heaving chested blank, and he was a dinosaur to her, and it shouldn't have mattered, it really shouldn't, for he had a wife whom he loved dearly and wouldn't hurt for the world. So it shouldn't have mattered.

But damn him for all eternity, it did.

It just did.

Chapter Nine

'Dad?' asked Tasha with what sounded like utter horror, 'Dad – what are you *watching?*'

She makes it sound like kiddieporn or a snuff movie, Colin thought with detached bemusement. *It's just an old black & white comedy after all.* 'Marx Brothers,' he said, smiling at his daughter. *'Day at the Races.* Forget your Jack Blacks, young lady, this is *real* comedy.'

'If you say so,' she sniffed. *And you've never been put down until you've been sniffed at by a nineteen year old girl.* She stared at the screen as Harpo chased a young blonde lady across a room. 'Oh, that's *so* sexist!'

'It was a different time, hon,' he said, making room on the sofa for his daughter. *And that's what my Dad used to say to me when I called him on those minstrels you used to get on BBC One.*

'Doesn't excuse it,' Tasha said, sitting next to him.

'Didn't offer it as an excuse, just an explanation.'

They sat in silence for a while – excepting Colin's stifled laughter as Groucho insulted Margaret Dumont – then Tasha said, 'This is a DVD!'

'Yep. So?'

She turned to him, her overly earnest face scanning his. *Oh Tash, he thought, when did it happen? When did the humour fairy visit and take it all away? What happened to the little girl I used to sit on my knee and tell stories to about Piglet and Owl? When did she become this stiff teenager with the dyed black hair and the face that never lit up? Who gave permission for that to happen?* And on its heels, *how long has it been since the two of you just sat side by side and talked? When did you become as a ghost to her? When?*

'You bought this?'

'Yep,' he said again.

'When? Today?'

'Yep,' he said a third time. Then he backed it up with, 'Hey, I've got to have *something* to occupy me with you at your dancing and your Mum at her acting. Even *I* get fed up sometimes.'

'Do you?' she asked, and her brow creased. 'Really?' *You're my Dad,* that crease said. *You're not supposed to be a real person.* In that second, Colin saw his daughter re-appraise him, trying to see him as something more than just the asexual lump that had once told her stories and now doled out cash. Something about that both bonded them and made him feel eternal.

'Yeah. Just sometimes though. Mostly it's nice to be shot of you both.'

She punched him on the arm then and, wonder of wonders, smiled. She was a very beautiful young woman when she smiled, so like Helen when he'd first met her that it almost made his heart break. *Who's after you,* he wondered. *What men? How many? When do I have to deal with that? How do I deal with that?*

Ah, that's easy surely? You just remember how you lust after your Nicola. She's Tasha's age.

But he ignored that, because it didn't matter, it was nothing. Instead he asked his daughter about the rehearsals for the show they were preparing, and she told him, they actually had a conversation, and when Colin obviously didn't know what she was talking about Tasha explained slowly, and that was a good time. Of course, when the black men on the film started singing *Ooo Dat Man* Tasha complained about its racism, and this time Colin didn't even bother with an explanation. He just agreed with her. It *was* racist. He'd thought that years ago.

'Hi you two,' Helen said as she walked in, a little later. Then, as she saw the TV, 'What are we watching?'

'One of Dad's old films,' said Tasha. 'Bit racist, bit sexist. But apart from that, it's OK.'

'I'm delighted to hear it,' said Helen. 'But it's almost eleven and I know someone who's got college in the morning and it's not me or your Dad.'

'OK,' said Tasha, and stood. She kissed Helen on the cheek, then turned and bent down to Colin. She put her arms around his neck and squeezed. 'G'night Dad,' she said, then kissed his cheek also.

'Goodnight hon,' said Colin thickly. He couldn't remember the last time she'd kissed him goodnight. Could have been five, six years ago. *Oh it's hard,* he thought as his daughter held him, *it's hard when they stop seeing you as their Dad and start seeing you as just a man. Oh God, stop this ride. Please. I feel sick.*

But then Tasha was going upstairs to bed, and Helen was in his arms instead. 'Good night?' he asked.

'OK,' she said. 'That new girl's good.' Then, good natured, 'Bitch.'

'You've got nothing to be jealous about.'

'Apart from the fact she's twenty odd years younger than me and is better than I'll ever be, no I suppose not. Maybe I'll trip her up,' she added thoughtfully. She snuggled into him, closer. *See what you have here, Colin? A beautiful wife who loves you.* 'God,' she said, taking in the film properly for the first time, 'I haven't seen this for *years!* What made you dig this out?'

'I didn't dig it out; I bought the DVD on my way home. Only a fiver in HMV.'

'Thought it looked too good to be that old VHS you had, you must've worn that out. Takes me back this,' she said, nestling even closer, 'you and me on the sofa with the Marx Brothers on the telly. When we were young.'

He said nothing for a while, he just let his wife of two decades wriggle against him, and soon she was nibbling his ear, and that led to them kissing, and that led to the two of them throwing off their clothes on the sofa...but before Helen's mouth did the thing he liked best, he thought, *I watched this film with you, yes I did. I remember that. But it wasn't* yours, *was it? It wasn't special to you like it was to...like it was to...*

But then Colin forgot about old films completely.

*

They're not in the pub now, not in any of their pubs, but in the gloom of the Refectory. Even in May, the place is gloomy. This part of the Tech, the old part, dates back over a hundred years or so some say. It was once part of a church (or maybe a monastery, Colin didn't really listen too hard when that piece of wisdom was being passed around) and it sure as hell hasn't decided to spruce itself up much for the latter part of the twentieth century. Its only concession has been the arrival of fluorescent tubes which dangle from the ridiculously high roof, but the light struggles apathetically to reach the long rows of dormitory style tables that clutter the stone, cracked floor. The windows are plentiful and no longer stained glass, but they're anorexic, arched, like arrow slits in a castle wall. It's always dark here, always gloomy, frequently cold (a monster of a room like this could never be heated)…but Colin loves it, because he loves all of it.

He loves it because it's always full. Even though lunchtimes are staggered in order not to overburden the canteen staff, it's always full. And even though his friends don't share all of his timetable, they're always here.

Always. It's impossible, but true.

They tell their jokes here, they speak of tutors and homework (and they always call it homework, like they were still at school, it's one of their 'things'), they speak of classes, they copy someone else's work, they speak of music they've bought or what was on the telly the night before. They speak and laugh and joke, and the gang's all here, roll out the barrel, for we'll have a barrel of fun.

Except they're not a gang yet, not just yet. They're friends, they laugh together, they've grown close since September 1983, but they're not quite a gang. It's May 1984, and it's exam time – the term's nearly over and they're about to have their last summer before they must Grow Up. Maybe they're all a little scared by the future, maybe that's why they're growing closer as the days grow longer. Who can tell?

Sophie's on his right, Howard's on his left, Joe (who is George here) is opposite, Carol's next to him (and their looks linger when their eyes meet, oh yes they do, it's not happened yet but it will, it will), there's a gap, then there's Brian. Howard's telling them all about the stash of **Penthouse** *magazines he found in his Dad's drawer one day five years back and about how sorry he felt for the ladies on the pages, all of whom appeared to have been razored in an* **extremely** *painful place, and, Lord, did they laugh?*

'OK, right, so that's funny to you, fine,' says Howard, and the tears are streaming down his own face despite his mock indignation. He's holding a chicken sandwich in his right hand, one his mother made. 'But look at it from my point of view. I was only fourteen, right? What did I know? How many naked women had I seen?'

Colin's pounding the table. He's got a plate of chips and shepherd's pie and it's going cold because he just can't find the time to eat with all this laughing. Part of him wants Howard to stop because his stomach muscles are complaining. Part of him wants Howard **never** *to stop. Part of him wants never to stop laughing.*

'By the time I was fourteen,' says Brian, 'I had seen **hundreds** *of women in the nack.'*

They howl at him then, howl in derision, they call him a 'lying hound', a 'big head', 'a faking fuckstick' (and look at Carol, her face is a little flushed, her colour a little high; Carol is the most prudish of them all, those almond shaped eyes of hers are wide and blue, part shock, part fascination…but she laughs all the same. Yep, they all laugh) but Brian just takes it in, lets the bombardment wash over him, and when they are quiet again he says, 'It's true. I found **my** *Dad's nudie book stash when I was nine!'*

They laugh again, and Howard throws a chicken sandwich at Brian, and Sophie yells about the starving Africans, don't waste the food, they're starving, and Colin looks at her; blonde, curvy, cat-like brown eyes, and something stirs beneath the table. She's not Carol, nope, she'll never be Carol, she's not as pretty as Carol – Carol's the prettiest girl he's ever seen – but Sophie…well, she's no longer a girl is she? Sophie's already a woman. And he notices. He's got eyes. Hell, they've all noticed.

He becomes aware Carol is looking at him, and he turns to her and smiles. You can't help but smile at Carol when she looks at you. She sees something in his eyes that she likes, and she smiles back, and just for a second the sun breaks through.

She does that to him, does Carol.

Then Brian says, loudly, 'Speaking of starving Africans, ladies and gentlemen…' and Colin wonders for the nine millionth time why that isn't insulting. It should be, because it's Emma coming back from the counter with her tray piled high. And Howard will say something like 'Jesus Christ, Red Rum couldn't jump that plate,' or Brian will shout 'Soylent Green is PEOPLE!' (and no one understands that, but they laugh anyway) but Emma won't mind. She won't. She'll shrug and say, 'Hey, I'm a growing girl' or 'So? I'm hungry.' Is it because there's no malice behind the words that she doesn't mind? Is it really true what The Fun Boy Three and Bananarama sang a couple of years ago? Is it really not what you say, but the way that you say it?

So Emma comes into view, and the laughter that rolls at Brian's remark would appear to wash over her like a wave on a rock, for she says nothing, she just sits between Carol and Brian, and the first thing Colin sees is the tray, and my Lord! It's piled with pie and chips and beans and bread rolls, it's a land mass, and almost in admiration (no, not almost, actually in admiration, for he loves Emma, he loves them all…Carol especially, but he loves them all) he raises his gaze, and he'll say something, something funny, but something non malicious, because he loves her.

But he says nothing. He says nothing because Emma Richards' face is as black as night, as black as space, as black as a vacuum. Her eyes have popped out of their sockets and rest listlessly on her cheeks. Gored, blooded, ripped eyelids flap horribly across her empty sockets. Something green – a waving flap of some waxed paper perhaps – pops from between her lips, like a perversion of a tongue.

Colin says nothing, because Emma Richards is dead. He says nothing because, even though dead, Emma is cutting open a bread roll and smearing butter on it.

Fixed, solid, immobile, Colin just stares. Then someone – he's no idea who - shouts 'OOO DAT MAN!' and as if on cue, the entire Refectory populace is up and dancing, dancing around their table, singing 'OOO DAT MAN!' And dead Emma just shrugs – there's no malice here, remember? – and keeps on spreading Kerrygold on her roll.

He's cold, cold inside, his world isn't right anymore, and he looks to Carol for hope, but she just shrugs. 'Eyes are bigger than her belly,' she says. And all he can do is sit, stone, as the room is filled with dancing, singing kids and a dead girl tries to eat her meal.

Chapter Ten

Colin turned off the radio and sat in the car park for a minute before opening the door. The flotsam that comprised the six hundred or so Allied Corporate's employees milled around him, some he knew by name, some by sight, the majority not at all. He supposed he should make some show of doing something – reaching in his glove compartment or rummaging under his seat – after all, just sitting in a car staring through the windscreen could at best be described as aberrant behaviour, but he just couldn't find the energy. *Let 'em look. It's just another of my sitting in a car moments. I seem to be making a habit of them recently.*

He turned his head and saw no one was paying him the slightest attention. They filed past him to the entrance, far too busy with what was in their own heads to care about the middle-aged man who sat motionless behind his steering wheel. He didn't know whether to be pleased or not.

You're carrying a heavy head these days, old son. Any idea why?

Answer came there none. And it was so *alien* to him. *I was always the one on the even keel, he thought. I was always the one with the clear, down-the-line thought process. I was always the dependable one. The Quiet One.*

Oh yeah? To whom?

What?

To whom *were you the clear, down-the-line one? To* whom *were you dependable?*

Well, to Helen. And Tasha. And…

And?

There was something there, something nagging…he'd been that to others once. Or had he?

'Maybe I'm sick,' he muttered to himself. 'Need a check-up.'

That could be valid. He'd not seen a doctor in years, and when you passed forty all sorts of things just started running down. *Maybe in your head, maybe a crowd of cells have started to go bad, Colin old son. Maybe that's how it starts, with Dem Ole No-Reason Blues.*

Yeah, maybe. But he'd felt OK when he'd set off from home, hadn't he? He'd been *zippedy doo dah,* in fact. This…whatever it was…had just dropped over him like a blanket during the journey to the Land of Corporate Banking, the Land of Oh Shit the Credit Crunch, the Land of the Shaky Investments, he'd felt it sink onto his shoulders as he'd listened to Radio Merseyside and took in the news. Job losses. Shop closures. Two corpses found in a burned out car identified as mother and son. *Maybe Dem Ole No-Reason Blues is just fear,* he thought. *Fear of the future, fear of losing my job, fear of losing my house, my marriage. Hard times have come to the world, Colin old Colin. No one's immune. Not you, not Nicola, not no one. Maybe that's all it is.*

He shrugged. Could be. Sounded logical. But there was no blinding light, no *Eureka!* It sounded fine, yes indeed (as Ben Elton used to say) but it didn't sound *right*.

'So what do I do?' he said to the empty car, unaware he was speaking aloud. 'What's the answer?'

You get out your car and do your job, he told himself. *And when you think no one's looking, you perv at your PA's tits. Or her arse. I'm not fussy.*

Though that thought made him feel dirty, it made him move. 'Sounds like a plan,' he said, and opened the door.

'Nicola,' he said as he shut the door behind him. 'You OK?' *Some reversal. Last two weeks she's been asking you the same thing.*

'Yeah, fine,' she said, raising her head and giving him a frankly ghastly smile. *Roots need doing,* Colin thought randomly. *See a little black peeking out there.* On top of that; *Oooh, girl's an aeroplane blonde! Ain't that nice?*

'You sure?' he asked. 'You look like –'

'Bad night,' said Nicola, cutting him off. 'Didn't sleep much.'

'Oh, right.' Colin put his man-of-the-world face on and sat down. 'I'll not ask then.'

'No.' But how forced was this today? Nicola didn't just look tired, she looked exhausted. Her beautiful blue eyes were puffy, bloodshot, her ash blonde with black roots hair clumped and…unwashed? Yep, that's how it looked. Her makeup was patchy, ill applied. *That's not like my Nicola at all.*

But she's not your *Nicola, is she?*
No. She isn't.

'Coffee?' she asked, standing. He blouse hadn't been ironed properly. And she wasn't playing the game.

'Love one, ta.' *What's up, Nicola? Trouble at home? Boyfriend problems? Rest your head on my shoulder, love. Rest your head and sit on my lap and tell your Uncle Colin AAALLL about it.*

Panicked and appalled, he thumped his left hand against his monitor, hard enough to hurt. Nicola, at the kettle, didn't seem to notice. *Maybe this is why you don't like coming to work, maybe this is why you feel bad. And you should, Colin. You should.*

You really fucking should.

He did feel bad. He felt awful. And still he couldn't stop himself checking out her arse as she looked out of the window waiting for the kettle to boil, for once not reporting on what she could see. He couldn't stop himself imagining bending her over and giving it to her right there and then.

Chapter Eleven

'Polly,' said Louise warningly, 'it's not polite to hog it all. You share, now.' Polly gazed up at her. The last thing Polly wanted was to give any of her cake to Basil. In front of them Pooh and Tigger were happily dividing it up – well, maybe Tigger's slice was a little bigger than Pooh's, but Pooh didn't seem to mind. He was a very gentle bear.

'Don't pout, Polly dear,' she went on, mellowing her tone. *You catch more flies with honey,* Louise's Mum had told her once, and like everything else she'd been right about that. Shouting never really achieved anything.

Sometimes, of course, shouting was all people understood. Sometimes you just *had* to raise your voice and give a big, bright yell before they took you seriously. Louise hated to do it, but – like her Mum had *also* said – *we all have to do things we don't like in this world.* But the shouting was for Outside. The shouting was for the Others; and even there, only rarely. *When you raise your voice you lower your standards,* that had been another Mum classic. Standards were important. Standards were almost all you had in this world.

But still Polly looked up, greedily. 'Polly, my love,' Louise said, stroking the dolly's shoulders, 'we're a family. Which means we're a unit. A team. Which means we care for each other, we look out for each other. We *share.* We share the house, and the heat and the love and the drink and the food.' Her brow furrowed as Polly spoke. 'No,' Louise answered her, 'we're not related. You're a dolly and Basil's a fox. Tigger's a tiger and Pooh's a bear. And I'm a person. But you don't have to be related to be a family. You see,' Louise went on, setting herself on the floor so she was eye to eye with Polly, 'a family isn't just something that you're related to. Just because you're born to the same gene pool doesn't automatically make you a family. There are *other* sorts of families. All sorts. A family is really just a bunch of people who hang together. Who care about each other. Who look out for each other, no matter the bloodline. Look at Basil now,' Louise reached out and turned Basil's head so it almost touched Polly's, 'doesn't he look *sad?* Doesn't he look *hungry?* That's how you've made him, because you want the cake all to yourself. Do you like that? Do you like Basil being all sad and hungry?'

Louise made Polly's head droop. It broke her heart to see Polly look that way, but sometimes these things had to be done. *A Mother's love must sometimes be hard love,* spoke that voice from her past.

Then Polly looked up at her, then at Basil, and then she sat back so Louise could cut the cake up. 'There,' she smiled. *'That's* what families do. Bless you, Pol.' She kissed Polly's head and cut the cake into equal slices. Then she made Basil kiss Polly on the cheek, and everyone around the table was happy.

Louise watched her children eat, and then she poured them tea and they all drank. After that there were games and stories, then bed. As Louise sank into the darkness to sleep the sleep of the just, she thought; *families. That's what they'll learn. They'll learn about what being a family* actually *means.*

Chapter Twelve

Some miles away, Colin Bryant lay on his back, staring into the night. Helen slept beside him, her low snoring which usually comforted him oddly irritating.

Their sex was over for the night, and – being a man – he should have just rolled over and checked in at Nod. But he didn't. He was too busy thinking of the over familiar curves of his wife's body, of its fleshy stomach and its wide hips and its cellulite. He was thinking of Nicola, of how young and fresh she was, how firm, how pert.

Oh God, take this cup away from me, for I don't want to drink its poison.

But God had clocked off for the night, so he was still thinking of his PA when sleep finally overtook him.

*

Howard is the first of them to leave home, the first of them to rent a flat, a bedsit in St Paul's Place, Southport. It's maybe fifteen minute's walk from the Tech, and it's January 1984 and paralysingly cold- when it comes to weather, 1984 is a year of extremes. They shiver together, they huddle together – and is Carol a little closer to him than she is to the others? Hard to tell, it's only January, and he's not yet nineteen, won't be for another five months, just after all the exams are done, and there is still much he doesn't know – but the important word is 'together.' It's a Saturday night, and they're filled with beer and crisps and nuts and joy. They're at Howard's flat, the place where there are no parents. They keep it down, they keep it quiet, for Howard is a tenant and they have no desire to disrupt the others in the building – besides, they're not a rowdy crew, not really. They're lively, they're funny, they're happy, but they're not rowdy, they're not disruptive. They've been well brought up.

So it's January 1984, and they're all young, and Howard – Howard who works the hardest, Howard who has the evening job as well as the Saturday job, Howard who is the most mature, Howard who has flown the nest - is talking.

'Look, I'm sorry,' he's saying, half laughing. He's talking over Sophie's howls of derision. 'That's just how it is. If it's on offer, a bloke will take it. We're dogs, us. We do what dogs do.'

'Oh, that's crap,' Sophie protests.

'It isn't,' Howard responds. 'I'm not proud of it, but it's what we do.'

'What about love?' Emma asks. It seems a loaded question, somehow. 'Where does that come into it?'

'Love,' echoes Howard. 'I don't think it exists.' Once more Sophie howls derision, Emma slaps him on the arm, and Carol calls him 'sexist.' George looks at Brian, and the two of them burst out laughing. Colin, however, says nothing. It's not his time to speak yet. 'Hey, don't shoot the messenger,' Howard smiles. It's a good smile, a winning smile. Howard's the best looking of the men. Tall, broad shouldered, light brown backswept hair. He will lose his virginity before any of them; Colin's prepared to put money on that. Possibly with Sophie. He's seen the way she looks at Howard, and no one could blame her. 'Love's just a word we use to excuse how we behave, to legitimise it. Lust? Fine, I'll agree with you on that. Affection? Check. Even fondness. But love? Nope. Love's an illusion, something to write songs about.'

'So,' says Colin, and everyone turns to look at him like they always do. He's The Quiet One of the group. 'You don't believe we're meant to be with one person for the rest of our lives?' Howard shakes his head. 'So how do you explain marriage then? Why do people do it?'

'Because they're scared,' Howard answers, and it's the first time Colin hears this argument, and it makes much sense to him. 'Nobody wants to live and die alone, everybody wants to think there's a special someone who walks the earth and is meant only for them. And when they find someone who'll half fit the bill, they jump and get that ring on their finger lickeddy-spit. Just so they won't die alone. But love? Nope. Love's the posh word you slap on it. Desperation, fear, loneliness, lust, affection – they're real. Love's nothing but a made up word.'

'Howie, you're a cynic,' Sophie says, and she's narrowed her eyes, but she doesn't fool Colin. Maybe she can fool the others, but not him.

'Yeah,' he agrees. 'But a fucking good-looking cynic. And that's the important part!'

They break up laughing then – quietly, for it is late, and they are not rowdy – but laughter is laughter for all that, and it is the nature of laughing people to double over, to roll, and does Carol roll a little closer to him than she does to the others? He can't tell, it's January 1984. The summer hasn't begun yet, but he finds himself thinking that, if she did, he wouldn't mind. He wouldn't mind at all.

'Hey,' says Brian, 'there's an old Marx Brothers movie on Channel Four tonight, we **gotta** watch that.' Someone asks why, and Brian answers, 'because, my friends, they're just the funniest things ever!'

It's Brian who introduces them to Groucho, Harpo and Chico, Brian who laughs the loudest of them all (but not too loud) and those three dead actors are somehow adopted by the gang…by the crew… as their secret code, their password. Even when they're a bit sexist, a bit racist, the crew don't care. They love those old films.

Why? Who can tell?

Chapter Thirteen

'Hey Dad,' said Tasha, stomping into the living room, more asleep than awake. *It's some form of miracle how she moves on stage,* Colin thought. *You'd never guess looking at her now.*

'Hi,' he smiled, crunching his toast, returning his gaze to BBC *Breakfast.* She schlepped past him into the kitchen and exchanged good mornings with Helen. In front of him the presenters gave their usual litany of terror; bombings in India, unrest in the Middle East, Chelsea signed another player, but Colin dialled it all down. *It was different then,* he thought, but didn't know why. *Back then, back in the heat, when we 'dug deep for the miners.' When we had Thatcher and Kinnock and…*

A proper enemy.

He stopped munching his toast and stared ahead. *Yeah, a proper enemy. We had right and we had wrong. Thatcher, wrong. The Labour Party, right. That's how it was then. She was evil, they were good. That's how we thought. Back in the Eighties, back when it could still be black and white, just after Toxteth, just before the Poll Tax. 'Axe the Tax!' we'd shout. 'Resist to exist! Can't pay, won't pay!' And there was more wasn't there? 'Jobs not bombs,' that was a favourite too, because back then – like now – there was a recession on. Back then, like now, there were hard times. Unemployment was on the way up. Three million, or something like that. UB40 told us they were 'One In Ten' – UB40, named after the unemployment card. My God, the things you forget!*

'Bye Dad,' said Tasha, making her way back from the kitchen, heading for the front door, interrupting his thoughts.

'Have you eaten?'

'I had a biscuit,' she muttered defensively.

'A biscuit's no good,' he called after her. 'Get something proper for lunch!'

She said something before the front door closed behind her, but Colin didn't quite catch it. He doubted very much it was 'You bet, Daddy–O.'

'She'll eat when she's hungry,' Helen said, kissing him on the forehead in passing.

'So long as she doesn't throw it up again.'

Helen stopped in the living room doorway, pausing in the act of checking her samples portfolio. 'You worry about her too much. She's a sensible kid.'

'She's a dancer,' Colin answered, swigging his coffee. 'Or will be. I don't want her neglecting her health just so she can fit into a leotard.'

'We raised her well.' Helen stepped forward and kissed him again. 'She'll get faddy like all teenagers do, but she'll get over it. She's our daughter, Col, and we did OK by her.'

Colin paused a bit before answering, taking his wife's face in. *I stopped looking some time ago,* he found himself thinking. *The russet hair, the deep blue – almost black – eyes. The wide, generous mouth and the thin nose, the dimpled chin. I stopped looking, the way you stop looking at the painting on the wall after a couple of months. It's just there. But unlike the painting, my wife is ageing. Many more crow's feet now. Etched lines around that mouth. That red rinse is a little heavier these days, isn't it dear? More work to cover the grey. We are not what we once were – does that ever scare you? Every second our daughter grows more into a woman is a second we grow closer to our graves – do you ever think that? Does that keep you awake as you think about the heavier foundation you use to cover the cracks which grow deeper every day? Do you mourn your departed waist? Do you clock your bigger arse in jeans and measure what you've lost against the inches you've gained? Do you?*

But he asked her none of these things. He reached up and took her head in his hands – gently, so as not to disturb her makeup – and said, 'You're a wonderful Mum, Helen, and I love you.'

A tiny twitch of surprise crossed her royal blue eyes. *I love you* had never been cheap currency in Colin's world. 'I love you too, hon.'

'You home tonight?'

'Uh-huh, sorry. Rehearsing till ten. Why don't you come along, see how it's going? We can get a drink after.'

And back to the game, an imaginary John Motson spoke up in his head. *Once more, Helen's made the 'come along to rehearsals' move, and once more Colin will make an excuse, and they'll both turn a blind eye to the fact Colin hates Amateur Dramatics and she knows it. It's fascinating to see how many variations they've managed on this play during the last two decades.*

'I'd rather see the full thing,' he lied, 'then it's a surprise.'

He saw the way she looked at him, the way Helen knew exactly what he meant, the way she didn't let the truth upset her. *That's how people manage to get along after so much time,* he thought. *We choose to ignore that which we don't like.* 'OK,' she said, and smiled. When she smiled he could still see the woman he'd met back in the last millennium. 'Be back about half ten.'

'Have a good day, hon.'

'And you, babe.'

Then she was gone, and Colin was left with the TV and ten minutes before he left for work, for the first time in many years actively thinking of his past. Not of the people, but the events. Of Helen and the strife in his youth, of his daughter and her future and her health. *The world has a way of sweeping you along. The world has a way of making you take your eye off the ball. Jesus.*

The local news was on by the time Colin reached for the remote to turn the TV off. Train derailed in Cumbria, six injured, two seriously. Air fares to rise. Police appealing for witnesses to the last movements of Emma Fillion and her son David, who were found dead in a burned out car.

Colin's thumb rested on the red button, and had his reflexes been just a touch sharper he'd never have seen the photo that flashed on the screen. But he was older now, and his thumb was too slow, and he saw a family grouping, three not too skinny people smiling into a lens.

The man and boy he'd never seen. But the woman...

Emma Fillion, they said on TV. He'd never known an Emma Fillion.

'Oh fucking hell,' he said, out of breath. His legs buckled and he sat down with all the grace of Tasha's slump through the living room minutes before.

Emma Fillion, no. Emma *Richards,* yes. There was enough of her left. Just enough that showed through the excess flubber. The green eyes. The turn of her head. 'Emma,' he gasped. 'Is that…?'

But the picture was gone, and the Indian woman was talking about some new shopping centre in Irlam. Colin sat in his chair, rubbing at his heart, unable to move. He sat there for an hour.

Utterly still.

Chapter Fourteen

'Allied Corporate, Colin Bryant's phone.'

'Hi Nicola, it's me. Colin.' He was amazed at how normal his voice sounded.

'You're late. Stuck in traffic?' A slight admonition in her voice, but that didn't mask the fact it was still colourless.

'Uh, no. I'm at home. Listen, I'm not going to be able to make it in today. Sorry.'

'What's up?' *Genuine concern?* Hard to tell.

'I think I ate something that disagreed with me, had bad guts all night –'

'OK, leave it there. Some details I don't need to know.'

'You got that right. Listen, Johnson's going to need the figures on the West thing. They're all in the folder. Just email them over and he'll be happy. Other than that there's nothing pressing.'

'Unlike your colon.'

'Unlike my colon, spot on. Just run interference, will you? Any major hassles call me at home and I'll try and get online to help. That all right?'

'I suppose it'll have to be. But you owe me, got that?'

'Got that. Listen, I'd better –'

'Yeah, sure. Get well.'

'Tomorrow,' he said, and hung up. Part of him felt bad about lying to her, but then he felt the contraction in his stomach and realised it hadn't really been a lie. He ran to the toilet and made it, but only just.

As the contents of his stomach exited his bowels, he groaned and thought, *Emma Richards. That was her. I'm sure it was her.*

Except he wasn't, not really. It *could* have been her - but when had he last seen her? He tried desperately to call that before him, but nothing happened. *She was one of us,* he thought, but didn't know why. *One of the gang. What gang? The gang. When? Back then. When did you see her last? Don't know. How did you meet her? She was at college, we had classes. Which classes? Don't know, can't remember, but I did know her...even if she's* not *that woman I've seen on the television, I knew a woman...girl...called Emma Richards. I did. Back then, I knew her. And others. We had a gang, we went places, we did things.*

What things?
Don't know.
Where did you go?
Can't remember.
What was she like?
Don't know.
WHY don't you know? WHY can't you remember?
Don't know.

He almost laughed at that, but the pain in his stomach trebled and another gallon of brown, foul smelling liquid hit the pan making a noise like shoes falling out of the cupboard. *It was back then, when we dug deep for the miners, when there was a dragon in Number Ten and we were all St George. It was back then, with big hair and shoulder pads and rah-rah skirts. It was back then, that's when I knew her.*

Are you sure?
Yes.

How can *you be? One random fact dragged out of a dark mass, like the dark mass you're producing from your anus, and you claim to know this as a truth. Remember what you were thinking the other day, about how sick you might be?*

Your point being?

Two hours ago you knew nothing of this woman, now you're certain you knew her once, you're certain you were part of a 'gang.' You? *In a gang?* YOU? *Consider that likely? When did you* ever *run with a pack? When did you* ever *have a gaggle of chums? You've always been the Solitude Dude, the Man of Few Words. When would you get a 'gang'? This could be nothing more than a 'false memory.' People who get false memories aren't necessarily considered in the best of mental health, Colin old Colin.*

But I – another torrent of diarrhoea ran down into the pan, causing him to shiver and groan. *I'm sure…*

Sure? Sure! *Sure you are!*

In a state of utter confusion, Colin held onto the side of the bath panel and decided to wait this out. Even if that woman who'd been murdered in her car did turn out to be Emma Richards, what of it, really? What did she mean to him anyway? He could hardly remember her. Tragic, yeah – tragic even if she turned out to be no one he'd ever set eyes on – but what did it mean to *him?*

Nothing, that's what.

Nothing at all.

He spent the rest of the afternoon on the sofa, BBC News 24 rolling on hour after hour, telling him the same stories over and over. Every half hour the local news popped up, and there it was, that photo again, the same request for information, and every time it did Colin would squint at the picture, trying to decide. He did know her, he'd *never* known her. She was part of his past that he dimly remembered, she was nothing, lines on a screen. He was reminded of that RSC production of *Hamlet* Helen had taken him to see many years back in Stratford. Four hours of a bloke being unable to make up his mind. *Just make a sodding decision,* he'd wanted to scream from their unfeasibly expensive seats, but now in late September 2009, he understood finally how the poor bastard felt. *It really is enough to drive you mad,* he thought, *and not just nor' nor' west,* properly *mad. Did I or didn't I? Did I or didn't I? And if I did, why can't I remember? What's* wrong *with me?*

But answers came there none, so he just lay there.

Chapter Fifteen

'Hush, Basil. Hush. No, I'll tell you the story later. Yes, I know Bulldog is hanging from his cuticles – and don't *oooohhh* me, young fox, you know very well that means fingernails, don't be rude – but he'll wait. He'll keep. No, that's not the story book, it's *Autotrader*. There's someone I want to call. I mean, my business is expanding, and I need a van. Don't I, Tigger?'

Tigger nodded.

Chapter Sixteen

'You all better?' Nicola asked as Colin stepped into the office. Then she took in his face and said, 'Stupid question, sorry. I mean, you look like shit. Sure you're OK to work?'

'Thank you for your vote of confidence, I hope I don't get a swell head.' He punched in his password.

'Sorry,' she said again. After a moment's hesitation she stood and took position at his shoulder. 'It's just you're still pale.'

'A day on the toilet takes it out of you.'

'There are some things I don't need to know thanks.' Then she did something Colin wasn't expecting, something that made him shiver all over again. She leaned forward and laid a cool hand on his forehead. 'Temperature's normal, anyway. But seriously,' she went on, taking that light, almost unbearably erotic pressure away, 'are you sure you're OK to be here? I mean, I miss you when you're not around but if what you've got is catching...'

'It's not,' he said, when he was sure he could trust himself to speak. Oh, that touch, that light, wonderful touch...*that* was a cure for what ailed him. How long had it been since anyone had touched him like that? How long had it been since he'd felt that way? Confused, he tried to conjure Helen's face before him, tried to remember her touch...*oh Colin old Colin, you're married, you're married, you're married with a daughter and you love them both very much, you do, you do. Don't be a silly middle-aged man. Don't. Just don't.*

Ah come on, so what? So what really*? Look at her, look at that vision of youthful beauty before you, look at the kid with everything still pointing forwards. So* what *if you think she's a honey – who wouldn't? Who* couldn't*? You think she would* ever *look at you and think the same? You're a Dad to her. At* most *that's all you are. What does she see? Man in his mid forties, grey at the sides, flabby in the gut, thin on top. Are you Colin Farrell? Hell, are you George Clooney? Nope, you're just a nothing, an old bloke she works with. So go ahead, drink her in, go all wobbly when she touches you. That's OK. Really. See, nothing will ever come of it, so it's OK, right? It's like looking at the Ferraris in the showrooms. You're free to dream.*

'You sure?' Nicola asked, breaking the train. 'Because the last thing right now I need is the backdoor trots.'

'I promise.' He gave the Boy Scout salute.

'Something you ate then? You ought to have a word with your wife about what she cooks you.'

'Helen's not there enough to cook my tea.' He saw Louise frown at this, almost disapproving. 'She does plays, Am Dram. They have lots of rehearsals.'

'So you poisoned yourself? Well done, you must be very proud.'

'No,' he said, then stopped. *Are you going to? Are you going to tell her? Are you going to tell her what you didn't tell your wife? Because when Helen came home from rehearsals and found you wrapped in the duvet on the sofa you just told her you'd had a bad dose of the squits, that's all, nothing else. You kept the rest to yourself. Oh, and by the way, when your wife knelt down next to you and took your hand and kissed your cheek and called you a 'poor baby,' what did you feel? Anything? Anything at all?*

But I've got to tell someone. Haven't I? Isn't that how it works? You tell people the things which are on your mind.

Yeah, you tell the people you love, not virtual strangers.

'No,' he went on. 'I saw something on the telly. On the news. Gave me a bit of a shock.'

'Oh? What?' She perched herself on the corner of his desk. Her skirt rode up a bit, exposing a sheer nyloned kneecap. He tried very, very hard not to look at it.

You going to do this? You going to tell her? Let her in on the secret you didn't tell your wife?

'You hear about that mother and son? Burned to death in their car?' She thought about it for a second, then nodded. Not a secure nod, but she was a kid. Kids didn't do News. Kids did *Big Brother* and *I'm A Celebrity...*One sure sign of growing old was turning on the News first thing in the day. 'I think...I think I knew her. Years ago, when I was a kid.'

Nicola's big blue eyes turned into perfect circles. 'Jesus! Really?'

'I don't know, not for sure. I mean, same name...but how many Emma's are there in the world. And it looked a bit like her, but...oh, it was all so long ago!'

'How long?'

He paused a bit, the anguish on his face replaced with a sort of sheepish guilt. 'That's another thing, I don't know. I can't really remember. It's like,' he went on, staring up into his PA's eyes, eyes that gazed down at him with compassion. 'It's like something I read in a book once or saw in a film. Stuff that gets buried, half remembered. But I saw her picture on the telly and...I don't know...it was like a key was put in the lock.' Then he laughed a little. 'That makes no sense, does it?'

'Not to me no,' Nicola answered, but she didn't laugh. She still looked down at him with understanding and sympathy. 'But it still must have been a hell of a shock to see that picture. If it *was* her. To think that would happen to someone you once knew. *Jesus!*' She shuddered a bit. Colin would have sold his soul to put his arms around her and take that shudder away, but souls were non-negotiable at Allied Corporate, so he didn't. 'OK,' she went on, stepping down, her skirt riding down over her knee, much to his regret. 'Today no flipping for coffee. Today I wait on you. Deal?'

Oh Nicola, the things you say in innocence...'Deal.' He tried to keep his eyes on the monitor as she made her way to the windowsill. 'How're you, anyway?'

'Me?'

'You. The other day you seemed a bit...distracted.'

She considered, opened her mouth, closed it. 'It's OK,' she said.

'Sure?'

Another second's hesitation. Then; 'Yeah, sure. It's probably nothing.'

'Well...if you need to talk, I'm here.'

Then Nicola did something that she hadn't done all morning. She smiled. She had the most wonderful smile, a smile that brought the sun out. 'Thanks,' she said. 'I will.'

But she didn't, not that day. All the same though, a thought kept crawling through Colin's head. *We've got a secret now, we've got a secret now, we've got a secret.* And with that thought went a terrible excitement.

Chapter Seventeen

At a little after midnight, a young, very stoned man was making his way home from a friend's house across a badly lit park. The man's name was Martin Styche. His friend Chris had bought a very big bag of weed from *his* friend Mike and he'd very kindly offered to share it. So Martin and Chris had partaken heavily of the grass, and now Martin was making his way back to his bedsit in Seaforth. It seemed to be taking an awfully long time, but then so did everything when you were stoned. That was one of the reasons why Martin loved it so much. It was like watching a movie on half speed.

Even when his foot caught on something and he went sprawling, it seemed to take him an hour to hit the grass. He lay there for a while – he would never be able to say how long – giggling. That was the other thing he loved about the rope-a-dope. It turned every day into a smiley face day.

He was still giggling when he realised he'd tripped over a man. He was still giggling when he eventually realised that the man he'd tripped over wasn't breathing. He only stopped giggling when he saw that the man he'd tripped over had a gaping hole where his stomach should be.

But he only started screaming when he saw that a dog had been stuffed down that hole, with its head sticking out.

The dog, however, looked like it was laughing.

Chapter Eighteen

'You kids today,' said Colin, fingers dancing over the keys, 'you never get enough sleep.'

'Have you been spying on me,' Nicola asked, likewise not looking from her monitor. 'I mean, how do you know if I've been sleeping or not?'

'It could be the constant yawning that's the giveaway. I mean, I'm not a detective or anything…'

'No, you're an accounts manager,' Nicola interrupted. 'And a very average one at that.'

Colin simply flicked her a V sign. 'You're like my daughter,' he went on. Part of him didn't like to talk about Tasha too much, part of him didn't want Nicola to think of him as being part of her father's generation, but all the same it kept the conversation going. 'In at all hours, up at all hours, hardly ever in her pit. And when she is in her room she's on that damned computer emailing her mates. And if she's not doing that she's texting them. Eight hours a night, that's what you need. You'll thank me in the end.'

'Time enough to sleep when you're dead, that's what my Mum always says.'

'And conserve your energy, that's what your boss always says. You think it'll last forever, you young people today.' He realised with some sour amusement he had dropped into an impersonation of his father. 'One day you'll wake up, go to the well, and bang! It'll be dry.'

'Do wells go bang when they dry up?' Nicola said, sitting back from her screen. Then she let out a jaw cracking yawn and gave a big stretch. Colin cut his eyes back to his keyboard immediately – he didn't want to get caught staring at how her blouse strained at the buttons. He saw he had misspelled the word *strategy*. He tried to think of Helen. He tried to think of Tasha. He tried to think of anything but his PA and her young, firm body.

'Don't give cheek to your elders.' He dragged the mouse across *staterguh* and replaced it with the correct word. 'And at least put your hand over your mouth when you yawn. No one wants to see your tonsils.' *Nope, not your tonsils. Your fine firm tits with their perky little nipples, yeah. But you can keep your tonsils.*

'A doctor would, if I had tonsillitis.'

'But *do* you have tonsillitis? I suspect not, judging by how much you're running your mouth off. And am I a doctor? No, according to you I'm a very average accounts manager.'

'That's not what you said. You said *no one* wants to see my tonsils, and I've just given you an example of someone who would. Which means I win, which means you make the coffee. *Boss.*'

Colin scowled at her, hit 'save' and made his way to the kettle, trying to ignore the way his heart was beating. Once more he tried to tell himself it was nothing, once more he tried to pass it off as a little harmless office banter. Not even enough to be called flirting, was it? *And even if it was,* he thought as he spooned Nescafé into the mugs, *what harm would that do? I mean, I've seen Helen snog other men on stage, play big passionate love scenes, entangle herself around some bloke from the newsagent's. Does that matter? Does that mean she's having an affair with everyone she has to make eye contact with and say 'I love you?' Does it? Nope, not at all.*

And yet, his mind kept turning to the dream he'd had the night before. He seemed to be dreaming a lot these days – even if he couldn't remember most of them - but dreams like *that* one he could take a lot of. He and Nicola had been in the office, it was dark, and he'd leaned over her to help her out with some report and she'd turned her face upwards and kissed him.

Soft, shy, hesitant at first – then harder, passion mounting. In seconds she'd been spread-eagled on the desk, blouse ripped open to reveal a black lace bra that only just managed to keep things harnessed, begging him to spear her.

So what? A dream is a dream, nothing but smoke. I used to dream I was an astronaut or a Formula One driver. Those dreams didn't come true either.

But the way she'd looked in his dream…blouse open, blonde hair tumbling across the desk, mouth and legs spread…

'You feeling any better then?' she asked, breaking his reverie.

'Hmm?'

'You know, that woman you thought you used to hang around with? The one who was murdered?'

Those huge blue eyes, moist, wild with anticipation…'If it was her. Which, face it, is unlikely. And even if it was, what can I do about it?'

'Still, you were very freaked about it.'

'Face from the past,' he said. 'When you get to my age, faces from the past throw up all sorts of feelings.' *Especially when you hardly remember your past. Especially when you never really give it a second thought.*

'Listen to you,' she chuckled. '"When you get to my age." You sound like Methuselah.'

'Feel like him most mornings,' Colin answered, dropping her mug off and returning to his computer. 'Old age is a guest you didn't invite and won't leave. He just hangs around the house making you slower and grumpier. He steals your hair and puts aches in your lower back. He makes you hate Kanye West.'

'That's not old age, that's good taste.'

'It'll happen to you one day.' She chuckled again, and Colin leaned forward. 'I mean it. One day you'll wake up and the grey hair fairy's been. One day you'll decide you prefer VH-1 to MTV. One day you'll realise that pizza after seven o'clock will keep you up all night.'

'Maybe it's not as bad as all that,' Nicola said, tapping a biro against her nose. 'They say experience comes with age, that's got to count for *something*. And you men are lucky, you get better looking as you get older. Look at George Clooney.'

'He's the exception that proves the rule,' Colin said, but all he could hear was '*you men are lucky. You get better looking as you get older.' Me? Does she mean me? Could she mean me?*

'Don't get too hung up on looks or age,' his only-just-out-of-teens PA told him with all her maturity. 'There's things that count more than those. There's kindness and humour and consideration.'

'The last refuge of the ugly,' Colin laughed.

Nicola didn't laugh back. 'No,' she said, and suddenly she was blinking a little too much. *She's upset. About what?* 'Yeah, OK, looks. Fine. I mean, you always want to fancy whoever you're seeing, I get that. But if that's all he's got…I mean, what if he's a pig? What if he doesn't *care* about you? What if he never calls just to see if you're OK or if he never tells you you're pretty? What if he just sees you as some jizz receptacle? What *then?* What do all his good looks count for *then?*'

She's been a bit off the last week or so, hasn't she? You noticed that. She almost told you something the other day. You noticed that, too. Face it, you'd notice if she developed a split end. When it comes to Nicola, you notice everything. *She had a breakup? Does she* want *a breakup? This is where you step in, Uncle Colin. This is where you put your arm around her and say, 'Hush now, sweetheart. Tell me aaaaaaalll about it.'*

No. As that old sign at the pop festival used to say, 'That way lies Madness.'

Still, she's upset. As a friend you can't ignore it.

We're not friends, we're just colleagues. Like Mrs Lewis from Finance.

And the last time you dreamed about Mrs Lewis lying across the desk begging you to fuck her brains out was when, exactly?

'Are you OK Nic?'

'Yes,' she said, dropping those huge lashed, impossibly gorgeous blue eyes from his. Then, after a second, she raised them again. A drop of moisture was dangling from the right. 'No. I split up with my boyfriend last week.'

'Oh hon,' he said, before he could stop himself. 'I'm so sorry. What happened?'

'He was…oh look; I don't want to talk about it.'

My God, she's just begging to be cuddled right now, just begging to be taken in my arms and comforted.

Right, and if the door opens and Big Boss McKenzie walks in, what do you say? Ah, she's just upset and I'm comforting her, Boss? Sure. You can say that all the way to the Job Centre.

'Sure, I understand. But if you do...'

Before he could finish his sentence with *I'm here,* a torrent of anger burst from her incredibly beautiful face. Hurt, upset anger. '*He slept around behind my back!* With my best mate! The *bastard!* The *bitch!*'

Colin sat there, stunned. But oddly the first thing that came to mind was not *oh, poor girl* but *come on, it happens.*

But it *didn't* happen, did it? It certainly hadn't to him. Nor to anyone he'd ever known. Until today.

This is where you do it, a part of him thought. *Look at her, she's distraught. You can't not do it. You can't just sit behind your desk and say 'dear dear, never mind eh?' You've got to comfort her.*

And you can, another part of him replied, but this part – the sensible, grown up part - seemed small and far off. *You can. But remember – there are rules! THERE ARE RULES!*

So he stood, Colin Bryant, forty-three, balding, slightly paunchy despite the care he took over his diet, and crossed the room to his beautiful, blonde haired, blue eyed PA. He sat on the edge of her desk and fished a clean handkerchief from his pocket. He tapped her lightly on the shoulder and offered it over. She took it and wiped her damp eyes, smudging the mascara that made those lashes even longer than they actually were. He waited while she composed herself. He sat there and watched her shoulders hitch.

If there was one moment where much was irrevocably lost, it was then.

Chapter Nineteen

'Are you sure your wife won't mind?' Nicola asked as he dropped their drinks onto the table. The pub was only half full. At half past four on a Thursday afternoon, he supposed half full was something of a miracle. 'What did she say when you rang her? I mean, I wouldn't want you to get into any trouble because of me.' She gnawed at a nail and looked about her. *Bless,* Colin found himself thinking. *All that's going on in her life and she's thinking of me.*

'She said, "Fine, don't worry about it, there's stuff in the freezer for tea,"' Colin answered truthfully. That had been exactly what she'd said. He saw no need to add that she'd said that in response to his 'Sorry love, I've got a bitch of a report to do. Might be a bit late.'

Lied to your wife. How's that make you feel?

Not good, but then in a marriage that'd lasted over twenty years it wouldn't be the first lie told, nor – in all probability – the last. None of them major, really, just stuff like 'Yes, I love that dress' or 'Your arse is fine, you don't need to lose weight.' Harmless stuff. Little white lies they were called. Like saying you were working late when you'd agreed to take your PA for a drink so she could unburden herself. To get things off her chest, so to speak.

'Good, that's good,' said Nicola. She breathed out heavily, and oh Lord did that chest heave. 'I couldn't have her upset with you because my life's fucked over.'

'We're not here to talk about me,' Colin said, sipping his half a bitter. 'It's you we're going to discuss.'

Another huge sigh. Nicola picked at her beer mat. 'I still can't believe it,' she said, more tears welling in her eyes. 'I mean, I never...look,' she was blushing now, 'I never once told him no, you understand?' Colin nodded, but the thought that ran through his mind was *the lucky bastard*. 'Not once did I tell him no. Even if I wasn't really...up for it,' that blush deepened, and she looked down at the table. *She'll freeze up now,* Colin thought. *This isn't the sort of thing you talk over with your boss.*

But she didn't. Still looking away from him, her hair spilling across her cheeks (and how he wanted to brush that gently away) she went on, 'I loved him. At least I *thought* I did. No, I *did*. I'm *sure* I did. I think I still do, even after...Alan, his name is. Met him at the youth club.'

Youth club? What youth club? Do they still have *youth clubs?* Oh, there was so much about this young woman he didn't know.

'You should have seen him,' she continued, probably unaware of that half smile on her face. 'He was...oh, I mean...like Pierce Brosnan meets Johnny Depp.'

Try as I might, I can't conjure that image up.

'I was playing pool. With Michelle.' He saw the way her lip pulled down on that name, and guessed exactly who this odd looking man with the square name had been playing away with. 'She's the good looking one out of the two of us. Tall, slim, brown hair. Men go crazy for her.' *Christ, she must be something else! She's the good looking one? Nicola, do you actually* own *a mirror?*

'But, this Alan...he seemed to be looking at *me*. *Me*. And him and his mate Martin come over to the table and challenge us to a game of doubles. Oh, Colin...I thought I was going to die!' She looked straight at him, and Colin knew *exactly* what she meant. 'He asked me out that night. Asked *me*. And I said yes. That was a year ago nearly. And I thought...' she trailed off, sipped at her vodka and orange, then started again. 'Not had many boyfriends, me. Davey Ablett back in school, but he was just a hand holding boyfriend, you get me? Bit of snogging, nothing much more than that. But Alan...he got what he wanted, when he wanted. Charming bastard he was too. Mum loved him. I think she saw him as the son she never had. And, God...I was besotted with him. Used to practice writing *Nicola Hickson* so I could sign things with my married name.' That small, bitter half smile dropped, vanished like an Etch-a-Sketch picture when the board was shaken. 'Stupid. Stupid *bitch*. Then a couple of weeks ago he's round at mine and his phone goes. Gets a text. Tells me it's from his mate Kevin, tells me Kevin's girlfriend's dumped him. Tells me he should get round there and sort it out. So I'm like, "OK, sure." He gets up, gives me a kiss, and he's off. Ten minutes later, Mum comes in and asks me to go to the shop for some milk. She works hard, my Mum, and she forgets things sometimes. So off to the shop I go, and who do I see drive past me on the street? Alan. With Michelle in the passenger seat. '

Colin winced. 'Oh Nicola, that's horrible.'

She gave a bitter smile. 'Yeah, isn't it?'

'Did you confront him about it?'

'Not right away, no. I kept telling myself it was a mistake, that it couldn't have been her in the car. Even though I saw her, clear as day. Could have been mistaken.'

'But you weren't?'

She shook her head, and sipped more vodka. 'Couple of days later, same thing. He's round at mine, we're watching telly – except we weren't *really* watching telly, understand? Even after I saw what I saw, I never told him no. Phone goes, another text, *oh dear Kevin's really down, best go and see him.*

'"I'll come with you," I said.

'"Nah, that's OK," he says, putting his shirt on. "Don't want to wave my girlfriend in his face when he's all upset and alone, do I? That's not nice."' Another bitter smile. 'No. It wasn't nice *at all*. So he gets off. I left it ten minutes and rang Michelle. She picked it up, and – d'you know, for a couple of minutes I thought, *oh thank God, he's not there. I got it all wrong, I did.* And we start chatting, just stuff, when I hear her doorbell ring. Then she couldn't get off the phone quick enough. Said another mate of hers was coming round to watch a film.'

'Could have been true.'

'Could have been, but wasn't. Because I got in my Vectra and drove over there. And whose car was parked outside?'

'His.' Colin felt sick for this poor kid. How could that happen to *anyone?*

'His,' she confirmed, her eyes glittering with tears.

'Did you go in?'

'Did I shite,' she exploded. More vodka, a gulp this time. 'I went round to his the day after, asked him how Kevin was. He said he wasn't doing so good. Said he might need a bit of propping up. So I said, "OK, that's fine. You prop him up all you want. But remember, Michelle fakes every orgasm. She's told me that. And she'll throw you aside when she's finished."'

'Jesus,' said Colin, impressed by her *chutzpah*. 'What did he say to that?'

More vodka sluiced down her oh so kissable mouth. 'Nothing, I turned and went. That was last week, a week ago tonight. Haven't heard a thing from either of them since. I hope they rot in fucking hell.' Then that bitterness turned to angry sadness. 'Oh, it's just…so *unfair! That's* what I hate most! Well, and the betrayal, obviously. But I've lost them *both,* my boyfriend *and* my best friend! What am I supposed to *do,* Colin? How am I supposed to *go on?'*

She looked so tired and vulnerable as she finished that sentence that he just couldn't help it. He reached his hand across the table and took hold of hers. She didn't pull back, she didn't resist. Her hand was blessedly warm in his. A tingle, a shock – something almost electric - ran down his arm and settled uncomfortably between his legs. *I love my wife,* he chanted inside his head, but the voice was distant, far off and echoing. *I love my wife, I love my wife.* True enough, of course he did, she was The One, The One to whom he'd promised his loyalty and fidelity. She was his woman and had been for two decades now, ever since they'd met in the long departed year of 1987. He'd taken one look at Helen and he'd known; *yep,* a little voice had spoken, *she's The One.*

But had there been *this* spark, this *tingle* when they'd first held hands, he and Helen, back when Berlin was still a couple of towns in Germany, back when Stock, Aitken & Waterman still ruled the charts, back when NICAM stereo was The Next Big Thing in home entertainment? Had he felt that shiver? *God, who knows? It was all so long ago.* True, it was – one long marriage and a teenage daughter ago.

But he *had* felt this before, hadn't he? This or something like it. Before Helen, before Kylie and Jason. Something like this with someone else.

He became aware that Nicola was staring at him –
not shocked, not upset, not angry at being mauled, just
staring, waiting for him to say something. 'You will,' he
managed after a gap of what seemed a million years. 'You
will. You just *will*.' He saw the dark look of scorn that
crossed her brow (but didn't cause her to pull that small,
delicate, warm hand away) and went on, 'I promise you,
you will. You've done it for a week, you've *gone on* for a
week, that means you can go on for another. And another.
Pretty soon it'll be almost nothing to you.'

'Oh, that's…' she started to say, still not
withdrawing her hand.

'It isn't, trust me. It isn't. It's the truth of the
world. Listen, when my Dad died back in 1990 I honestly
thought I'd *never* get over it. It was a shock, a big shock.
But I did. I did because your life takes over, it gets in the
way, it smothers the pain and lets you move on. And
you'll be the same.'

'Yeah, but – no disrespect – this is different.' Still,
she kept her hand where it was.

'Only in the circumstances. Grief is still grief, and
that's what you're doing now, grieving. And it hurts like
hell. But as each day goes on it'll hurt a bit less. That's
maybe the only good thing about growing old,' he went
on. 'The older you get the more days you have to smear
over what's hurt you.'

For a second it looked like she was going to
dispute this again, but then she considered it – Colin could
see her turning it over in her pretty little head – and she
shrugged. 'OK, if you say so. But I warn you, if it doesn't
I'll hold you responsible.'

What'll you do my angel? Spank me? 'I'm never
wrong.'

Nicola took her hand away then, and how bereft
it made him feel. She checked her watch. 'Oh look, better
make a move. Got Mum's tea to make. She works hard,
Mum. She's always too tired when she gets in to cook.'

'OK, that's fine.' Except it wasn't really fine. He wanted to sit across from this young woman for the rest of the night. *Hey, bless what you got.*

Yeah. I got the empty house to go back to. I got a wife at Am Dram and a daughter at dance class. I got the Marx Brothers on DVD or Billy Joel on CD. That's what I got, pal.

They made their way to the door, and stood for a second by the Cancer Lepers huddled around the wall mounted ashtray. *Back then pubs were full of smoke,* he thought randomly. He saw Nicola shiver a little. September getting ready to quit, October's warming up in the wings, gargling with warm lemon. *The years, oh they do fade fast once you give goodbye to your twenties, don't they?*

Then she turned to him and hugged him – a full hug, not one of those bowed at the waist hugs you gave to or received from your wife's friends. A hug that started at the shoulders and ended at the ankles. He felt her young, full breasts pressed against him, he smelled her perfume. *I love my wife, I love my wife,* he tried to chant, but it turned into *I love my wife but oh you kid.*

Then she was gone, out of his arms, leaving him light headed, horny…and a little relieved. *If she'd been there for just one more second I'd have had to pretend I had a Mars bar in my pocket.* 'Thanks Colin,' she said. 'Thanks a bunch, love.'

'Any time,' he heard himself say. And oh dear God he meant it. 'Take it easy.' *Love. She called me…*

'I will.' She gave him a smile. It was the bravest thing he'd ever seen. Then she gave him a look, a long, searching (yearning?) look, a look that made his stomach flip and his dick twitch again. 'Oh Colin,' she sighed. 'Why can't I meet someone like you?'

But you have *met someone like me,* Colin thought immediately. *You have, in fact, met* me. *And I'm here, right in front of you. With an empty house we can go back to…*

Stop it, stop it, STOP IT, some other part of him commanded. *Leave it, she's young –* too *young, she's upset, and she doesn't know what she's saying. So leave it, stop it, and* go the fuck home! *Have a wank over that hug if you want, fine, who cares about that…but* no more!

'What,' he said eventually (and did she notice how uneven his voice was?) 'someone old, baldy and grey?'

'Don't,' she said, eyes narrowing and oh dear Lord sexier than ever. 'Don't put yourself down, Colin. You're…' but she seemed to think better of that, and simply said, 'Tomorrow.' Then she was gone, walking to her car, and he was alone. Quite alone.

Chapter Twenty

In 1984, everything was different. And so it is with this dream, because this is different from the others he's had recently. In this one he is outside *of his younger self. In this one he can look* upon *rather than look* out.

Colin sees himself as he once was – fresh, clean, and smart. He's wearing a very fine Top Man suit - and it comes to him, suddenly, that he was always *in a very fine Top Man suit. Or jacket and trousers. Often a tie. The Quiet One, the Responsible One…and the Smart One too. For 1984, he's looking quite the man. He has lots of hair back then, and it's combed straight back from his forehead in a sort of bouffant style quiff. Sophie sometimes calls him Cliff Richard or Pete Wylie. He doesn't mind. He doesn't mind because he's with his people, his crew, and his older self, the one who looks upon, wants to shout out to his younger persona, wants to tell him to remember every moment of this, every special moment, because times like this don't come back. Ever.*

He sees himself sitting at the table in The Houghton, and Joe, who is George here, has just returned from the video juke jingling a pile of those brand new pound coins – the ones Colin had called 'a Thatcher, because they're hard, brassy and think they're a Sovereign.'

He doesn't speak often, Colin – he's the Quiet One, after all – but when he gets a joke off, it's the best of them all.

George is grinning an evil grin, a naughty grin. They know what this means, and they're proved correct for the nine millionth time that summer as The Longest Time by Billy Joel fills the room. He looks on, an old man now, as his younger self slumps with his head in his hands, as Sophie exclaims 'Oh for fuck's sake!' As Brian mimes slitting his wrist, and Emma cries 'Bagsy next with the knife, Bri.' As Carol snuggles her so beautiful head into his shoulder, as Howard stands and says, 'I swear to God, George, you do that one more time and I will cut you.'

'Your trouble,' says George, 'is that you have no appreciation of fine music.'

'No no,' says Howard. If Colin is slim, then Howard is positively emaciated. The oldest of them all – and, it must be supposed, their leader – he is the one to whom they all defer. Howard is the one who decides which pubs they will meet in, he's the one who says which live bands they go to see. Howard is slick, he's confident, and he's the boss. 'Our trouble is we actually have an appreciation of fine music. Which you keep ruining by playing this shit.'

'To be fair,' says Brian. Brian is The Mad One of the gang. His sense of humour is what they call 'surreal' in those days. 'George does suffer from that number blindness thing. I mean, he honestly can't see that there are other numbers on the juke. We shouldn't really have a go at him, it's a medical condition.'

'You two hold him down,' Sophie says, 'I'll operate on him.'

'Oh please,' says George, 'Sophie, I would pay good money for you to operate on me!'

'I'd pay good money to watch,' says Colin, and they laugh. They laugh longer and harder when Colin makes a joke, for Colin is The Quiet One. When they're together they're *together*, *they're a unit, a solid team, a* gestalt. *Their words tumble one over another, conversations never really start or finish, they just roll over each other into a mass like a snowball tumbling downhill, it's chaos, it's joy. But Colin is always just a step outside of the others, just a step apart. He's almost their arbiter, their referee. He doesn't say much, but when he does, they listen. And when it's funny – like it was then – they appreciate it all the more. It's like a dog walking on its hind legs. Rare, but it happens.*

This must be June, *he thinks in his dream as he looks on at his crowd.* June 1984, when Thatcher and Reagan ruled the world, when they were united against Brezhnev, when you couldn't spit without hitting a hundred Citroen 2CVs with NO NUKES stickers in their windows. This must be June, early June…look at us, look at Carol and me. See that look she gave me when I made even so much as an oblique remark linking Sophie and sex. Doesn't she *know* yet? We're close, closer than everyone else, but this must be early June and nothing's *quite* happened yet. It will, it's in the air, and surely everyone else has noticed. Everyone but us, it seems.

'My lords, ladies and gentlemen, a toast,' Howard says. He stands, and my God you can almost see through him. His white, capped-sleeved T-shirt looks like a sail, he looks like a scarecrow. 'To George, and his woeful music taste!'

They all stand, because Howard's their leader, and they echo 'TO GEORGE!' Even George joins in. No one cares about being ribbed here, they all have their turns being the butt of the joke.

But as Brian sits, Colin – both Colins - notice something. A huge bulge has formed under Brian's Jackson Pollock T-shirt. It inflates like a balloon. Then it bursts. A thin runner of blood slashes across the material. And there's something inside, wriggling, as if he's giving birth.

1984 Colin and 2009 Colin both gape in horror – the bloodstain is widening, deepening and something is poking out at the seams of Brian's T-shirt, something furry – but no one else notices, not even Brian. He opens his mouth to swig down some more lager and an enormous gout of blood is vomited across the table, but no one notices, no one cares, they're young, they're out for a laugh, and who cares that their friend is being ripped apart from inside by something furry, something making wet, awful snuffling noises?

No, someone other than Colin then and Colin now notices. Carol leans to him, closer – so close you couldn't slide a credit card between them (not that any of them had credit cards in 1984) – and she says, 'Brian's having a blood baby.'

It's a terrible phrase, an awful phrase, a meaningless phrase, and 1984 Colin turns to her, silently begging an explanation, but she just shrugs her pretty shoulders as the bulge in Brian's T-shirt finally explodes, showering them all in blood and gore and the thing that was inside him leaps onto the table, and it's a **dog**, dear Jesus a small **dog**, covered in blood and dripping entrails, a wet mass, and it starts tap dancing amid the ashtray and glasses.

'A dog on its hind legs,' smiles Carol, and she starts clapping, then they all join in, even Colin, because despite this monstrous horror he is with his gang, his people, it's 1984, and when one starts something, everyone joins in.

It's the rules.

*

He sat up, afraid he had screamed. One look over at his huddled wife told him he hadn't.

Dear God, Colin thought, rubbing his hands over his head. *Dear God.*

Sleep was over, at least for a while – there was no way he could close his eyes again and risk seeing that puppy, dripping blood and entrails, dancing around on a pub table like Snoopy, flecks of matter spattering his friends as they looked on and clapped – so he gently slid back the duvet and padded downstairs in the chill September dark. He flicked on the living room light and checked his watch. 4.32.

Dear God, he thought for a third time and managed to flop onto the sofa. *What* was *that? What was all* that *about?*

But although the house was dark, silent…an answer bloomed like a light. *Carol, Emma, Howard and the rest of them…all of them, all of us, back in the pub. When we were kids. Jesus, I haven't thought of them for, well, years.*

Except when you might have recognised Emma. On the telly. When you mentioned it to Nicola but not to Helen.

He sat up straight at that. Yeah, that had started something. And after all, hadn't he been talking about it today? Hadn't Nicola brought it up? Of course she had, they'd discussed it before (*before you took her to the pub and kept that from your wife as well*) before they'd talked about her problems.

That must've been what set it off, 'faces from the past.' *Yeah, that's what did it. Still…Jesus! Who'd have thought one little conversation could have brought* that *nightmare up?*

But that's all it was, a nightmare. Everyone had them from time to time, just like everyone has a sex dream or sees themselves scoring the winning goal in the World Cup Final. Dreams and nightmares meant nothing, no matter what Dr Freud might have said. Your brain just vomited something during the night and made you watch. Inconsequential, that was the word.

Yeah, talking about the old days with Nicola just triggered something – an old memory maybe - that popped out of your head in a manner that Edgar Allan Poe might have appreciated. No sweat, forget about it.

You've done a bit too much of that, Colin.

That was an odd thought, and Colin, who had been preparing to go back to bed, sat back and considered it. Yeah, forgetting...he'd forgotten all about his old friends, hadn't he? All the old crew, all the old times. Howard and Brian and George (that wasn't his name though, just something Howard had bestowed upon him, and he'd never, ever had the reason explained), Sophie and Emma. And Carol. Yep, most of all, Carol. *I forgot her,* he marvelled in the silence. *I thought your first love was supposed to live with you forever. Isn't it supposed to be the best love of all? First kiss, first grope, first shag...I mean, weren't they supposed to be indelibly wired into the hard drive of your brain? How could I forget* her? *How could I forget* them? *My people, my crew. What went on? Who gave my brain permission to jettison all that? I never did!*

But permission granted or not, that's just what had happened. He'd forgotten them. He hadn't spared them a thought in...hell, it had been so total a blank he couldn't even recall the last time he'd recalled them, the last time he'd brought them up in conversation, the last time he'd drunk enough bitter to say, 'Oh hey, I remember one time...'

Howard was the boss, he was our leader. Brian was his sidekick. George was the little kid, the one who got into scrapes and had to be rescued. Sophie was the sexy one – and my God, wasn't she just! Emma was the mother, the compassionate one. And Carol? Carol was our moral compass, the one who wasn't quite with the kick and rush of the rest of us. She didn't drink too much. She was never sick in the bushes. She was the one who said 'Now that's enough' when it all got a bit too risqué for her. And yeah, Sophie was the sexy one, no doubt, those oval brown eyes of hers that lazily scanned you up and down and made you just sell your soul for a smile, but Carol...that morality of hers made her so very vulnerable somehow. You felt like you had to protect her. She couldn't seem to see how bad it could get out there. She had the blue eyes of innocence, of honesty, of trust...but trust was dangerous, trust could get you hurt. So we'd looked out for her, made sure she didn't get too upset or offended, made sure nothing trampled over her. And over time, over quite some time, you stopped wanting just to protect her. Oh boy, yes.

And all of this I forgot.

All of this and more.

That was right, that was spot on. There was more he'd forgotten. How they'd met, for a start – it was at college, yes...but what made *them* a crew, and not the hundreds of *other* students? Why had they just blown away like dandelions, never to meet up again. We were everything to each other back then, one for all and all for one. But it just ended. Why? What happened?

Nothing came back to him, nothing at all, so eventually he went back upstairs and climbed back into the warmth of his sleeping wife.

But it was not his wife he thought of in the dark, nor about those long forgotten but now remembered names from his past. He thought of his PA, he thought of Nicola, pressing herself close, asking why she couldn't meet someone like him, telling him not to put himself down, because he was...

What? What was she going to say?

There was so much in his head right now, so much confusion that Colin lay there staring into the dark, listening to Helen's faint snoring, troubled and unhappy.

But also excited.

After an hour or so, he slept.

Chapter Twenty-One

'You in tonight?' Colin asked Helen as she sat next to him at the table. Ahead of them, but dialled so far down the importance scale it might have been invisible, BBC *Breakfast* gave the world cause to be fearful over their cereal.

'I'm afraid so,' she answered after swallowing a mouthful of toast. 'You'll have to put that wild orgy off.'

'It's really short notice, but I suppose I'll have to.' He slugged some tea down his throat and hoped Helen wouldn't notice how forced his early morning badinage was.

'Still, if you're very good, you might get lucky with me.'

'Oh, guh-*ross*!' exclaimed Tasha as she stomped in from the hallway. 'That's five years in Therapy right there.'

'You'll have to pay for it yourself, young lady,' said Helen, 'those dance classes are going to put us in the poorhouse.'

'It'll be worth it when I'm touring with P Diddy.' She plodded into the kitchen. Colin could hear a carton of something or other – fruit juice, most likely – being pulled from the fridge.

'And that will make it all worthwhile,' Helen went on, popping more toast into her mouth. *How many times have I kissed that mouth*, Colin wondered. *How often has it had my tongue or my cock inside it?* 'Watching you mime having intercourse with the Invisible Man behind some unbearably rich black man with a mansion in Beverly Hills who's singing about how hard life is in the ghetto.'

'I can't begin to tell you how many things are wrong in that sentence, so I'm not even going to try.' Tasha slammed the empty glass on the table. 'OK, I'm off. Bye.'

'Hey,' said Helen, indicating the glass, 'put that in the sink.'

Colin opened his mouth to tell her to eat something before she went, but he didn't. Instead he stared at the TV. 'Jesus,' he said. 'Oh dear Jesus.'

'OK, OK,' said Tasha, 'sink it is. God, Dad, don't be such a drama queen.'

But Helen, at least, was looking at her husband. She saw the colour drain from his face – such colour as there was, Colin didn't look like he'd had the best night's sleep ever – and said, 'Hon, what is it? What's wrong?'

Colin couldn't speak. He just pointed wordlessly at the TV screen. A blurred photo of a middle aged man was staring back at them, taken at what looked like some party or other. The newsreader was saying, '...appealing for any witnesses to what Police are calling a particularly brutal murder.' The camera switched to something taped on location, a stretch of park. A square area of grass was staked out with 'CRIME SCENE' tape. A disembodied woman's voice said, 'This is the area of Seaforth where Brian Collins' body was found early yesterday morning. Collins, an advertising executive with his own firm in Southport, was reported missing late the previous night by his wife. It's thought he was on the way to collect his dog which had been lost that afternoon.'

Brian's having a blood baby, Colin thought, and shivered. Dimly he felt Helen's arm on his shoulder, he was aware that Tasha had crowded behind him. Both of them were asking what was wrong, but to Colin they seemed to be in another room down a long, empty corridor.

The picture switched to a telephoto shot of some uniformed officers scouring the scene. 'Police say they have several leads they are investigating, but some people have commented that this is the third brutal murder in the area in the last month that the Police appear to be no closer to solving.'

Then the camera cut to a tall, thin man with a sour, weasel face. He had small, beady eyes. Any milk of human kindness he might have possessed had long since curdled by the look of him. 'Our investigations are ongoing,' he said, as the caption 'Det Insp Michael Walker' appeared under his face. 'We're not, at the moment, at the point where we can make any arrests, but that day isn't far off now.'

'So you'd say you're making good progress on these murders?' the off-camera woman asked.

'We're making progress, certainly,' the copper obfuscated. 'Slow, but steady progress, yes. That's not to say that we wouldn't welcome any help from the public.'

Oh Det Insp Walker, what you do to the English language, Colin found himself thinking. A giggle almost burst from his throat, and he struggled to keep it down. If that came up, so would his breakfast.

The camera was on the woman now, a pretty young Asian. She had the appropriate look of gravitas. 'Police have set up a Hotline number for anyone who has information to contact, or they may call Crimestoppers if they wish.' Two 0800 numbers flashed up on the screen. 'All information will be in the strictest confidence. But for now, all Mr Collins' wife and family have is questions. Questions which they only hope will be answered swiftly.' Another picture, this one horribly familiar to Colin also, the large woman with her family. 'Nor are they the only ones who wait. Emma Fillion and her son Kevin were also murdered eight days ago in brutal fashion; so far no one has even been so much as called in for questioning. Though there has been no official connection between these cases by Police, it's unusual to say the least that two such extreme acts should occur in such a short space of time in such a small area. And then there is this man,' a third picture, a man with thinning blonde hair and glasses. 'Joseph McGovern, 44, murdered and left in a field in Lancashire just over two weeks ago.'

'George,' Colin breathed. 'Fuck. Fuck. George.'

'No Dad,' Tasha corrected. 'Joseph, she called him.'

Colin turned his awful, sick face to her. 'We called him George,' he whispered.

'You knew him?' asked Helen.

'I knew them all,' Colin answered. 'George. Emma. Brian. I knew them all. I just forgot about them till last night. Oh fucking hell.'

Then he could hold it no more, and he collapsed forward. He cried. Great wracking sobs burst from him, each one agony. His family held him as the TV droned on, they held him and they comforted him as best they could.

And part of him – quite a large part – wanted Nicola.

Chapter Twenty-Two

'Yes sir?'

Colin stood at the station desk, mouth dry, almost overwhelmed. *Too much, all too much. Nicola…my friends from the past…*it was as if he'd been stuck on the Waltzers for an hour or two and spun round by a particularly vicious Gypsy. *Last month all I had to worry about was balancing a spreadsheet and finalising a budget, but now…I can't cope…*

'Can I help you sir?' the pretty PC asked again.

'Yes,' he said finally. His mouth was dry and his head was a Magimix, but he managed to speak. 'There've been some murders…I saw, on the telly this morning…' *Look at where the pretty PC has put her hand, Colin. Under the table. Resting on a panic button, you reckon? Get your shit together, son. You're rambling.*

'You have information, sir?' *Any minute now, Colin, a silent alarm will ring, and Regan and Carter will come bursting through that door…*

Colin sucked air through his teeth, held it for a second, then let it out. He smiled as calmly as he could. 'I'm not sure. But I knew the victim, Brian Collins. Also Emma – only I knew her as Emma Richards. And –'

'Joe,' said a voice from the doorway. Colin spun around as quickly as he could, and saw a tall, slightly lopsided figure standing there. Hefty, slightly pop-eyed, all baseball cap and faded jeans. 'We knew Joe as well. Only I called him George. We all did, back in the day.'

Colin gaped at this stranger, who lurched across the Police station foyer towards him like an overwound toy. *Who the blinding fuck is this?*

'Would you gentlemen stay here a minute, please,' said the PC. 'I'll get Detective Walker. Your names are?'

Colin opened his mouth, but the other man spoke first. 'He's Colin. Colin Bryant. And I'm Howard Miller. We were at college together. All of us.' Then, as the PC left the desk and moved into the back room, this overweight man smiled, and Colin saw – yep, that was Howard. Howard with the ghost of an old man overlaid, but Howard. After all this time. Howard.

'Jesus fucking Christ,' breathed Colin.

'*Almost* how I'd put it,' said Howard, 'but not quite. How's it going, Colin?'

Chapter Twenty-Three

Colin had made two phone calls by the time Howard had returned from the bar and placed two bitter shandies before them. The first was to Helen on her mobile. Yes, he'd been to the Police. No, they'd told him nothing. Yes, they were grateful for the little he'd been able to tell them.

'Do they think,' she'd asked, her voice hitching, 'that you're in any...?'

Danger, she was going to say. And what was his answer to be? The truth? Frankly love, they don't look like they've got a clue about what's going on. By the way that rat faced Walker was firing questions about like an epileptic with a machine gun I'd say they considered the entire population of England as either a potential victim or a potential murderer. 'It's doubtful,' he said, carefully. He wanted her aware, but not scared – not until, at least, he knew there was something to be scared about. 'They showed us a picture though,' he went on, 'an e-fit they called it.'

'Us?'

'Sorry love?'

'You said they showed *us*. Who's *us*?'

And for one horrible second, one awful, eternal second, Colin didn't really have an answer. *Who's us? Is us me and you, my old love? Is us me and you and Tasha, our only child? Is us me and the total stranger who has now replaced one of my oldest and dearest friends, who is even as we speak lurching his way to the bar? Or is us me and the young lady I held in my arms yesterday in this very pub? Who's us? Who're you? Who, for that matter, am I?*

But that terrible second passed, the way all seconds – terrible and marvellous alike, pass. 'Another of the old crew turned up at the station – he's been watching the news as well. Howard. We hung around a lot back then.'

'Right,' she said in his ear, but you didn't stay married for twenty years without picking up what was happening. She was dubious. And, sure enough, 'Bit of a coincidence, isn't it?'

'What do you mean?'

'Him turning up at the same time as you. I mean…look, those murders…I'm not saying…'

Howard, he almost laughed. *Howard? Aw c'mon, love – if you knew him…*

But she doesn't *know him. Come to that,* you *don't know him. You did, quarter of a century ago, but have you any idea how much people change, Colin old Colin? He hardly even looks the same –* you *hardly even look the same. Something could have got in, changed him. After all,* someone *appears to be knocking off the class of '84…why* not *him? What if he got himself a good dose of the psychos between then and now? Thanks for that, love. I really needed to be just that bit more scared than I am now.*

'Point taken, hon. I promise you, I'll be careful. But only if you promise it right back, OK?'

'OK.'

'You blow off rehearsal tonight, you hear me? You come straight home. And Tasha, she does the same. I want you all around me tonight.'

'Sure, no worries. Love you, Col.'

'And you hon. Love you loads.'

He hit the red DISCONNECT button on his phone, hesitated, then scrolled through the numbers. *What did you just say to your wife? 'Love you loads,' wasn't it? And do you? Do you love her loads? Of course you do, Colin old lad. After all these years, how could you not? But still...you appear to be calling...*

'Hello,' said Nicola.

'Hi...' there was a second – maybe less - where he could've just rung off. Except he couldn't, not in this wonderful 21st century where everyone's number and name were recorded on screens. She'd know who'd rung. 'It's Colin.'

'Hey,' and her voice in his ear was so sweet, so welcoming, so warm...so young. 'How's things?'

Oh you kid...'Pretty crazy right now. But never mind that, how're you?'

'I'm...OK. Pretty much.' And then she sighed, deep in his ear from miles away. 'I mean, I'll cope.' *Is she thinking about what she said yesterday? Is she thinking about how she held me? Did these things mean anything to her?* 'What's crazy?'

'Hmm?'

'You said stuff was crazy right now. And, by the by, no one says "crazy" anymore.'

'Tell you tomorrow,' he said, catching sight of Howard – or the man who'd replaced Howard, anyway – awkwardly stuffing change into his jeans pocket. 'I just wanted to...' *what, hear your voice?* 'Make sure you were OK. And apologise for leaving you in the lurch again today.'

'So you bloody should, that place is as boring as hell without you.' *Oh, I heard* that *right enough...but what does she* mean *by it?* 'And I'm fine. Thanks. Thanks for caring. That means...well, it means a lot. Thanks.'

For a brief, wonderful, awful moment the memory of their embrace – full body contact – swept over him. In that second, had Nicola been before him he would have pushed her onto the table and had her there and then. *I love my wife. I love my wife.*

'Hey,' she went on, 'can I hear pub noises in the background? Is that what's crazy? Are you back in our pub, developing a drink problem?'

I got no problem with drink, said a long gone voice in his ear. Brian, he thought. Brian the slightly mad, manic one, whose left leg seemed to be constantly twitching. *I just pour it in my mouth and it goes down sweet.* Then, *our pub? Our pub?*

'Yeah, I'm back there. Just catching up with...' *a total stranger who stole the face of an old friend but finds it doesn't fit right.* '...Someone I used to know. Guy called Howard. We were at college together.'

'Well, you two have fun. Enjoy talking about Billy Joel. As if *anyone* can enjoy talking about Billy Joel.'

Joe could...except he wasn't Joe, he was George and nobody ever knew why.

'I'll try my best, sweetheart. See you tomorrow.' Once more, DISCONNECT, and as he pocketed the phone, he shuddered. *Ah Colin...did you hear? Did you hear what you called her? Did you?*

Too much, thought Colin as Howard weaved his way back to the table, two pints of bitter shandy to the good, *too much. Overload warnings on the screen. How am I supposed to be able to cope with all this?*

'What do we drink to?' asked Howard as he wheezed down into the chair. 'Absent friends? Times gone by? The end of Kajagoogoo?'

'To the last, yeah,' said Colin. Then simultaneously they raised their glasses and chinked them. And then burst out laughing.

'We got hit with sticks,' said Howard a couple of minutes later, after that strange almost hysterical fit had passed.

'Say what?' Colin replied, then almost boggled. *Say what? When did you last utter 'say what?' The 1984 way of asking someone to repeat themselves.*

'What I said,' exhaled Howard, and yep, there he was underneath the unhealthy, sallow skin and the Marty Feldman eyes, the teenager he'd once been. 'Is that someone got the sticks out and gave us a good whacking. Me, I got the Shit Thyroid stick. Got whopped with it 'bout six years ago. Mr Thyroid took a look around him, weighed up his job, decided he didn't like it much and fucked off, leaving me with a figure that makes me look like the Staypuft Marshmallow Man.'

'Hey,' said Colin, the way you do to strangers, 'you don't look so – '

Howard cut him off. 'Colin, I look like fucking shit. You know it, I know it, my wife knows it, my cat knows it, total strangers know it. As yet undiscovered tribes in the Amazon know it.'

They laughed again at that. *As yet undiscovered tribes...*Colin thought. *He used to use that all the time. Pilfered it from somewhere, I remember that, but Christ how it used to make us laugh.* But under that laugh there was a deep, despairing sadness, the sound of a clunking coffin lid. *It's here, in front of me. Mortality. We're not teenagers anymore and we never will be again. All we have left is the inevitable race to our own deaths.*

'You,' Howard went on after sipping more John Smith's, 'got hit with the Middle-Aged Businessman stick. OK, so there are worse sticks you can get hit with – the Cancer stick, for instance, will never be beaten – but *man,* you took a walloping. What are you? Accountant? Insurance?'

'A banker,' said Colin, and – of course – they laughed at that. 'A *corporate* banker. You?'

'Nothing, at least not anymore. I was a teacher – History was my chosen specialised subject, Magnus – but when Mr Thyroid decided to hand in his notice I got stuck on the disability train. These days I can quote chapter and verse on the ITV4 schedules. Not to mention exactly when you can catch a *Top Gear* repeat on Dave.'

'Hey, I'm sorry,' said Colin.

'There's worse things,' answered Howard. 'Like finding out someone's killing all your old mates.'

'Yeah,' said Colin. 'There's that.'

And once more, they burst out laughing.

'So, Mr Corporate, what the fuck do *you* think is going on?'

That strange fugue had passed – but had it, really? Weren't *all* his days strange fugues now? 'Don't have a clue. I mean – and try not to take this the wrong way Howard, but I hadn't thought about you guys in a Trojan's age. And now, bang -'

'Hey, don't sweat it. It was a couple of decades and change ago. Who really wants to carry their past around?'

'Yeah, but…we were solid, weren't we? We were a gang.'

'No man, we were a *crew*. That was Brian, remember? Never a gang, always a crew. And yeah, we were tight, we were solid…but we were young. Teenagers, hadn't even lived two whole decades. We grew up, we moved on – like Freddy Mercury sang, we got mortgages and homes. Me, I got sickness in the bones. It happens.'

'Yeah,' said Colin, 'that makes sense. But Howard, it all just *went*. All my memories of us. Blew away like a kite. How? Why?'

'Hang on, let's try my telepathy,' said Howard, furrowing his brow. Then he relaxed again. 'Nope, that must've got fucked along with my thyroid. Pity. Look,' he went on, 'it'd be unhealthy it if *didn't* happen. Growth is what we humans – and I'm assuming you count on this score – are all about. Dragging your past with you? *Unhealthy*, man.'

'But just to *forget* everything...c'mon, that's not right.'

'Maybe, maybe not. Who can tell? *I* didn't forget us, I just didn't think about us. Maybe if I heard an old song or took a drive past the Tech something would pop up. But we were all nineteen, mate. Your last year of being a kid, isn't it? We were all off to universities or jobs – if you could get one. We had one final blowout that summer then all shook hands politely and got on with the business of living. You keep in touch with anyone?'

Colin shook his head. 'You?'

'No. And you guys, all of you, were great. But we didn't exchange numbers or arrange to meet up for a reunion. OK it was harder in those days – no social networking – but we *could've* made the effort. We didn't.'

'Why? Why, do you think?' This was very, very important to Colin.

'Maybe...maybe because somehow, on some level, we knew that time was special, that it was right, that it was some never-to-be-repeated offer. Maybe because we knew it could never be recreated. Same reason The Beatles never reformed, what d'you reckon?'

Colin gave it some thought as he sipped his pint...damning himself for the faint tingle of suspicion that ran across his brain. *What if he's poisoned this?* 'I suppose you could be right.' Then, angry, 'there's just *so much I can't remember!*'

There was a silence then, broken only by the sound of the fruit machine and the low babble of conversation around them.

Finally, Howard said, 'And now out the blue someone appears to be lining us up and knocking us down, and I don't mind telling you, man, I'm fucking terrified.'

'To quote my daughter, I passed terrified three exits back. I mean, why? What did we do to deserve this? I mean, we didn't do anything bad, did we?'

'Not unless you count Joe putting *The Longest Time* on that video juke nine million times a night – which frankly *was* a crime – but enough to wipe us out one by one? Doubtful.' Howard leaned forward then, slack faced, skin yellowish as if his liver was about to follow his thyroid into oblivion, and Colin could see how scared he was. 'We were *nothing*, Colin. Just a crew of kids. We drank a bit and laughed a bit and screwed about a bit – hell, you should know more about that than any of us, you lucky bastard – but *bad?* No. We didn't murder a hitchhiker and bury his body in a wood. But someone's killing us and there's *no fucking point to it!* And you know what scares me the most? That fucking copper *knows* there's no point to it. And he's got no suspects. *None at all.* You, me…Carol and Sophie, wherever they are…we are liable to be in a whole world of pain soon. And I don't think anyone's got a way to stop it.'

'Fuck,' said Colin.

'Fuck II, The Adventure Continues,' agreed Howard.

Once more, they burst out laughing.

A question bubble burst in Colin's head. *What do you mean, 'you should know, you lucky bastard?'* He was about to ask it when Howard's mobile rang.

'There's not much I miss about my youth,' said Howard, scrabbling in his jacket pocket, 'but one thing I could go back to quite easily – along with being able to run up stairs – is being uncontactable. You can't go fucking nowhere these days without people on your case.' Then he flipped open a prehistoric Nokia and said 'Hi honey.'

Colin turned down Howard's conversation and tried to focus. He found he couldn't. *Too much,* he thought again. *Too Goddam* much. *Ghosts from my past, crowding my head. And we're in danger, a whole world of hurt. Me. Colin Bryant. A nobody, a zero, a fucking Corporate Banker, a survivor from the days where no one had a mobile phone, when VHS was still a luxury, when dinosaurs and Thatcher ruled the Earth. And I'm* in danger. *Jesus – why? Why me? Why us?*

Howard muttered, 'Yeah babe, on my way. Love you,' and snapped the phone closed. 'The missus wants me back, and I can't say I blame her.' He stood, painfully, slowly. 'Listen man,' he said, and his eyes were suddenly glistening. 'It's been good to see you again. Maybe…maybe we should get together again? Safety in numbers, get me?'

Thing is, man…*you may be a killer for all I know.* Instead he said, 'Yeah. That sounds like a plan.' He stood and extended his hand. 'Good to see you Howard.'

'Fuck that shit,' said Howard and clumsily embraced Colin around the table…and for one terrible, hateful second Colin found himself braced and awkward, expecting a knife thrust.

But there was nothing, so instead they made their way outside.

'Let me give you my number,' said Howard. 'Keep in touch. We have to. 'Cause this shit is *real.*'

'Yeah. It is. I'll get a pen.'

So Colin reached into his pocket and missed seeing the battered and screeching Chevrolet as it mounted the kerb and drove straight at them. Howard saw it though. He saw it and pushed Colin away. Colin fell to the floor and smashed his elbow. A shaft of white pain ran up his arm. *Howard*, he thought.

Howard couldn't move fast enough. His body was too fat, his legs too underpowered. The Chevy hit him at over forty miles an hour and he bounced over the bonnet, over the roof, and hit the ground with a wet *smeck!* sound that Colin never forgot.

The Chevy never slowed. It turned off the pavement and swerved back into the road. Then it turned a corner and was gone.

Somewhere, someone was screaming. As Colin lay on the ground staring at the dead body of an old friend he'd shared one last drink with, he realised it was him.

Chapter Twenty-Four

'Take a good, hard look,' said Walker, with all the sympathy and compassion of a man who'd no idea what the words *sympathy* and *compassion* meant. 'Was this person driving the car?'

'I didn't see,' said Colin, hands shaking as he once again held the e-fit. Even if he had seen, that thing would've been no use to him. Like all of those damned things he'd seen on *Crimewatch* it bore the closest resemblance to Christopher Lee as the Frankenstein Monster.

Walker snatched it back impatiently. He then thrust it towards Helen. 'Have you seen this person hanging around recently?'

For a minute, Helen didn't look at it. She just stared at her husband, as if expecting him to jump up and shout *April Fool!* Then she'd laugh, hit him in the ribs, and express her relief that this *wasn't* actually happening, that there *weren't* two Police officers in their front room, asking questions as they drank the coffee she'd made, that she, her husband and daughter *weren't* being asked to identify 'a suspect,' that her husband *hadn't* seen an old friend knocked down and killed in the street like a dog.

Colin saw all that in her eyes – they'd known each other so long he could read every flicker and expression in them – and, if it were possible, he'd have driven that fear away. *That's what you do when you love someone. You drive their fear away.* But he couldn't. This was all horribly real.

Eventually, she looked at the page, went to shake her head in negation, then looked again. She frowned a bit. Then the frown went away and she handed it back. 'No.'

'You sure?' asked Walker. 'You had to look twice.'

'I wanted to be certain. No, could be anyone.'

Colin saw Walker tense. *If he could ram that paper down her throat right now, he would. He's a man with a whole heap o' nothings being pressed for a resolution. And it looks like he doesn't take pressure well. Way to go for finding the right job, man.*

That thought almost made him burst into tears. It was such a *Howard* thing to say.

Walker snapped his gaze back to Tasha. 'Told you before,' she said, 'never seen him.'

'And I told *you* before,' said Walker, on the last page of his self-control manual. 'We believe it's a woman.'

'Really,' said Tasha. Then muttered, 'What a moose,' under her breath.

Walker actually sat up at that, and for one more horrible second in a life that suddenly seemed crammed with horrible seconds, Colin thought there was going to be a fight in his living room. But then the other copper – God alone knew what his name was – coughed quietly into his hand, and Walker somehow managed to settle himself. 'If she is, as you say, a "moose" then hopefully she'll be more identifiable. But for the moment, she appears to be our only lead. Someone fitting this description was seen accompanying Mr McGovern from a lapdancing club in Liverpool on the night before his body was discovered. Someone *also* fitting this description bought a second hand van from a ratboy...' another cough from the Anonymous Copper, this time ignored, 'in Bootle the day before Mr Collins' body was discovered. Said van was found burned out and abandoned two miles from the scene. At the moment we're searching for the Chevrolet Lacetti that ran over Mr Miller, but I've few hopes that even if we do it'll tell us anything. This person, whoever is committing these murders, is clever and sadistic. This,' he said, waving the piece of paper like Chamberlain coming back from Munich, 'is the *closest* thing we have to a clue. And it's fucking *nothing*.'

This time Detective No Name didn't bother with the cough. 'Mike,' he said. *Shut up* was the subtext.

'No,' said Walker. 'Bollocks to it all. We've got a psycho on the loose – a very clever and cunning psycho – who appears to be working his/her/its way round a group of people who knew each other twenty-five years ago, and we've got fucking *nothing*, so it's time to stop arseing about and get serious.' He turned back to Colin, his eyes wide and furious. 'Let me tell you *exactly* how your friends were killed, just so you get an idea of what we're up against. Mr McGovern's heart was hacked out.'

George is just heartless, thought Colin, and turned cold.

'Mrs Fillion was choked to death with a bag of frozen peas, and her son had his brains battered in. Both of them had their eyes gouged out post-mortem.'

Eyes are bigger than her belly. Colin went colder.

'Mr Collins' was the most elaborate,' Walker ranted on, remorseless. 'His dog went missing on a walk. Mr Collins was distraught; according to his wife he loved that animal. Phone rang in the night – traced to a call box in Litherland – voice says "I've found your dog, got the number from the collar, come and get him." So he does. Last time he's seen. Didn't tell his wife where he was going, just "someone's found Sparky!" Next time we see him, he's gutted like a sea bass and the dead dog's stuffed in his chest cavity.'

Brian's having a blood baby. Colin shivered, his teeth chattered. 'Jesus,' he heard Helen mutter.

'But this other bloke,' said Tasha, 'what was his name, Dad? Howard?' Colin nodded. 'Bit of a switch, wasn't it? He was just run down in the street.'

'Yeah,' said Walker, so clearly wanting to kill Tasha right there and then. 'And the only one in broad daylight. Which we think means whoever is getting bolder. They maybe don't need to be so fucking clever anymore.'

'Would you mind not swearing so much,' said Helen, quietly. 'We try not to use language like that in front of our daughter.'

Walker's right fist balled up. *He is two seconds away from self-destruction, he has absolutely nothing left.* 'Of course, Mrs Bryant. I'm sure your daughter has never encountered such talk before.' Then, before Helen could respond – and she had a temper on her when pushed – Walker was back to Colin. 'From what you said earlier today, there are now just the three of you from that old gang left, yes? You, Carol Smith and Sophie Brown.'

'Yes.'

'And you've no idea of their whereabouts?'

'None whatsoever,' said Colin, slightly nonplussed.

'No contact through Facebook or Friends Reunited, anything like that?'

'No. None.' *And I'd never even thought about it. But then, I never thought about* them, *did* ?

'OK, great,' said Walker, sighing. 'We got a Smith and a Brown – except that won't be their names any more – a rough year of birth and the fact you all attended Southport Technical College in 1984. Should be a piece of piss, this.' Then he stood up, and strode to the door without so much as a *thanks for the coffee.* The other copper stood still for a second, as if to apologise, then just walked silently after him.

There was a very long pause. Colin felt Helen and Tasha looking at him. He wanted to say something reassuring. But he couldn't.

It was Tasha who broke the silence, with one of her rare jokes. 'Do you think he kept the receipt from the charm school? He's going to need a refund.'

Chapter Twenty-Five

Today was a special day. Today was Bounce's birthday.

Louise had all the toys lined up – the whole family – on the edge of her bed. They were Bounce's guard of honour. As she led Bounce to the front, making him nod his appreciation, all of the other toys clapped and cheered. Tigger did an extra special series of – well, bounces.

That's because Bounce was the Biggest Toy of them all, the oldest and the most revered. When other toys had arrived into the family, they all had to pay deference to Bounce. He would welcome them with a smile and a paternal handshake, he would inform them of the rules, gently but firmly, and then receive them to the fold.

He was loved by all. Pooh virtually *worshipped* Bounce. Even Tigger and Basil – the cheekiest of the family – were silent and respectful whenever Bounce was around.

In truth, Bounce didn't make too many public appearances these days. He was eighteen today, and eighteen was old for a bear. His fur was worn smooth from all the hugging he'd received, and in some places his skin was patched. Many, many years ago, he'd had an accident and lost an eye. He'd received a button transplant, and though he said he could see quite well enough out of it, thank you, Louise knew it troubled him somewhat and it could hurt on a rainy day.

These days, Bounce mostly sat on a shelf, away from the other toys, looking down in a stern but loving fashion. He would allow for the energies and eccentricities of youth, but when the others went too far, he would step in with a word or two of admonition. He wasn't the Supreme Voice of Authority – that would be Louise herself, not even Bounce outranked *her* - but usually a gentle growl from him was enough to keep the others in line.

Louise loved all her family equally. Oh, sometimes she loved Polly best, because Polly was sensible – if occasionally a little greedy. Sometimes she loved Pooh best, because he was so caring. At other times, Basil and Tigger's relentless good energy and downright naughtiness made her love them best (even if they could be a little wearing) but she genuinely loved them all the same.

Except for Bounce, because she loved Bounce the best, because Bounce was the first.

Sometimes she felt a little bit guilty for that. She knew that, really, it was wrong to have favourites. But then she remembered one of her conversations with Mum, after lights out, in her bedroom, when Mum had said, 'You always love your first the best of all. Maybe you shouldn't, but you can't help it. Maybe it's wrong, but you're powerless. The first is what matters the most. First go on the swings, first drink, first child, first love…' (at that point, her Mum had gone all far-away looking) 'doesn't matter. It's something you can't recapture, you see. Yes, you can go on the swings again, and you can love it every time, yes you can have lots of children if you like, and you will love them all, but you can't re-create the first time, can you? That's what makes the first so special. You may never remember the *ninth* time you rode a bike without stabilisers, but you'll always remember the first. And I want you to never, *ever* forget that. That's why, no matter how many children your Dad and I have, you'll always be my special one, because you were the first.'

Had Louise glowed at that? Oh yes, she had! No matter who else was to enter the house, no matter who else would fill the nights with cries or fill their nappies with poo, she, Louise, would always be special, the best, the most loved.

But there had *never* been anyone to share the house with, had there? Just her and Dad and Mum. After Dad had gone to Heaven, there'd been only Mum. So Louise had *always* been special – just like Bounce.

All the other toys stopped applauding – even Tigger settled down. Bounce bowed low (as low as he could with his aching back) and the others bowed in return. Then Bounce looked at Louise and asked, 'Why did you change your routine with the last one?'

Polly gasped a little. Polly was easily shocked. But Louise was not in the least put out – the question hadn't been impertinent, just curious. 'Because I had an opportunity, dear. I had to think quickly. And it was only Howard, Bounce my love. And he wasn't really important, you know.'

Bounce nodded, thinking it over. Then, frowning, 'But I thought he was their leader – the oldest?'

'Certainly *he* thought that,' Louise replied, gently. 'But he wasn't. He proposed nothing in the sight of God. He had a big head and a bigger ego – he thought all the girlies loved him. Oh, Emma the Heffalump did, but again – what did *she* matter? The ones who mattered didn't look *twice* at him. They loved the only man left. And *he* certainly loved them, didn't he? So Howard wasn't worth any effort. It's the others who will suffer big. Oh, and when we get the last of them, Bounce...oh, what a party *that* will be! The like of which you will have *never* seen! Not even in *your* long life!'

At that, Bounce let out a growly cheer – old as he was, he still had a mighty roar at times – and all the other toys joined in. And they had a special birthday tea for their king – with fairy cakes and Jelly Tots and even ice cream!

Louise was never happier than with her family. The plotting was fun, and the killing was *great,* but she loved her children with all her heart.

Chapter Twenty-Six

It was eleven thirty, and both his wife and daughter were asleep above his head. He knew they were, because (a) he'd just looked in on them and (b) he'd ground an antihistamine each into their cocoa. It had taken some persuasion to get them to drink the cocoa in the first place (and Colin knew damn well that Helen knew damn well what he was up to, oh how they knew each other!) but finally they'd acquiesced and now Colin was sitting in his own front room, scared and twitchy.

Nothing about this makes sense. Nothing about this comes within a country mile *of sense. Like poor bastard Howard was saying,* what *were we? Kids, just kids, a crew who blew together for a few short months a quarter of a century ago, then blew apart, never bothering to keep in touch. We just...had fun.*

You certainly did, you lucky bastard, said Howard's voice in his memory.

So you say, but what do you mean? Yeah, OK, I've got it now – Carol and I, we did go out for a while. And we had good times – but...

Colin sat up then, suddenly remembering his past. Yes, he had gone out with Carol – he'd asked her out one day, magnificently casually (after a shared History class, as he recalled). 'Hey, listen Carol,' he'd said, as if his heart wasn't pounding. 'How's about, one night, you and I go out for a drink, eh? Just the two of us, without the rest?'

She'd blushed a little (had she, or was he inventing that part?), looked at the floor, (really?) then said, 'I'd like that, yes,' and he'd taken her hand (maybe) as they'd walked the corridor...and that had been it, they'd been a couple, they'd been boyfriend and girlfriend.

Sort of. For the truth of Carol, apart from her raven black hair and enormous blue eyes, was that she was Not That Kind of Girl.

. Yeah, that was the truth of it, Colin thought. *She wasn't. And we all kind've knew that, didn't we? There was a certain…prudishness about her. Not in a nasty way, not a scolding, disapproving Old Maidish way…she'd just been brought up to believe she should go to her marriage bed a virgin. And you know what, we didn't care, none of us – hell, we loved her more for that, didn't we? It made her…special, particularly in the (just) pre-AIDS eighties.*

'Yeah, we went out,' he said to the empty room, 'and we snogged, and there was a fair amount of what we used to call "heavy petting"…but sex? No. I think I got a handjob once or twice…and I'm sure the way she used to rub herself against me would finish *her* off at times…but sex? No. So why call me a "lucky bastard", Howie? I'm sure you got up to much, much worse.'

The mention – out loud – of his old friend, a man he'd caught up with for maybe an hour, who had died right before his eyes, caused him to tear up. *Maybe I should grind up a few antihistamines myself and mix up a batch of Cadbury's Drinking Chocolate,* he thought, but then answered himself with a *fuck that, there's a bottle of whisky in the cupboard and I need to get* seriously *pissed.*

Just as he thought that, his mobile rang. He fished it from his jeans' pocket, and there was a name on the screen. NICOLA MOB CALLING it said.

Feeling insanely guilty (why? He'd done nothing wrong, had he? Ever?) he hit the green button. 'Hi,' he said.

'Hi yourself,' said his young and beautiful PA in his ear. 'Thank God you answered. You OK to talk?' *Is your wife listening, that's what she means. No, she can't mean that. That'd imply something secret, and we have no secrets. Well, none that count.*

'Yeah.'

'Good. It's just…I saw the News. Bloke called Howard got run over in town. Police don't deny it's linked to those other murders…and you said…'

'That I was drinking with an old mate called Howard. Yeah. It was him. I was next to him when it happened.'

'You're fucking *joking!*' Colin jerked the phone from his ear. 'Jesus! You OK, hon?'

You heard that, Colin. You heard what she called you. 'Yeah, physically. Got a sore arm from where he…pushed me out of the way, but…'

'What do you mean?'

The whole thing flashed again in front of him – like it would do forever. The car, screaming towards them. Howard shoving him. The horrible, damp sound as he hit the pavement.

Suddenly Colin wanted very much to vomit. Vomit, and hold his PA very, very close. *And your wife asleep upstairs…*

'The car would have hit us both, but Howie…he saw it first. He saved my life. Poor bastard.'

There was a pause, then; 'I'm glad,' she said, low. 'I mean, I'm sorry for your mate, but I didn't know him. I know *you* though, and I…' The line went silent.

'Nic? You there?'

'I don't want anything to happen to you, that's all.'

This time Colin went quiet. *What does she mean by that? Nothing, other than you get on. Nothing, other than you're her boss and she looks upon you as a father figure. I mean, she never mentions her Dad, does she? Mum, sure. But Dad? Nope. So you're her surrogate. That's how it is. That, and nothing more.*

Which is why she calls me 'hon,' presumably.

'Thank you, neither do I. Listen, I may be taking some time off – I'll have to square it with the Big Boys but I think it'll be OK. There's just no way I can concentrate with…all this, you know?'

'Course you can't. And don't worry, I can cope without you. Just. I'll miss you though.' *Please stop, I can't deal with this confusion on top of everything else. Please* don't *stop. If nothing else, it distracts me.* 'Is it all right for me to call, see how you are?'

Is it? 'Of course you can. I'd like that.'

'Then I will. Take it easy, Col. G'night, babe.' With that, the phone was dead. *G'night babe,* she'd said.

A terrible wave of the shivers ran through him. *G'night, babe.*

Oh God, he wanted to hear her say that again. In person.

G'night, babe.

'Jesus. Jesus fucking Christ.'

The day really did catch up with him then, and he made it to the sink in time to see a thin line of gruel eject from his throat. As he washed his face, he felt his phone vibrate. A text message. From Nicole. STAY SAFE MY LOVE it said. With a kiss.

Hon. Babe. My love. My God, what am I to do?

Chapter Twenty-Seven

He was no wiser in the morning – unsurprising, really, as he'd managed no more than maybe an hour's awful, tortured sleep. Every time he closed his eyes, he saw his old friend bounce across a car bonnet, or hear Walker's strangled tone of bitterness and rage say *choked on a bag of frozen peas…eyes gouged out…gutted like a sea bass.*

This cannot be happening he thought over and over. *It's impossible. Shit like this does not happen to real people. Shit like this only happens to made up characters on TV. We* can't *be going through it. We* can't.

Only it appeared they were.

The closest thing to a plan his tired, abject mind would concoct occurred while he was in the shower; he would keep his family locked away in their house until such time as Walker rang him with the words, 'We've got the mad bastard locked up in a cell, and we're working him over with the rubber hoses.' He put it to his family as they sat at the kitchen table, not eating breakfast. Helen seemed OK with it, but Tasha...

'Dad, I just *can't* stay here for God knows how long,' she said. If she'd been standing instead of sitting at one of the stools she'd have stamped her foot. 'I've got essays to do, classes, and my dance...'

'And your Mum and I have work,' said Colin, trying not to snap at her. It was hard, he was tired and stressed, but he managed it. Just. 'But we're calling in sick for as long as we can swing it.'

'You heard the policeman, love,' chipped in Helen.

'Fascist pig,' muttered Tasha, and horribly Colin almost laughed. *Fascist pig. How eighties.*

'He wasn't my favourite person either,' said Helen. 'But this is real. If it wasn't for that man Howard...' She caught a breath, then steadied herself, 'then we could have lost your Dad yesterday.'

There was a silence, then a large tear dropped down Tasha's cheek. She hopped down from her stool and ran to Colin, hugging him so tight he thought he might suffocate. Then Helen started crying too, and *she* hugged him.

My God, thought Colin, as it truly, really struck him. *I could have died. I could have died.* I could have died. *Nobody leaves my sight. Nobody. I will keep them safe. I will keep them safe.*

Chapter Twenty-Eight

All of her family – even Bounce – cowered in the corner. Pooh had his paws over his eyes and Tigger was nearly crying. Only Basil tracked her movements – back and forth, back and forth - his bright, alert eyes ready for any sign she might turn on them. She never had, ever...but then they'd never seen her like this.

'Cancer!' Louise screamed. 'Fucking *cancer!* How *dare* she? *How dare she??* I hope the bitch *suffered.* I hope she suffered *plenty!* I hope she fucking *screamed* as it ate her up, the *fucking whoring bitch!'* Then she stopped as a sudden, very warm thought occurred to her. 'Of course, *that's* what did it!' She smiled, her storm over like the flick of a switch. 'Ovarian cancer, that's what her husband said. Ovarian cancer...which is often caused by *promiscuous sexual activity at an early age!* Yes. *Yes!* It all makes *sense!* She fucked and she fucked and got *cancer* for it, the fucking *whore!'* Louise sank down on her knees, and looked to the ceiling. 'See? Yeah, I didn't get to kill her, but the cancer did it for me – the *whore cunt cancer!* The cancer she probably got from *him! I* didn't have to kill her, Mum – *he* did! He did it *for* us!'

Then she started to laugh. It was, oddly, a very pretty laugh. High, light and infectious. Even the toys weren't immune. Basil, of course, started first, because he had the loudest laugh of any of them. Then Polly. Pooh uncovered his eyes and goggled about him, then started to chuckle. Even Tigger stopped wanting to cry and joined in. Finally, Bounce bounced from the shelf with a mighty growl.

'Oh loves,' said Louise. She crossed to them, still on her knees, like that Frog painter with the beard. 'I'm sorry, Mummy's sorry. Mummy got angry at someone – not at you, not at *any* of you, just someone. She died before I could kill them, and that made me frustrated – like when you can't get that last jar of honey from the shelf, Pooh. You understand?' Pooh nodded. He thought about it first, obviously, but he nodded. 'It's OK now,' she went on. 'There's still one more. One last one. The worst of them all. And boys and girls...we are going to enjoy this more than we've enjoyed any of them. Mummy's going to put on a *special* show.'

Chapter Twenty-Nine

'Is that Mr Colin Bryant?' said the lady on the phone.

If you're about to tell me I can save ten pounds on my car insurance I shall hunt you down and fucking kill you. 'Yes?'

'WPC Belding here from Southport Police Station, sir,' she went on. 'We're holding a suspect in connection with a series of related...events to which you may be connected.'

Colin felt his heart speed up. It had been two days since he'd enforced house arrest on his family and, if truth be told, things were growing pretty fractious. The tension, the not knowing, the constant jumping at every phone call and knock (the first time the postman had dropped a bank statement and flyer for Sky TV through his door had triggered a wave of hysteria he *never* wanted to see repeated) not to mention the imposed proximity had caused them to circle each other like wary panthers. *And we all love each other*, he'd thought. *Imagine if we didn't.*

'Oh yes?' *Could it be that this nightmare was over so soon?* Could *it? Please God.*

Things hadn't really been helped by Nicola's texting. She hadn't done it often, but it was the…well, tone (if texts could be said to *have* a tone) that had been the issue. HOPE YOU'RE ALL OK, MISS YOU COLIN. Or CAN'T STOP THINKING ABOUT YOU (not 'you all,' 'you') HOPE YOU'RE SAFE. Or I COULDN'T COPE IF SOMETHING HAPPENED TO YOU. Maybe - no, surely he was reading too much into them – but still, they weren't messages he was comfortable showing to Helen. 'Who's that,' she'd ask every time he received one, and he'd had to fob it off with an *oh, just my PA, something she can't deal with* and a raise of the eyes, as he sent back a reply. Innocent stuff. Really, what was incriminating about MISS YOU TOO?

'Yes sir. We'd like you to come down to the station and view the suspect through the two way glass and see if this in any way jogs your memory of the person who was driving the car during the RTA a few days back.'

'Well…' said Colin, torn. 'I don't really want to leave my family…I mean, just in case.'

'I appreciate that sir, and completely understand. However, for your protection we have stationed an unmarked car in your street for the duration of this investigation. There have been two trained officers maintaining surveillance round the clock. They will maintain this scrutiny during your stay at the station, which should be not in excess of half an hour. And your presence here could expedite matters.'

Of course – police protection! Of course they'll have set that up. And probably a tap on the phone as well. OK, so maybe we should have been told, but that dick Walker didn't look like he had 'people skills' as the first line of his CV. 'Yes, of course then. As long as my family will be watched, then yes. I'd like to get this over and done with.'

'Of course you would sir, as would we. Shall we see you in an hour? Ask for me, WPC Belding, at the front desk. I'll escort you through.'

'Yes, an hour. Fine. And thank you.'

'No problem at all, sir,' said the woman, and hung up.

Colin did likewise, and turned to see Helen and Tasha staring at him. 'Police,' said Colin, and he saw the way their shoulders tensed. 'They think they've got a suspect, they want me to go to the station, see if I recognise them.'

Tasha's eyes widened. 'Dad, you can't,' she said. 'You *can't* leave us! What if something happens to you?'

'Hon,' said Colin, and hugged her. 'This may be all over in a couple of hour's time. It may not, but it could be. All I'm going to do is drive to the station in Southport and back. I'll be in my car for most of it and surrounded by fascist pigs the rest.' He'd expected a giggle at that, but it didn't arrive. Maybe no surprise, all things considered. 'And you two will be safe – did you know they've had a couple of coppers sat outside the whole time?'

'No,' said Helen, ever so slightly pissed off. 'You'd have thought they'd have told us.'

'My thoughts exactly, but they didn't. Anyway, I know you two will be safe, that's all that counts. So I'll…'

He got no further, as the phone rang again. 'Hello,' he said into the receiver.

'Hello,' said a young girl's voice, 'could I speak to Helen Bryant, please?'

'Yes, of course,' said Colin, and held the receiver out. 'For you,' he said.

He led Tasha into the living room, leaving Helen some privacy after hearing her say, 'Hello?' Then warmly, 'Oh, *hi* Louise!'

'Do you have to go Dad?' Tasha begged. She looked very young.

'No,' he said. Reluctantly, but he said it. Honesty was his preferred tactic at all times...well, nearly. Excepting calls/texts/drinks with his PA, but they didn't count. 'But if I do, it might speed things up. *Expedite matters,* as they said on the phone. And...oh face it, love. We can't go on living in each other's pockets, can we?'

'S'ppose not,' she mumbled, looking at the floor.

'You're a good girl, Tash,' said Colin, and his daughter smiled a little at that. 'I do love you, you know. You'll be safe here, and I'll look after myself. I promise. And I also promise that when all this is over you can take my Billy Joel and Bruce Springsteen CDs and burn them in the garden.'

That tiny smile almost widened. 'You promise?'

'Cross my heart,' he said. He found he meant it. He really had fallen out of love with his past over the last few days.

Helen joined them, closing the door behind her. 'That was Louise,' she said. Then, at the blank stares that met her, 'the new girl in *Dangerous Corner.* Wondered why I hadn't been at the last couple of rehearsals.'

'What did you say?' asked Colin.

'Some crap about being under the weather. She asked if it was OK to come over so I could hear her lines – said it probably would be.'

Colin sucked air through his teeth. 'Well, I'm not sure...'

'Oh come on, if it's safe enough for you to leave us, then it's safe enough for a young kid to come around here and read aloud. *Plus* she's only about six stone soaking wet, *plus* there'll be me and Tasha here, *plus* the two boys in blue across the road, *plus* I know her and she's all right.'

Colin looked her full in the face, and once more was struck by the telepathy that long time marrieds grew. *Plus I'm tired and scared and for just a little while I want to forget about all this shit, make tea, have a gossip and recite some JB Priestley, how's that?*

'Yeah, sure. Be careful though, won't you?'

'I will. But if you'd ever *seen* Louise...'

Colin kissed her, then made his way to the front door. 'Here I go then. When she knocks,' he said to Helen, 'make sure it's her and *only her* before you open the door.' Then he widened his gaze. 'Take care of each other. I'll be back in two hours, maximum.'

The women in his life – two of them, anyway – nodded back, said their goodbyes, and he closed the door behind him and stepped into the sunlight. Momentary agoraphobia engulfed him – it was terrifying to think how small his world had become in just forty-eight short hours – but then he sucked it up and made his way to the car.

Just before he climbed inside, he had a quick scan to see if he could spot the protection. There was a car – a Vauxhall Vectra by the looks of it - parked at the bottom of the road that looked like it had someone in it, but he couldn't be sure. Then again, these guys were trained to be – what was the word? – 'covert,' weren't they? Attracting attention wasn't in their brief. *The policewoman told me they'd be there, so they are there, that's enough for me,* he thought.

Then he started the engine and drove off.

Chapter Thirty

He'd driven no more than five yards when he felt his phone vibrate, making him panic. *God, something's happened*, he thought as he pulled over. *That mad bastard's knocking the door down and Helen's calling for me to help and I should never have left them –*

But that thought cut off abruptly when he saw the screen. NICOLA MOB CALLING, it said. 'Hi,' he said.

'Hey you,' she said in his ear. No, that panic was gone now, and in its place was something much worse. Just those two words, low and whispered into his ear, were enough. *Why can't I help this? Why?* 'How're things?' Then, more quickly, 'Are you OK to talk?'

Why does she ask that? Why does she think I need to keep this from Helen? She's my PA, it's natural she should ring from time to time...isn't it? Y'know, work related stuff? 'Yeah, fine. Not for long though, I'm on my way to the police station in Southport.'

'What's up?' Definite urgency and concern in her voice. 'Is everything OK?'

But she never used to ring me about work related stuff. She never used to ring me at all. Or text. Or anything. *And if they were all so perfectly innocent, why have I never told Helen?*

'We're all fine,' he said, hating himself for wanting to hold her, to put his arms around her while he said that; to comfort her the way he'd comforted her over her cheating boyfriend. But that hating didn't make the desire go away. 'The police may have a suspect, they want me to give him the once over, see if I can identify him.'

'Oh, thank God,' she breathed. 'Thank God. Please, *please* let it be him. Please God you can put all this behind you and get back to work.' That other voice, low, breathy, secret. 'I really miss having you, Colin.' Then her voice sped up, embarrassed. '*Here.* Having you *here* – y'know, about the place. It's like, dull, without you. Is what I mean.'

Is it? Is it really? Do you remember the way we held each other? Do you remember that look in your eyes – the one that I know was in mine, too. Do you remember what you said? Oh, Nicola – this is dangerous. Too dangerous. For both of us. Your Freudian slips are showing and I'm sat here developing a semi while not twenty feet away my wife and daughter are cowering in fear. This can't go on. It just can't.

Trouble is, I don't want it to stop.

'Yeah,' he said. 'Must be a bitch having to actually do something for a change. Look, sooner or later things will be back to normal and then we can have a…' *good hard fuck over the desk* 'chat and a catch up. How're things with you?'

'Oh, who cares?' Her voice was back to normal. 'I just want you back here and safe. And your wife and kid too. Obviously. Though not back here.'

'Yeah. That's what I want too.' *In all sorts of ways that just confuse my poor bloody head.* 'Listen, I'd better run. Sooner I'm there the sooner this may all be done and dusted.'

'Yeah, sure. Speak to you soon.' Then, low, almost inaudible; 'Love you, Col.'

Like that, she was gone, and Colin was left holding a dead phone. *Oh now Nicola…what do I do* now?

The question he didn't think to ask was *why am I smiling?*

But smiling he was as he put the car in gear, checked the mirror and drove off.

Chapter Thirty-One

'Help you?' said the desk sergeant, nearly forty minutes later. Traffic had been a bitch.

'Yeah, Colin Bryant.' No recognition flickered over the policeman's face, so Colin tried again. 'I received a phone call from you – well, not you exactly, a WPC, but from this station – to say you'd a suspect that you wanted me to help identify.' Still nothing on the copper's face. He felt himself starting to heat up. *There's something wrong here,* he thought.

'Could you be more specific, sir?'

'Yes. Um…' He started to sweat. *There's something wrong here.* 'About an hour ago, I got a phone call from a WPC at this station saying they – you - had a suspect in for questioning that they wanted me to identify. In connection with the…murders, you know?' *No, look at him. He doesn't know. Something is very wrong here.* 'The…connected murders. The ones that, um…' *Christ, what was that miserable angry bastard's name?* 'Walker! Detective Walker is investigating.'

Jesus, there's nothing on this bastard's face! Is he some sort of fucking robot? 'You received a call, asking you to come here and identify a suspect? Is that what you're saying, sir?'

Yes! Yes! Yes! But his voice was small, his face hot, his heart rate insane. *Duped,* a voice said, far off in his mind. 'About an hour ago. From a woman.'

'Well, first I've heard of it sir, but still…' he gave a *you know how it works* chuckle and tapped a password into a computer screen. *Duped,* that voice spoke up again, a little louder. Sweat was running down his face in streams now. 'Your name again, sir?'

'Colin. Colin Bryant,' he whispered, throat constricted to the size of a bean, whistling like a kettle. *They've a suspect in for questioning…*and they want you to look at him through the two way glass, *eh? Is that ethical, do you suppose?*

I don't know.

Does it sound like normal police procedure to you?

I don't know.

Have you ever seen it on one of those police shows?

Colin swallowed hard. *No.*

Duped, that voice said again. *Fooled. Tricked. Made an arsehole out of.*

'I'm very sorry, sir,' the sergeant was saying. 'I've no record of this on the system. Do you recall the name of the officer who you say called?'

Who you say called...not who called, *who you* say *called.* 'No. Sorry.'

The copper stared at him for a moment, then said, 'Would you like to take a seat, sir? I'll just check.' With that, he walked through the door into the station, leaving Colin – who was totally incapable of moving anywhere – quite alone.

And it's not just you who's alone, is it? There's Helen and Tasha...you've been nicely separated...

SHUT UP, SHUT UP, SHUT UP!! Colin screamed at himself. *There's just been a...minor communications breakdown, that's all. C'mon, happens all the time. How often at Allied Corporate do phone conversations start with 'did you not get the email?' Ten times a day? Fifty? Someone didn't press 'send', that's all. Any minute now, that copper's going to walk through that door and say, 'Sorry about that, Mr Bryant. Would you care to step this way?'*

Yeah, sure. 'Come and take part in a completely unethical identity parade.' Meanwhile, you stand here, waiting. While Helen and Tasha are miles away.

Yeah, with police protection outside. Who's going to attack them with two officers on guard, eh?

Of course, the police protection. I forgot about that – the way they forgot to tell you they were setting it up. And this'll be the police protection that a random woman's voice told you about? The random woman's voice who's led you here, on a wild goose chase? That police protection?

Shaking, sweating, struggling for breath, Colin reached into his jacket and pulled out his phone. *Here,* he thought, *I'll prove to you that they're all right! I'll call home and they'll answer and they'll be fine and then the copper will appear – as if by magic, like the 'Mr Ben' shopkeeper, and say, 'Right this way Mr Bryant' and all of this...paranoia...will have been for nothing!*

So he hit the green button, and in his ear his home phone rang.

And rang. And rang some more.

'Jesus fucking Christ no,' he breathed, and ran for his car.

Chapter Thirty-Two

Panic swamped him on the drive back. He floored the accelerator, pushing his car as hard as it would go. He tailgated, switched lanes without looking, was nearly sideswiped at least three times, all the time his heart pounding in his chest to a terrible rhythm. *They're-DEAD,* it beat, *they're-DEAD, they're-DEAD.*

He slammed the brakes on outside his house and was nearly catapulted through the windscreen – clipping the seatbelt on had seemed a waste of time. He flung open the door and didn't bother to close it. He ran up the driveway, fumbling for his keys, screaming his wife and daughter's names.

But as he got to his front door, he went very, very quiet.

His front door was open. Just a bit, maybe an inch…but open.

'Helen?' He said. Or maybe sobbed.

Then he stepped inside.

Chapter Thirty-Three

Helen wasn't there. But Tasha was. She was sitting on the sofa. She'd have looked perfectly normal, perfectly lovely, if it wasn't for the blood that oozed from the back of her head.

Oh, and the two five inch nails which had been hammered into her eye sockets.

'Tasha,' said Colin. His mouth fell open, and he was unable to close it. Spit began to pool on his chin. 'Tasha,' he mumbled again.

Tasha said nothing. She just stared outwards through two sharp pieces of iron. Her face – her beautiful face, so like Helen's, was reposed, peaceful...but desecrated.

'Tasha?' he asked...then started to cry. His legs gave out, and he sank down onto the carpet. 'Tasha,' he said through his tears. 'Tasha.' Over and over again, he said his daughter's name.

But no matter how often he called to her, she didn't reply.

Chapter Thirty-Four

In 1984, they didn't have mobile phones. The technology was being developed, George had said he'd seen something about them on Tomorrow's World, *but they were a way off, and were going to be cripplingly expensive. There was no way some poor bloody students could ever afford them. Ever.*

Since they didn't have them, they were often uncontactable. You could phone various parents' houses – but if the teenagers were out, they were out, and that was that. Sometimes, that was a good thing – during the summer, when he and Carol were often out on their own – they didn't want to be disturbed. Other times, it could be an annoyance. Sometimes, for no very good reason, you'd just want to call them up – any of them, Brian, Howard, George, Sophie, Emma – just for a chat. 'Hi, how's this, how's that, did you see, so did I, well I never, no, did they?' That's how it is with friends. Maybe that's how you can define *a friend – they're the ones who call for no reason. Who can tell?*

Colin can't, not in this...dream? Not quite. It has the textures *of a dream, but it feels...deeper, somehow. Simultaneously heavier and yet more fragile. It's a little like coming around from anaesthetic – there's an awareness of a bigger, more corporeal space around him, but it's fogged. It feels dangerous out there. This space, this* place, *even though it feels like a dream, is safer. Cosier. He wants to stay.*

Why shouldn't he? He's sat inside one of the shelters on Southport promenade, and before him is the sea, painted a stunning boiling orange by the sunset. It's beautiful. Not real, but beautiful, so he looks at it.

He's younger here, he knows that. He's thinner. He always wore suits back then. Even though there was a heatwave in the summer of 1984, even though there were drought warnings, he always wore a suit and was never uncomfortable.

He feels a warm hand take his. He looks to his left and there's Carol, and oh God, what she does to him. Maybe not everything he'd like her to do to him – they're going out now, oh yes they are, hot 'n' heavy – but still, one look at her and his breath vanishes.

He loves her, and she loves him.

It's obvious. 'Lennie fucking Peters could see it,' said Howard, when Colin had told the rest of the gang that he and Carol were a couple. 'We just had bets on how fucking long it would take!' They'd all been happy for them, Colin remembers that now, all of them. They'd all wanted these crazy kids to get together.

No, there'd not been a bad word or a bad look at all, and now here they are, Colin and Carol, Carol and Colin, the two 'Cs', sitting together hand in hand, staring out to the sea.

'I'm very happy,' whispers Carol.

Colin leans down and kisses her. He could never get tired of kissing her. It's the most wonderful thing ever invented. 'Me too,' he says.

'Do you think we'll be together forever?' Carol asks, those huge blue eyes of hers looking out into the future.

'No,' he says, but the look on her face breaks his heart. It's crushed, desolate. He speaks quickly, he wants that look to vanish. 'I only meant you'll get bored of me and run off with someone much sexier.'

'I'll never get bored of you,' she says, with a confidence so fierce it's frightening. A little. 'I love you. You're the one. You'll always be the one. If anything, you'll get bored of me.' That almost ferocious confidence is gone. She looks scared now, almost ashamed. 'Because of...you know.'

'Shh, love,' he says and holds her close. Because I don't let you stick your dick in me, *is what she means – not that she'd ever be so coarse. Besides, does it matter? Really? That's just Carol, that's just how she is, it's what separates her from other women. Women like…well, Sophie for instance. Sophie's got that whole languid, feline sexuality thing going on, and by Christ does it work for her…but Carol's, well…unique. That strangely old fashioned way of behaving just makes her more desirable. Who knows why? Who cares why? 'I love you,' he says, and means it. He does. He loves her. He loves her like a nineteen year old boy loves any girl, deeply, sincerely, passionately, devotedly.*

He holds her close, and it's a warm summer's evening in the year of all years, 1984, and he's never been happier. They're alone, uncontactable, and even though he loves his friends, his gang, his crew, he loves Carol more, and here they are, watching the sun and the sea, in love, and utterly alone.

Well, except for that odd, trilling noise.

Colin looks around, thinking maybe it's some new kind of ice-cream van bell. That'd be cool, they could get a King Cone each and wander across the boating lake bridge. Hand in hand, eating ice cream, young, healthy and in love.

But there's no ice cream van around, and it's getting dark. The sun has crossed the horizon to start waking up some Australians. It's starting to get chilly. Time to make our way to the station, *he thinks.* Time to get the last train home, to walk her to her door, to…what the bloody hell is that noise?

'Aren't you going to answer that,' asks Carol, and Colin notices he has something in his right hand. Something roughly the size of a cassette cover, but much slimmer. It's black, but there's a weird sort of display on it, the like of which he's never, ever seen before.

The display reads NICOLA MOB CALLING.

'What the bastard hell?' he mutters, then turns to Carol to apologise for swearing. But he doesn't speak, he screams instead. He screams because Carol has nails for eyes and blood is spouting from the sockets.

Chapter Thirty-Five

Colin screamed himself back awake, his phone trilling away somewhere in the distance. *What the fuck – why am I on the floor?* was his first tired, confused thought. Then he remembered everything.

He called his daughter's name again, crawling across the floor to her, his tears still damp on his cheeks, his phone, his bastard phone ringing, ringing, ringing. But despite the noise, Tasha was still silent. Silent and dead. His far too serious daughter's face would never crease in one of those rare smiles again. She would never roll her eyes at him again. She would never give him an infrequent hug again. She would never do anything, ever, again.

Dead, and not yet twenty.

His phone kept ringing. Louder now, because it was somehow in his hand. When had he taken it from his pocket? No idea. But he had, and on the display were the words NICOLA MOB CALLING.

With no more thoughts in his head, maybe not for ever, Colin Bryant – never once looking away from his daughter's destroyed face – said 'Hello?'

'Hey love,' said Nicola, quietly. 'Sorry for whispering, I'm in the toilets. You OK to talk?'

'I'm…I'm…I'm…' said Colin. It was the best he could do. *Tasha,* he thought. There were nails in her eyes. Iron nails. Someone had hammered nails into his daughter's head.

'Colin? Babe? What is it?' Still whispering, but urgently now, concerned.

'Ta…Tash…'

'Tash? Tasha? Your *daughter?* Is that what you mean?'

'Yuh…yuh…'

'What is it, sweetheart? What's happened?' Still whispering.

'Duh…duhd. Duhd. *Dead!*' It snapped into place, the word popped out of his mouth. '*Dead!*'

There was a moment's awful silence, then; 'No. Please God, no. Oh fuck no…' A sniffle, still hushed. 'Where are you?'

'Huh…huh…house.'

'Helen? Is Helen there?'

'Don't…don't know.'

'Is she missing? Is that what you're saying?'

'Don't know.'

Another silence. Then, 'Colin? Are you alone in the house?'

He froze. *Was* there someone else here? *Was* there, apart from the corpse of his only child? Helen, for instance? Where was she, anyway? Had she *(my God please no)* also been killed? Killed and placed somewhere else? Upstairs, maybe?

'Don't know,' he managed to say.

'Have you called the police?'

'No.'

'Right,' said Nicola, brisk, efficient, businesslike…but still hushed. 'Get out of the house now. I'll get to you as soon as I can – I'll just leave. I'll call the police on my way to you. But you, for God's sake, darling, *get out of the house!*'

Then the phone was dead, dead like his daughter, and the house was silent, save for his breathing.

And the thump from his bedroom.

Colin's entire body twitched in shock. Someone had moved up there. It was a footstep, a definite footstep. Not a heavy tread, but still someone moving.

Helen!

That galvanised him. *Helen!* It *had* to be Helen. This...this *whoever it was* had lured him away, got in, hurt (killed) Tasha and had...what? Tied Helen up? Hurt her too? Maybe his coming home had startled the fucker, made him run...maybe Helen was upstairs, hurt, bleeding...*but still alive!*

He ran as best he could to the stairs, screaming his wife's name. He bounced off the walls, as if his house was a ship in a storm, he nearly fell over the banister rail, but he kept going. Somehow he kept going. He had failed his daughter, but he would save his wife.

He *would.*

He *just fucking would.*

He lurched across the landing to his closed bedroom door, still calling her name. He put his hand on the doorknob. *Let her be all right, let me be able to save her, let her live, please...*

The door was opened from the other side, violently. Colin tumbled into the room, falling onto the bed. He struggled upright. 'Helen?'

'No,' said Nicola, who for some reason was standing in the doorway. Colin stared at her, mute. 'Helen's waiting in the car,' she went on. 'We finish this off at mine.'

'Wha...' was all Colin could say.

'Shhh, lover,' said Nicola, as she raised what looked for all the world like a hammer. A hammer with a much bloodied head. Then she ran towards him, the hammer descending in an arc, screaming '*Iiiiiiiiiiiiiiiiiiiiit's SHOWTIME!!!*'

Then his head exploded, and Colin went into the dark.

Chapter Thirty-Six

He's kissing her, kissing her all over, he's young, horny, and frantic. And so, perhaps more importantly, is she. She can't keep her hands off him! She's rubbing herself against every inch of his naked body, fingernails digging, teeth biting – she's animalistic, she's experienced, and he isn't. But what he lacks in experience he makes up for in enthusiasm, and that seems to make her happy – judging from the noises she's making, anyway.

*There's not a bit of her he's not had his mouth around, and oh God if she doesn't finish him off soon he'll die. He may die anyway when he shoots his mess, he feels so…wired, so alive, like he could just…fucking…*explode…

He's never gone this far before, never had his fingers or tongue inside a woman before, and it's joyous, it's wondrous, he can't believe he ever made it to nineteen, nuh-nuh-nuh-nuh-nineteen without this. He wants to do this forever. Forever.

And so does she.

But he knows he can't go All The Way, he knows that's forbidden, it's always been forbidden before and so must be forbidden again. Just before he reaches the terminal point, he pulls back, pulls away from her, from her mouth, from her hands, just like he has a thousand (maybe) times before.

But this time, she won't let him. This time, she locks her hands around his neck and stops him going away. 'It's OK,' she says, and she's smiling – breathless, but smiling. 'Do it. Please. It's OK. I've taken my pill, it's OK, do it, please…do me.'

And with a thrust, he does. He doesn't even care that the woman underneath is blonde, not brunette, that her eyes are brown, not blue, that she's called Sophie and not Carol.

At that precise moment, as he rides deep in the wetness of a woman for the first time ever, Colin Bryant couldn't care less.

Somewhere off in the distance, he hears Howard calling him a 'lucky bastard.'

Chapter Thirty-Seven

The sound of a laughing fox brought Colin back into the real would. *What the fuck?* he thought as best he could through the headache – no, *incapacitating pain.*

He opened his eyes, and right in front of him was Basil Brush. He felt more of the world slide away. *Basil...Brush?* Basil's brown eyes stared him unblinkingly down, and as Colin watched, the fox's head was thrown back, and once again it gave that trademark laugh, the one that had delighted him as a child, the raucous, slightly dirty laugh that ended with a screamed *BOOM-BOOM!*

But then the fox dropped from his eyeline, and his view was filled by Nicola – blonde, blue eyed, impossibly beautiful Nicola, the PA who had so recently told him she loved him, the PA who had filled so many salacious thoughts...

The PA who had hit him across the jaw with a hammer, knocking him unconscious.

'I say, Miss Louise,' said Basil to Nicola. Except, of course, Basil was just a glove puppet, and Nicola had her arm up its arse, and she was doing the talking for both of them.

'Yes Basil?' she answered herself.

'You know that man there?'

'Yes Basil.'

'The one trussed up like a Christmas turkey?'

'Yes Basil?'

'I was just wondering,' then a little pause, and Nicola waggled her fingers in the fox's snout as if it was thinking, 'what we're going to *stuff him with!*'

Once more, that laugh – so delightfully infectious when Colin had been a boy, now rendered terrifying beyond belief. *What...the fuck...is happening,* he thought as clearly as he could.

This time, however, as Nicola made the puppet's laugh reach its apex, she clamped down on its snout with her left hand. 'Quiet, you nut!' she snapped, appearing both irritated and amused at the same time. Basil wriggled a bit under the pressure, but she kept him restrained. 'Mr Colin is a guest on the show, Basil, and should be treated with some respect! We'll see him do his act in a minute, and the audience will all applaud,' she broke off here, looking above and beyond Colin's head, 'won't you, boys and girls?' Then she nodded, as if receiving confirmation, and turned back to the still trapped puppet, 'and then we'll *fucking rip his head off and piss down the hole!* Sound good?'

Nicola let go of Basil's snout. Basil leered unpleasantly in front of Colin's face. 'Yes, yes,' he said, greedily.

Colin screamed.

Chapter Thirty-Eight

'Oh, hush now, you big baby,' said Nicola as she moved away. Colin tracked her, and noticed for the first time where he was. In a bedroom – a child's bedroom. A narrow single bed, above which was a shelf filled with Enid Blyton's *Famous Five* and *Secret Seven* books. The walls were covered in paper showing Disney's Snow White and her dwarves. A row of teddy bears sat on that spinster's mattress – Pooh, Tigger, a bear, a rag doll – staring at him like some kapok stuffed jury. Nicola sat Basil alongside the rest, then turned back and smiled at him. 'Are you sitting comfortably, Colin?' she asked.

Colin wasn't. He was lying on the floor facing the bed and the doorway, hands and ankles tied by something that felt like rough nylon – clothesline? *Possibly.* His jaw hurt from where the – no, could this be right? *Really?* – hammer had cracked him.

But he said nothing. He couldn't answer – not because he was gagged (which he wasn't...and how unsettling was *that?*) but because the whole thing had moved up into a gear beyond insanity. *Maybe I died, maybe on the way back from the police station, when I was driving 'without due care and attention,' I hit another car and died and this is all some terrible final nightmare.*

I've a horrible feeling that's both right and *wrong. This* is *a terrible nightmare. But you're not dead.* Yet.

'Then I'll begin,' said Nicola, as if he'd agreed.

Chapter Thirty-Nine

'Nicola,' Colin managed, then stopped. He had no idea what to say after that. Just like when he'd...he'd found Tasha. All of his processes were locked down, frozen like a computer that couldn't run the programme.

Nicola looked over her left shoulder in confusion. Then she looked over her right. Then she shrugged those shoulders that Colin had imagined kissing on more nights than were healthy, and turned to the toys on the bed. 'Nicola?' she echoed. 'Nicola? Are any of you called Nicola?' She reached out and made each one of the toys shake their heads in turn. 'Sorry, Colin old chum, old mate, old lover – well, nearly - there's no Nicola here. No Nicola *anywhere. Never* been a Nicola,' then, with a slight tilt of that elegant, long neck, she looked to the ceiling. 'Except in my head. Except in the *oh so easily* forged employment records of Allied Corporate. I mean, *honestly* Colin - you should check just that little bit more *thoroughly* before you employ somebody! Check their qualifications! Ask to see certificates! Phone the bloody referees! But you didn't, did you?' Then, horribly, in a gruff (but somehow bubbly amused) voice, 'Why didn't he, Mummy?'

'Oh, Tigger,' she continued, in her own voice, 'you're a bit too young to appreciate this but…because he fancied me, that's why.' Back to Colin. 'That's right, isn't it, lover? You didn't give two *shits* about whether I could use Word or Excel, did you? All you cared about was looking down my blouse or staring at my arse as I made the tea. You think I'm *stupid*? You think I'm *blind*? I'm neither, you sad, pathetic fuck. Do you think I don't *know* what men will do for a flash of tit? *Anything,* that's what they'll do! *Anything!* You can turn up at an interview with a CV made of lies and a made up name, but so long as they think they're in with the merest *hint* of seeing your bra they'll give you a three month trial! Useless,' she said, tossing her hair back. 'Utterly fucking useless!' Then, back to her toys, 'Sorry about the language, children – but sometimes things must be blunt, as my Mum used to say. We'll all have ice cream later to make up for it – what, Polly dear? Yes, Neapolitan. That's fine.'

Oh dear God, thought Colin. *Oh dear God.*

'So that was that,' said…well, whoever she was. 'Fake name, fake references, fake account – and yeah, I went to a lot of trouble setting that one up, but it's the details that count in the end – and there I was, your PA. Months of sitting in the same office as you, having to put up with you raping me with your eyes, having to feign interest in your pathetic little life, having to pretend to laugh at your frankly rather shit jokes. And you know what? Your Groucho Marx voice *sucks.* I know. I've got *all* their films. My Mum gave them to me. She'd watch them over and over – when Dad was out, Dad was no fun at all, that's why we killed him – and we'd laugh and laugh and laugh, but *you*…God, you sounded like Colin Bryant with a head cold!'

That's…why we killed him?

'Me and my Mum. I loved my Mum, Colin. Loved her with all my heart and soul. I cut her down after she hanged herself and I rocked her from side to side, and I remembered everything she'd ever said to me, about you and your gang and what you'd done. And I swore to her that I'd see you all in the ground. And I very nearly have. You're the only one left, Colin. I did it all for her.

'For my Mum, Carol. Because my name is Louise. Louise Hill, but that's only because she took his name when they married. Her maiden name was Smith.' Then she bent low in front of him, her long blonde hair (dark at the roots) almost brushing his face. She looked quite, quite mad. 'Get it, now? Do you get it?'

Chapter Forty

Colin didn't get it. Colin didn't get it *at all*. Colin's brain – which, after all, was programmed to deal with spreadsheets and balances and transfers and bill payments and a boring middle-class life – was in *no way* set to process what was happening to him. How *could* it? How could *anyone's?*

This blankness must've shown on his face, as Nicola/Louise/whatever heaved a huge sigh of irritation. 'Oh come on,' she said, almost stamping her foot. 'It's nimps. *Simple-pimple!* My Mum was your old girlfriend, Carol Smith. After you…betrayed her, she met my Dad. And they had me. And from the moment I could listen, she talked. She talked about all of her friends from the old days…Brian and Howard and the one with two names and Emma-Fenella. And you. And the whore. And the times you had and the laughs you had and how you were her first big love, Colin oh my Colin. She told me after that summer you all fucked off from her – though she wasn't a swearer, my Mum. She was polite, she was well mannered. But you all just…*went away*, didn't you? *All of you?* None of you kept in touch, none of you wrote a letter or a card, none of you later looked her up on Facebook and hit the Friends Invite button. None of you could be bothered, that's what she said. You just got on with your little lives and your little dreams *and left her behind!*'

In his head, dimly, Colin heard Howard say *who really wants to carry their past around?*

'That was bad enough,' this woman went on, 'that *alone* was reason enough to do what I did – I mean how *dare* you leave her behind – but when I found out about you and that Brown woman…'

Howard again, in his head, *screwed about a bit – hell, you should know more about that than any of us, you lucky bastard – but bad?*

But I forgot about that, he heard himself thinking. It was wrong to be thinking like this, he knew that – there were more important things to be thinking, like *how do I get out of this?* and (most important of all) *where's Helen?* – but there was just too much white noise between his ears. *It just went. I forgot and moved on, the way I forgot all my old mates. It just happens sometimes. You don't mean to, you just have other stuff to deal with. Like the present.*

'That's when I knew,' the woman he was almost coming round to thinking of as Louise continued. 'That's when I *decided*. When I cut my Mum down, and I held her cold body in my arms, when I rocked her and sang all the old songs, *The Longest Time* and *Thunder Road* and *Electric Dreams. That's* when I began to work out what to do. And the mechanics of it all were oh so simple, Colin my love. I had my weapons already.' Hands moving so fast they were a blur, she reached up to her gore soaked blouse and ripped it open, buttons popping everywhere. The white cotton fell apart, revealing a black lace bra, *exactly* like the one he'd imagined she'd wear. 'Tits, Colin.' She said. 'You stupid arsehole men will do anything for a pair of these.'

Chapter Forty-One

'Joe or George or whatever the fudge he wanted to call himself wasn't my first,' she said, sitting on the bed and gathering her children to her, arranging them on her lap. 'You don't mind them listening in, do you Colin, my angel? They've heard it before – haven't you? – but it's a favourite story, and a favourite story, like a favourite song, bears repetition. There was Dad. But Joe or George was my first *solo* effort, like *Careless Whispers* was to George Michael. Mum really deserves the credit for what we did to Dad. I mean, don't get me wrong, he wasn't a *bad* man – not like you – but he was…well, *boring*. He didn't tell stories or play tea parties. He *hated* the Marx Brothers! He liked *classical* music! And jazz! *Jazz? Jizz,* more like!' Then, to the toys which had made no noise whatsoever (how could they?) 'Don't snigger, you lot. I know you don't know what that means. And Mum was…OK, yes, eccentric. In a nice way, in a fun way. She knew *all* the best games and stories! She'd play with me and the toys all day, but then Dad would come home and she'd have to be…well, all grown up then. Like a proper housewife. But she *wasn't* a proper housewife, do you see?'

No. She sounds a model of sanity and respectability, Colin found himself thinking – and was he deluding himself, or were his thought processes actually shaping up? Were they starting to file logically again?

'She was the Best Mum Ever,' said Louise, looking off into the far distance, her eyes moist, and – if not for the torn open blouse and the Ann Summers style bra – she would have looked all of six years old. 'And Dad was an Old Poop. Sooner or later, she said, he'd leave her. Sooner or later, *everyone* left her. And when he did that, Mum would have to go out to work – oh sure, he'd pay his maintenance, he wasn't a man to shirk his responsibility – but that wouldn't be enough to keep this place on. But if Mum went to work, who'd be here to play games with me? Who'd be here to have set a game of Hide the Bounce when I got home from school? She'd be too tired to have tea parties or tell me stories of the Hundred Acre Wood or what Polly had got up to while I was working at my algebra.'

Listen to her. Listen to all this. She sees nothing wrong in the way she was raised. Face it, mate, your ex was a wacko and she did a number on her daughter.

Yes. And your daughter too, don't forget.

The image of Tasha – beautiful, serious Tasha – threatened to overwhelm him (and on top of that, the question of his wife and her safety) but he struggled to stay as focused as he could. Focus he was going to need.

'But,' Louise was saying, 'the fact he was an Old Poop we could use, she said. He was insured up to the nose. *This* insurance and *that* insurance, accidental *this* and personal injury *the other*, so that...well, if we kind've made it look like an *accident*, we'd be quids in for the rest of our lives.' Horribly, terribly, she giggled, covering her mouth like a naughty schoolgirl. 'So we loosened the wheelnuts on his car one night, after dark. Me and Mum. Well, she actually did the loosening, but I kept lookout. And the next day he drove to work and the wheel came right off! His car went out of control! Flipped over! He died and we were rich – rich and free! Free to play all the games we ever wanted! Free to listen to our favourite songs and watch our favourite films! *Free to eat jelly!*' She was laughing uncontrollably now, the toys jiggling and joggling on her lap. '*No one* suspected us! The Police said it was kids, probably, mindless vandalism, so sorry, never mind. That's when I knew, you see, that's when I knew that murder was easy – just as long as you're clever, and dedicated. And I'm both, Colin oh my Colin.

'I'm both. But I think you know that, don't you?'

Chapter Forty-Two

'So we kept on playing our games, and she kept on telling me her stories. Some were made up, and I loved those, but the ones I loved *best* were when she'd tell me about you lot. I knew you all, long time before I met any of you. I knew your music, your clothes, your films. I knew what you said and what you drank. I knew that Mum had the best time of her life back in that hot summer of 1984. She had her friends. Her *crew* as that fucking dog-lover Brian called you.' Her voice rose, her face became savage and dark. '*SPAR-key*,' she shouted, making Colin twitch. '*SPAR-key!*' Then, in her normal (if *anything* about her was normal) voice, 'Stupid, stupid man. Letting a dog *like* that off its lead. Terriers! Little shit weasels, that's all *they* are! But he loved that dog, probably more than his wife and kids. Anyway, I'd seen him for months walking that fucking useless animal. Talking to it. Running around with it. *Singing* to it, for flip's sake! I'm patient, you see. Patient, clever and dedicated. I study. So I watched him for months and I saw how *he* was and I saw how the dog was – badly trained, naughty, no recall – and, one night, I bought an old van with my wages, went to the park where he walked the dog, waited till it was off its lead, grabbed the little shit, drove off. Then I rang him – Brian – in the middle of the night – and, Colin my Captain, you should have heard how pathetically grateful he was! "*Oooh, you found my doggy, fank yooo, I wuff my doggy wots and woads!*" Of course, the bastard thing was long dead by then – I mean, it had widdled in my *hall*, Colin – but…oh, it was funny, when he came here, and saw it, saw it with the nails driven into its eyes…'

Like my Tasha, Colin thought, once again almost overwhelmed by grief. Once again, he tried to keep it under control.

'He cried,' said Louise. 'Then I stabbed him in the heart and slit him open. Pulled his guts out. Made a mess, but I always put polythene down first. Mum was a Girl Guide. *Be Prepared*. For a laugh I stuck the dog in the hole. It was only a little dog, but I had to cut its back legs off first. Oh, my lovely, lovely Colin…*that was a scream!*'

Scream. Yes. If this goes on much longer, I will.

'It was only him and Howard I didn't use my tits on, one way or another,' Louise reflected. 'Emma's son, for instance. Fat bastard, like his Mum. Never get a smell of *ein fraugarten!* Until I started hanging around him. He went to your old college – how's that for irony? Some nights, after work, I'd potter down to their library. Useless security at that place, anyone can just wander in. Pull out some books. Sit close to him. Thrust my tits in his general direction. One day I ask him out. Virtually comes in his jeans. We hang about a bit. I have to put up with him pawing at me, slobbering in my mouth, the dirty birdie. But eventually, he invites me home to tea…' She broke off again, smiling. 'Tits. Tits get you everywhere.

'Joe or George…he was just a loser. Wife left him ten years ago. He spent all his dole in lapdancing clubs. Disgusting places. But still, if you're a woman, with tits, and you walk into a place like that…oh, men just think it's *Christmas*. Well, he did, anyway. I made all his wank fantasies come true. "Do you like them?" I whispered in his ear as he watched the strippers – *no* Basil, not paint strippers – "I can do that better, and I'll let you touch me." Back to my place in twenty minutes flat. Tits.

'Howard…well, why bother with him? You know, Mum never talked about him much. She didn't think he was important. Just ran him down with a stolen car.'

Not important…but he was our leader! How can she say…?

Colin, I'm not sure that's the issue right now.

'I was disappointed in Sophie, dying on me like that – oh, you don't know, sorry. Cancer got her. But, as I said at the time, cunt cancer means too much pokey-proddy as a youngster.

'Hell, maybe you gave it to her. Again, a little irony is good for the blood. Or potential irony anyway. I *do* feel a bit cheated, yes, but as my Mum said so often, "when life gives you lemons, make lemonade." She was a wise old thing, my Mum.' Then tears, huge and soft, trickled down her cheeks. 'Wise, but sad. Even the games and the stories couldn't cover it all, not at the end. You all up and left her, and she loved me, but maybe…maybe I *wasn't enough for her. I tried to be!* I tried to be *everything* she ever wanted me to be…but maybe I didn't try *enough!* She really, really wanted those days back again, for things to be like they were before…but the music and the clothes and the films weren't *enough.* They *couldn't* be enough. I don't know, maybe having me was the thing that just tipped the scales. Maybe when she looked at me I just reminded her that now wasn't then and never would be. Maybe *I'm* the reason she hanged herself.'

Once more, Louise stared off into the distance, lost in her memory. For just a second, Colin could almost feel some sympathy for her. She was damaged. She'd been beaten around by a psychotic mother, drip fed lies and insanities. Who could have escaped *that* intact? She'd been entrapped in patricide, for Christ's sake! She'd been made to think of murder as some sort of…complicated game, almost, like Cluedo. She was a mad dog, sure – but who made the dog mad in the first place? Why, the owners, of course.

But regardless of the blame, mad dogs still bit. Mad dogs still killed. Mad dogs had to be destroyed.

Louise controlled herself with an effort. 'But still, you and your lot...what you did...specifically what *you* did, with her *best friend*...you're the *real* reason all this happened. OK, granted, I was the tangible sign that the old days were never coming back...but you...oh, *you pokey-prodded her best mate!* And you had the fucking *temerity* to just *forget it all*, to go on with your twatting useless *life! That's* why I had to save you till last. *That's* why you were my most elaborate plan. Working with you, teasing you...tits, you see...making up a whole host of shit about cheating partners – and you *still didn't get it*, did you? "My boyfriend's shagging my best mate," I said, looking right at you, and there wasn't even a flicker of guilt, you fucking *cunt!*'

No, there wasn't. But there was a 'hey, these things happen' moment, wasn't there? A tiny bubble from my subconscious.

'And then there was the new girl at *her* Am Flipping Dram society.' Louise waved a hand under her nose, as if wafting a bad smell. 'Oh, did they *stink!* But then, you knew that. Helen told me. We got to be quite close, you know. She talked about you a lot. How you *put up* with her hobby – such a *magnanimous* man! How you thought it was all "a bit silly." On that, you were right. It *was* silly, and they *did* stink, and *she* was the worst of the lot. A plank. Utter pooh-shite. Compared to me, anyway. I blew those bastards away, Colin. Why not? I've had practice. I am a *fucking brilliant actress!* So we became close. Me and your ugly wife. Close enough so I could phone her up and ask to go over my lines with her. At your house. After I'd got you out of the way with a fake phone call. *Told* you I was good – you didn't even recognise my voice! Oh, I'm a *brilliant* actress, Colin my Colin! I missed my vocation, didn't I? Then a call as me to your mobile to make sure you were out…and *bingo bango*, as they say. In I come, Helen smiles, shows me into the front room, I knock her and that miserable bitch of a daughter out with my *BANG! BANG! LOUISE'S SILVER HAMMER*…and pretty much, that's where we came in, I think.'

'Helen,' said Colin. 'Where is she?'

'I *told* you,' Louise sighed, 'in the boot of the car – I *did* tell you, didn't I? Still alive. Tied up well, but still alive. For now. You'll both be dead when the police find you, but that's OK because I will be too. Like mother, like daughter. After I've killed you both, I'll hang myself.' Then she leaned forward, and gave him the most terrifyingly salacious wink he'd ever seen. 'But before all the nastiness, you and me are going to have some fun.'

She blushed, giggled, then removed the toys from her lap and stood up. She moved to her bedside table drawer and reached in. 'You know,' she said, 'these aren't my *only* toys. I mean, I'm a grown woman. I have needs. Just *different* needs to any other woman. And different needs require different toys to satisfy them, don't you think?'

From the drawer, Louise produced two objects. The first was a terrifyingly big dildo, pink plastic with a black base. The second was even worse. A long, serrated butcher knife. Thick maroon blotches that Colin could not tell himself were rust smeared the blade.

'Oh lover,' she breathed. 'We're going to have a lot of fun.'

Chapter Forty-Three

Panic overcame him then, as Louise knew it would. As ever, warm ecstasy welled up inside her. Although all parts of the game were fun – tiring, but fun – this bit was her Big Favourite. Watching their pointless thrashings and struggles was as funny as…well, as funny as Basil Brush! This time, though, it was tempered with a certain sadness.

This time was, after all, the last time.

It was like going to the park, she thought. When she was young, her Mum had taken her to the park every day. They'd ride the swings and the slides and the roundabouts for what seemed like forever, but then, eventually, Mum would say that it was time to go home, that it was enough for today, young lady. And Louise would pout her bottom lip, and her Mum would always say, 'All right then, one more go on one more ride, but then we go home.' Louise would clap her hands and skip to the roundabout (because the roundabout was her Best Ride, she loved the *pulling* of it once the thing really got going) and she would savour every second of it, making it a film in her mind, cherishing it, because she knew it was the last time, and the last time should be the Best Time.

In another way, of course, it wasn't like going to the park at all, because there was always another day at the park, always. But once Colin was history, once he was nothing more than bits of meat and gristle and eyes that stared into the dark like those of a teddy bear, there'd be no more fun for Louise Hill.

A life without fun was no life at all.

So once Colin was done with, she would line up her children, kiss them all, tell them she loved them all forever, then walk downstairs and into the kitchen, stand on the table, and put her head in the noose she had set up the night before.

You just couldn't live without laughs.

So, just as in the past a young girl with pigtails and a joyful look in her saucer shaped eyes had run to the roundabout for *just one last go*, Louise advanced on Colin.

One last time, before she went home. Forever.

Chapter Forty-Four

Colin was on shutdown. A red wave of terror blotted his vision. He couldn't even scream. With his hands and ankles tied the most he could do was buck his hips up and down, like Helen as she approached orgasm.

Helen, he thought, like a flash of lightning.

Hurt, he thought in another flash.

Die, he thought.

From somewhere off in another universe, he heard Louise speak. 'You never did get to fuck Mum, did you, lover? You went off with her best mate and fucked *that* slag instead. I'd ask why, but I think we both know why, don't we? Because dogs will stick it where there's *any* hole, that's why. And you never got to fuck me either, though by *Christ* you were begging for it. *Begging.* But I got to let you in on a secret, Colin old Colin my babyluv, I ain't never not been fucked by no man neither.' She was bending over him again, blouse falling apart like curtains. 'And never will be. I'm the original dead letter, returned unopened. But, I am going to have a little sextytime fun.' She held up the dildo. 'I'm going to flip you over and play the B side, Colin.'

Chapter Forty-Five

Oh, look at him go!

The giggle made her chest heave, the sight of him made her nipples ping, hard against her bra, like…well, like bullets, she supposed. She'd never really given a thought to the whole sex business – from what her Mum had told her it all seemed a bit wet and nasty – but just right then, looking at him, *him,* the worst, the most evil of them all, do the Victim Flop on her bedroom floor (and he was the only man *ever* who'd been allowed in here!) suddenly prompted a whole series of ideas and images and rushes of heat that she'd never experienced before. She'd told him she'd had needs, but like so many other things she'd told him that had been a lie. The only need she'd ever had was to kill the people who had betrayed her old Mum.

Now, maybe, she could see what all the fuss was about. Now, maybe, she could think of one final thing to do before stepping off that kitchen table and feeling the rope bite into her neck…

But that was for later. For now, she bent even lower over him and, dropping the dildo onto the floor and ignoring his frankly pathetic thrashings, unbuckled his belt, popped his trouser button and yanked them and his underwear to his ankles.

Then – and even *she* knew this was bad form, but she just couldn't stop herself - she burst out laughing. 'Oh, bloody hell,' she managed, eventually. 'Is that *it?*'

Could that – that tiny, flapping, maggot sized noodle - *really* be what all the fuss was about? Is that what all the girls in her Mum's old *Jackie* and *Just Seventeen* annuals had been so obsessed with? It was nothing! *Nothing!*

How the hell does a baby come out of that? she wondered, giggling like she had done all those years ago as the roundabout went faster, faster, pulling her outwards. Then she decided she didn't care.

There were, after all, things to do.

She reached out and grabbed Colin by the shoulders, and flexed the muscles which had been built up beautifully over the past few weeks, effortlessly flipping him onto his front. She heard a faint clonk as his nose hit the carpet, and that set her giggles off again. *You think* that hurts, *Colin my lover,* she thought. *Allow me to broaden your…well, horizons. Amongst other things.*

She picked up the dildo (bought from an Ann Summers shop the day before, and mercy weren't they *expensive!*) and caressed it between his bucking buttocks. 'Easy lover,' she breathed, the title of one of her Mum's old songs. 'Easy.' She lightly traced it backwards and forwards, forwards and backwards…then she located his bottom hole and rammed the bastard *right* up.

Chapter Forty-Six

Agony.

A terrible swelling filled him from behind, a sense of violation, abuse, invasion, a feeling that he was about to burst. Then a ripping, a rupturing, a searing, white hot torture the like of which he'd never known existed…never known *could* exist. He couldn't even scream. Tears rolled down his cheeks. Sweat poured down his forehead. He felt the thing withdraw…then thrust back again. Withdraw, then thrust. He felt something deep inside him sever, and a wet gush warmed his thighs.

Bleeding. Blood. Bleeding. Please God. Make it stop. Please God…

But it didn't stop. It went on forever.

Chapter Forty-Seven

You little bugger, Louise thought, and laughed again. The blood coursing down his legs was making it easier to slide the dildo in and out of Colin's arse, which was nice. Anything that made her job just that little bit easier was welcomed. Not that she was a slacker – Lord no, anyone who'd been on the receiving end of her work recently would testify to how much of a grafter she was – but still, a shortcut every now and then was welcomed.

But after a time, and she'd no idea how long (*time flies when you're having fun,* her Mum had said so often) the blood started to congeal, become sticky and icky, and the dildo started to catch. *Roundabout's winding down,* Louise thought to herself, and resigned herself to one last, extra hard *push.* One she put *all* her weight behind.

Chapter Forty-Eight

A deep *rip* set his world alight. He'd heard the phrase *blinding pain* often enough in his life, but finally he understood the truth of it. White fire exploded across his retinas, scarring them. He hissed inwards, biting at his bottom lip, his back arched and spasming.

Then there was a splattering noise, and more warmth on his legs. Not blood this time. Not with that smell.

Chapter Forty-Nine

'Oh, you *dirty* piggy!' Louise said in horror and pulled the beshitted plastic cock from Colin's anus. A perfect torrent of rusty brown, foul smelling water was cascading down his legs and puddling on her carpet. She wrinkled her nose and stepped back in a hurry. She didn't want any of *that* on her. Oh yes, she'd seen enough of it recently – when people died, they died smelly – but that didn't mean she'd have to *touch* it!

She began to wave the dildo about, to get rid of the filth, then thought better of it and looked for something to wipe it down with. Then she thought better of *that*.

She knew the perfect cleaning method.

Chapter Fifty

Colin thought he was crying. It was impossible to say for sure, but he was making some noise, and crying seemed to describe it best. That thing was gone from inside him, but there was a pulsing hot throbbing somewhere below his stomach, a spasming, and the smell of his own shit and blood was nauseating.

Helen, he thought. *Tasha. I'm so sorry. I let you all down. I couldn't help you. I'm sorry. I'm going to die and God help me I* want *to die Helen I'm sorry I can't help I'm sorry I'll never see you again I'm sorry…*

Then he felt her strong arms underneath him, and once more he was flipped over. The harridan he'd once idly (or not so idly) fantasised about was above him.

'Lover,' she said. 'Lick the bowl.'

She punched him hard in the stomach. His mouth opened in reflex, trying to suck in more air.

Which is when she rammed the blood and ordure streaked dildo in his mouth.

Chapter Fifty-One

You never know how long you have in this life, her Mum had said, more than once. *So you must make sure you enjoy every good moment when it comes along. Cherish them.*

Oh boy, was Louise cherishing this. Ramming that filthy, diseased, plastic cock down the dirty piggy's mouth was the funniest thing she'd ever seen – and she'd seen some stuff in her time. This was funnier than Groucho insulting the fat lady. This was funnier than Basil interrupting the story. This was even funnier than the look on the doggy's face as it popped out of Brian's chest. Watching Colin choke on a dildo covered in his own blood and poo was *just priceless*!

'Suck it down, lover,' she called, as she bashed all thirty pounds worth of Ann Summer's finest against his teeth. 'Suck it on down! *Swallow it*, you dirty piggy, swallow it *all!!*'

Oh, it was such a shame all this had to end. It really was.

Chapter Fifty-Two

Colin, repulsed beyond belief, felt his gag reflex twitch as the bastard thing was rammed towards his tonsils. *At least she didn't get to stab me,* he thought crazily. *At least I just get to choke.*

Then, with what he was sure was his final thought, he once again apologised to Helen.

He spasmed, violently, and prepared to die.

Chapter Fifty-Three

Ah, Louise thought as the brutal contraction wracked Colin's body, *I may have misca –*

But then she lost her concentration, as an especially vicious seizure struck him. She was bending right over him, after all, so much the better to see his face turn purple, so much better to see the alternating brown and red smears bubble off his lips, and as he gave that involuntary lurch forward, he butted her in the forehead.

Stars exploded in front of her. Once more he bucked, somehow twisting onto his side as he wretched a great pool of vomit. Louise, already off balance and stunned, felt her left leg pushed to one side. She tumbled, helpless, and tried to get her right hand out to cushion the fall.

She didn't quite make it. Her head connected with the wooden frame of the bed, and a sharp red pain ignited inside her. Her world went grey.

Some might have said it had been that way for quite some time.

Chapter Fifty-Four

His stomach voided, Colin opened his eyes.

He was alive. Still. Broken, bleeding, suffering…but *alive.* He'd literally no idea that he'd butted his torturer into semi consciousness, none at all, he'd been almost in the black by then, his body working strictly on primal survival instinct. Apart from a vague notion that his head hurt (but where *didn't* hurt now?) all he really registered was that the attack was, at least for now, over.

So what? part of him thought. *It'll start up again soon enough. She's taking a break, having a Kit-Kat, she'll be back. Mad bitches like that are* always *back. And I* can't *do a thing, anyway. Tied up, trousers round my ankles…where am I going to go?*

Then another part of him thought, *Helen.*

She was still alive, in Louise's car, waiting. Dark, cold, scared. Waiting for this lunatic to kill her. *Do something,* this part of his mind said. *Do something!*

Breathing thinly through his mouth (Christ, the *stench* in that room – all of it from him, all of it from his fluids) Colin just about managed to contort his body into a sort of question mark. The effort was agonising and set off a fresh spurt of rectal bleeding. *Something's ripped badly back there, I'm like that poor bastard in that comedian's swimming pool.*

But then he saw Louise, and for a second all his pain vanished. *Dead,* he rejoiced as he saw her lying at the foot of the bed. *Ding, dong the bitch is –*

But then her eyelids fluttered – the way they'd fluttered at him so often as they'd sat opposite each other for eight hours a day, five days a week – and she let out a sort of moaning rumble. *Fuck. Might have known. She's going to come back like some low-rent horror movie monster and finish me off and there's nothing I can –*

Which is when he saw the knife. On the floor, where she'd dropped it. The huge serrated knife.

It was maybe only six inches away, but it seemed like six miles. His hands tied at the wrists, feet tied at the ankles – never mind the whole Brian Rix trouser arrangement – how was he *actually* going to get to the (literally) bloody thing? What would he do with it even if he *could* reach it?

Don't know. Don't care. Going to do it. Going to get it. Then I'm going to free Helen. Then I'm going to save my wife.

Inching forward like a slug – a slug that was leaving a trail of blood from a ripped open arsehole – Colin Bryant gritted his teeth, ignored his pain, and tried to reach the knife.

Chapter Fifty-Five

Things have never gone wrong before, Louise found herself thinking from the Land of the Grey. *Why now?*

Perhaps surprisingly, she heard her Mum answer. *Because this one's the worst of the lot,* she said. *He's the embodiment of all evil – he pretended to love me and then threw it up my best friend. You know that, I've told you that. He's cunning and scheming and unfaithful. All you had to do was smile and bend over and he'd already committed adultery in his mind. Several times. He's a man, and* all *men are evil, but he's the* apogee *of men, the 'poster child' as you'd call him. He'll take more killing than the others. But how greater the satisfaction when you do. How sweeter the rest you'll then take will be.*

Is it like how much nicer the jelly tasted when I'd eaten all my broccoli?

Yes, dear.

How I slept much better after I'd tidied up my room?

Yes, dear. You were always a good daughter, a good listener, a good friend in all our games, and I loved you so much. If you love me half as much as I loved you, you'll wake up now. *Wake up, and kill the bastard.*

Yes Mum, said Louise obediently, and opened her eyes.

She hissed in horror. Colin was almost at the knife. He had his fingertips on it. Another second and –

But she wasn't going to give him another second. Ignoring the dull aches that ratcheted through her head, she leapt at him with a growl, and sank her teeth into his fingers.

Chapter Fifty-Six

Needles of agony shot up Colin's arms. Any shred of beauty had long since departed Louise's face – she was feral, rabid, savage. Some terrible, terrifying sound of rage and hunger was spouting from her throat; not even a snarl, something more primal. Tiny pricks of blood oozed their way down his arms.

But he didn't care, mainly because he was halfway to being insane himself. Anal rape and being forced to swallow your own blood and shit had that effect, it seemed. All he saw was Helen, alone, afraid, trapped. All he cared about was rescuing her, seeing her again, making sure she was safe.

Louise was gnawing away at his fingers, but his wrists were still tied. This turned his hands into one single unit, one single club. Muscles shaking with the effort, he put all he could behind that club and raised it.

She bit in, dug deeper as his hands forced her head up six inches from the floor. A great gout of blood shot up, and Colin screamed. Screamed, but didn't stop. Her arms and legs – her *unfettered* arms and legs - thrashed wildly about, like the Tasmanian Devil on those old cartoons he'd loved as a kid. A stray blow or two slapped him about the face, but he hardly noticed.

He focused everything he could onto raising his arms. Eight inches…ten…

Then something snapped – his right index finger – and a lance of pain almost engulfed him, almost caused him to faint dead away.

Almost. But not quite.

He kept on raising his hands. Twelve inches. Fourteen. Her head, deeply buried into the meat of his fingers, kept on whipsawing away, shaking like a terrier shakes a rag. But he kept going. For Helen, he kept going. Sixteen inches. Eighteen. Soon enough he'd have raised her head far enough off the ground. Then he'd find a way to pull out of her grip and smash the fucking thing to the carpet.

Chapter Fifty-Seven

She felt something plop into her mouth, and had no idea what it was for a second. She wasn't aware of much now, just the imperative to destroy this man, to finally even the scales.

Then it suddenly occurred to her what it was - the tip of Colin's finger! *Well, you may be about to die,* she thought, *but you did finally get a finger inside me.*

That was a deliciously funny thought, and she laughed. Just a little, a chuckle really, but that was enough to send the fingertip sliding down her throat.

Where it lodged.

Chapter Fifty-Eight

Louise suddenly spasmed, and barked a muted cough, like a silenced gun. Flecks of blood – *his* blood – flew from her mouth. A strange *what's this* expression crossed her mad face. Then it was replaced by something else, something Colin would have recognised if there'd been a mirror handy. Panic.

Chapter Fifty-Nine

No, she tried to scream, but she couldn't catch a breath. That thing, that lump of alien meat, was stuck at the back of her throat, in her windpipe, and she couldn't displace it. She coughed. Nothing. She coughed again. Still nothing.

No, no, no – this doesn't happen. THIS DOESN'T HAPPEN!!!

But it was, and it was happening to *her.*

She let go of Colin and staggered to her feet, gripping at her throat, almost strangling herself. Black lines were tracing the edge of her vision. *No. NO!* He *dies first, he* has *to die first, then my work is done…my children…my family…they can't see this…*

She was dimly aware of Colin, somewhere in another universe, scrabbling about on the floor – but it was dim, hazy, slow. All she could think of was her family, how they would see her die – choked to death on a fucking *fingertip!* All she could think of was her Mum, who she'd so badly let down at the last hurdle. *All but him, Mummy, all but him I'm sorry Mummy I'm sorry…*

Hush now, said her Mum. *It's not over yet. It can yet be saved, you can* still *win. Remember the day after you joined Allied Corporate, remember that Health and Safety at the Workplace seminar you had to attend? Remember the Heimlich manoeuvre? Remember how to perform it on yourself? You do, dear. You* do.

Yes Mummy, she thought, hoping she was still strong enough. She balled her hands into fists, popped up her right thumb, and smashed it under her breastbone.

It worked like a charm. That hunk of meat shot from her in a fan of blood, spit and vomit. Louise staggered, still faint, pulling great searing lungfuls of air into her body. *A second,* she thought. *A second. Then I'll slice the dirty piggy into bacon. Ready or not, Porky, here I come.*

Chapter Sixty

There wasn't time to even think about his good fortune. Colin hardly registered that Louise was choking to death. If he had he wouldn't have even stopped to celebrate. He had to get that knife. He had to cut himself loose.

To the background of her wheezing, Colin managed to wriggle to it and finally get his hands – his wrecked, wretched hands – on the handle.

Easy, he thought. *Careful. This fucker's sharp.*

Gently, ever so gently, he grasped it as hard as he could in his ruined hands and started to cut the rope at his ankles.

Chapter Sixty-One

She leaned against the wall and sucked every bit of oxygen she could down. Gradually the room swam into focus.

Oh, the dirty –

He was hunched up on the carpet, cutting away at his ropes. He was almost through. *No, my love, no.*

She took four wobbly strides to him and kicked him in the temple.

Chapter Sixty-Two

Colin's brain took a bang against his skull, and colours he didn't know existed exploded across his vision. But still, he heard the rending tear of nylon. But still, he felt his ankles separate. He'd done it.

He rolled across the carpet – thankfully throwing the knife away, he could easily have impaled himself on it – and tried to sort out his mind. It was easier said than done – the room was slippy, slidey, all of a tumble. The floor was writhing and undulating. He felt like he'd just walked off the Daddy of all Waltzers rides – the sort he and Carol had enjoyed so often in that long, hot and dead summer of 1984.

But his ankles were still free. He was halfway home.

He seemed to see Louise advance upon him, stalking across on mile long legs. He didn't think she had the knife in her hands, but how could he tell? How could he really tell *anything*, with his head pulsing like that?

But his legs were, after all, still free.

One good kick deserves another, he thought. He pistoned his leg up and cracked her on her right kneecap. She screamed (or did she? Did he just *think* she did?) and tumbled to the ground. *C'mon, Colin, keep it together. The knife. Where's the knife?*

Something glittering dully to his left, by the foot of the bed. Colin scrambled to his feet and staggered towards it like a sailor in a hurricane.

Chapter Sixty-Three

It was a weak kick – the kick of a man in his middle age, a soft man who played no sports and drank one too many beers of a weekend – but it still hurt all the same. More pain to add to the list – her head, her lungs, her throat, her knee. And the pain he'd caused her Mum.

All the sweeter jelly will taste, Louise decided. She clambered upright and turned to him.

He turned back.

She smiled.

So did he. Between his tied wrists, he held the knife.

Chapter Sixty-Four

It was his turn to run. It was his turn to be an animal. *Just don't fall over your fucking trousers...*

He didn't care that his world view was still skewed, he didn't care he was still leaking blood, all he saw was her, open, defenceless, shocked...afraid.

All he cared about was Helen. All he cared about was Tasha.

He screamed in rage and sorrow. He ran, and for once his luck was in, and he didn't fall. He rammed the knife hilt deep between her breasts, breasts he once dreamed of kissing, of licking, of fondling.

Chapter Sixty-Five

Mummy, thought Louise as that bright, piercing bolt of torture struck home.

My children, she thought, as blood flew down her chest.

I'm sorry, I wasn't good enough, she thought, as the dark encircled her.

But then she saw her Mummy, and her Mummy was in the park. Her Mummy was beckoning her. She was standing beside the roundabout. She'd lined up Polly and Pooh and Tigger and Basil – and Bounce! And Bounce was *young* again! Bounce had fur *everywhere!* Bounce had *both* his eyes!

'Come on, dear,' said her Mummy. 'Never mind the nasty man. In the end, you won. You did, you know, and that's good enough for your old Mum. We're all here now, all in the park, and you can play forever and never have to go in when it's dark.'

'But Mummy, he killed me. He's still alive. How could I have won?'

'You'll see,' said her old Mum, Carol Smith, and...oh, that *smile!* 'We'll *both* see. We'll look in on him every day...between trips to the park.'

'Can I have jelly, Mummy?' said Louise. 'I've eaten *all* my broccoli.'

Carol smiled wider. It crinkled her nose and made her eyes light up. 'We'll see.'

Louise knew that meant *yes*, and with a happy yelp she ran to the roundabout and gathered all her toys in her arms and her Mummy pushed her and pushed her forever and never grew tired.

Chapter Sixty-Six

The murdering bitch died.

Colin looked at her and laughed as she jittered and jived on the end of the knife. He laughed as a torrent of thick black blood splashed over his hands. He laughed as he rammed the knife further and further into her heart. He laughed as her eyes grew still, fixed, waxen.

He laughed and laughed. Just like the old days. Like when he was young.

Chapter Sixty-Seven

How long he stood like that he'd never know, but eventually the weight of her became just too much and her corpse slid off the knife with a tearing damp sound and collapsed to the floor.

He looked down on her and kicked her in the head. Then he kicked her again.

He'd stopped laughing, but he still kicked her a third time before thinking, *Helen.*

In the car, the bitch had said. *But it'd be locked. Logical.*

Got to find keys, thought Colin. He dropped the knife to the ground and somehow made his antique, badly abused body move.

But first, he pulled his trousers up.

Chapter Sixty-Eight

The keys were on the kitchen table. They were coiled inside a length of nylon rope, the same rope he'd been bound in, the same rope his wrists were still bound in, rope she used to furnish that noose that swung idly from the ceiling.

Saved you some trouble, didn't I? He glanced around him, then saw the dribbling patches of blood he'd leaked down the stair carpet. *How bad am I hurt,* he wondered. *She ripped something badly up there.*

Never mind that now. Time for that later. Now he had to rescue his wife.

Chapter Sixty-Nine

There were two doors in the kitchen. One led to the hallway and the front door beyond, the other to a garage. He took the garage door. *She'd park in close,* he thought. *She wouldn't want the neighbours seeing her drag her victims up the driveway, would she?*

Part of him expected the door to the garage to be locked, but it wasn't. *No reason to. She was going to kill me then herself. Why bother locking up after you?*

Filling the space was a Vauxhall Vectra. He reached out and pressed the key fob. There was a *twip-TWIP* noise, and then the sound of catches being released.

'Helen,' he said, as loudly as he could, making his way to the boot. 'Helen?'

He lifted the boot lid and looked at his wife. She looked back, but didn't see him. How could she, with two five inch nails for eyes?

Are you surprised? Did you expect her not *to lie? Of* course Helen *would be dead. They're* all *dead now. All except* you.

Enjoy your life, Colin.

Chapter Seventy

The ones we love come back to us in dreams.

Chapter Seventy-One

Colin Bryant never really recovered. No one – not his doctors, his psychiatrists, not even Detective Walker – was in the least bit surprised. He lived out the rest of his life in a secure ward in a hospital not too far away from the college that he and his friends had attended, many years ago.

He could speak, he just chose not to very often. He could eat (and, after a while, even be trusted with cutlery) he just didn't very much. After a year or so, he even stopped crying. Of course, he'd always have to shit in a bag and carry it round with him – the damage up his rectum was astonishing, and his blood loss had been Promethean – but hey, there were worse things. *You're lucky to be alive at all,* someone had told him once.

Yes. Very fucking lucky.

He was asked all sorts of questions, and sometimes he answered them. He genuinely answered them to the best of his ability. The most asked question was *why? Why did she do it, Colin? Why?*

Because I had sex with her Mum's friend when I was nineteen, he said. *Because we got on with our lives and her Mum didn't,* he said. *Because she was raised to hate us all and me in particular,* he said.

People shook their heads at those answers, and once Colin overheard one policeman say to another, *there has to be a real reason, a* proper *reason.* The other one had asked, *do you think we'll ever find it?*

Colin hadn't heard the answer, but didn't care. No, they'd find no other reason. In the end, there was nothing else to find. Everything she'd done, all that brutality, she'd done because once, as a young man, Colin had committed an act of betrayal he could hardly remember.

Except in his dreams. Except in the dreams where he and Sophie are drunk, alone, and just pissed enough to think a bad idea is a good one.

How had they come to be alone? He had no clue. Where were their friends – the gang, the crew, Carol? He had no idea. He just couldn't remember. But alone they had been – her house, his house? Who could tell? And there'd been some beer and some talk...

Then they'd just sat a little bit closer...

Then they'd...

Sometimes he could remember the event, the time he'd lost his virginity to his girlfriend's best mate (hell, one of *his* best mates) but most times he couldn't. One thing he could *never* remember, no matter how often he tried, was how he'd felt afterwards. Guilty? Disgusted? Smug? He'd no idea. Damn him to hell forever, he'd no idea. And how had Carol found out? Had he told her? Had Sophie? One of the others?

I'll never know. There's no one left to ask. No one but me, living in a ward and carrying a bag of my own shit around. The last of the gang, of the crew. We laughed, didn't we? We laughed and thought we'd never stop.

Laughter was nothing but a memory now. Memories like those of 1984, when it was hot, when they were all friends, when...

*

A middle-aged man lies in his hospital bed, and dreams.

He's nineteen in 1984, and it's summer, high summer, the highest, hottest summer there ever was and ever will be, and he sits with his friends in the Houghton pub in Southport. The Longest Time by Billy Joel plays on the video juke over and over again, but no one moans, no one laughs, because his friends are all dead. Everyone is dead here; Joe who was George, Sophie, Howard and Brian.

Of Carol, however, there is no sign and never will be. She's never in the pub anymore. Sometimes he is sad, because maybe – just maybe – if he just sat her down and explained things then this nightmare would end. 'Carol,' he would say, 'I'm sorry. I was young and stupid. That's all I can say – no, I was young and stupid and horny. In the end, the lust just overcame what I felt for you. And I loved you, I did – so did Sophie and the others, we all did. But when you're nineteen, nuh-nuh-nineteen sometimes your hormones just take over. I'm sorry. I'm sorry I did it. I'm sorry I forgot it. But I did, I did both of those things, and I was wrong, so wrong. And I'm sorry.' Would that be enough for her? Would she understand?

But she never turns up, so he never finds out. Yes, sometimes that makes him sad…but mostly he is scared that she will turn up, turn up angry, turn up with her daughter from the future and…well, do things.

So he sits surrounded by the corpses of his friends, of his past. And at the bar, two women, mother and daughter, sit on stools. Their names are Tasha and Helen.

They're dead too.

In the background, Billy Joel sings on. The Longest Time. Colin thinks that's just about right, and cries a little in his sleep.

Afterword

Old Bones Lie Still was first published as an eBook back in 2012. Preparing this paperback edition has given me the chance to re-read these stories for the first time in three years. I've resisted the temptation to update anything, which explains references to The Saturdays and Andy Carroll (who?) in an England shirt. I hope these anachronisms don't irritate you too much – but I felt if I started down that line, I may never stop.

Some of these tales go back a long way – *The Start of Another Week*, for instance, is almost old enough to buy a legal drink – others aren't yet ready to start shaving. Some, I think, are better than others, but all of them gave me a laugh when I wrote them.

I hope they gave you some laughs as well. A life without laughs is no fun *at all*. Ask Louise Smith.

T.K. June 2015

Printed in Great Britain
by Amazon